GARBAGE BOY

Michael McMullen

#8/2000

One Printers Way
Altona, MB R0G 0B0
Canada

www.friesenpress.com

Copyright © 2023 by Michael McMullen
First Edition — 2023

All rights reserved.

This work is a book of fiction. The characters, names, business entities, events and outcomes are all the product of the author's imagination. Any semblance to actual persons, living or dead, or actual events is purely coincidental. The use of terms and language reflects the time period of the book, the early seventies. Descriptions and words used that are derogatory are chosen to depict and illustrate the bias, racism and social class oppression the characters would have faced in this time period. The inclusion of this content is to introduce these difficult topics and grapple with them. These words and descriptions are not condoned, accepted or used by the author at anytime.

No part of this publication may be reproduced in any form, or by any means, electronic or mechanical, including photocopying, recording, or any information browsing, storage, or retrieval system, without permission in writing from FriesenPress.

ISBN
978-1-03-916505-2 (Hardcover)
978-1-03-916504-5 (Paperback)
978-1-03-916506-9 (eBook)

1. FIC043000 FICTION, COMING OF AGE

Distributed to the trade by The Ingram Book Company

GARBAGE BOY

THE *High* BAR
OF
LOW EXPECTATIONS

MICHAEL MCMULLEN

FOREWORD

The first version of Garbage Boy: The High Bar of Low Expectations was completed in April of 2020. I have been "living" with him and his circle of friends, enemies, and others since then. The pandemic actually slowed down my writing progress although I did finish another book 'Leaving Lisa' in the summer of 2020.

Fast forward almost four years and you might ask what happened to Garbage Boy in the interim? An important step taken in the summer of 2022 was to link up with Friesen Press and get professional guidance for my writing, the construction of this book and the story. That process has been invaluable. The Friesen relationship brought the polish and professionalism to the writing and the publication of the book.

OK but what happened to the story of Garbage Boy in those four years? The story grew. The characters grew. The ending became more evasive. It still is! Garbage Boy is elusive.

What you will read will be the sixth full version/revisions of the story. The theme 'The High Bar of Low Expectations' started to embed itself deeply in the second/third iterations and jumped to star billing in the title. The strong cast of characters surrounding Garbage Boy deserved to have their back stories illuminated. Mister and Stone Pony's backgrounds and key turning points in their lives revealed themselves in trip number three to the writing well. In the fourth version the supporting cast of secondary characters that populate Garbage Boy's world such as the FBI, The Whities, The Brownies, Mr. Clampett and Ms. Cecilia Annamoosie become a little more real as they briefly share how they were shaped and formed.

When I am writing these characters 'talk to me' and reveal themselves sometimes in quick bursts and sometimes reluctantly. That was the case with Mister's silence as a grown man. Why was he quiet? Then he told me about his childhood. Ms. Cecilia Annamoosie is a brilliant, barrier breaking Indigenous woman. Why would she get hooked up with this crew of low means and low social standing? Then she whispered her path from lacrosse player to corporate lawyer to outcast. Even Garbage Boy's father, who had deserted the family years ago, gets dragged back into the fray. He talked me into four brief chapters to provide a glimpse into his perspective. He thinks he's funny. We will see what you think of his humour.

The story kept on pulling me into deeper troughs, twists and turns. I should have expected this when I mixed the selling of weed, motorcycle gangs, garbage routes, high school elections, racism, bias, social stigma all in a time of social and cultural upheaval. Ah, the early seventies, how things shifted.

I hope you enjoy reading Garbage Boy as much as I have enjoyed living with this crew and telling their story. They have talked me into the follow on sequel. Lost And Found: And The Shot Gunning of Mrs.D. Together with SCARRED (published in 2019), that now serves as a prequel to Garbage Boy, there will soon be three books in the Newspaper Crew Chronicles.

Sincerely,
Michael

CHAPTER 1

Notoriety

This wasn't going to end well.

I knew the likely outcome before I entered the classroom. I knew full well that this peacock was going to bait me, taunt me, and attempt to humble me. I knew that silence was my best approach. Just let him huff and puff and blow his wad of intellectual venom, sarcasm, and ridicule. I knew how to deal with all that. As a garbage boy, I got that every day. Nothing new here. Keep quiet and let it roll off my back. This was not a fight I could win. This was his territory, and we both knew it. *Just keep your cool; your silence will suffice.*

Fat chance of that happening. My silence, that is.

"You're seven days late, and you're officially notorious. Your two dubious appearances on national TV, the esteemed CBC no less, have provided you with immense notoriety in these parts and also a certain undeniable minor-celebrity status."

"You make notoriety sound like such a negative, sir."

"I do? Really? You think when I use the word 'notoriety' in your case my intention is to create a negative impression?"

"Not to be out of line, sir, but yeah that's exactly how it sounds to me, sir, negative. Maybe we could survey the class on how it sounds."

"Great suggestion! Surveys are good. Catch the sentiment of the crowd. Get a feel for, what is it, 'the vibe' in the air? OK, let's have a simple show of hands. Was my tone and the use of the word 'notoriety' in reference to, what do we call you, Scarface or Garbage Boy? Doesn't matter at the moment. We all know who you are. Class, was that descriptive negativity implied? Hands up. Congratulations! Every one of you, including the notorious Garbage Boy himself, all perceived my tone and phrasing correctly: negative. Extremely negative, in fact."

"Thank you for the clarity, sir."

"Ah, I hear sarcasm from Scarface. How precious!"

"Sir, I'm guessing you have a point to make, or are you just ragging on me for your own enjoyment?"

"Garbage Boy, you radiate a whole gamut of expression. You're displaying a lack of sincerity, and I detect an intended undertone that demonstrates a lack of respect due to the way you call me 'sir.' I detect disdain, subtle aggression, the aforementioned sarcasm, and humour in an attempt to be cool. I'm sure I have missed a few. Perhaps a good exercise for your classmates would be to list all the attitudes and expressions you're conveying."

"That might beat what you originally intended for the class, sir. Luckily I showed up today to lighten your lesson-plan load."

The class couldn't contain themselves after that comeback. Loud guffaws, laughter, and I believe a verifiable snort were elicited, but they soon trailed into apprehensive giggles, smirks, and even wincing. The class assumed that "Sir" was about to deliver a death blow.

"Garbage Boy."

"Yes, sir."

"Get your bedraggled late ass out of my class, and get down to the VP's office now."

"Yes, sir, and, sir, I'm really sorry you have never been on CBC."

"I'll not tolerate any challenge to my professionalism, and you, young man, are both way out of line and wayward."

"Yes, sir. Will I have the pleasure of your company soon, sir, or do I self-report my behaviour?"

"Wait outside his office until I arrive at the end of the class."

"Yes, sir. Looking forward to our get-together."

My walk to the VP's office was a stumble, at least mentally. My steps were solid, but my thoughts were cloudy, and I had an undeniable lurch in my gut, the fog and fumble of foreboding that this could all turn out very wrong.

There is bullshit and then there is absolutely pure bullshit. This guy thought he could bruise, poke, and ridicule me, and I would take his crap. Maybe I should have. I usually would, I think. My family and I had been pushed around enough by those who thought they were superior. At least that's what I told myself as I sat outside the VP's office. I never knew what was going to set someone else off or set someone against me, but man, the CBC appearances had this guy fairly rattled, or so I guessed. I didn't think I came into the classroom acting like all that and a bag of chips! Who knew how I was perceived? Who cared? I had spent most of my life just trying to stay under the radar.

The session with the VP was straightforward and crisp. The VP was one of those men who was originally a tech or a shop teacher who had been required to go back to school to get his BA in the summers and take some night classes. He was a hard-working straight shooter, who was involved in the community.

He took no crap and genuinely seemed to give a damn.

Summation of the session: I was an out-of-line young asshole. It was not expressed in those exact words, but that was the general drift of the conversation. Well, it wasn't much of a conversation, considering my input was allowed to be less than negligible.

Some details of the session. It seems that "Sir," according to Sir and several other teachers, thought I wasn't going to amount to much. I was singularly insolent and disrespectful, an extremely bad example, and a disruptive influence, harmful to the general well-being and behaviour of the student body. In short, if I was to paraphrase: a "fucked-up piece of work."

Sir provided a career trajectory for me as well, which was very thoughtful of that righteous asshole. In his all-knowing and all-seeing view, because he had dealt with my kind in the past, I would, in roughly this order: drop out of school, matriculate from garbage boy to garbage man, and other than likely criminal activity, garbage man would be the highest station I would achieve in life. Therefore, to expedite my path in life, the best course for all was my immediate expulsion. It certainly appeared that he felt good when he pronounced his sentence. The VP simply nodded and thanked him for his input.

Sir vacated the VP's office with an overwhelming sense of self-righteousness, his dignity and pride intact, with a smug sense of the aforementioned superiority. Before I even looked at the VP he said, "I know; I'd like to kick his pompous ass as well."

I didn't know whether to shit my pants or shine my shoes.

"I would appreciate it if you kept that comment between us," the VP continued.

"Absolutely."

"Now, son, you have a problem. Your notoriety and popularity notwithstanding, do you know the nature of your problem?"

"I think so. I come from a poor family that lacks a certain social acceptance in town. I work picking up other people's shit, and I'm not really a favourite son of the city, except with a group of cops and some coaches. My best friends are dope dealers and longhairs. I have acne and scars, and I couldn't get a date to save my soul."

"That truly is an impressive 'woe is me' list. You rehearse that, son? Do you really live in that frame of mind? Because it's a pretty pathetic whine, and I'm not buying it."

"I may not dwell there in my head, but I know that description is a pretty accurate view held by many of the 'well to do' in this town."

"I still don't buy it. Want to know why?"

"Yes, I do."

"OK, here goes, and don't let this inflate your ego. I've seen you work, and I have seen you compete. I have seen people throw garbage and destructive comments out their car windows at you. I have seen how your shoulders slump, and your head goes down at first. Then you square up and stare at the car. In that moment you show no fear. You rise up and meet the nastiness of the ugliness. You show strength."

"Thank you."

"You know the next thing you do in those situations?"

"No, I don't."

"You go and pick the garbage up because that's your job, and that's what's expected of you. You might have tremendous disdain for what you're paid to do, but you do it."

"I wait until the car has driven far enough away, so they don't get the pleasure of seeing me pick up the crap they throw."

"OK, you protect your pride to a degree, but then you do your job. You fulfill your task, your commitment. That, young man, is good stuff."

"Thank you."

"We have all seen you run on the garbage route. Son, in some circles you, the Indian and the big black man are the main topics of conversation."

"You mean the Newspaper Crew?"

"What?"

"Black and white and 'red' all over."

"That's hilarious! Did you come up with that?"

"No, it was the garbage men on another sanitation crew."

"You mean the other garbage men?"

"Yes."

"How did your crew take that?"

"They stared them down. Scared the shit out of them. Not one of them laughed when that supervisor presented us with our nickname. Mister and Stone Pony scared the absolute bejesus out of them."

"So, they don't usually call you that, at least to your face?"

"No, they don't, but Stone Pony told them we liked the name. He told them it was a good solid name. He also told them we thought the name was fitting because we were the only sanitation crew who could read. A couple of days later, Mister added the fact that we were the only crew who actually knew what to do with newspapers—to actually read them, not wipe their asses with them like the rest of you morons!"

"Son, there are a bunch of tough men in that sanitation group. Was there a fight?"

"Not a thing! They hold these guys in awe and I think fright. Mister and Stone Pony are nothing but muscle and mystery. They don't speak much."

"Do they scare you?"

"Not a bit. They have my back one hundred percent of the time."

"Let's get back to your problem. Your problem is your associates, your friends. Your garbage crew is scary, different, and, therefore, way outside the norms of the populace. It doesn't mean they're bad men. They are just so different that embracing them and their embrace of you makes you different. Absurdly different from the standard. The truth is, few of the town's white folks, and they're all white folks, have any close friendships with the Indians. Unfortunately, you're judged by your associates. It may be bigotry, but our town isn't any different from most small towns and cities. We just don't find it easy to embrace what we don't know. It appears you have. People see your crew smiling at each other when you finish all the barrels on a street. You genuinely like each other."

"I like them. I love the feel of that work. I don't know if they like me. As I said, they don't say much. If people judge me by my affiliation with Mister and Stone Pony, they must love my relationship with Bogeyman and Scarecrow."

"Is that what you call them?"

"Always have."

"They're scarier to most folks than the Newspaper Crew."

"Really? They are just long-haired dopers who mean no harm."

"Do you know how intelligent they are?"

"I know they are smart guys. They work on their vocabulary all the time."

"No, I mean really smart, brainiacs, so much so I had them re-tested in grade ten just to verify."

"Did you tell them?"

"Yes."

"What did they say?"

"They asked me if I could just keep that to myself."

"Were they surprised?"

"Not at all. They both said they knew they had an uncanny ability to figure out how things worked and how people thought. They also figured it was a great advantage to be constantly underestimated. They, like you, have a pretty good understanding of their rung on the social ladder."

"They are clever collectors."

The VP looked a little perplexed at this comment. "What do you mean 'clever collectors'?"

"They collect everything and all for profit. From bottles and cans to people's thoughts, actions, and behaviours. Before they dropped out, they could tell you who every single person in this town was screwing, who beat their wife, who was cheating on their spouse, and anything you wanted to know about any of our teachers' private lives. Including you!"

"Including me?"

"Yes, including you. You came out as a stand-up, solid citizen. Fairly trustworthy for an authority figure, which is high praise from those two."

"That was the full report on me?"

"Yes, all good. According to Bogeyman and Scarecrow, you're the real deal. They trust you. It must be nice to have Bogeyman and Scarecrow's stamp of credibility."

"Actually, it is. I believe that to be true about me, but back to you. Bogeyman and Scarecrow are dope dealers or are assumed to be."

"They are."

"Well, you know, them being your best friends doesn't bode well: guilt by association and all that."

"I don't deal."

"I didn't think you did, but why not? Your friends are globetrotters and seem to have girls hanging off their arms."

"They won't let me. They say our little trio needs a straight man, and somehow, they know Mister and Stone Pony would not react kindly to me getting involved in their business."

"Do your mutual friends know each other?"

"Yes, but they never associate together in my presence. They have a strange mutual respect, probably based on them all being outsiders."

"That would presumably be a big part of it. Is there more to their relationship?"

"Probably, but I don't want to know how Bogeyman and Scarecrow and the Newspaper Crew intersect."

"Neither do I. Your four closest associates are extremely different. They virtually glow with notoriety, and you bask in the glow of national news coverage. You're on a path that looks to be strewn with potential trouble."

"So, what do I do?"

"I don't know. I wish I had something for you here. I hear in your tone and in your words and I see in your expression that you're loyal and you care for these four men."

"I do."

"Just be careful, OK? Step back once in a while and assess where these four are heading, good and bad, then adjust your course accordingly. Can you do that?"

"Yes."

"Now, last topic. Competing. I have seen the fire and passion in you and the ability. You're a good teammate and a fiery competitor. Your teammates follow you and trust you."

"Thank you."

"Keep competing. There is none of the 'woe is me' mindset when you compete. The playing field is level and equal, and in that environment you take ownership of the diamond, the rink, the field. In those arenas of competition, you have the right to force your will, to exert your will over others, and to exert your force and you have the will to inspire and lift your teammates. You have the right to compete in all areas, so compete fully. Exert your presence and be substantial on the fields of play. Be solid, be bold, be relentless. This I have seen in you. Rise above the taunts, the jeers, and the cruelty of personal attacks. Be better than that! Realize for you there is a need for constant proof. You can't rest on your accomplishments. Failure to perform to expectations will be jumped on with glee, and it will fulfill the prophecies of all those who have set for you the high bar of low expectations. All of this is based on your maligned status, your associations, and your character flaws. Don't look for sympathy for your lot in life. It isn't coming, and you don't want it anyway. Sympathy can manifest as a rationale for failure. Do not get trapped in self-pity. You're stronger and smarter than that. Compete. Go at it!"

"Thank you. No wonder Bogeyman and Scarecrow gave you a solid approval rating."

"Thank you. You're welling up on me, Big Boy. Don't go all soft and mushy. It's not a luxury you can afford."

"I won't."

"Good. Don't. One last thing you might want to consider."

"What would that be?"

"I think it would help your image, your perception with the townsfolk and all, if you got a haircut and shaved that scraggly beard."

"Well sir, I really like growing my hair and look around it's not like I am in the minority. I think the hair fits who I am and I think it's important to be true to myself. As for the beard it helps cover the zits and the scars. I have put almost six months of hard work into this beard and having it referred to as scraggly is hurtful."

We both chuckled at my feigned hurt feelings about my truthfully scraggly beard.

"Those scars are never going to be covered by anything, at least in this town, given how you got them. That's a good point about the zits though. The hair is up to you. It's just seen as rebellious and defiant in some circles."

"I don't travel in those circles, sir. I do appreciate where your advice is coming from and I thank you for looking out for me like that."

"OK, let's move on. Now for your punishment."

"Punishment?"

"Yes, discipline for your aggressive, disrespectful engagement with Sir."

"OK, I can do the time."

"Yes, you can. Your time is every school day from here to eternity or graduation because I'll not let you drop out. You will be in my office at 8:15 a.m. You will lead us in the Lord's Prayer, 'God Save the Queen,' and the morning announcements until further notice."

"God damn it, that seems a little more punishment than the crime deserves."

"Justice is mine in this case, not the Lord's, and stop using His name in vain. By the way, do you know how big a victory this is for Sir?"

"It's a freakin' feather in his cap."

"Wrong; it's a whole war bonnet. He never expected me to suspend you. He just wanted an audience for his fire-and-brimstone theatrics. When he thanks me for my handling of your case, dealing with a problematic individual like you with harsh, appropriate discipline that will, hopefully, save your bedraggled ass, I'll try not to laugh."

"Why not laugh? It seems to be a good joke on me."

"No joke on you, son. The victory here is mine, again, with no offence to the Lord."

"How is it your victory?"

"At 8:15 every morning, I get to look you in the eyes and see if you're on track. You get the chance to ask for help, guidance, or a way out. Every morning we will share those opportunities. Every morning we will get to chuckle just a little at that pompous ass who brought us together. Fair deal?"

"Absolutely. Thank you."

I left his office. Feeling up. Feeling good. *Hold your head up boy. Hold your head high.* Thank you for those song lyrics, Argent.

Life could be good. I wanted to live life feeling good. Just live with my head up. I didn't need a great life. Good was good enough. You know, just normal. What would that feel like? What would that life look like? Well, a girlfriend would be nice. Fewer zits would be unreal. That would be really good. I knew good things had happened for me already. Mister and Stone Pony were good for me. They treated me well. We ran barrels and that had built me up physically. Screw Charles Atlas and weightlifting. Try running garbage cans on a garbage route. That will build you up: all that running and the lifting.

The money they paid me was unreal. When I got back from Winnipeg, I missed the whole first week of school because they gave me a hardship absence. My family was poor, so a full week of work eased our hardship. The farm kids could get a hardship absence, so they had to give it to a garbage boy. So, that was all good stuff. Not normal but good, especially if I could look past the disdain held for me and the Newspaper Crew.

What was not normal and caused me to miss two more days of school was a boil on my ass. I told my mom I had a sore on my butt, and it hurt like hell when I sat. She finally convinced me to show her my wound. She held a mirror, so I could look over my shoulder and see the damage. There it was, a boil, yellow, full of puss, and almost four inches long running along the top ridge on the right side of my ass crack! *Come on, God*, I thought. *This is ridiculous Old Testament biblical shit. That's kind of funny, God. A boil on your ass crack is funny shit, right? Hey, Lord, stop trying to be a comedian if you're just going to be a pain in my ass. Now that thought cracks me up. Get it, Lord Almighty? Cracks me up! Maybe you and I should pair up and go on the road as a comedy team.*

Anyway, I'm way off track here. It was hard to get to good or normal with an infected, pus-filled boil on the ridge of my ass crack. As it turned out, it was an abscess, and I needed surgery. They put me out. When I came to, I tried to fondle the nurse. Nurse fondling isn't normal behaviour, and news of the incident quickly spread through town.

My mom had to dress my surgical wound. The best thing for dressing the wound was to insert a tampon in the incision, cover it with gauze, and tape it up. I took baths in Epsom salts. Mom had to change my "dressing" like she was changing a baby's diaper, using tampons to stick in my ass. God, that was not normal, but still would be funny if I heard it happened to someone else.

So, again, I just wanted a good life. Simple. No notoriety. No tampons up my ass. Maybe even a tad less of the spotlight.

I just wanted things to end well.

Good People

Dear God

You know, Lord, I just need to thank you,
You keep putting good people in my path.
The VP, Lord, he's the real Mohican.
Thank you.

You and I may disagree on this, but Bogeyman and Scarecrow are good people.
Same said for Mister and Stone Pony,
Though most don't see those four that way.
But you're omniscient and all knowing, right?
You see that. I mean you have the bright, shiny light into peoples' souls.
So, you know these are good people you put in my path.
Anyway, thanks.

God Almighty, one big question.
Did you intend to create people with a stick up their ass who are hell bent on demeaning others?
Or is 'sir' just a mistake?
Just asking, no offence intended. Well, maybe a little.
Lord, can you help this guy lighten up or at least lighten up on me?

Thanks for listening.
Looks like I'll be saying your prayer every morning until hell freezes over.
That's funny stuff right there, God.

All the best,
Amen.

CHAPTER 2

Under the Radar

The note from the school wasn't surprising. That it came from the vice principal was a bit of a shock. I wasn't surprised because a lot of people were talking about my son and his CBC appearances. Not many people from our town ever make the national news, let alone twice in just over a month! There was a lot happening in the summer of 1970, and still my son was on the national news twice.

He seemed more confident in himself than ever before. That was a good thing, but I hope not too much of a good thing, and maybe it was all just for show. I was feeling that was at least part of his story. When I asked him about the note and his punishment, he laughed it off and said the VP was a good guy. I pushed him about the teacher he disrespected, and I didn't like his answer.

"That guy's an asshole, Mom, a real conceited prick. He tried to embarrass me and put me down. I'm not taking that shit anymore, Mom."

"Teachers should be respected, and you need to be the bigger man and rise above the put-downs, not provoke or fight back. You're not on equal terms, and authority wins. If you're smart, you can fly under the radar."

"Mom, this guy is going to push me. He wins if I stay quiet and take his crap."

"No, son, a man like that is already small on the inside. If he can't get you to become angry and mouth back, it just makes him look petty and small. The harder he tries and the less you rise against him, the sooner it will get old for him."

He nodded and said he would try, but it wasn't going to be easy. I knew it wasn't going to be easy for him. Stay low, son. Don't stand straight up in a low-ceiling room. No sense banging your head for no good reason or outcome.

I had been trying to stay under the radar since the day I was raped and beaten. Even more so since the man who raped me died, and my son and I were suspected in helping speed his departure from this world. Keep your nose clean. Focus on the things you can win or make better. In my case, my kids and my home were my focus and where my victories would be won. However, if that prick of a teacher rode my boy for no reason, I would march into the VP's office and speak my piece, which wouldn't be so peaceful.

We were still in the shadow of my ex-boyfriend's death. We needed to stay low. Low but not broken. I wished my son weren't in the spotlight, but I would never hold him back. There seemed to be some invisible hand or wave sweeping him forward and up. He needed to be careful. Our safety net was not deep, wide, or strong.

I just wanted to be free of a few things. Mostly free of fear. I feared payback was always out there, and I was not even sure why. I wanted to be free of debt. Free of worry would be good. Worry was part of a mother's world, so maybe not to be free of worry. My kids and their well-being were what I should worry about. Maybe I could flip that around and think of my feelings as caring, not worry. That made sense, didn't it? If I cared a lot, if I was caring all the time, well that sounded a lot better than worrying all the time. It even somehow felt better and lifted my spirits when I thought that way.

I knew I was a caring person, so I chose to care and think that way. I also hoped that the coroner's report on my rapist boyfriend's death came back and cleared all suspicions about my boy and me having any connection to his demise.

Stay under the radar, son. Fly, but fly low. Keep the ground in sight and your head on straight. As for me, I was going to try and keep him flying straight, providing him with a safe landing space in our home and in my care.

I hadn't been praying much lately. I never asked for anything for myself when I did pray. At least I never asked for stuff or things. I wanted to provide for myself and my family without any intervention, divine or otherwise. I don't know if what I did even qualified as praying. I didn't go to church. I couldn't afford to. That would require nice clothes, and I would have been expected to put a donation in the prayer basket. I figured if the Lord existed, he would hear what I had to say from right where I was, beside my bed on my knees. My little church of one.

I said what I had to say and then climbed into my bed, thinking about what I'd said, just in my own head. Then I felt some sense of peace. It was good to give even a silent voice to my concerns, hopes, and wishes.

Common Ground

Dear God

What's that verse?
Though I walk through the valley of the shadow of death, I'll fear no evil.
Well, that one death does hang over us like a shadow,
And I do fear that dark cloud.
Can you help me with that?
Don't bother; that's my darkness to burn away.
So, you're a caring God, not a worrying God.
I'm going to be a caring mom, not a worrying mom.
There you go, some common ground for us,
We can care together for my kids.
I do think I'm going to need some help on this.
I have foreshadowing thoughts of bad things around the corner.
So, if you can just give me a heads up,
That's all I need,
Just fair warning, a "whether" report,
Whether to lift up or lie low.
Just give me the warning thunder before the lightning.
Amen.

CHAPTER 3

Celebrity Status

You know, I would have really liked the opportunity to have a good look at the CBC segment from Man-Pop and Winnipeg. That whole episode in front of the TV cameras was so quick and in the midst of a swirling mayhem of humanity. If I did have more than one momentary glance at the fifteen to twenty seconds I was the focus of the camera and the interviewer, then I might have had a better appreciation for my minor celebrity status. I mean, it was such a brief segment on the CBC national news, and Crazy Horse was the star. My celebrity probably sprang from the mystery surrounding the meaning of my answers to the questions I was asked by the CBC. I answered "golfed" to the question of how I got to Winnipeg.

Crazy Horse and Scarface on national TV. A Metis kid nicknamed after a famous Indian chief and Scarface, being me, were the centre of the main story aired by CBC about Man-Pop. The Manitoba provincial government had allowed Man-Pop to happen as a gift to the youth of the province in celebration of the province's one hundredth anniversary. Over twenty thousand kids attended the party.

An impromptu parade occurred on the day of the concert. And who was leading that parade? Crazy Horse and Scarface, of course. Who else but two teenagers who had met just three days earlier? We led that parade from the Manitoba Legislature, with Golden Boy's glowing approval, all the way up Portage to the Blue Bomber Stadium. That was an attention getter. They tell me the CTV piece was longer and better, but I haven't seen that one. I'm still not clear how Crazy Horse organized the ten Cree warriors, the six dancers, and four drummers, led by Crazy Horse and me in our buckskin vests and boots, bare chests, and painted faces. The cops didn't know what to make of us, but since the parade was peaceful, and there might have been ten thousand kids walking up Portage, most of whom didn't have a clue they were in a parade, stopping us wasn't really an option.

At the stadium when the CBC interviewer asked me where I was from and how I got to Winnipeg my answer was spontaneous. "Somewhere in Ontario, and I golfed my way here."

The interviewer choked on the second part of my answer. "You golfed here? Golfed?"

"Yes. It turns out I'm a particularly good putter, and I just nail it on the seventh holes."

"Golfing" was instantly and widely assumed to be some new hippie term for some form of drug or type of drug use. The RCMP and narcs across Canada were immediately informed that golf references were almost definitely a new drug slang. These good officers were instantly charged with the mission of uncovering the meaning and connection of golf references to the drug and hippie culture. I'm sure officers would be awarded bonus citations if they could sleuth out whether "putting" was a special derivation of drug or drug use and if the seventh hole was another code word. As far as I know, I still think only two blondes from BC, a couple of younger Ontario cops, and I fully understood that all golf referred to was me getting lucky on three golf courses on three nights on the seventh greens of courses as I hitchhiked my way to Winnipeg and Man-Pop. That answer caused Canadian law enforcement to get very active and curious on a wild-assed tangent!

My popularity, notoriety, or celebrity status, whatever it was, at school and in town was firm with groups and individuals who had one if not all three defining characteristics. They were either lower to low middle on the rungs of the social and economic ladders in our fair town—sorry, city. (For the centennial year in 1967 the city fathers had upgraded our town to city status.) Second, those individuals who had a less than religious inclination, and last but certainly not least, those whose behaviour and character traits were embracing a looser moral standard. A lower moral standard could be easily judged by long hair on boys and braless girls. Clearly those signs were definitive and obvious statements of moral standards gone to hell in 1970 small-town Canada. The kids who were embracing whatever this current social and cultural shift was all about saw me as immensely cool. At least for the moment.

On the other hand, I got a few messages from some old friends, including some of my hockey teammates. Simply stated, their parents were not comfortable with any association they might have with that "Scarface, Garbage Boy, hippie."

Shit, what did that mean? Well, it was a two-way street because I sure as fuck wasn't comfortable around their parents! Actually, it was far worse than just feeling uncomfortable. I had been declared *persona non grata*. Those parents declared I was forbidden territory. Wow, I felt kind of like the apple in the Garden of Eden or as Iron Butterfly sing in their song "In-A-Gadda-Da-Vida." You know, the forbidden fruit. Iron Butterfly played at Man-Pop just before Led Zeppelin and before Man-Pop was moved from the outdoors at Blue Bomber stadium, because of torrential rain, to across the road at the arena, the home barn of the Jets. Crazy Horse even got us backstage with the bands, mostly the Led Zeppelin roadies, but Page, Plant, Bonham, and Jones were in the vicinity and walked right by us twice. Cool as hell even when soaked to the skin. I was, in fact, a bigger fan of Iron Butterfly than Zeppelin before the concert. The two drum solos during "In Da Gadda Da Vida" and "Moby Dick" by Zeppelin convinced me to switch allegiance to Zeppelin.

Celebrity perks! You bet! I had never been invited to so many parties. I had never had so many girls talk to me! Girls actually initiating contact.

My morning intonement of the Lord's Prayer and the morning announcements added to my aura. The story of how I earned the morning duty was circulated instantly. Every one of Sir's classes had become somewhat silent and surly. Of course, there were students who were oblivious to the powerful undercurrent of sentimentality flooding in my direction. The support was unspoken—just known. The oblivious minority in Sir's classes saw the silence as an opportunistic vacuum to raise their participation grades. They took full advantage and did not understand how they were increasing the growing rift in the social classes and behaviours in our high school and town. The oblivious ascend. The aware stew and stir.

Nothing is fully intentional, and then again, nothing is fully unintentional. We all steer in certain directions, knowingly and unknowingly, conscious and unconscious, walking down paths lined by our parents, families, friends, activities, and associations with narrow or wider circles. Church, school, subjects we study, sports, groups, clubs—we bounce into and off things. The walls are everywhere and everything. Social, class, emotional, physical, psychological, and self-perception walls. Hell, there were probably way more walls and paths that influenced what we were becoming and how we acted and reacted than I could imagine, but act and react I did.

So, here is the interesting thing. Some people liked me. Some people disliked me intensely. It seems the like and the dislike were for the same reasons.

People who liked me thought along the lines of: single-parent family. Mother and kids deserted. Hell, that boy has got an uphill battle, and he fights it, clubs it head on. People who disliked me thought along the lines of: that family is fucked up, has always been fucked up, and that boy will be a fuck-up, especially with his disrespectful attitude. No wonder the dad had the brains to leave. Who does he think he is? Counterbalanced by, he will not let his circumstances limit him. Contrasted by, that disrespectful pissant thinks he has the right to question everything without any right to. Contrasted by, he has the courage to challenge everything, especially the status quo. He has grown a pair.

Well, I probably saw those counterbalances and contrasts through a biased filter. Not probably; I did. So, that was the terrain I navigated, and I was creating the disruptive vibes.

For reasons unbeknownst to me, the elections for student council were postponed in the spring to be held in the third and fourth weeks of school in the fall. I was nominated for president on the first day of nominations. I accepted, and things rolled from there. The election period was only ten days long and included two after-school, all-candidate presentations, with questions and answers and a full school presentation, two separate assemblies with about one thousand kids in each. My celebrity status was immediately valuable. I had an organizing committee of fifty before noon. I had a campaign manager and cut the campaign committee enrollment at fifty members, so we had a half-assed chance of having an organized organization! By the end of the school day, there were fifty or sixty unauthorized renegade posters throughout the school, touting me for president! So much for flying under the radar!

Much of the sign material was created in grade nine and ten art classes. The art teachers created a free period for artistic expression, and I was the beneficiary of that creative freedom, that liberation movement! Overwhelming! As in, not one of the other two candidates received a single creative piece of free expression. By 3 p.m., the rumour mill had it that another candidate's younger sister had produced a poster expressing support and love for me. My first experience with politics making strange bedfellows. The other candidate's grade-ten brother was even better for my candidacy. Having seen the previous grade-nine art class troop out with several posters supporting my candidacy, he reacted poorly. After the art teacher announced the free creative period, he stood up and told the class that posters should not be allowed until the allotted time, starting at 8 a.m. the following morning. Candidates were allowed only fifty pieces of Bristol board from school art supplies, and campaigning was not permitted during class time, including creating candidate propaganda of any type, especially posters.

The art teacher shrugged. "You heard the young man."

However, one of my fifty campaign committee members, whom I had never met but had ogled discreetly, asked what the boundaries were for free creative expression. Did artistic expression not include art as the core voice for all types of expression, especially political? She was not only beautiful but intelligent as well!

The art teacher reveled in her statement. Art cannot be bound, constrained, or ruled. Have at it! Art transcends rules!

That class produced more campaign posters for my candidacy than any other. One round for free expression and the advocacy of anyone, anything, anytime, anywhere.

My organizing executive and I were summoned over the PA system to come to the VP's office at 3:10 p.m. I was extremely interested because I didn't know I had an organizing executive, nor why we were being summoned.

The VP welcomed us and congratulated me on my nomination and organizational skills. "Be bold" was ringing in my ears from our previous conversation. Then he proceeded to give fair warning and expectations. He said my behaviour should be cautious, respectful, and beyond reproach at all times.

"The start of your campaign has already broken several rules. First, class time was used to produce campaign materials. Second, your limit of fifty school-supplied Bristol boards has been exceeded by twenty-two, and third, your campaign material was posted before the allotted time at 8 a.m. tomorrow morning. Now, who on the executive committee is responsible? Who initiated or directed this campaign?"

At that moment I found my executive lacking in knowledge but consistent in their acknowledgement of lack of knowledge. All of them denied any knowledge or action related to the spontaneous campaign. The VP just shook his head. I knew he knew more than he was letting on.

"Let's take this one step at a time," he said. Then he went through my executive team one at a time. They were equally befuddled and found not responsible, consistently expressing awe at the spontaneity of the support. Befuddled and consistent were the hallmarks of our campaign up to that point. In that session of the unaware and uninformed, I took the opportunity to introduce myself to the co-chairwoman and each of our two secretaries and two treasurers, whom I had never met. This crew, as a whole, was a fine mix of outsiders and insiders. I was impressed by the diversity my candidacy had elicited.

The VP put some tractor-beam eyes on me and in his best Ricky Ricardo voice told me I had some 'splaining to do.

"Well, sir, as far as I can tell, the art teachers turned their classes over to free artistic expression without boundaries. In fact, when students who were blood relatives to other candidates stated that suppression of artistic freedom was in order, I was propelled forward as the primary beneficiary of the artistic poetic license."

"Did B and S teach you all of this vocabulary?"

"More or less."

The B and S reference puzzled my executive team, except for the one ninth grader who was Bogeyman's cousin. The "Mor or Les" backstory was not known by any of these folks, including the VP, so that reference fizzled as well.

Then the VP launched into an apparently predetermined, prescriptive course of action. "One, you and your large executive team will remove all seventy-two posters before you leave the school today. Mr. Von Huben is outside the main office with stepladders and scrubbing supplies to aid in your efforts.

Two, your campaign owes the school sixteen dollars and fifty cents for material use beyond the allowed limits. Three, the use of class time as sanctioned by members of the arts faculty cannot be held against your organizing committee. This was a privilege granted by faculty and supported by the administration; however, you will be monitored closely. As you know, the number of posters produced on material provided independently by students on your committee is not restricted. Additionally, this package arrived for you at 2:30 p.m. I think you and your team should look at it together in my presence." He handed me an envelope. "I have looked at the contents."

I opened the envelope. It held $250 in twenties, tens, and fives. The bills were crinkled and appeared old and well used. It appeared these bills had traded through rough hands. A piece of foolscap paper was also in the envelope. I unfolded the paper, and two words were penned meticulously in a flowing, elegant, cursive writing about two inches in height: "WIN IT." That was it. No signature, no exclamation point, just those two words. It felt like an executive order.

"So, what are you going to do with the money?" the VP inquired.

"Two things. Pay the sixteen-fifty immediately, if the front desk will be so kind as to give me proper change. Then we will have a quick meeting with the executive committee and decide on what to do with the funds."

"OK. Keep me informed on disbursement of the funds. With two treasurers that should be easy. In tomorrow morning's announcements, you will apologize for the early placement of your posters. I'll review your written script prior to the announcement. Your executive team is dismissed. They can wait for you with Mr. Von Huben."

He started immediately as the door hit the last executive's ass. "Is this drug money?"

"I don't think so. B and S are out of the country."

"If it is, don't use it. Donate it to charity or something outside of the school. Use the money for good."

"What if it isn't drug money? What then?"

"Where else could it come from?"

"I think it's garbage money."

"What?"

"Stone Pony and Mister. This is something they would do. How did the money get to the school?"

"A taxi driver dropped it and didn't tell us anything."

"Probably my very different associates. So, if it's garbage money, can I use it?"

"Absolutely but spend it in a manner nobody would expect."

"OK, I'll try. They'll never confirm it's from them. You need to understand that."

"I get it. My guidance is for you to be clever and generous to all."

"That isn't providing me with much direction or clarity."

"Just be as clever as I think you can be."

When I reached my executive team they were standing with our head janitor, Dutch Von Huben. Bogeyman's ninth-grade cousin pulled me away from the group. "Look, I'm sorry, but I can't stay," he said. "I have to go right home or all hell breaks loose." I knew his family and realized things were not simple or easy for him. Bogeyman's family tree had a lot of violence and bad shit circling at all times.

"OK, take off. See you tomorrow when we put these freakin' posters back up."

"Thanks, but here's the thing. Call this number. Scarecrow checks in with his mom every morning at about 11:30. She already heard about your candidacy. Scarecrow sends her money. She has three hundred dollars to give you. B and S are supporting your campaign."

"OK. Shit, this is a bit of a predicament. The VP said not to spend the two-fifty if it was drug money."

"Well, it ain't. B and S are running American tour groups in Mexico, Brazil, and Columbia. This is tourism money. That's what Scarecrow told his mom."

"OK, get home."

My executive team and I pulled down the seventy-two posters in record time. Anyone who asked us what we were doing and why, we told them the truth—on direct orders from the VP. One of my treasurers counted forty people helping us and just as many promising to make posters at home that night. My campaign was steamrolling.

We had an executive meeting at 4:15 for the remaining four team members still at school. Two had already left to catch a school bus home. We established a 7:15 a.m. start time to rehang the posters and talked about best spots, where most students would see them. Places like the entrances, cafeteria, stairwells, some real basic tactical thinking. My campaign manager (who nominated me and I think appointed himself as campaign manager) was all over this. He had written out phone chains in what he called cells. The cells were assigned to all members of the executive team, including me and two other friends of the campaign. This guy who I had always called "the Rave" was an organizer beyond anything I had ever encountered. Each cell consisted of four names. Ten people would call four people each. Forty total! We would ask each person we called to do two things. One, call four other people. Two, make a poster, and come and hang posters in the morning. The Rave wanted a report of everyone who was called. The original cells of four were organized by grade and study streams. He estimated that by morning there would be about 120 calls, another 30 posters, and about 25 people at the school, and they would be ready to hang posters. He had a campaign desk that would be set up just outside the main exit from the administration area. Everyone was to check in through that desk, and the campaign team would staff the desk and direct operations from there. I was instructed to write a campaign platform. Five to seven points—short, descriptive, and catchy. We would get them printed and ready to distribute later in the campaign. We would keep the platform secret until we were ready. I would greet everyone personally by name the next morning and every day thereafter. I was to go home and study last year's yearbook and memorize as many current grade ten and eleven names and faces as possible. He figured I had a pretty good handle on the twelves and thirteens.

The Rave had created a machine, and I told him so. He said this campaign was against the machine. The usual machine elected someone in grade thirteen based on the sway of their seniority and presumed maturity and influence on younger siblings, cousins, teammates, club mates, and all the normal big cheese bullshit. The Rave was hell bent on getting grade twelves in charge. He figured we were a brighter, more tuned in group. *OK*, I thought, *let's go with that*.

I didn't phone anybody. Our phone rang all night. The Rave phoned four times. He was predicting a landslide. "You're a bona fide phenomenon, a shooting star celebrity," he said. "You're a minor pimple-faced god. The fourteen- and fifteen-year-old girls seem to love you. God knows why. The sixteen-year-old and older women appear too smart to be smitten by you. Just don't fuck this up and stay cool. That ain't too hard, is it? Study names and faces. Listen. Don't speak. You'll just fuck things up if you talk."

Seventy-seven poster hangers, 124 recorded phone calls, and 113 posters or various forms of art. One amply endowed grade ten drew a heart on and through her cleavage. In the centre of the heart she wrote, "Scarface for president." It was a big heart at the crest of her cleavage. She was told to wash it off before the morning announcements by the VP, who whispered in my ear shortly after the ordering of the cleansing that I should refrain from any suggestion that free speech was being suppressed in this case.

"Well, sir, I guess she had to get something off her chest," I remarked. He couldn't suppress a snicker.

The morning announcements went well for the campaign. When I said, "Good morning," several classrooms cheered and three broke into a chant of "Scarface for president": the Rave at work, all orchestrated. The guy was a fuckin' genius or a fuckin' asshole, depending on one's political stripe.

The first week of the campaign went extremely well. I decided, without the Rave's input, to distribute the $233.50 remaining to the other candidates. I doled out forty dollars each to the two other presidential candidates and twenty each to the three treasurer candidates, three secretary candidates, and two junior VPs. My campaign was officially $6.50 in the hole, not counting the $300 in tourism funding I picked up from Scarecrow's mom.

By the end of the week, a few disturbing things emerged—that were all minor according to the Rave. A few groups came out against me, mostly led by grade thirteens, which was to be expected. The wrestling team made it known that I was a poor choice or, as they elegantly put it, a fuckin' wimp. The student newspaper was against my presidency. I didn't even know we had a student newspaper. This was a group primarily composed of honour students who were extremely smart and not too popular. Their diatribe actually sparked a second newspaper published by a group of non-conformists, tenth grade hippie chicks. Well, hot damn! I knew who I wanted to hang with between those two groups. The four young women were vocal and intelligent. They were writing stories on all the campaigns and about issues they thought were important. Some liked me. Some preferred the other candidates.

The first all-candidates' meeting, open to all students, was held on Thursday after school. Two hundred or so politically minded individuals were present. I guess I fared well. The Rave conducted a poll on Friday morning. According to the poll, I was getting seventy-six percent of the vote. The other two candidates were at twelve percent and ten percent, with only two percent uncertain or declining to comment. The survey was 120 kids proportionately selected by grade representation. I was running away with grades nine, ten, and eleven. I held a decent lead with my grade-twelve peer group, and I was in solid third with the grade thirteens and the wrestling team.

The Rave suggested—actually, he highly recommended—that I host a party on Friday night. Good idea. Keep the momentum flowing.

We should have put some more thought into the planning phase. We decided on a bonfire in the woods at the cow pond located just across the highway from the school. Two hundred or so politically-minded individuals showed up, and probably 150 of them were underage. Fire management and noise management were not our strengths and had certainly not been considered in the extensive three-minute planning phase. The smoke from the fire could be seen above the treetops, and the noise drifted across the highway to Scott Lane and beyond.

I was comfortable at the bonfire, although some underlying tensions could be felt between the supporters of the opposing presidential candidates. Rave and I had a cooler with twelve Molson Exports and were sitting on a big log at the south end of the cow pond. We were in the act of what the Rave referred to as political glad handing. Most kids came by and said "Good luck" or "You have this in the bag," regarding the election. It all felt good. I was leaning back against a branch on the log and feeling really good. Solid. I was thinking about the previous February and the Saturday afternoon we had spent there playing hockey, roasting hot dogs and drinking a couple of beers. The cow pond was a perfect rink. The farmer who owned the land, Mr. Murphy, had made the pond 50 feet wide and about 150 feet long. It was a bitch to shovel, but with a bunch of kids looking to play hockey, that work went fast. There had been about thirty of us: half from a couple of streets on the edge of town where we lived, the neighbourhood kids. The other half were country kids from the third and fourth county lines. We divided naturally on town versus country teams and played for three to four hours. A light snow was falling, and a few girlfriends and others kept a fire going. It was perfect. Scenic, Christmas-card stuff. Like this night, the whole thing felt good—just teenagers kicking back, doing what teenagers did. No problems, just fun. Some kids sat on the case of beer they'd brought, some passed around brown paper bags of Ruby Rouge or Four Aces, and others passed joints. Perfect.

Rave kept on leaving and then coming back with one or two kids. I always said hi, but I didn't recognize half of them. Rave let me know that he was recruiting votes to our side. All good with me. The Ex was cold, and a couple of the girls that the Rave brought over were hot. I was more than willing to share a spot on the log with them.

The local police and the fire chief were alerted to some serious shenanigans and arrived shortly after eleven. Maybe it was just the smoke signals coming from the cow pond. The flashing lights and sirens gave the attendees early warning of the pending arrival. Our gathering was blessed with the presence of both the fire chief and the police chief's offspring.

All hell broke loose. The voters headed west or north in the general direction of the lake outside of town or into some open fields. We had told everyone to park no closer than the strip mall, almost a mile east and south of the woods. Those driving were heading away from their potential getaway vehicles.

The Rave and I were surprisingly calm. Well, the Rave was. We led a small group, maybe twenty or twenty-five, north and east through the woods right to the edge of the highway and then took a sharp right. The few posters brought to the non-partisan event, or so we claimed it was, had been put in the fire before we left. The amount of beer and booze bottles left behind was staggering.

The sharp right headed us directly toward the cow tunnel. Before we entered the cow tunnel, we could hear and vaguely see the police coming out of the woods and heading back to their cars. They drove up the highway where most of the politically-inclined would be emerging from the woods. The firemen were employing a bucket brigade. They still had buckets on their trucks. Who would have guessed that?

With the excitement and the fire both dying down, we marched our little troop through the cow tunnel under the highway. We dispersed at the top of the hill in the field across the highway. I got through the fields behind my street, through the bush, and down the hare line straight to my house. The hare line was the almost mythical strip of land between two families on our street. The Hair clan was on one side and the Hare clan was on the other side of this pathway. Both families were blessed with four attractive daughters, whom I had no chance of dating.

My mom asked me if I knew about a big fire across the highway in the woods.

"No, Mom. Not a thing," I replied.

The police arrived at the door about ten minutes later, as the Rave had predicted they would. When I answered their knock, the officers were shocked to see me. No potential lawbreakers had passed the police or firemen heading in our direction.

The young officer from my last law enforcement interview, about ten days earlier when I had arrived home from Winnipeg, couldn't restrain himself. "Scarface, how the hell did you get here?"

"Well, I live here."

"You know what the fuck I mean. From the woods. From the cow pond. How did you get here?"

"Well, if I was in the woods, I would have crossed the highway and gone through the fields. Then through the woods across the street, then down between the Hares' and the Hairs' houses, and voila, home with my mom."

"Listen, you little prick. You were hosting that so-called big political rally in the woods. Kids are falling out of the bushes and fields all along the highway and township lines. We have a cruiser sitting on the twenty-three cars abandoned in the parking lot at the strip mall. So, all I want to know now is how the hell did you get home without us seeing you? Every kid we scooped up said the political rally was organized by you and your campaign manager."

"Well, I can assure you that my campaign manager is at home with his mom, as is your chief's son and the fire chief's daughter, and all I can tell you about getting here is I would have had to cross the highway right in front of you."

His partner went back to the car. The police radio hadn't stopped spitting out sounds of fury, static, and expressions of disbelief since they arrived.

"How did you get by us?" my police friend asked me one more time.

"Officer, how did the chicken cross the highway?"

"Stop fuckin' with me, Scarface. You might need a friend or two in my workplace."

"Officer, how did the cow cross the highway?"

"Scarface, you clever little prick." He had to laugh.

"You beat the confession out of my hide, officer. Good work."

"The two chiefs' kids were with you?"

"We call it political foresight."

"Fuckin' brilliant, Scarface. Fuckin' incredibly brilliant! Win the fuckin' election! See you later!" He went to leave, then stopped and leaned in close. "Listen, Scarface. Keep it straight between you and me at all times. Here's some advice: don't go golfing with anybody's daughter who is well connected. You're not a favoured son in the upper end of town. Win the election. Show them! But for God's sake, keep your nose clean!"

CHAPTER 4

Flirting with Disaster

I was proud that my son was running for president of the student council. I didn't think he had a chance at all, but he was standing up. That had to be a positive, although he was not exactly staying under the radar. There was such a change in him. His little sister came home on Wednesday all excited because all the big kids in grade seven and eight at her public school were talking about the high school elections. She said no one from our part of town ever got elected for anything, or so she'd heard.

This was a big deal for our little family. His big sister called on Friday night. She usually called on Sunday before the *Ed Sullivan Show*. She wanted me to tell her brother she was very proud of him. We all were. He was out somewhere at a party.

For me, life wasn't returning to normal. My son was bringing some previously unknown force or foreign feeling into our lives. It felt like we were driving fast on less than a quarter tank of gas or near empty. What if he lost the election? Things were still stacked against us. What if he ran really hard and his tank emptied? I tried to tell him not to get too far ahead of himself. He just laughed and said he never thought he would get this far, so why not push a little further? And that rang true. It reached way above the low expectations many in town believed he could achieve.

Everything else in our lives felt sort of stable, if not normal. We were not used to much light, let alone bright ones. The lights weren't burning away all the dark in my past or the future shadows our past lives could cast. I was wondering if this was all too much too fast for him, for us. I was turning this over in my mind for the umpteenth time, like I did on my lonely weekend nights, after the little one went to bed—she wasn't so little at almost ten years old—when he came striding in the back door. He was smiling. I could see he had had a couple of beers and maybe had been running. He was wearing a grin. What he would call a "shit-eating grin." I never got how that kind of grin was a good thing, but that's what he was wearing.

"You're home early. Why such a big grin? Have you been running? Drinking?"

"A little bit of both, Mom. You feel like a beer?"

"OK. If you tell me what you've been up to."

"I will. It's very high level, presidential stuff."

He laughed and told me he had to pee and to please open the beers and he would be right back. I got two bottles of my favourite beer, Labatt's 50, out of the fridge and opened them. I poured them into two frosted mugs I kept in the little freezer at the top of our fridge.

He came back, and we sat at the kitchen table and clinked our glasses. We made eye contact as we took our first sip together, as we always did.

"Cold beer. Thank you."

"You bought them, so thank you. What were you up to, and why are you home before midnight on a Friday night?"

"I just wanted to spend some time with my dear mom."

"Now you're sounding like a politician."

"Well, to tell you the truth, I'm home a little earlier than planned for political reasons."

"OK, now this is beginning to sound like some political nonsense or crap. By the way, your older sister called and said she's very proud of you. Now tell me some truth."

"That was great she called. I love that she feels that way. So, Mom, here's the story."

"I don't want a story, son. I want the truth."

"Mom, Mom, Mom, just trust me. I'll make this as truthful as possible with some minor parts of the story left out for your own good."

"For my own good?"

"Yeah, in case you get asked about it later."

"Son, this is starting to go in a direction I don't like. I hope you aren't flirting with disaster, acting like a big shot."

"Mom, I might be a little on the edge here, but there were about two hundred others sharing in the shenanigans."

"If that's supposed to be comforting, it's not."

"OK. Let me tell you what every other kid will be telling their parents tonight and tomorrow morning—if they choose to tell any of the truth."

"That sounds like a good start, son, and we will take it from there."

I was thinking to myself, *Dear God, don't let him fly too high and get burned*, which seemed to be the perfect cue for what came next. Before he could get started on his story, I heard a car pull into the driveway, and a few seconds later there was a knock on the front door. I could see the outline of the officer's hat, uniform, and holster. A shadow from the recent past at our door.

"Son, what have you done?"

"Mom, this is OK. I have this."

He strode to the front door, seemingly without fear or any hesitation. He welcomed the young officer and his partner into the house. Neither one of them chose to invite me into the conversation. I heard it all. When the officer left, my son came back into the kitchen and asked if I wanted another beer. I said yes and I asked him if he wanted some popcorn. He poured the beer as I stood shaking the popcorn pot on the stove. We didn't talk until the popcorn had popped. I salted it and put it in two bowls and poured some melted butter on top.

"Mom, let me explain."

"Son, I think I wanted popcorn because I feel I was just at the movies watching a bad scene unfold in my hallway."

"So, pretty entertaining then?"

"No, not entertaining. Goddamn frightening and scary. Making the popcorn helped me calm down a bit. Son, you can't flirt with disaster like this. You can't invite shit into your life. If you take chances there are only so many times you will walk away safely. I can't . . . I won't get by. I won't make it if you get in trouble or hurt or worse. That current would be too fast. It would sweep me down the stream, and I wouldn't have the strength or the will to swim back."

I started to cry. He remained quiet. I looked at him through the haze of my tears. Shadows. His image wasn't clear. I couldn't make him out.

"Son, you cannot put yourself in harm's way. You know from our past that shadows hang over us. Don't invite darkness, son. For the love of God, please. Forget God, son, for your love of *me*, please don't. Please don't."

I cried some more. We sat in silence and nursed our beers. We had lost our appetite for the popcorn.

He finished his beer, got up, and then bent over and kissed my forehead. "Mom, I'll be careful. I won't invite darkness. I love you."

After he went to bed, I stayed up a little longer and finished my beer. The stairs up to our bedrooms seemed long and steep that night. My feet felt heavy and my bones weary.

Disaster tugged at my skirt, but only for a while, then it ripped my skirt off and raped me of my life. This was the disaster that landed and when it landed on me, it pounded away, and there was nothing I could do.

And still no coroner's report.

Fair Warning

Dear God

Knock some common sense into him.
Show him some way forward without breaking him.
You don't need to lay him low.
We don't have that much lower to go.
So, give him a little bit of your light.
Give him some of your infinite wisdom.
Was the cow-tunnel escape part of your greater plan?
Is that infinite wisdom or a light?
In this case the light at the end of a cow tunnel.
Well, thank you for that.
Sorry I took your name in vain,
But you didn't give me fair warning.
Or maybe you did.
In the future if you send messages make them a little clearer or louder.
Other than this we're all fine.
Maybe this too shall pass.
I can't remember the story.
Was it one of your angels or just a myth about the angel who flew too close to the sun, and their wings burned?
If my son flies too high, please don't let him burn.
Don't let him crash to the ground.
Or give me fair warning,
So, I can come catch him
If you won't.

Amen.

CHAPTER 5

Cottage Country

It was all good that Friday evening ended with an earlier-than-expected voter migration. Stone Pony and Mister, as promised, and as usual, were at my door at 6 a.m. on Saturday morning. The coffee in the thermos they brought me was strong and black, even though they knew I took milk and sugar.

We were doing a cottage run. The gentlemen of garbage had a year-round weekend business with over 350 pick-ups on Saturday and another 150 on Sunday. They had aggressively promoted their business over the past spring and summer and added almost two hundred customers. I'm pretty good with numbers. My crew was charging between ten and twenty dollars per pick-up depending on remoteness, load factor, length of driveway, and general accessibility. They were taking in roughly $7,500 per weekend through the end of October when their year-round clientele dropped to two hundred or so at about twelve dollars per pick-up. We were running garbage barrels fifteen hours every weekend. My take was an incredible $225. Fifteen bucks an hour! And we ran hard. The truck would remain parked on the road, and the three of us would disperse down cottage laneways, often to multiple households, and wheel back barrels. *Wheel* is a bit of an overstatement, as we tilted them on their edges and rolled them that way or carried the pails. Less than a handful of our customers actually had wheels on their barrels. Stone Pony and Mister had what they referred to as "preferred-customer houses" where only they did the pick-up. They said those were the houses where the women were frequently scantily clad. They described this clientele as "white trouser snake teasers who hoped they could make a black or a red man hard with glimpses of white wanton flesh."

The preferred-customer lanes and driveways seemed to be longer and more secluded, so I didn't give a rat's ass about their preferred pick-ups. It was tough work. The driveways were often rough and full of ruts and grooves. The barrels did not easily wheel or roll, and the bottom rims of most pails were damaged, uneven, or broken. Stone Pony and Mister carried their pails, and I was getting strong enough to do the same. I earned my money. It was sometimes scary and was definitely "shit" work. We encountered two bears, four or five porcupines, raccoons, deer, and a fox on my first Saturday. That would be just an average "wild kingdom" set of encounters as it turned out. Stone Pony saw two bobcats, a marten, and a weasel and swore he got a glimpse of a badger once. He told me I wouldn't ever see these animals with my ignorant white-man eyes. He said Mister was showing promise as a potential Indian despite being a shuffling negro of a barrel-runner. Mister countered that he had seen three beavers and two wonderful sets of white breasts. Not bad for a guy who was told never to even make eye contact with white women as a youngster growing up in the southern states. Mister said he loved that slice of segregated, racist bullshit. Who wanted to look at their eyes when the good parts were all there to gaze upon? My mind couldn't stop working the math! Ten weekends at $7,500, plus twenty winter weekends at $2,400, and then the full twenty-two weeks at $9,000 per from mid-May to Labour Day. Stone Pony and Mister were pulling in $321,000 a year in cottage country. If I worked every weekend, I was going to make well over $10,000!

By the end of the day on Saturday, I was done. I just wanted to get a shower and sleep. Mister announced pick-up at 7 a.m. on Sunday. Stone Pony said with luck, we would be done by 11, and they would still pay me for five hours. Mister told me half my pay would be by cheque, the other half in cash. They had formed a company and were keeping records for tax purposes. They were entrepreneurial businessmen.

By the third weekend I recommended a trend-setting innovation for their business. Hefty Bags, fifty for $6.99. If our customers used the bags, we wouldn't need to run the barrels back to their bins. Our time would be cut in half.

Stone Pony and Mister contemplated my proposed innovation for the remainder of Saturday and most of Sunday. At the end of our route on Sunday, we pulled the truck into a small restaurant and went in for a business meeting. Stone Pony and Mister didn't order. They just nodded at the waitress, who owned the restaurant with her sister, and Stone Pony said the white kid would have the same.

She squinted at me. "Well, if it isn't the infamous Scarface himself. Started any forest fires lately?" My companions snickered at her joke, and I couldn't help but break into a shit-eatin' grin. The bonfire left unattended in the woods at the cow pond, through the exaggerations of the town gossips, had been blown so out of proportion that it was now described as a potentially devastating forest fire that could have jumped the highway and burned the entire town to the ground.

Mister started in. "How do we convince them to start using these bags?"

"We tell them they save wear and tear on their garbage pails."

"Why would they pay seven bucks for the bags when they don't have to?"

"Give them the bags for free."

"That's an expense. Multiply five hundred customers times seven dollars for a box of bags. That's thirty-five hundred bucks!"

"Just one percent of your annual revenue."

"How do you know what our annual revenue is?"

"I did the math."

Stone Pony took over for his partner. "I still don't think they'll use them. And why give these pricks anything for free? We've already undercut every other garbage pick-up service north of the town."

"OK, give them ten or twenty free to get them started and charge them less for bag versus pail pick-up."

"Now you're eating into revenue."

"Tell them a two-buck price increase for pails is starting January first. If you're the cheapest then you can take a price increase. Start the new system in November when our customers drop to two hundred. Let's see what happens with them first before we go full route in May."

Stone Pony nodded. "OK. We can give this a shot."

"One more thing," I said.

Mister raised his eyebrows. "You've got another innovation?"

"Yes, a pay raise."

"What?"

"Of course! That's what innovators get."

"How much?"

"Four hundred dollars per weekend"

"You're crazy! Three-fifty."

"Done."

And then the biggest plate of food I had ever seen in my life arrived and was placed in front of me. Stone Pony and Mister didn't say boo during the meal. They just ate.

Then the oddest thing happened. Two minutes into our meal, the waitress, Jeannie, came by. "Meals OK, boys? Fine, good to know. More coffee?"

"Yep. You're welcome, Jeannie."

"Papers, boys?"

"Yep."

"Yep. I'll add that to the bill."

"Thanks, Jeannie. Best pancakes ever. Yes, indeedy."

"More bacon and sausage?"

"Yes."

"Two strips and a poke for all three of you big, strappin', loud-talkin', never-shut-up gentlemen?" "Yes, that will be fine, Jeannie. Now piss off and get the papers and the grub."

"Nice talkin' with you boys. And keep recommending the place to all your customers."

Mister and Stone Pony never said a word, grunted, or even looked her way through the whole conversation that the waitress conducted with herself about the meals. Then, Jeannie just walked away.

The papers arrived followed shortly thereafter with a refresh of meat and coffee. I started to say something, but Mister put his hand up in the classic stop-sign manner.

"Shut up, stay quiet, read, and educate yourself," Stone Pony said. "Start with the *Globe* business section, not sports."

We ate and read. Nobody talked. The business headlines were vaguely familiar. I had probably heard snatches and pieces related to the articles on the CBC. I did look through the local paper every day, but this stuff was largely foreign to me. We had five papers—the Saturday and Sunday *Globe and Mail*, the *Star*, and the local paper, the *Racket and Crimes*, as we hip youngsters called it. There was no local Sunday paper.

When it looked like I was finishing the Sunday *Globe* business section, Mister passed me Saturday's *Globe* business. The sports sections were kept beyond my reach. I could see pictures of Ullman against Mackie and one of Jean Beliveau; the stories were probably all some pre-season NHL hype. Most likely about the Leafs' chances of winning the cup, because that's just how the big-city papers were slanted.

We ate and read in silence for over an hour. Jeannie came and went, talking to herself, refilling and replenishing as she saw fit. Mister leaned back and, on cue, Jeannie produced the bill. Mister put a fifty-dollar bill on top of the cheque, and we got up and walked out. The total on the cheque was $31.50. I just shook my head and thought I had underbid my collection services. We quietly got in the truck, with Mister driving. In thirty minutes or so, we pulled up to my house. Stone Pony and I had both been snoozing.

Mister peeled off $225 from the big wad that Stone Pony had pulled out of the truck's glove compartment. They took turns giving me the following directions, starting with Mister, then Stone Pony.

"You give your mother fifty dollars every weekend."

"Your cheque, we deposit for one hundred and seventy-five, less government deductions when we deposit our own cheques. We have set that up with the bank already."

"Go to the bank every couple of weeks, and get your passbook updated. The money is in your savings account."

"There's an extra fifty dollars in cash this week for all the crap that is coming your way."

I was going to ask how they set up a bank account on my behalf, but Mister's hand went up, and Stone Pony gave me my next direction. "Don't spend your money stupidly. Every couple of weeks, put some of the cash we pay you in your checking account. When you get over five hundred dollars, move at least half into savings. Sign up for the driving course at school tomorrow. We're going to need at least a second truck and crew. Learn to drive and get your license soon. Tell no one about our route, our business, and especially our revenues. Got it? Just nod if you do."

I nodded, still somewhat overcome by my newfound wealth.

"Good. One last thing. Maybe two. Maybe three. That party on Friday night. Never do that shit again, or you're fired! Got it? Just nod! Second, start studying, and get your fuckin' grades up. Got it? Good. You're getting the drift of this! Third, buy a bunch of heavy-duty bags. We'll roll this innovation out in a couple of weeks. We'll reimburse your expenses. Give us the receipts. Finally, drop a subject and pick up grade-eleven bookkeeping tomorrow. Got it?"

They went silent.

"Anything else guys?" I asked.

"Keep your fuckin' nose clean," Mister replied. "You ain't all that popular beyond grade ten. Any other questions?"

"No, but you know what's really cool?"

"What?" they both asked with eyebrows raised.

"We were the Newspaper Crew, sitting there at breakfast. That was cool."

Stone Pony and Mister didn't smile much. I knew without knowing they both got there travelin' down some hard roads. These guys had taken beatings in more ways than one. But they smiled at this.

"Yes we are, Scarface, and it is cool. You know why?"

"Why?"

"Cuz it's just the three of us in on it, and that fuckin' yakky Jeannie."

We all smiled and laughed. That laugh felt good, as did the $225 in my pocket. I needed a little smile after the roller coaster two weeks of the election.

My popularity was indeed not universal. My mom had experienced some reactions from parents and some town officials. It would be good to hand her a hundred dollars. Stone Pony and Mister didn't know I had already been giving her fifty dollars a week for the first two weeks from my cottage-country work.

First stop was the bathroom. I had to take a look at my beak! Too many people had been telling me to keep my nose clean lately. People who I believed cared about me—so I knew my nose had better be spotless.

CHAPTER 6

The Cow Pond Catastrophe and Desecration

The Monday morning after our little political rally and bonfire was eventful, even prior to the morning announcements. The VP called our house on Sunday and told me to be in his office by 7:30 a.m. for a counselling session. The principal, the police chief, and the fire chief would be in attendance.

Of course, most of the shit broke out on the weekend. By late Sunday afternoon, rumours had moved from the credible, reality-based events of Friday's cow pond party to a macabre description of what must have been a hallucinogenic-induced surreal event. I learned two of those bigger words over the weekend. At least I was getting some educational benefits from my experiences.

Amongst the total roller-coaster emotions over the weekend was the behaviour of the police chief and the fire chief. Initially irate and suspecting that their own children had been in attendance at the cow pond catastrophe and desecration, they switched to a calmer demeanour when they learned their perfect offspring were safe at home. The cow pond catastrophe and desecration was seen as violating everything we held holy in our town and the adjacent township lands. (The cow pond and the woods were just over the town line.) The chiefs, the white chiefs anyway, had initially reacted with extreme vitriol, with most of their anger aimed in my direction. That young, arrogant prick Scarface leading our youth into a bonfire of adolescent misdeeds, misdemeanours, sin, and corruption. That misbehaving, fatherless, little asshole has led our innocent children astray. I think they were blaming me for every single flaw known to mankind and throughout the greater metropolis of our city. Increased flatulence, belching, acne, premarital sex, masturbation, bralessness, marijuana smoking, and hallucinogenics on the streets! Of course, this was all within the first two or three hours of the cow pond catastrophe and desecration, when early reports were coming in from the first attendees rounded up by our fire, police, and ambulance crews. The early reports included eyewitness testimony that offspring of the fire and police chiefs, the mayor, two councillors, the township reeve, several lawyers, prominent business persons, doctors, tinkers, tailors, and so on had been enthusiastic attendees, except for, as it turns out, the Indian chief's little darlings.

When it turned out that the chiefs'—the white chiefs', which in my case were the right chiefs'—little darlings were at home with their mothers, as was the mayor's extremely well-built fifteen-year-old daughter, then my crimes against the ruling class were deemed not so extreme. The mayor's daughter? How did I miss her? I mean, she was built like a brick shithouse. I don't even know what that means or how it fits as a description of that very shapely, good-looking young woman, but that was how she was commonly described.

Anyway, it seems that because their progeny, another good word I learned, were not at the CPC&D, at least at the time of arrival of the town forces of officialdom, safety, sobriety, and social sanctity, then it was a less serious situation. It helped that I was officially at home as well, which was duly noted in the two officers' reports. (Two more cynical cops stopped by twenty minutes after the first two departed to verify it was actually me at home with my mom and little sister.)

"Holy crap, Batman! He's home. He's actually at home."

"I don't know how that little fucker made it here, Robin. We better get back out there and find our own daughters before our wives get even more pissed at us."

"Yeah, why are they pissed at us? They should be pissed at him and them! What the Sam Hill did we do wrong?"

"Well, Robin, it seems men like us have not done enough to curb and eliminate the action of brash peckerheads like Scarface. That's our crime."

"We need to eradicate this bullshit from our town, Batman."

"Bullshit, Robin. We were all out drinking and trying to get laid when we were their age. Scarface ain't the problem, so don't go all righteous on me. You know there are a lot of prominent citizens in this town who party, drink, and screw around. You scapegoat that kid—that's just too fuckin' easy, and it solves nothing. Get your head out of your ass and concentrate on your own house."

At least, I hope that's how the conversation went. Call me an optimist.

Mom and I took a few late calls from angry parents. The police chief dropped by at a quarter to one. He looked me over rather angrily but showed courtesy to my mom. He pulled me to the side and let me know a few things. He knew I had probably pulled a fast one and thanked me for pulling his kid out of the fire, so to speak, but I should not count on Houdini-like escapes in the future, and for the love of God, keep my nose clean.

He said one other thing: "I'm going to take you back to a dark place. You ready? Yeah? You think you're ready? OK, two words: Nick Ages. Nick Ages for you again, Scarface. You remember how bad that situation was that led to your mother choking out those words, Nick Ages? Remember? That's good. Don't get yourself in places that can lead to that pain again. No charges are going to come of this. The rumours and yelling will be loud, but there will be no charges. I cried that night when your mom was lying there on the floor. You cried, my officers cried. Never seen anything like that. So, stay away from events that bring that world down on you and yours. Got it?"

"Yes, sir. Thank you, sir."

Those two words filled me with dread, remorse, pain, and worry. Stiff, sobering, icy, and gut wrenching. Nick Ages. No charges. My mom's mouth was so broken that when she tried to say, "no charges" after being beaten and raped, it sounded like "Nick Ages." The cops actually searched for someone named Nick Ages.

Being in cottage country all day Saturday was an escape from the storm that raged over the cow pond catastrophe and desecration. The local radio station, CFOR 1680, had a Saturday-morning talk and call-in show for local events. Early on, it got hijacked by callers who called the CPC&D a cataclysmic event where all hell and evil had broken loose. Callers even pitted our high school against the other local high school. Our high school was portrayed as full of lowlifes, NDP leftists, anarchists, hippies, and general scum. The other high school apparently had a caller or two who saw this incident as a clear indication of the superiority of the education, moral teachings, and guidance provided by the high school from where they had graduated. The newer high school, ours, opened in 1961. The old one had opened in 1914. Our school was staffed by young, liberal, tolerant, left-leaning teachers who were deemed weak on values of the traditional variety. That absence of values was the root cause of the incident in the woods. One caller described the events as an official massacre of morals and used it as a platform to advocate for a separate Catholic high school. That led into an open debate about Catholic versus Protestant morals, ethics, and teachings. The morning radio show went to mid-afternoon before the mayor phoned in and asked for calm on the airways. Behind the scenes he phoned the owner of the station, a curling and golf buddy, told him to get that fuckin' nitwit running the show to shut it down. The religious debate had not been helped by the hourly announcement of Mass times at Guardian Angels Catholic Church on the town social calendar.

My mom stopped listening after the first hour and left the phone unplugged, a wise move after the previous night's late calls. Mom passed on her weekly shopping trip. Many of the callers asked the radio talk show host to bring me on live. The host couldn't get a hold of anyone at our house despite several efforts.

Some callers indicated that I had left town. Some said the police chief had taken me into custody, and some even reported that I had suffered severe burns at the bonfire. A response to that call suggested my looks might have then been improved somewhat. That was a tad cruel. My friends and the Rave were eating this all up, and as I learned later, they and everyone within listening distance stayed tuned in to the show for the entire six hours it was on the air. That was four hours longer than normal. CFOR announced a special four-hour show the following Saturday to follow up. The only institution that complained about that was the Royal Canadian Legion, who saw their afternoon bingo attendance drop by more than half and feared another cash shortfall the following weekend. They later cleverly announced they would reschedule bingo from 3 to 5 p.m. the following Saturday and advertised the timing change on the radio's social calendar.

Notoriety seemed to be winning over celebrity.

Saturday night, I laid low. Mom and I watched a John Wayne movie, but I kept falling asleep. The late-night, early-morning, and hard work were more than catching up to me. I took a bath instead of a shower when I got home. Mom was right; a bath was relaxing. She had to wake me up to prevent me from drowning. We laughed that it would be an interesting twist to the story. From hellfire pit to drowning pool in twenty-four hours.

Sunday, I was off barreling with the crew. We were done by 11, and Mister handed me the $225. That was staggering. A bonus of fifty dollars. When I asked what it was for, he said it was for dealing with all the bullshit I would be facing. He said that Stone Pony and he preferred to read the papers in silence, and that would have been impossible if I had been yakking about Friday night. So, the bonus was also for staying quiet during our breakfast. Jeannie didn't stay quiet, but they had the uncanny ability to completely tune her out.

After breakfast when I came in the door at home, I asked my mom if she felt like Chinese food for an early dinner. We phoned our order into the Golden Dragon, known locally as the Rusty Reptile, and I took a quick shower and then rode my bike downtown to pick up our food. Mom plugged the phone back in to call the Rusty Reptile, and it started ringing as soon as I hit the shower.

Nobody noticed me on my bike as I went right down the main drag to the restaurant. A couple of heads turned in the restaurant, but I managed to enter, pay, and exit without incident. When I rode by Little Hendri Park on the way back, a few local heads were gathering, probably for the first shared joint of the day. They were a little slow on the uptake as I pedaled past, so I was twenty or thirty yards beyond them when one managed to gather his wits. "Peace, brother, and fuck the establishment!" he shouted.

I realized then that the local heads were with me.

At home, I dished out the plates for the three of us. The phone was once again unplugged, so we could eat in peace. I had tucked two twenties and a ten under my mom's plate and a fiver under my little sister's. They spotted them at the same time. When I explained that there was good money in garbage, my mom was already in tears. Money had never come easily, and although we were OK and gettin' by, it was still a struggle. My little sister told us about all the different ways she was going to spend her money. That fiver was spent about ten times. Mom said maybe I got the garbage money distribution mixed up between the two of them. We all laughed.

The meal was the calm before the storm.

Sunday evening, the storm came full bore. About 5:30 p.m., a group of ladies from the church arrived at our front door. My mom and I met them on the steps together. They had come directly from a lady's church tea and were there to offer support and advice. One of the good God-fearing women asked Mom if she was going to invite them in, as a good hospitable Christian woman would. Mom's knees buckled a bit. I had seen and felt the strength of such words as they knuckled into my gut and sucker-punched my spirit. Mom held her ground and said her house was too humble for women of such high purpose. There were no high teas to be had there. She thanked them for their support and said she was seeking advice directly from a higher authority. Then she looked upward and wished them a pleasant Sunday. They seemed frozen in place, but the arrival of a police car broke their trance.

My officer friend got out of his car, introduced himself, and explained the ladies should leave, so he could conduct a routine police follow-up. They disbanded stiffly but orderly, got in their late-model sedans, and drove away. The officer waited for their complete departure before telling us we had some friends on our street. They had called in a complaint about a bunch of snooty, busybody hypocrites harassing people in our peaceful neighbourhood. He said good day to my mom and asked if he could take me aside for a little chat.

We moved into the backyard, out of earshot. "Listen, Scarface, there's a general uproar," he said. "The chief knows what you did for him and some others, but don't over-play that card. Maintain a low profile. Be polite and apologetic about everything and anything. Your high school VP, the chief, and others will be meeting with you tomorrow morning at 7:30 a.m. Miracle of miracles, the meeting is definitely not connected to the pious biddies who were just here."

The rest of Sunday evening was quiet. We kept the phone unplugged. The Rave dropped by for a brief strategy discussion on the upcoming candidate meetings and the election assemblies to be held on Thursday. Our street had far more traffic than normal. We peacefully watched the *Ed Sullivan Show* and *Bonanza*, and I read a couple of chapters in English and history.

At 7:30 a.m. sharp the next morning, we were in it deep. The admonishments were plentiful, repetitive, and laced with dire warnings. The gathered collective brain trust had not connected the dots and figured out the escape route from the cow pond catastrophe and desecration. My officer buddy had not revealed the Houdini technique I'd used. There was a good deal of consternation, condemnation, and confoundedness in the room. Dozens upon dozens of fleeing "cow-ponders" had said I was there and had told their parents I had been there. They told the whole town on the radio call-in show, told God in church on Sunday, and told each other. *Scarface was there!* Much to my joy, they also said that many children of the town officials and dignitaries as well as other members of the "hoity-toity, high-falutin' elite" had offspring in attendance as well. The cow pond catastrophe and desecration would land in the lore of our town in mythical proportions and distortions for decades. Much like the recounting of the first night when the drinking age was lowered to eighteen, with allegedly thousands drinking at the Refuge despite the bar having a legal capacity of 237 total in all three drinking rooms combined.

I was asked how many kids had been at the cow pond. Sort of a trick question, because if I provided an answer, it would confirm my attendance. I said I had heard around two hundred. My estimate was derived from some of my acquaintances, who'd heard from some of their acquaintances, who had talked to people who actually had been in the woods at the cow pond, so my information was fourth-hand at best.

The VP called bullshit or cow shit, though he didn't word it quite that crudely. He told me to fess up and get on with telling a little truth. He said they had all heard a number between 450 and 500 had been in attendance.

So, I told them a lot of truth. An all-candidates gathering had been rumoured and spread through the school like wildfire on Friday afternoon. That was maybe eighty percent true. It had started as a campaign rally for *moi*, but the Rave had deduced that that might be a problem, so the communications team he had assembled adjusted the scope of the meeting to be all-inclusive, and spread the word accordingly. My interrogators had heard this. I had been there. Truth rating: one hundred percent! There were no arguments from anyone in the room on that one. They verified the veracity of my words.

Next item of business: I dealt with who had been there. I informed them that many children of well-known, well-positioned townsfolk had been in attendance. Truth rating: one hundred percent! There was zero to little eye contact and no verifications on this one. They knew.

Now that I was sharing some truths, I wanted to be helpful. Would they like a list of cow ponders in attendance? Apparently, that verification wasn't necessary, and I felt it would definitely not be appreciated. Truth rating: one hundred percent!

I informed the group that I thought the gathering was getting a little out of hand, so I convinced a number of others to leave with me. That was before the police and firemen arrived at the cow pond. Truth rating: fifty percent, well, sort of. We had convinced about twenty scared-shitless cow ponders, some hand-picked, to follow my lead, or in reality, the Rave's lead. At that specific time, the police and fire vehicles were on the highway—they had not officially arrived at the cow pond, so it was technically true. Although this fact could be verified by at least three men in the room, they chose not to validate my story. Silent acceptance was all I needed. They'd probably heard some variant of that truth from their progeny.

Stern warnings followed. Surprisingly, I was not asked about booze or drugs at the cow pond catastrophe and desecration. The amount of stuff left at the scene was staggering, so I'm sure that was sufficient evidence and required no additional verification. The beer and liquor left behind was substantial, but the amount had become an immensely exaggerated part of the legend.

Just for fun I asked how many people were there when the police arrived. They estimated 450 to 500. Skating the edge of what I could get away with, I told them there had been two hundred at most when I had left. Wow! It had gotten out of hand!

The assembled officials departed, leaving me and the VP in his office. His first words, when we were alone, surprised me. "Thank you for getting my daughter out of there. You know, she's only fifteen. Her getting caught would have caused a great deal of consternation in my household. I dropped her off at the mall, so she could do some shopping with a couple of girlfriends. They were supposed to get some pizza downtown and be home by eleven. She was just a bit late. She was so scared when the police arrived that she confessed to me the next morning. Her girlfriends got caught, and she heard all the calls I took throughout the weekend. I was handling the first of those calls when she walked in on Friday night."

"You're welcome. I should get ready for morning announcements."

"Yes, you should. By the way, she doesn't remember how you smuggled them all out. She did say the children of the mayor, the chief of police, the fire chief, and several other prominent citizens were herded to safety by you and the Rave. You're showing some real political acumen, I guess."

I thought it was all a little bewildering. First, I didn't even know he had a daughter. Second, given where the VP lived, any of his kids would go to the other high school. Third, how the hell had the Rave gotten this select group of kids organized to follow us? He had worked a miracle. When we'd exited the tunnel and let our saved souls flee toward home, the Rave had said that our exit strategy showed brilliant political maneuvering and foresight. I had let that slide because I was happy not to have been found at the cow pond catastrophe and desecration.

I was feeling bewildered and was wondering if there was a higher being or beings to talk to. And I don't mean Bogeyman and Scarecrow when they were stoned out of their gourds and higher than kites. Although they did reach a stage of being truly higher beings. They called it being "blissed out."

My mom got down on her knees from time to time and prayed quiet little words of thanks for whatever good fortune came our way, but mostly she asked for troubled and troublesome people to just pass us by. Me? I lay in bed and contemplated how things unfolded and sent some thoughts skyward. Like Mom, I didn't ask for fame, money, or material things, and certainly not for notoriety or any of the accompanying shit. Just peace, and to be allowed to make our own progress without the judgment of others wreaking havoc on our hopes and weighing us down. Because those were heavy, heavy weights. The high bar of low expectations. People don't expect you to be much, so they don't let you be much. Prayer or just contemplation sometimes helped me through this bewilderment. Bewilderment about why others, who were doing OK, would want to keep me down.

Mysteries and Miracles

Dear God

Mysteries and miracles,
God, that's your territory, not mine.
The way things are unfolding,
I wonder, do you have a hand in all of this?
Some things are divine, others, not so fine.
Things just seem to be rolling and
not many of them under full control.
Thanks for money in my pocket,
Especially being able to help my mom.
Thanks for friends.
Thanks for sense and nonsense.
I have to ask you why I'm learning
exactly how not to act with charity and grace
from those who supposedly seek and are blessed by your grace.
You know the ones,
The old biddies at my mom's door
Those casting stones on the radio show.
They may be pious, but they certainly aren't kind or generous of
faith and spirit.
Not for a second.
They hold themselves as being close to you and clutch onto your
teachings as if some special lifeline is reserved for them and only them.
God, does their clutching and self-righteous grabbing at you leave a mark?
Well, bless you, God, for putting up with their shit.

Amen.

CHAPTER 7

Driving Between the Lines

There was a song out called "Stuck in the Middle with You." I thought it was perfect, except for clowns and jokers all around.

I liked being in the middle—you know, not too high, not too low, but just right. Not full of myself and not down on myself, believing in myself but being humble and grateful.

My son was doing well and not. He was running for president and working hard. He was making good money. Boy, did I appreciate what he gave me! It helped a lot, and it meant more.

I didn't like the police showing up at our door. They were becoming regular visitors. All in all, they had been fair, and they meant no harm. I felt they actually cared about us. Well, some of them did.

The thing with the bonfire, the radio talk show, and the visit from the high tea, crumpets, holier-than-thou ladies was more than unsettling. My son seemed to be a magnet for situations that got attention. Heck, that cow pond had seen more parties over the last decades than anyone could remember. For everyone to act all surprised and like it was some unnatural disaster and calamity was far more surprising than the fact that there had been a party. They say that idle hands are the devil's tools. I think idle minds of the self-righteous are the devil's playground. The devil stirs them up with thoughts of wrongdoing, sin, and evil ways. How did they so easily make those accusations? Unless their holy selves had minds full of evil. I thought their own temptations must be many. Anyway, that was my thought on the matter.

My son probably had a lot to do with that party, but nothing bad happened. The radio talk show was entertaining and would have been a laugh to listen to, except that my son was the central story.

Some of the comments were hilarious and hypocritical as hell. Many of the people calling in had likely been at more than one party at the cow pond themselves. The catastrophe was supposedly that young people had partied, drank, and had probably been smoking marijuana. Well, teens and young people had been partying and doing illegal things forever, like drinking underage and, heaven forbid, having sex. Some callers were treating this catastrophe as the first of its kind ever in the world. That the party had ruined our town and all the reputations of the good sons and daughters of the outraged, beyond-reproach, indignant callers. Such a load of crap!

Desecration? I still can't figure that description for a party. It was a cow pond, across the highway, in the woods. How could anyone desecrate that? I knew they meant something like the moral fibre of our youth—but come on, desecration? People liked to exaggerate, but that was a real stretch.

When my son arrived home earlier than expected, I knew something was off.

The police arriving just confirmed my suspicions. When I think about it, the church ladies should have viewed that night as "the miracle of the cow pond." It had to be a miracle. How else do you explain all those children from prominent families supposedly at the party and in their loving parents' home at the same time? A miracle, a bloody miracle! Hallelujah! My son should have been receiving high praise because he and the Rave were the miracle-workers. I knew he received some quiet thanks and grudging admiration from more than one authority figure.

"Try to keep yourself on the straight and narrow," I told him. My son wanted to get his driver's license, so I talked to him about driving and about life. "Son, keep your car on your side of the road. Stay between the lines of the ditch on your right and the head-on traffic on your left. That will keep you safe and out of trouble. You hit the ditch when you're driving recklessly, not paying attention, or just being stupid. Veering into the other lane is just acting dangerously. You're trespassing into someone's space. You have gone into the wrong lane knowing there is nothing but a whole bunch of bad waiting ahead. Son, the ditch or the other lane is trouble. Live between the lines. That's where we can be all safe and happy, and I don't need to worry."

I hoped he would learn and take to heart my parallel story as well, as he needed to learn parallel parking. I never did.

The coroner's report was well over a month later than expected.

Desecration and Grace

Dear God

A desecration can't be a cow pond party, can it?
Lord, if that event is catching your attention, you might be missing some bigger things down here.
Not my place to suggest, but I think Vietnam and crooked politicians could use a little more focus.
Not much of a prayer so far.

Lord, can you please give your ladies of the high teas and crumpets a lot less religious fervour and outrage?
They could use a dash of grace.
That would be nice for all of us, including them.
That's a hell of a way to live (sorry about cursing),
Telling others how to live and raise their children.
I'm not listening to them at all.

So, you're not getting any benefit from their high and mighty work that they profess to be doing in your name.
That's how they described their mission to my house, your work.
God, maybe they should live between the lines of care for others and demonstrate some actual grace and forgiveness instead of the fire and damnation of the ditch
And their end-of-the-world proclamations when someone veers onto the other side of the road.

God, I can almost guarantee everyone, including the crumpet crew, would be a lot happier if they just focused on grace.
Give it some thought and steer us all in the right direction.
Still not much of a prayer; sorry about that.
I appreciate your hands on the wheel.

Amen.

CHAPTER 8

The Vote

My "Good morning" over the school PA system at the start of the morning announcements elicited cheers in many of the classrooms. Apparently, it was a well-known fact that a significant meeting had been called to determine my demise. The two police cars, the fire chief's truck, eyewitness accounts of the mayor, the Catholic priest, and a united church minister having entered the school office had solidified the fact and the intent of the meeting. No fellow students had seen me arrive at 7 a.m., nor had anyone seen me enter or exit the administrative office. Given that half the school was aware that a special meeting had been called, my future was being widely discussed, and the outcomes were not predicted as positive. I found out later that the dominant theory circulating was that I had been led away in handcuffs. The handcuff speculation was aided by the arrival of my friendly law-enforcement contact. The young police officer had arrived on scene in his patrol car with lights flashing. He had a habit of leaning against his car, spinning his handcuffs around his index finger, and whistling. He later told me that those considering criminal activities found the twirling and whistling unnerving and reconsidered their wayward tendencies. My demise was held as a certainty in some quarters.

The cheers might have been a bit of relief on behalf of the student body, because if I wasn't busted, it was unlikely the fifteen percent of the school in attendance at the cow pond catastrophe and desecration would be charged or incarcerated. A collective sigh of relief was heard throughout the town and township.

I heard later there were a minority of home rooms where some booing occurred.

The second candidate's meeting was scheduled to start at 3:05 p.m. sharp. The meeting was set up in the northwest end of the cafeteria, which could be partitioned off and hold about 250 people. This was a meeting with the candidates running for the office of the president. The Rave and I had gone over my platform briefly on the weekend. He had written a seven-point plan, and we went over it at lunch and in a spare. I was ready and pumped. All the bullshit surrounding the CPC&D had somehow shot me with a will to win this thing. I think I was mostly motivated by the pious, sanctimonious bullshit of a town where a class structure was so freakin' evident I could taste the stink of it.

We drew cards to determine the speaking order. I lost, and the others chose to go first and second. That left me batting in a power position. Drive in some runs. I was good with that. It is an open and direct competition.

The grade-thirteen candidate would be batting lead-off. The session was being supervised, guided, and steered by the assistant wrestling coach and history/politics teacher. This was not a good omen. Several teachers were in attendance as well. Every seat was taken. The student body lined all available space along the walls, two-deep in most places. There were close to four hundred members of the student body in attendance, about the same as the overestimated attendance at the CPC&D. Actually, double the real attendance of the cow pond get-together. Who would have guessed?

The three candidates and their campaign managers, including the Rave and me, and the moderator/teacher were seated at the front. The candidates each had ten minutes to speak and then the floor would be open for questions.

The graduating senior was introduced by his campaign manager. The introduction included his impressive scholastic record, including his early acceptance to Queen's in engineering, the bursaries he had been awarded, his Ontario Scholar status, and then his athletic prowess. The intro took almost three of his ten minutes. I leaned over to the Rave and suggested his intro for me would be about a hundred times quicker. The Rave laughed at that and was quickly and loudly admonished by the moderator. I must admit I was impressed by my fellow candidate's credentials. He was one smart dude. But he looked like crap in a wrestling singlet.

He started great, quoting Sir John A. McDonald, further impressing the hell out of me. He was nervous and uncertain. I didn't blame him for that; this was intimidating. Once he got beyond the Sir John A. quote and one more by Octavius Caesar, he was stumbling on about ability versus popularity and academic credibility versus adolescent capers, when the moderator gave him his two-minute warning. That rattled him. I got that he was contrasting his smarts compared to my idiocy, where he had a substantive case, but then he went rabid. Literally, he foamed at the mouth and went on a two-minute rip on what a disaster I would be as president. I think he said I had the morals of a monkey, the principles of a porcupine, the social consciousness of a squirrel, the intelligence of an insect, the backbone of a beaver, the character of a can of worms, and he rattled off a number of other animal-oriented comparisons. He wasn't making much sense, but he sure as hell was animated. He was red in the face by the one-minute warning and appeared exhausted as he was nearing the end. I'd have thought his wrestling training would have given him a smidgeon more stamina. That's when the Rave whispered, "At least he didn't say you have the dick of a donkey."

I looked at Rave. "I wish," I replied, and we both lost it. We couldn't hold back the laughter. The Rave was tearing up but still wondered how my opponent had missed mentioning my blatant bestiality.

The moderator signaled the end of my opponent's allotted time, and the crowd was stunned. The only sound that could be heard was the Rave and me laughing. The candidate barked at me, red-faced and foaming, "Garbage Boy, you find this funny? Politics are serious business."

"As serious as squirrel shit on a sunny Sunday," I replied. (I had no idea what I meant.) "I think you just went batshit crazy there!"

The room erupted in laughter and cheers. The teachers looked perplexed. The moderator cautioned me on language and on personally attacking another candidate's character. I guess he missed the five-minute-plus character attack followed by the two minutes of animal analogies directed at me that had been voiced by my fellow candidate.

My next fellow candidate received a more modest introduction. He and his campaign manager shared the normal intimidation of stepping up in front of the school, their anxiety fueled by an atmosphere now fully charged with some intense negativity and growing animosity. This guy was just going to be the mustard on a meat sandwich, between the foaming wrestler and me. He started surprisingly strong by simply saying, "Well that was interesting." The room loosened with a wash of relieved laughter and polite applause. He quietly presented a strong platform based on what he represented and what he would attempt to achieve on behalf of his fellow students. The whole time he was speaking, I could feel the room warming up in anticipation of all hell breaking loose when I talked. Mr. Mustard received the two-minute warning, and I saw one of the shop teachers slip out of the room. He was a good guy, coached the high school hockey team, and was well liked. I thought it was a bad sign that he was leaving before I spoke. My opposition was winding up early when the VP entered the room. The second presidential candidate concluded with kind words of respect and admiration for the courage of all the students running for the various offices and wishing his opponents well.

His speech was not stirring. He didn't lose any votes, but he didn't gain much ground either. The Rave's polling had him a distant third. He might have won just a few votes with his speech.

The moderator was at the podium and was just finishing complimenting the second candidate on his respectfulness, courtesy, and focus on his fellow students' rights and needs. For good measure he added that the speech should be an outstanding example for others to follow.

Since I was the only speaker left, I would have bet dollars to donuts (another phrase that made no sense to me) that the moderator's message was aimed solely at me and the Rave.

Before the Rave could get out of his seat, the VP's voice rang through the room as he pointed in our direction. "You two with me, now! We'll be just a moment, Mr. Moderator." The VP exited through the side glass doors and stood about ten feet outside the doors to the cafeteria.

When the Rave and I arrived at that spot, he began gesturing wildly with his hands and arms. His expression was stern, and his whole manner commanded our attention. His words and tone of voice were completely incongruent with his physical gestures. His message was straight and plain. "You two are going to take the high road. No personal attacks, no character assassinations, no grandstanding, no swearing, and nothing but respect. You're taking the high road. Got it?"

"Yes sir. I got it."

The VP pointed at the Rave. "That goes for you, too. Do not embellish Scarface's credentials. Do not say one thing about another candidate, and do not go off on any tangents that can be construed as assaults on others. Got it?"

"Yes, sir."

"Scarface, be genuine. Be as bold as you can be. Do not give them grounds for attack. You're on thin ice. A number of teachers and parents want you removed from the election and from the school. Take the high road."

"Thank you, sir. I'm not even sure what the high road looks like."

"Son, this is easy. Just be yourself. You can be likable. You do a mean Lord's Prayer. Your 'God Save the Queen' needs work, but you have the rest of the year for that. You can be funny, and you can be sincere. Your opponent probably defeated himself. By the way, CBC from Toronto is here to interview you about the cow pond incident after this meeting."

I was thinking the CBC ought to start paying me royalties! With that said, we all walked back into the room, which was buzzing. The air felt electric. The Rave went straight to the podium. He was quick, polite, and respectful. He mentioned a few things I had done in school organizations and sports. He drew a laugh when he mentioned my scholastic performance was not reflective of my true academic abilities or potential, and then I was on stage.

Just before I started to speak, there was a shout from the back of the room, a big tough townie. "Rip him a new one, Scarface!" The pent-up tension was pricked out of the room, and the laughter again was a relief. Some teachers smiled. Mr. Moderator was pumping up to unleash a tirade. The VP caught his eye and waved him down.

The townie provided me with the introduction I needed. "Rip? Heck, we rip on each other all the time. I think that's a high school thing. Rip on these guys up here with me? No, not going to do that. I would like to, because there was a little bit of poking the bear earlier. But here's what I know. My opponents are good people and good students. They do many admirable things at school and outside of school. Me? Well, I do a few things as well. Maybe not as good as them in some respects, maybe better in other areas. So, let me tell you why I'm up here. I've had some experiences in life that have taught me some lessons, and some of these were hard lessons. Some of you know the hard lessons I've lived through. These lessons have never really kept me down. You all know I'm the Garbage Boy. I pick up trash in the parks. People throw trash out their windows of their fancy cars at me. I run barrels. You know that I run them on the weekends. We need the money. I pick up what people throw out. As president, I can relate to what is the best of in all of us, and I can deal with the worst stuff and keep showing up every day to try to make the best out of any situation. I pick our town parks clean. I do my best at a job nobody else wants. Why? Because that's who I am. You can trust me. Vote for me, and I'll come to that job every day with my best. And I'll pick us up. I promise to encourage and support you and work with and for you, so we collectively can be our best. Our best as individuals, teams, clubs, classes, and most importantly, our best as a school. Over the weekend, we took some shots to who we are as a school. Some of those shots were spiked by some of my activities, along with apparently a few hundred of my closest friends on Friday night. But we are not who some callers say we are. We're good people. I'm proud to be part of our school. I'm honoured and privileged to be a candidate with these two good members of our community up here with me and all the other candidates running for office.

"Rave, I'm sorry I didn't have time to lay out our seven-point platform. Today it was important for me to say who I am, the Garbage Boy or Scarface, or a wise ass. Sorry, I meant wiseacre. You know some wiseacre called to me from a Mustang convertible as they drove by and threw some garbage out their window.

They said, 'You're a shit stick, crap with a stick.' That's not who I am. I'm strong enough to take that shit and any other crap that comes my way or our way. I'll do my best for you. I'll take great pride and be honoured to represent you, and I'll not tolerate anyone putting us down. Thank you."

Then came the applause. It felt like thunder. I didn't notice when the room went totally quiet, but I knew at some point in time the silence was deafening (another expression I don't get).

In the question-and-answer period, I was in a bit of a haze. I know I answered a few questions, but nothing harmful or hurtful to any of the candidates came up. The tension balloon had been thoroughly pricked and deflated by my speech.

Afterwards, the Rave asked where that inspiration and those words had come from. I told him I didn't have a clue, except that I did clean up after other people made a mess. I was the Garbage Boy. I also told the Rave it was the first time I'd ever called myself that. Called myself the Garbage Boy. I didn't feel ashamed about that. Any work could be good work.

Now, the CBC. Something told me those guys were underemployed, or there were too many of them. *Here we go again*, I thought. I wished Bogeyman and Scarecrow were there to facilitate and moderate. We were set up for the taping in the VP's office. The Rave was with me. He was dying to be in the national spotlight. The VP had already finished his portion of the CBC interview.

The first question was what one would expect. "What was your role in the massive party held at the cow pond on Friday night?"

"My role? Not much. It was an all-candidates' gathering outside of school hours. So, I was there early in the evening along with a few friends and my campaign manager, the Rave, who is here with me now."

The Rave tried to look all serious and professional when the camera tilted his way, following my acknowledgement of his presence. He couldn't maintain his serious nature, however, and a smile consumed his professional demeanour like someone chowing down on our school's famous Wednesday lunch, shepherd's pie.

"What exactly happened when the police, fire, and ambulance arrived?"

"I don't know. A group of us left when we thought things might get out of hand. That was before the police arrived at the cow pond. What I've heard is that everybody in attendance scattered in all directions, and the police talked to more than a few individuals, but no charges were laid. That would indicate to me that the gathering was relatively tame and those in attendance were well behaved."

"How many students were at this gathering?"

"When we left, there were fewer than two hundred."

"Then why are the official estimates somewhere between four and five hundred?"

"As I stated earlier, we left, as we thought things might get out of hand, so it's possible more people arrived later. I really don't believe the crowd got that big."

"With the fact that this cow pond gathering has garnered so much attention, including hours on local radio and the national spotlight, do you feel this puts the youth of this town, and particularly your high school, in a bad light?"

"No, I don't."

"Why? How could it not?"

"Simple. Have you ever been on Yonge Street or in Yorkville on a weekend? Or, for that matter, any day of the week? There are thousands of high-school kids scoring dope, getting stoned, drinking like fish, and getting busted by narcs and cops. Compared to that continuous crazy scene, we're not even trying to misbehave. What about Oakville? The number-one drug capital in Canada? Are they too rich for you to investigate? How about Markham? What was that article in the *Star* last week, 'Markham: Mayhem on Main Street'? If you believe the *Star*, we held a Sunshine City social compared to the mayhem in downtown Markham. We gathered less than two hundred people. There was some beer and cheap wine going around at a bonfire, and somehow, that was a big deal? So, no, I don't think comparatively it puts our town or our school in a bad light. Look in your own backyard. Look across the country. We're not worse nor better than any youth in Canada, and trying to portray us as anything else is just wrong and as hypocritical as hell."

"That's not what we're saying. We're just curious."

"Curious about what? Whether we were the first kids acting like typical teenagers? Because it feels like you're trying to paint another picture."

The VP cut the interview off there. It was then that I appreciated the genius he had shown by inviting our own film and camera club into his office to learn from the best, the CBC, and they were able to tape the interview as well.

The CBC crew packed up quickly. The interviewer left in a huff. One of the cameramen had been with the CBC crew in the summer. "Great work, Scarface," he told me after the interview. "Keep telling it like it is, brother. Tell Bogeyman and Scarecrow to call me. I need to hook up with those dudes again. They're seriously bad men." He was grinning the whole time.

As everyone else departed, the VP motioned for me to stay behind. "Scarface, you sure have made things more interesting around here. You're a one-man lightning rod for attention, wanted or unwanted. The CBC is not going to air much of that clip, maybe none of it. The interviewer had a whole list of questions she never got to. It was likely to paint us in a bad light. Is that stuff about Oakville and Markham true?"

I nodded.

"Well, how about that! My mother-in-law is from Oakville, and she's always crapping on our little town. That insight into Oakville is a sword I'm going to strike on her shield of sanctimonious superiority. I think you might have saved our town and our school a lot of embarrassment. That reporter isn't happy, so it's still going to be a negative piece. I'm going to alert the mayor."

The remainder of the day and the following day were uneventful. There were a lot of congratulations for my speech. Home rooms cheered loudly when my good morning came over the speaker for the next couple of days. Well, as a matter of fact, that was the one dark part of the day. The righteous grade-ten brother of the wrestling candidate petitioned to have me removed from the announcements for the remainder of the election period. Three mornings of a little extra sleep would have been OK by me! The VP never let that happen.

The CBC piece appeared on the evening news and later during the nightly news. After the intro to the cow-pond segment, where it was clear the reporter was somewhat agitated and still in a huff, my interview was first. They only played the questions and answers on when the police arrived, how many kids were there, and whether it put the town and the school in a bad light. They did not include my words on Toronto, Oakville, or Markham.

The mayor and the police chief came off as defensive and apologetic. The VP's interview never made airtime. The Rave's somewhat bewildered and smiling face was on screen for my whole interview. He was the only one ecstatic about the whole experience.

The VP handled the next morning's announcements and criticized the CBC report. He announced the full interview would be shown at all three lunches. After school was the last of the all-candidates' forums with all people running for all offices having three minutes to speak and then a short Q and A.

The filming of the CBC interview by our own camera club was a bigger hit than Wednesday's shepherd's pie or Friday's fish and chips, served up in the cafeteria. The camera-club film was narrated by a very serious grade-eleven librarian's assistant, who wore glasses and looked sexy in her white turtleneck shirt, short skirt and platform shoes. I just wanted to replay her part over and over. The Rave was equally excited about his own appearance. He was new to the spotlight. The camera club interviewed him for the piece, and man, did he make us sound good. It was right then that I thought—and it wouldn't be the last time—that the Rave should have been the one running for election.

The cafeteria went crazy in all three lunch periods. I had last lunch that day, and the northeast corner had close to seven hundred people jammed in. The first two lunch periods had ended in standing ovations. By the time the third showing cued up, everybody was already standing except those at the first seven or eight rows of tables.

Man, did I sound fierce! I came off as this great protector of our school, our town, just our teens being teens. Not special, not different, not better, but certainly no worse than anywhere else. It had felt good when I said it, and it felt even better afterwards. This stuff was true and right. Where it came from was dawning on me. It came from deep within my heart and gut, and somehow, I managed to express my inner hurt and rage in an articulate fashion. I also realized, looking at myself on that big white screen, that my apparent anger was only inches from tears. I gulped at that. I know someone at some time had told me that emotions run a whole spectrum. I just didn't know that anger and tears were neighbours on that emotional block—at least, on my block.

The cafeteria went crazy at the end of the film. No one heard how the gorgeous librarian finished the piece as she rekindled my libido. Yes, Scarecrow and Bogeyman had added that word to my vocabulary. It was obvious that it was not only me who thought and felt that small-town people were regarded as hillbillies, a bunch of Jethros and Ellie Maes doing as Granny bid them: "Wave goodbye now, y'all." I had hit some core belief or chord of discontent felt by a lot of us in that room. It's still funny and strange to me how I came to be the one who covered that shared sentiment. What was that feeling all about? Resentment, being put down, or just the uneasiness of it all as we navigated being teens? We were all just growing up, and the majority had our doubts, uncertainties, and worries. I guess the common thread is we didn't need a private school, U of T journalism grad kicking crap all over us. By the way, I don't know if she went to private school or attended the U of T or whether U of T even had a journalism program. I asked the Rave about that later. With a puzzled look, he told me U of T didn't do journalism. They were better than that!

The election was over. I think everybody sensed it. I felt it. The Rave was glowing over it. At the all-candidates' meeting, everything felt warm and fuzzy.

No outbreak, no attacks. The "peace in our time" Neville Chamberlain quote came out in that meeting—at least I think it did.

Thursday was non-contentious. The one candidate from grade thirteen was removing all his twenty-three posters after school. We talked. He was surly and subdued, which seemed like a strange combination. That was even before the election assemblies.

The assemblies were carefully planned with detailed time allotments. The junior vice-presidential candidates were allotted four minutes, as were the secretarial candidates. The treasurer candidates got six minutes and the presidential candidates ten minutes. The assembly was scheduled for ninety minutes. I again drew the low card, and my opponents elected to go first and second. Both had bands as their intros. Some of the other candidates had skits. One treasurer had a band, and a secretarial candidate sang; she was really talented. A couple had short films. They were all nervous. They were all good, and some were great. Getting up in front of a thousand-seat auditorium is never easy, but in high school, as teens, it was nuts and intimidating.

The bands were all fantastic! Rock music in our high school gym—nothing better! Of course, they shouted their candidate's name at the beginning and end of the song. The treasurer's band did "Gloria," her name. I'm sure she won on that basis! The other grade-thirteen candidates for president surprised me. His band played "Bron-Y-Aur Stomp" by Led Zeppelin, an interesting, non-political choice. He subtly attacked. His line of reasoning was that fame could go to people's heads. The job didn't require someone who sought and enjoyed the spotlight. Such types focused only on themselves. They became non-interested in the hard work or the heavy lifting. They quickly became self-centred, self-interested, and self-serving. They forgot who they represented, as they were constantly and shamelessly representing only themselves. Every morning, every day, every time, and in everything.

"I, on the other hand, get up every morning and do chores. We milk the cows, slop the barn, and feed the pigs and chickens. We do the work every morning, every day, every time, and every chore." It should be noted here that half the school was bussed in from the surrounding countryside. He was trying to nail the farm and rural vote. Smart. "I do my schoolwork. I get decent grades. I might even apply to U of T. It is very hard to get accepted there and even harder now for people coming from this school, or so I hear." That deserved and got some laughs. "I play sports. I belong to clubs. I go home and do chores and schoolwork. I even attend social events like the cow-pond party. I didn't leave early either. My cross-country training came in handy." More laughter, stronger this time. This guy was the real deal! "So, I'm going to come in every day and work hard for you. I won't grab the spotlight; I don't need it, but I'll turn that spotlight on all of you because that's where it should shine."

Wow, that was good!

The other grade-thirteen candidate's band played Kelly J. and Crowbar's bar anthem, "Oh What a Feeling... What a Rush." Man, I love that song! So did the audience. After the song he was very subdued. I think he was so worried about losing it again that he seemed sedated. He was wearing a Che Guevara beret. His manner, his voice, and his words were incongruent with his look and the musical intro. I felt sorry for him. The impact of his platform and speech were interfered with and made less effective because his grade-thirteen classmates, who had taken over the front row, burst into cheers and stood up and applauded after every five or six of his sentences. It appeared planned, and it was. Choreographed, as the Rave later informed me. The thirteens supporting him were imploring the rest of the crowd to stand when they did. That backfired badly. I learned right then that clear passion is an absolute necessity if you want to move people. Either he didn't have that passion, or his tank was empty. He had spent that the previous Monday, and it hadn't worked out for him. He was a smart, caring guy. He deserved better, but then people don't often get what they deserve, and I knew that more deeply than most. I was hoping that he and I could have a cold beer together sometime on a back road and just talk all this bullshit out.

Now it was my turn. No band, no skit, no film, and much to the Rave's chagrin, no intro. None needed.

The grade-thirteen class in the front rows stood up and booed, made thumbs-down gestures, and actively encouraged others to boo. It didn't happen. The Rave ran on stage and yelled at the moderator. I grabbed him and looked him square in the eyes. "It's alright, brother," I said. "This too shall pass." The Rave didn't know whether to shit or go blind, so he just walked back onto the side of the stage. I turned and had a big grin on my face. I began to clap and point at the thirteen class. I was smiling, clapping, and pointing. The VP came up behind the moderator, grabbed his elbow, and said something in his ear.

"Sit down!" the moderator yelled. My reaction created chaos in their ranks. They looked confused, disconcerted, pissed off, and discombobulated. (That last word was sourced from my mom, not from Bogeyman and Scarecrow's vocabulary tutoring.)

For my opening line, I quoted Stephen Stills from Woodstock. "Hey, man, this is the first time we've played in front of people, and we're scared shitless."

"Stop that vulgarity!" the moderator screamed into his microphone. That ended any chance he had at moderating anything except chess club competitions at the school from then on. The crowd instantly responded by jumping to their feet with an instant standing ovation, with the exception of the front rows.

"Sorry, sir. What I meant to say is, this experience is like Crosby Stills, Nash, and Young when they performed in front of a large group for the first time at Woodstock. It is an intimidating experience. I talked off-stage to many of the other candidates, and we're all a little rattled. I'm so proud of how everyone has conducted themselves, and I hope I can measure up."

It didn't feel right just repeating what I had already said in the all-candidates' debate or to the CBC, so this was new territory.

"I never thought I would be booed while standing on this stage. Frankly, I never thought I would be standing on this stage. My applause for the grade-thirteen class who booed me is about recognition. You demonstrate a passionate commitment for what you believe in, and in this situation, it is your fellow graduating classmate, my opponent. Commitment is to be applauded, I think, so I applaud you. Confidentially, I really wish you could find another way to show your commitment rather than booing me. Oh, I guess that wasn't so confidential!" People laughed. The mood, I felt, was turning, but there was an air of uncertainty in the auditorium. I was uncertain how things were going to go.

"Commitment is an interesting thing, isn't it? I don't have much going for me up here. No band, no skit, no film, no intro, just me. Hey, Rave, what kind of campaign are you running?"

There was lots of laughter.

"Here's what I know about commitment. I commit to do the best job I can. I commit not to even try to do it alone. I commit to work with all of you—every one of you. I understand that to get things done requires commitment of not one but everyone. I'll encourage you and assist you. I won't be milking the cows tomorrow, but if we choose to support milking cows every morning to lift up our school, our teams, and our clubs, then I'll commit to milking cows alongside you. Someone would have to show me how. Any volunteers?"

Many hands shot up, even a couple in the grade-thirteen class. There was laughter. Man, laughter really does ease tension. I pointed at one of the thirteens whose hand was still raised.

"Hey there, this means you and I would be mooin' not booin'!"

More laughter.

"Of course, you haven't seen me milk yet, so there still could be some booin'!"

More laughter.

"Hey, I think you're laughing with me, not at me, and I think when most of us get up here, whether you choose to vote for us or not, one thing should be clear about all of us, all the candidates."

I paused, and the room went quiet.

"We're with you. We're for you, and we're one with you. We hope for your support and pray we don't receive your disdain, anger, or apathy. We're part of you. When you vote, please remember we're here for you, all of the candidates are here for you. There are no bad guys or gals here. There is no evil intent. There is only a willingness to commit and serve. I think in some small way this is noble and worthwhile, to stand up in front of all of you and say I commit to serve. I commit to you for you and for us. We took the stage. We publicly demonstrated our commitment. Judge us not on that because that commitment is clear. Vote for who you think can best deliver on their fundamental commitment. We all thank you in advance for a vote cast with that spirit and understanding. That's a vote of grace, wisdom, kindness, conscience, and respect for the candidates you choose as well as the candidates you pass over. That's a vote cast with good intent and a better chance of landing the right candidate for you and for all of us.

"Yes, these roles come with a spotlight. The spotlight is bright, and you can get caught in it, burned by it, enamoured with it, and, yes, you can try and live in it. Getting seduced by the light doesn't occur unless you let it. In my case I was interviewed by the CBC at night, and the next morning I was back at it, picking up garbage in the park and scooping up dog shit. Sorry about the language, sir.

"Running barrels from rich people's cottages on Saturdays and Sundays. Yep, the spotlight has really led me to an incredible lifestyle. Actions, everyday actions, getting up and doing the work. I'm that guy. Seven days a week, as it turns out. I'll be that guy as your president. Thank you."

The audience sat in stunned silence for a moment or two. My voice was cracking, and my words were coming out slower and quieter at the end. I was struggling to keep my emotions in check.

Then the audience exploded. They roared. They stood. They bellowed. They mooed. They laughed, and they were touched. It wasn't just the words. It was how they came out. I don't even know how they sounded. I only know how they felt to me. They felt real, and they felt tinged with anguish, sorrow, and a whole lot of truth. That's what I felt, and no matter what happened with the vote, I felt good.

The second assembly went much the same, except for the scared shitless line, which I left out, and the booing. My speech was roughly the same without the obvious reference to booing and mooing.

The voting started in the homerooms at 8 a.m. on Friday and closed at 9 a.m. after the morning announcements. Late arrivals and those with opening period spares could vote at the main office up until 10 a.m. At about 11 a.m. as I walked by the main office, the senior administrative secretary, who worked for the VP, waved me in. She was in her sixties and tough on truants and miscreants, as she liked to say. She bent over the counter and motioned for me to lean in.

"Never liked you much, but you do say a good Lord's Prayer," she whispered. "I always thought you were a little full of yourself, but the way you took that CBC witch on, I couldn't help but smile and start to like you!"

"Thank you."

"By the way, you're winning by a landslide. You're going to win. Let me be the first to congratulate you."

"Thank you."

"Now get out of here. I don't want to have to write you up because you're late for class."

The halls were empty when I left the office except for one friend who had worked on the campaign. I approached him and told him that we had won and won big. His reaction was surprising. He looked guilty.

"Good. Gotta get to class," he said.

As planned, the announcement on the new student council would be made at the end of the 11 a.m. class, just before the first lunch. I sat in class with my head down and avoided eye contact for almost the full forty-five minutes, trying to subdue my elation. I was elated, elevated, and inebriated. I stood up. I had taken the shot and given my background, it was such a stretch, but we had won!

They always announced the student-council elections by what they call the electoral roll call. Each candidate by position by grade, starting with grade nine, the junior VP post. Grade nine cast 563 votes. I received 452. Grade ten cast 500 votes. I received 397. With the two classes I had over 800 votes. I knew I needed about 1,050 if the whole school voted. I kept my head down. The Rave was standing up with his fists clenched. Grade eleven, 448 votes cast. I received 332. "One thousand one hundred and eighty-one! Scarface in a landslide!" he shouted.

Cheering erupted in the room. I kept my head down. Grade twelve, 338 votes cast. I received 277. "That's now one thousand four hundred and fifty-eight," the Rave said.

Grade thirteen, 154 votes cast. I received 82 votes. That shocked me—stunned me, actually! The Rave was yelling that Scarface took every grade, 1540 votes, over 75 percent of the votes cast. Landslide. Tidal Wave. Wipeout!

The room was loud. Then the VP announced the student's council. The big surprise was the main grade-thirteen candidate had only tallied 157 votes. Something about my margin of victory and his third-place finish seemed odd, wrong, foreboding, and just not right. He deserved better.

The new student council was required to report immediately to the principal's office. The VP formally congratulated us and handed us our role descriptions and a copy of the student council charter and bylaws and told us our first meeting would be Monday afternoon with our advisor.

When we were finished, the VP pulled me into his office and shut the door. "President Scarface!" he said, grinning. "President Garbage Boy." He laughed. "Good for you. Well done! You know, I'll be on your case the whole way, but I have your back. Now get out of here!"

That felt good.

CHAPTER 9

Fame Fizzles

Premonition, that's what it was. I had a premonition of something bad coming out of the rival candidate's third-place finish. A few weeks into my term as the new student-council president, a new student newspaper emerged. The editors and writers were anonymous. The paper was called the *Raging Rag*. The title was on the money. They were mostly raging about and ragging on me. After reading the first two articles, even I didn't like or trust myself anymore. My feelings were more than hurt, and anxiety and anger were growing. Four of the seven articles were about my failures, inadequacies, and broken promises. The other three articles respectively faulted the electoral process but praised that year's basket drive and the choice for that year's student musical, *Oklahoma*.

I had clearly underestimated two things when I ran for president. First, the job was time consuming. Second, fame can bring some animosity or at least natural adolescent jealousy to the forefront. That being true, I still liked the role, the interactions, the opportunity for leadership, and the fact that I had done several interviews with the beautiful student librarian with the glasses. Now, *that* was outstanding! And I was still running barrels every weekend, so that was good for the wallet.

The *Raging Rag* set me back, though. There was some vicious shit being spread. Most of it wasn't true, just a very slanted perspective. My initial reaction was to lash out. Find out who these pricks were and call them out. The VP called me into his office as soon as he saw the *Rag*. His guidance was needed, because the Rave and a few others were going nuts. The Rave and his crew were openly declaring a war on the one failed presidential candidate and his cronies. Cronies? What the heck was a crony? Was that like a witch from *Macbeth* or what?

The VP was a calming influence. "Are you angry?"

"Yes!"

"Really angry? Pissed off?"

"Yes."

"What's your planned response?"

"I don't have one yet."

"Good. Want an idea?"

"About how I should respond?"

"Yes."

"Well, I have nothing now, except the Rave and a bunch of friends going batshit crazy."

"Batshit crazy? Well, that's an interesting reaction. Do you think that will help anything or shut this paper down?"

"No, probably the opposite."

"OK, then. How about this? Do nothing."

"What? I have to fight back."

"Why? Figure this out. You already won. These guys lost. Now they're hiding behind some bushes and throwing stones. They're anonymous. Their teacher advisor condones their secret society, and the principal won't change that. So, you have to learn to handle some irritants."

"And how do I do that?"

"Look, I have to handle you, and you're as irritating as hell, so it's possible."

"You know, sir, with all due respect, humour maybe ain't your strong suit."

"Come on, I made you lighten up a little."

"Yeah, you did. So, I do nothing?"

"Let it ride. Take the high road. Be gracious. You won. Figure out a response. Check in with me tomorrow before announcements. Stay calm. Stay quiet. That will drive them crazy. Pull the Rave and the Ravenettes back into a calm place."

"The Ravenettes? Wow, I think some of the guys are not going to love that nickname." "Call them the Ravers then. That's got a ring to it and sounds a bit out there."

"Well, the Rave is going to love both those names for his group. So, I stay quiet?"

"Don't let them see you break a sweat. Water off a duck's back."

"The more I think about it, the more I like it. Not responding will show it didn't get to me and that will drive them batshit crazy."

"It probably will. Then they're likely to fire up the rhetoric even higher."

"Rhetoric?"

"Look it up."

"So, they're probably going to get nastier?"

"Likely."

"Are you going to get involved if they do?"

"Not likely."

"I don't know if I can stay calm. I might have to send the Ravers into action."

"Don't. Grow a hide. Thick skin. They want you to react. Don't give them what they want or expect and keep doing the job you're doing. Talk to everyone. Take time for everything. Show up for all school events."

"So, I take the high road publicly?"

"Exactly! Visible and unrattled."

"Sir, again with all due respect, that's easier said than done."

"That's precisely the sum of it all and what will differentiate you as a leader and not as an easily antagonized adolescent."

"I thought you were going to say . . . asshole."

"Look, these guys want to provoke. They want you to act like an asshole. Heck, son, half the staff and the principal think this is going to get out of hand. You are the defining catalyst of what happens from here forward. You have all the power to control and command this situation. How do you fight a fire?"

"You pour water on it."

"Get your rubber boots and the fire hose, son, and douse these invisible pricks with a cold, calm, and collected response. Water on fire. Water on fire. I'll allow you a one-paragraph response to the Raging Rag on tomorrow's announcements. I'll sign off on your written response before you go live, right?"

"Right, sir, and thanks."

"Now go find the Rave and the Ravenettes and tell them to cool it."

"Got it. And can we stick with Ravers?"

"Sure."

I found the Rave and a bunch of our friends just outside the cafeteria. The high-road message didn't sit well at first, but after we talked it through, the Ravers got it. We won! "We" is such a powerful word. "You guys won! You pulled this off. We annihilated them. You did this! Now, we can take the high road. I need a one-paragraph response for the morning announcements, three or four short sentences. Can you guys put something together for me? I might be preaching the high road, but I'm having trouble thinking of how to express that. You might also draft a letter to the editors of the *Raging Rag* along the same lines, taking the high road."

Not entirely intended, but I had replaced our group's rage with a mission. I also transferred ownership of the solution from me to us. Belonging was important. Trust was important. I was learning. I filled them in on the VP referring to them as Ravers and Ravenettes. They settled on Ravers. The Rave was beaming. He had hated his nickname until then, but now it was a group. A team. A team with a fierce degree of loyalty and purpose. A purpose centered on them and not someone else. The Ravers were growing as a force for collective action.

The response was a thing of beauty.

The VP reacted with what he called incredulity. "Look the word up. You had help with this, didn't you?"

"Well, sir, the Ravers wrote it."

"You're kidding me. You delegated this, and they got it?"

"The Ravers were on a high-road crusade." I handed him the letter to the *Raging Rag* editors. He was blown away.

"This is good, son. This is very good. You're creating a real team, aren't you?"

"Sort of serendipitous, sir. Look it up." We both chuckled about that.

"OK, morning announcements. Let's go."

"Any changes to the response, sir?"

"No, read it verbatim. Look it up. No deviations."

So here it is: "In response to the first issue of the *Raging Rag*, I would like to congratulate the anonymous editors on their engagement in our school. Although your articles are primarily derogatory and certainly defamatory toward me, you have the right, and I certainly respect, defend, and support that right to share your views and opinions. However, I would encourage a tad more accuracy on your facts. Thank you for the encouraging support to our faculty and friends engaged with *Oklahoma* and the acknowledgement of our school's successful basket drive. I also want to thank those who put together this response." I named eight Ravers. "Please look forward to their non-anonymous letters to the *Raging Rag* editors. Everyone, please enjoy a great day!"

I heard that the homeroom reactions varied from astonishment to applause. The editors of the *Raging Rag* were all hunkered down in one of the grade-thirteen home rooms with their faculty advisor. They were stunned. They didn't know whether to shit their pants or wind their watches. I think the original expression might have been wind their watches or shine their shoes, but I prefer the shit-their-pants version.

A fight almost broke out in their home room. As soon as I finished, a big burly farm boy with the most incongruent afro in the world spoke out. "You egg-headed assholes. That boy just crammed your own bullshit right down your throats. He totally wiped you out!"

Their response was something mature like, "Did not," which, of course, can only be responded to with a "Did too!" followed by, "I'll beat the snot out of you and your did-not," countered by, "I'll smack the poo out of you and your did-too."

Well, that's probably not how it went, but that would have been the general drift of the back and forth.

I walked down the main hall after the morning announcements. Mostly ninth and tenth graders were there. I was getting applause, pats on the back, and "atta boys" all the way. At least three teachers stopped me to shake my hand and congratulate me on the positive nature of my response. I let them all know we had good guidance from the VP, and that the team had helped me overcome the initial urge to respond negatively.

Fame was fizzling, but it was still incredibly interesting. The faculty advisor calmed the rival thirteen factions down, avoiding fisticuffs. When he settled that potential donnybrook, he headed to the principal's office and demanded a meeting with the principal and the VP. The principal agreed and called in the head guidance counsellor.

The VP let me in on the outcome the next day in our morning get-together before the announcements. The principal had flattened the faculty advisor. The advisor started the meeting by declaring that the VP should never have allowed me to use the morning announcements to respond and that my tone was a tongue-in-cheek, derogatory, and sarcastic attack on the principled editors of the *Raging Rag*. The VP told me he had a hard time not exploding at the pompous prick, but the principal handled the situation in a straight forward, clear manner.

The principal said that the response had his blessing and was a course of action that he and the VP had agreed on in advance. The VP had guided the tone and nature of the response. The response was drafted by a group of eight students of equal status to the advisor's anonymous seven.

"Are we clear on those facts?" the VP said. "That isn't a question, by the way. Are we clear?"

"Yes."

"Furthermore, the president of the student council, fairly elected by a landslide, has done nothing derogatory in the month following the election. In fact, he reached out and asked your defeated grade-thirteen candidate to be a special advisor to the council. The request was summarily rejected. Are we clear on those facts as well?"

"Yes."

"The response was well crafted and admirable. An element of humour was present, but certainly nothing derogatory or defamatory in nature was included. Your seven brought this on themselves, and you have an unmistakable hand in their behaviour. You have an opportunity to learn from the example provided on this morning's announcements. It would be advisable to utilize that example in your guidance of the *Raging Rag's* editors. We'll see if you have the capacity and willingness to influence and elicit a more positive approach. Additionally, guidance will be setting up counselling appointments with the students listed here. The VP is aware of some of these names. The other names are my best guesses at who the primary writers of the *Raging Rag* are, and these are the students I believe could best receive value from some counselling. The objective is to help them find a more positive, beneficial, and factual way to channel their rage and intellect. Any objections? That isn't a question either."

Man, when I heard this from the VP, it felt, well, righteous, brother. I went all hippie there.

Things settled down quickly after that. We did not see another issue of the *Raging Rag* until just before the Christmas break, almost two months after the first. In the interim I was fulfilling my role, enjoying leadership and what felt like acceptance, and I was growing my hair even longer. The beard was a continued work in progress. Fame had turned to trying to be a leader if not a role model. I was secretly happy about my weekend work and playing hockey with the school team. We weren't good, but we cared. The teacher who intervened with the VP after the thirteen candidate's meltdown was the coach. Another good man. He knew I needed lots of that "good man" influence in my life. My previous role models, as were Bogeyman's, Scarecrow's, Stone Pony's, and Mister's, had all been shit. I think shit begets shit, which begets shit, like all that begetting in the Old Testament. Someone needs to intervene, get involved, take an interest, or just give a shit to stop the begetting of shit! I vowed never to beget shit!

Why was I happy about early Saturday and Sunday mornings? Because what seemed like the majority of my old friends and fervent supporters were getting shitfaced and stoned beyond comprehension from Thursday through Sunday. Working those long hours on the weekend running barrels provided me a legitimate reason to bow out of the brain-cell bacchanalia that was occurring. Scarecrow and Bogeyman told me their out-of-the-country trips were a full-throttle onslaught to surpass Bacchus's reputation. They insisted their activities were also exercises in business development and personal growth. My boys, B and S: completely full of BS.

Ah, B and S, my now-mythical brethren. How deep and dangerous was the shit they were into? I had a premonition that B and S were begetting a lot of shit. Their fame had not fizzled.

Yet.

Thanks, Man

Dear God

I can never remember that poem or saying about granting serenity, calm, and whatever, but thank you for the cool head on the VP's shoulders.
Thank you for friends.
Keep a kind, forgiving eye out for B and S.
Thank you for Stone Pony and Mister and hard work.
Be kind to them too, because I know they have lived hard times, felt hot stares and cold words.
We mean no harm, and
We beget no shit.
At least intentionally.
Don't think you have to judge us too harshly.
We have plenty of lesser beings with more immediate earthbound powers doing that,
But it's OK if you look out and over us a bit
If you have the time, big fellow, no pressure.
And thanks for hard barrel runs; money in my pocket; the soft looks of Ms. Librarian; the VP; decent, caring people; and my mom.
I probably haven't thanked you much lately
Or ever, but right now I feel a little calm.
So, just in case you have anything to do with that, thanks, man.
And I'll do my best not to beget any batshit craziness.

Amen.

CHAPTER 10

Tugs

I feel a lot of different little tugs. Sometimes on my purse strings, sometimes on my heart strings.

There are the tugs from my friends. Which way to lean? Which path to follow? What trouble and temptations to try or avoid? All these little tugs and pulls. How much effect do they have? How far can they pull me off course? Into the ditch or worse?

Can I muster the strength of character and belief in my own path to ignore the tugs? The pulls? Do I even know my own path well enough to figure out which tugs are good and which tugs are bad? A number of tugs are fun but not necessarily good for me.

There are often tugs on my purse strings. Things I would like to have or things the kids need. I don't mind these tugs, and I try to loosen the purse strings when I can. The tugs on the heart strings pluck notes of love and care. Sometimes the notes are sad because although the strings would love to provide the sounds that take away the sadness, the heart strings can't create that music. The strings are being plucked to a melody of sadness. The joy is when the heart strings get tugged, and they can play the music of love and care that provides comfort.

My kids are the musicians who tug at my heart strings and make me want to give them the music, the sounds that they need to hear for comfort, relief, assurance, joy, care, and so much more. The only guaranteed note they pull out every time is love.

Sometimes it's the only note I can muster.

My son is being tugged in many ways. The whole town is bubbling with the uncertainty created by drugs and the lowered drinking age. Everything is more accessible. The kids are just being kids and doing what teens and young people do. They party, they drink, and they "experiment" with drugs. Experimenting is a term that had to be dreamed up by the richer families to explain the behaviour of their own children who were doing drugs. Experimenting has a lot more class than just saying, "They do drugs!"

When I asked my son if he and his friends were experimenting with drugs, he laughed and explained that this wasn't a lab assignment for a science class. Kids were getting high, stoned, wasted, and spaced out. They weren't experimenting. They knew exactly what they were doing.

Then he asked me flat-out if I wanted to know if he was experimenting, and he laughed again. He wasn't being cruel or mean. I told him I didn't want to know but to be careful.

He laughed again and said he promised to use the scientific method and be very careful if he conducted any experiments. We both laughed and decided a cold beer was necessary at that moment, but just for scientific purposes. We laughed more.

Tugs. Did I want to know or not? I didn't actually care to know, but I did care. I decided ignorance was bliss for the moment. He was growing his hair long—and that beard. People in town were saying the "longhairs" were all likely doing drugs. That was a tug. Part of me didn't want people thinking of my son that way. I'd seen and felt enough judgment from others about me that I didn't care what people thought of me, but my son? Tug, tug, tug.

I saw his friends around town from time to time, looking like ragamuffins and rock groups but mostly acting happy. Mellow. Were they stoned, high, wasted, whatever? I don't know. They always said hi and smiled. These were good kids, maybe experimenting a little too much. I wasn't going to judge them because I didn't want my son judged.

My son was working crazy hours on weekends and almost making too much money. I loved that the hard work kept him in the house on weekend nights, as he was too exhausted to go out with his friends. I was one of the few women at work who had her son home almost every Friday and Saturday night. He should be out having some fun, but having him home safe without all that temptation swirling around feels comforting and then some. Tugs.

The rumour about his bosses, the Indian and the black man, were swirling all around. How much money they must be making and what they were doing with all that cash. How they lived, where they lived, and who they were. They were men of mystery. People were more than curious. The rumours were not kind. The exact opposite. Cruel and vicious. That was a gnawing tug. Was my son working for bad men or good men? I chose to believe in good. Most people in our town were blinded by colour. Blinded by white light. "If you're not white, you're not quite right."

I didn't want to believe or listen to any of the gossip, the whispers, the so-called theories, or the wild stories. I was constantly asked, "What does your son say about them?" I always replied that they worked hard, long hours and mostly for very demanding, rich, big-city customers. I also said that my son was too exhausted to go out much or say much, that they treated him well, and the pay was OK. I knew they wanted more, so I gradually gave them less. Tugs. These men were a mystery to me. My son clearly had respect for them and seemed incredibly loyal and certainly appreciative.

My life? Good. Getting ahead. No men in my life. I missed the company of a man but not the headaches and heartaches. The tugs only a man can introduce into my life.

Life is fine and good. Why do I always expect to get tugged hard into some troubles? Well, we do have a bit of a track record with some bad tugs. I guess I have that premonition from the past. Does that even make sense? I tell myself to breathe past the terror of all the possible tugs of hurt and pain. Breathe through the tug. Of course, the coroner's report continually tugs at the corners of my mind. Is that my premonition of something bad lying on the coroner's table? That tug could finish us.

Tugs

Dear God
You know all the tugs
All the things that could pull and tug us. Damage us.
There is no good reason for us to be pulled down or tugged to the ground,
Is there? So let these things pass us by.
That's in your power.
Just let us miss out on any bad stuff, if just for a while.
We've had our fair share and then some.
Let us catch our breath, get our feet on the ground.
Thank you for this current calm in our lives.
Thank you for this progress.
Guide my son and thank you for the guidance he gets from good men.
We're safe and happy.
We don't ask you for anything special.
So, in fairness, don't visit any harm upon us.

Or do you deal in fairness much,
Or just judgment and rewards in your kingdom?
If you can, let the coroner's report pass us by.
We didn't kill that man.
And Lord knows, he might have needed killing.

But that's on you, right? You would know that.
You would never let us get tugged down by that, would you?
That would be innocent lambs to the slaughter.

I'm just asking for a breather from bad tugs.
Not asking for riches, fame, or even a place in your place
Just a little breather from bad.
Sounds like a fair deal and a small ask
Lord, don't tug us down.

Amen.

CHAPTER 11

The Cabin

When the garbage route cut back to the winter-season customers, we still did garbage runs on Saturday and Sunday. We could have done the whole winter route in seven hours on Saturday, but Mister and Stone Pony insisted that customers who wanted Sunday service got their Sunday service. This seemed odd and out of character for these two men, who were extremely efficient in all things, especially work. On the other hand, what did I care about the efficiency of garbage collecting? I made more money just sitting in the truck driving our routes in two days of runs than the actual time running barrels and bags. I was less exhausted with the workload spread out over two days and was even venturing out to some parties on the weekends.

Mister and Stone Pony still had "their" laneways and barrels. I was sure they were all shorter runs than mine, but it seemed to take Stone Pony and Mister longer than I thought necessary.

I was so excited in early November when the first decent snowfall of about three inches arrived. The snow was that soft, fluffy kind that had fallen overnight. I was excited not by the snow but by the tracks I saw right at the top of one of my longest runs. The lane was about three hundred yards long and curved. Usually, I ran that lane hard, but not that day. They were cat tracks. Stone Pony had told me what a bobcat track looked like and showed me track pictures in the *Beaver* magazine. I walked slowly, one eye on the tracks, one eye searching the lane and the bush ahead, which isn't possible, but most people know what people mean when they say that. More of a look down, look up, repeat process.

Halfway up to the house where the lane curved to the right and around the bend, there it was: a big, beautiful, male bobcat with the distinctive tufted ears. It stared at me over its shoulder, then did a three-quarter turn to face me directly. We were maybe thirty yards apart. I was fast, but I knew he was faster. I wondered what the hell I should do. Stone Pony and Mister had been clear on this: "You get the barrel. You always get the barrel." This was again a case of wind my watch or shit my pants. I wasn't wearing a watch, so the choice narrowed to a sphincter decision. Well, my sphincter slammed shut, and my balls retracted to somewhere in my gut! The bobcat continued staring and then slowly turned and sauntered toward the house. I followed slowly with my slammed-shut sphincter, no balls, and all. The bobcat veered about twenty yards from the house and then disappeared into the dense pine woods. I lost sight of him when he was less than a few feet into the woods. I ran to the side of the house, grabbed the barrel—it was freakin' full—and hightailed it down the lane. My crew was waiting impatiently and looking perturbed. I was holding up their Sunday-morning breakfast.

"Bobcat, big bobcat, up there near the house!"

"Well, what did you do with it? Fuck it? That bobcat ain't the kind of pussy you spend time with on this job." Mister laughed at his own hilarity.

Stone Pony was right there with him in his humour. "I don't know how the bobcat reacted to your encounter, but one white boy just got whiter."

They were both enjoying themselves, and I couldn't help but join in.

"Hey, Mister, is it possible for someone's balls to disappear inside them, like, forever?" We all enjoyed my agony. Then we ran barrels hard and real fast. They wanted to be done early. The Sunday run was from pickup at my house at 6:30 and finished before 10. We could have started earlier, but we had to wait for some semblance of daybreak. We were done today by 9:27, a new best. Stone Pony and Mister kept records of our times. There, see that focus on efficiency? So, why would we spend the extra time driving over two days? That answer was above my pay grade.

We didn't stop for our usual breakfast. "Different breakfast plans today," Stone Pony said when we drove by the exit. Jeannie would miss our talkativeness and stimulating conversation.

We turned off the highway, down some concession roads that I had never seen before. The roads were not plowed that early in the morning, but the truck could drive through and over almost anything. Stone Pony and Mister had jacked up and reinforced the suspension by adding coil springs, strut spacers, and lift blocks which added about a foot of height to their beast. They'd also added suspension coils under the bed and a fortified chassis that allowed the eight-tonne-capacity truck to haul maybe another two tonnes of payload. The truck was a beast! Not that I knew a damn thing about that stuff, but it sure seemed way more capable than our garbage business required. They called her "Miss Bump and Grind."

As usual, I was in the middle of the cab, and despite all the bumps, turns, rumbles, and ruts, I was nodding off when we came to a full stop. Mister elbowed me awake as Stone Pony jumped out of the truck. Mister told me to get out and walk back about a hundred yards. I was to say hello to Mr. Clampett back there and not to be afraid of the shotgun. "Tell him you're with us and tell him who you are, although he probably knows that already," Stone Pony said. "Be respectful, and always call him Mr. Clampett. He's a war vet."

Stone Pony closed the gate after Mister drove through to the other side, and then jumped back in Miss Bump and Grind. I was sad to see the big girl drive away. Or anxious. Mr. Clampett? Where was I? This felt ominous for no good reason. Except for the sound reason that I didn't know where I was or anything about a war vet with the same name as the TV Beverly Hills family. Should I call him Jed or Mr. Clampett? The shotgun reference had me leaning heavily toward "Mr. Clampett, sir."

I went back down the most unambitious lane I had encountered to date. Deadfall protruded onto the road, along with big boulders. It had potholes and even a little creek running through it. I came over a bit of a rise, and on my left about fifty feet into the bush, I saw a cabin. Thin grey smoke was wafting out from the silver stovepipe. Twenty feet farther I saw a small lane that headed to the cabin. I turned up the lane and was peering through the woods trying to make out more of the cabin when I heard the voice.

"That's far enough, son."

For the second time that morning my asshole shrank and slammed shut, and my balls retreated somewhere north. That voice was all gravel, whisky, tobacco, and incoming hurt. Worse yet, I had no idea where it was coming from.

"Well, son, you got a story to tell, or do I just start shooting for the goddamn pleasure of shooting?"

"Mr. Clampett?" I asked meekly.

The voice boomed out a laugh. "Those fuckin' misfits call me Mr. Clampett? What a beautiful fuckin' irony that is! Those two are the only fuckin' hillbillies in the neighbourhood, and the neighbourhood has gone to hell since they moved in. So, you must be Scarface, the Garbage Boy, the apprentice. The white in the black, white, and red Newspaper Crew. The CBC celebrity. Shit, son, I love my CBC, and you have been as entertaining as a raccoon with the shits and a hard-on. Come a little closer to the cabin, son, so I can get a close up of your presidential stuff and CBC stardom profile and bask in your presence."

I was at the steps and still couldn't see him when I felt a tap on my shoulder. If my ass wasn't cemented shut, I would have shit my pants for sure, and the spring on my watch, if I was wearing one, would have burst. The fact that the tap on my shoulder was with the business end of a double-barrel shotgun didn't ease any pressure off the escapism and shut down mechanics of some of my vital organs.

Mr. Clampett walked by me and up the steps before he turned around. When he did, my eyes met a combination of Daniel Boone and Tonto. Buckskin boots up to midcalf, fringed buckskin pants, then a dirty, grey T-shirt with the sleeves cut off, and on top of his head, a coonskin hat with full face and tail. His dark face was framed with a rough, short, grey beard. He had a massive chest and arms.

"I'm a veteran of three wars," he said. "Two you've heard of and only one anyone gave a good goddamn about. I've trained with the Yanks and the Brits in their special forces. I still get called in occasionally to consult. If necessary or required in my consulting work, you're dead when I'm already somewhere else. I'm a spook's spook. That explains how I can speak from everywhere and come out of nowhere. Now you know more about me than you do about the fuckin' twins down the street, Mister and Stone Pony. They're twins of the mind, more brothers than brothers, and very tough mothers. So, the great Scarface. How's it hanging?"

"Not hanging at all right now, Mr. Clampett. My dick seems to have followed my balls somewhere internally thanks to that friend of yours tapping on my shoulder." I motioned carefully to the shotgun.

"Keep calling me Mr. Clampett; I like that! You have a sense of humour, too! That's good. You'll need it. How's your mother doing?"

That caught me by surprise.

"Good, Mr. Clampett. Thanks for asking. You know her?"

"No, but I know of her. Know what happened to her. I know and have felt and experienced small-town piety and pettiness myself. I know how the self-righteous not only hold you down but also kick you when you're down. Your mom took all that shit and keeps rising up. That's a good, strong woman you have for a mother, Scarface. You get that, right?"

"Yes, sir."

"OK, you should also know my role with my neighbours. I'm advanced security. Hopefully, you never have to see my security force in action. Part of my security responsibilities assigned by my neighbours are the safety of your mom and family. No ill will comes her way without immediate and preferably pre-emptive security enforcement measures. The neighbours pay me for this as well as other security and intelligence services. The task assigned regarding your mom I would do without a fee."

"Thank you, Mr. Clampett."

"Now, get up the road. Smells like the rest of your Newspaper Crew are cooking breakfast. The gate will be closed. Climb over it. Don't go around it. Their cabin is about half a mile up. Nice talking to you."

"Yes, sir. Thank you again."

When I was about ten feet from the gate, Mr. Clampett's voice came from somewhere up ahead in the trees. "Over the fence. The middle of the fence. Then follow the tire tracks. That bobcat scared the crap out of you, but it sure is a beautiful animal. I can smell him on you, and I'm getting a little whiff of fear as well. Fear can be a good thing. It keeps you alert and wired. See you around, Scarface."

Then silence. I started over the exact damn centre of that fence. I heard the voice. He was now standing less than four feet behind me. "But you won't see me around." By the time I was twenty feet past the fence and turned around, he was gone. It was not only scary but irritating. A big man like that couldn't just disappear. I walked back to the fence and looked around. The only visible signs of humanity were the tire tracks and my footprints. There was no sign of Mr. Clampett. No footprints, nothing. How was that possible? I walked what I thought was way more than the half-mile indicated by Mr. Clampett. There were tracks in the snow—deer, rabbits, raccoon, a moose, a fox, some smaller animals, and what could have been a bear. The lane got narrower and more rutted the farther in I went. It took a sharp right turn, and I was in a large clearing. Standing on the front porch of a phenomenally huge log cabin, a freakin' log mansion, was my crew. Both of them were wearing Hawaiian shirts and shorts. They said "Aloha" and beckoned me in. They were wearing leis around their necks.

"Good morning, Scarface," Mister said. "It took us three years to build this place. You're only the fifth person to see it. The third person is right behind you."

I sensed before turning around that Mr. Clampett would be there, and there he was, dressed in a Hawaiian shirt, shorts, shotgun, and a smile.

"Come on, Garbage Boy. At the back of the cabin is a bathroom with a shower and breakfast attire waiting for you, so get a move on."

Up the steps and in the door I went, feeling like Dorothy in *The Wizard of Oz*.

"No, Toto, we're definitely not in Kansas anymore," I said. All three men laughed loudly at that.

"Good one, Scarface," Stone Pony said. "Now get showered, so we can enjoy our feast."

The place was spectacular. A thirty-foot-tall fireplace going up a full three floors to the peaked roof, filled one end of a huge living space. At the other end was a full kitchen with what looked like brand-new appliances and a dining area for twelve, with comfy armchairs around a long, beautiful, carved wooden table.

"Stop gawking, and get cleaned up," Mister barked. "We'll explain some of this place to you over our meal."

I was directed down the hallway, past a huge bedroom on the left, and then a bathroom on the right. On the left it looked like a door to another bedroom, but straight ahead a massive open space with a huge window led to a screened-in porch. The furniture was all rough branches woven into the shapes of massive couches, chairs, and coffee tables, and another impressive stone fireplace right in the centre. Wow! I showered quickly and put on my shorts and Hawaiian shirt. There was even clean underwear for me and a pair of sandals—but no lei.

When I came back into the great room, the big, open space seemed so fantastic, so freakin' grand. And it all seemed unreal and incongruent with the knowledge of whose place it was. Mr. Clampett provided the background narrative. "They found it rundown and framed. They built it all except for the electrical, plumbing, and heating. They brought people in from west of the big city, all the trades for everything. Most of the folks were Indians from the Six Nations, no locals. This place, on a lake, in a few years, will be worth millions. Quite the spot! All the security work, personally done by me. Anyone trying to sneak up on this place would encounter a few surprises."

The meal was centred on a big ham that was adorned and cooked with pineapple rings. There were grits, scalloped potatoes, corn, peas, and a bowl of bacon. "Well, it is breakfast," Mister offered as an explanation for the bacon. There were also hot rolls, which turned out to be bannock, and cornmeal muffins. The grits were tasteless gruel for me, but my breakfast companions ate them up like they were a dessert. Talk was mostly gibes and laughs. Drink was coffee. I felt good and warm. I knew I was with a group of companions. I wasn't their equal, but we were connected. Misfits, oddballs, non-conformists, rejects, and outcasts who actually knew that about themselves and, more importantly, about the group, but no one gave a shit about how they were viewed except me. It's hard to describe, but I felt comfort, tranquility, and ease here with these men—and yes, peace. I felt quiet in my brain and in my gut. My arse loosened, and thank the Lord, my balls were back.

The quiet of trust, the calm of companionship, the serenity of safety. I sensed that Stone Pony and Mister's cabin would be a safety zone for me for a long time to come. I don't know why that feeling came so quickly and with such certainty, but it did.

When we finished breakfast, it was time for a tour of the property. We threw on our boots and went for a walk. There were four outbuildings. Mr. Clampett told me three of the outbuildings had been constructed by the previous owner. Some big-city lawyer who had gone missing and his money had disappeared. There were lots of rumours and theories about whether he was alive or dead. Mister and Stone Pony bought the place for a song about five years after his estate and grieving widow put it on the market. Rumours also spread that buying the property was strongly discouraged by some criminal elements.

The place had a two-storey, four-vehicle garage. The upstairs had two huge bedrooms and a big, open living area with a good-size kitchen and a full bath. They referred to it as the guest quarters. The garage was laid out like a mechanic's workshop, with a hydraulic lift and a full range of equipment and tools. There were two snowmobiles and two Indians—the motorcycle kind. The second outbuilding we only viewed from the outside. It was about two hundred yards deep in the woods, about fifty feet long, and almost as wide. It looked like a greenhouse, and I was told that was the main function. That's where our vegetables had come from for our breakfast. These guys grew potatoes and peas. Go figure. Sure enough, what I could see were climbing vines. I surmised my crew had green thumbs.

The third outbuilding was a two-seater outhouse, because one never knew when the plumbing was going to break down, and a man always needed a place to dump a load.

The fourth building was recessed into the woods on the opposite side of the house. It was referred to as the shed. We went in. There was lots of mechanical stuff in there, along with a boat, canoes, and motors. There was a two-hundred-gallon gas tank with a pump and, out back, a launching ramp. A large stream flowed by the shed, a perfect place for launching the boat. Stone Pony told me the lake was over a half a mile away, and that was by far the largest stream running into it on the south side of the lake. Mr. Clampett said I would probably know it as Black Cedar Creek. I realized I knew that creek as "Shit Creek." In the spring run-off, the lake was filled with brown water flowing from the creek. The soil was a darker shade, and the erosion from the spring run-off created a significant, dark stain on the lake.

I asked how big the property was and was stunned by the answer. "Just over three hundred acres," Stone Pony said. "Mr. Clampett has another three hundred acres. We have no neighbours except for that hillbilly."

"Do you guys own all of this?"

"Mostly. The bank has some claim with the mortgage they carry, but we're working that down."

"How long have you had this place?"

"We bought it in sixty-five, after we worked city garbage for about a year. Then we started buying the surrounding land. Look, the land is dirt cheap. We don't own down to the lake, but no one is ever going to want that land. There's no beach front, just rocks and trees and all kinds of marshy areas and bogs. Right now it's Crown land. If it comes up for sale, we'll buy it."

"So, this isn't the spot for the next wave of cottages for the big-city folks."

"Not likely. We're just north and east of the reserve here. We don't have the appeal like the other end of the lake. So nice and quiet. Let the animals and Mr. Clampett roam!"

When we returned to the cabin, Stone Pony and Mister toured me through the rest of their home. A second hallway led past two huge bedrooms and one bathroom. Beyond that was an open room full of weights, punching bags, and other gym equipment. Also in this space was a sauna made of cedar.

"You lift, right?" Mister asked.

"A little. Not as disciplined as I should be."

"We lift seriously here," Stone Pony said. "At least three times but maybe as many as five times a week. You should get serious about your strength. We'll give you a program. We do a big lift on Sunday afternoons, starting at about four o'clock. You should join us."

"It would be tough getting out here."

"Ride your bike or get a car. We're paying you enough."

"I'm saving for university and helping my mom out."

"You need a car. We'll look around for you. We'll find something reliable and cheap."

"OK, thanks, but I don't know if I'll be able to afford it. Another slight problem. I don't know how to drive."

"Learn! We're going to run a second truck by late spring. You might even get to drive. Sign up for driver's ed tomorrow!"

Truth be told, I was dying to learn how to drive. Our family had never had a car. The Vancouver blondes had asked me to drive a couple of times on our little golfing tour the previous summer, but I had said I wouldn't be comfortable driving their VW.

We took it easy in front of a big fire in the great room. I fell asleep and woke up at around 3. Mister said I should stay and lift, then they would give me a ride home. The lift was a trip! Bench press, squats, deadlifts, standing curls, overhead triceps curls, preacher curls on the bench, three sets of eight to ten each. No breaks. We started with bench and ended with bench. The finishing set was reversed. High to low weights, five sets, each to failure. All lifts in our Hawaiian shirts, shorts, and sandals. Mr. Clampett was doing his own thing. Some martial arts movements, very rhythmic—and he worked himself into our lift sequence at times. He lifted mostly light reps and periodically a heavy rep. Mister bench-pressed 400, Mr. Clampett, 340, Stone Pony, 320, and me, 175. They told me in two months, I would be at 250.

We made massive ham-and-cheese sandwiches after lifting. When they dropped me off, my legs felt like jelly. I mumbled a bit about my day to my mom and the little one and then went up to my room. After tucking one hundred dollars under my mom's pillow and twenty dollars under the little one's, I fell asleep quickly. Thoughts of the cabin and Mr. Clampett were playing on the back of my eyelids. My last thought prior to slumber: *a greenhouse?*

CHAPTER 12

The Rat Bastards

They're all rat bastards. My two brothers and their bitch wives. Those two witches wouldn't piss on you if you were on fire. They blame me for their husband's drinking and all their badass behaviour. As if it was my fault. The youngest brother. Who the fuck do they think taught me to drink? Well, our old man and his brothers mostly, but I looked up to my brothers. They were both taller and stronger than me. They were naturally better baseball and hockey players, but I worked harder and outshone them for a time. I also drank harder and scored more putang than those tall fucks. All that was long ago and long gone.

My rat bastard brothers put me on a train with a one-way, non-refundable, non-transferable ticket to Vancouver. Coach class; no sleeper for Art. That was about three months after our failed mission to plant me back with my family. That didn't go well. We should not have been drinking on the drive to my old house. I had cleaned up good too. I was thinking how great it would be to see my son. I had heard he was a good athlete and not a fuck up. Yet.

Legend has it that my brothers and I were fourth-generation hardcore drinkers. That blend of Irish/Scottish heritage was hard on livers, bodies, and wives. Historically, we didn't have good track records as family men or long lifers. I was hoping that my son would break that pattern. The men in my family had not ended life well through the generations—and often far too early. It appeared that my brothers' sons were on their way to break the pattern. That would be good.

Credit their wives. Those hard-faced, hard-hearted bitches steered their offspring onto good paths. They were probably right; I definitely was not a positive influence.

My cleaning-up and drying-out period of five days before our mission to regain my family was freaking agony. My brothers were forced to participate in the five days of cleansing. The cap was off the whisky bottle ten minutes into our three-hour drive.

My son stood up. He knocked me down at the back door. He bloodied my lip. I bloodied his nose. He put me on my ass. We left, and my last words to him, probably ever, were, "Fuck you." His last words to me: "Hey, Dad, you forgot the loaf of bread." That jogged a memory. When I left, when was that? Like eight years before. I said I was going to the store for a pack of smokes, and my wife asked me to get a loaf of bread. She even gave me a quarter to cover the cost of the bread, and I just loafed it on out of there.

My brothers' wives greased my exit. They did research and got me to sign some papers. They said they could get me some money for being a war veteran, more if I had a disability. They sent me to a doctor. He said I had some physical damage caused by war. I qualified for disabled veteran benefits. Cash was on the way. The wives got me a bank account. They were some kind of custodians, and there were some constraints on me accessing the funds. I didn't care as long as I had some whisky money coming in. My ambitions were focused if not extremely limited.

They gave me an allowance for about four months. It was just a trickle of cash to a thirsty man, but I managed. I was living on a cot with a camp stove in the basement of my oldest brother's home. The basement was just concrete, filled with junk and a furnace. At least I was warm. I even had my own private piss bucket. I was allowed to go upstairs to shit. I washed up in the laundry tub. The cat came down regularly but not to visit me. She came to visit the litter box. It was the first pussy I had coming my way in a long time, and she was not interested in me at all, just like any other pussy I had encountered recently. The cat came down to shit. I went upstairs to shit. Sometimes we passed on the stairs. Two shits passing in the night—well actually, on a flight of stairs. Fuck, I can be funny. I used to work that humour on the ladies. Now, a rummy like me doesn't do funny. At least not well. Not funny enough to get some skirt or a free drink anymore, or anything of anything.

It was the end of my second day, and the bar car on the train had already devoured my cash in hand. I thought I would get off the train in Winnipeg, get some cash, get some booze, and stay for a couple of days. That's when I discovered the non-refundable, non-transferable, and non-redeemable wording on part of the train ticket in Winnipeg. It was late October or early November. Who remembers? Who knows? Who gives a flying fuck?

Winnipeg was a bit of a surprise. I mean, they had stuff that fit my taste. Cheap bars with fifteen-cent drafts and fifty-cent shots in the afternoons. A flophouse for six bucks a night. Hookers for five or ten bucks. Prices went up at night for everything except the five-buck hookers.

The CN ticket clerk told me my ticket to Vancouver was good for fourteen days. That gave me ample time for play time in the Peg.

Winnipeg was also where I found out the constraints on my bank account. My account was not allowed to go under a $500 balance without the permission of the account custodians, my two bitch sisters-in-law. I was being treated like a twelve-year-old with my own money. When I got off the train in Winnipeg, the first bank teller informed me that I had $1,107 dollars in my account and asked if I would like a passbook to keep track of my finances. Well, yes I would.

Six days later the account was at $507, and I had $30 in my wallet when I got back on that westbound train. How the hell did I blow $600 at 50 cents a shot, 15 cents a draft, and on $5 hookers? I guess I had myself some fun.

The bank teller was kind enough to inform me that I would receive my next veteran's disability cheque on November 15. I was getting $534.17 per month. I figured I could almost remain flush if I managed myself with some restraint. Less rye. More Four Aces. You know, belt tightening. I'm a funny guy. At least I make myself chuckle from time to time.

Winnipeg was the high-water mark of my low life for the foreseeable future. The fifteenth was only six days away, so I invested wisely. Cleaned up and showered at the downtown Y for seventy-five cents, got a hot meal at a mission house, and bought three bottles of Four Aces for the trip. The old reliable "Come alive for a buck five." That would get me to Vancouver in prime form in two or three days.

I hit Vancouver with only ten bucks, with three days until money day. I had some soup and a grilled-cheese sandwich on the train, maybe a whisky shot, a double. Big spender, cash coming in and all. I got myself to a run-down, five-storey apartment building around the corner from the train station. The place cost $150 per month, and I got myself a penthouse with a window. The room had a toilet separated from the rest of the space by a thin piece of particle board. A man could crap in the relative privacy of his ten-by-twelve domain. There was a kitchen sink, hot plate, a tiny fridge for an extra five bucks a month, a bed, a chair, and a folding table. Handy to have that folding table for working on my monthly budget and other important household affairs. I could just fold it up to get it out of the way for dancing when company came over. Gave myself another good chuckle with that thought. I used to be a good dancer. That's what my mom told me growing up. My wife did, too. At least I think they did. Swept some Italian whores off their feet during the war and a few Indian girls at the Retreat. Now, the Retreat was and maybe still is a good bar for fuckin' and fightin'—but dancing? Not so much.

I got myself a couple of blankets, a pillow, some sheets, and a couple of towels at the local thrift shop, all for a few bucks. Two bucks left and two days to go. I knew where the nearest bank branch was. I could have walked there with my eyes closed. I was working up a big thirst. My passbook with the recent withdrawal and balance history got me my penthouse without an advance, but three hundred was given right to the landlord from my next payday. I had been on the streets enough times to know that a room would be the difference between living or dying, at least in the short run.

Made it to payday, settled with the landlord on the first and last months' rent. Two hundred and thirty-four dollars and seventeen cents, plus the seven bucks already in the account over the required minimum balance. The next month was going to be tight and dry as well as drizzly in Vancouver, but I'd done longer with less.

I sat in my room a lot, nursing the Four Aces, playing solitaire on my folding table, and cooking the odd grilled-cheese sandwich. The frying pan, some dishes, and cutlery set me back four bucks. I was going to splurge on a toaster the following month.

Drank my Four Aces right from the bottle. No need to be all pompous and drink from my cup, but I did take the bottle out of the brown paper bag. Looked out my window. I had quite a view. The decrepit and decaying buildings of East Hastings. Glorious in their fall from grace. Occasionally took a drag on a smoke, blowing the exhale through the sliver of space of the raised sill of my window. I was thinking of those rat bastards, those bitch sisters-in-law. Dreaming how one day I would go back and show those sons of bitches that I could make it on my own. That Art wasn't a total asshole, a total fuck up.

Almost made it through the month before it hit. No, not the shakes—or what did they call them? The DDTs? Nope, just blew some smoke out the window, watching the rain and seeking solace from a saucy little rosé I found priced at only a buck ten. Then, my son popped into my head. His nose bleeding, maybe a bruise around his eyes, both from me. Not a bad-looking kid, despite the scars. My brothers told me they called my son Scarface. Even drunk, I could see why, poor kid. Took another little swig of the rosé and started to cry. Raggedy shitstorm of a cry. Sobbing, chest heaving. Hard to catch my breath. Thinking when he was born how I wanted to be a good father. Teach him to play ball. Catch, run, hit. Saw myself strong and smiling, watching him try, learn, and then get it.

Fuck me. Art, the good father. If I were making a confession, I would say nothing more than "Father, my great sin is not ever becoming the father I saw in my own head for my son. The father I wanted and hoped to become. I compare this vision to the failed father I am. That's it; there you go, Father. Just the enormous sin of being a failed father." That broke the weepy-sister cycle from sob to a wet snicker.

Took a last drag of the tobacco, blew out the smoke, and through the fog of the rosé, the tears, and the cigarette fog, I accepted that this view of the decrepit street was the best view I would likely get and would be lucky to have on the day I died. That's as well as I could end if I could even end that well. And to that end, I would drink.

The chances of this father rising were slim, none, and fat. I didn't want to live with that, so I thought I'd better drink that dream into oblivion and beyond. Tomorrow was the fifteenth, so all was well that ended well, at least on the fifteenth of every month.

CHAPTER 13

Weekly Write

Now that celebrity had faded to normality, things seemed to be more routine. Morning announcements, lifting before school three days a week, student council duties, hockey practices, and one or two games a week playing for the high school team. We were barely competitive, but a good bunch of guys mostly, and we had a great man coaching us.

Most of our team had given up playing for—or were never good enough to play for—the town all-star travel teams. Only three or four of us could have skated at that higher level. Our coach was so down to earth. He worked hard at our practices and games. We were all motivated to play for him. I played defence instead of forward, giving us a slightly better chance at being competitive.

School was OK. I was studying. Mister and Stone Pony were grilling me to get good grades to give me a chance to get into a university.

I decided to start writing a weekly student-council news and views. Turns out I liked thinking and writing. The topics were based on upcoming events, student-council decisions, and actions, along with two or three paragraphs on my thoughts and perspective. I called the column the "Scarface Sagas," which was probably me slipping into pretentiousness.

Part of the writing was just for me. I guess you could call it a diary. I was beginning to keep notes about my life and my thoughts. The writing covered my feelings, thoughts on family, wonderings, as in things I wondered about, and some short stories. Some of the stories made their way into the Scarface Sagas. Most didn't. The diary posts could really have been titled, "The Route of the Newspaper Crew. Red, White, and Black or Black, White, and Red." Whatever connected us was much deeper than our garbage route. The guys acted more and more like big brothers. I was OK with that. I liked that. I needed that, and there was comfort in that.

I guess I was writing a bit of their story. Mister and Stone Pony were still a mystery to me, but what a mystery! It wasn't really their story but more my recording of their extraordinary ways. Their house, their security, their strength, their wisdom, and Mr. Clampett.

These two were known by everyone in town and beyond, without even doing anything to draw attention to themselves. They were not in the public eye except when running barrels.

There was a mystique surrounding them. It was beyond the quiet strength. It was beyond the dignity and work ethic that they demonstrated as garbage men. They had this thing about them. My English teacher described watching us run barrels as the actions of warriors. He said there was an animalistic power and fierce pride in our movements. He called it the "ballet of the barrels, the strength and the symmetry of sinew." He waxed a little too poetic at times, which would cause his students to shut him out.

The weekly writing even had me thinking and sometimes sharing thoughts on good governance, relating, and working with others. It also had me praising various activities, teams, and people in our school. That was particularly enjoyable.

I liked spotlighting others who were achieving, contributing, and striving. I did it with some humour, such as assigning nicknames, but was very conscious not to slip into ridicule. Just building people up. This was well received, and people looked forward to it.

The more I wrote, the more I thought. I was thinking a lot about how people got along, who hung out with who and why. Some of this thinking entered my creative writing assignments for English class. Our teacher took that as a springboard for him to introduce social structures, classes, and class thinking into our discussions of novels. Then he asked us to relate those concepts to our town and write a five-page "class" story.

I thought it was a cool topic, and so did more than a few others in the class. He was asked if the paper could include thoughts on the role of religion, town politics, dope, booze, sex, and the different groups within our school. He'd hit upon a theme that had some appeal he had not anticipated. He was ecstatic. Given this abnormally receptive and enthusiastic response, he thought he was becoming inspirational in his teaching. He gave us one ground rule: "You can share your perspective, but you cannot attack any group in your essays."

Fair enough!

He said it was good to wonder, to be inquisitive, to share our perspective about institutions and the class structure and the things people did.

I had lots of thoughts on all of this. The hippie-type classmates thought it could be "far out." Some planned to write their essay while stoned for a mellower or giddier perspective.

Our teacher said we should use a filter, a lens, a conduit, or some device to structure our perspective to write through the eyes or from the shoes of some other person. "You're writing what you think they're thinking when they think about you." That line was enough to get those who liked to toke up halfway stoned already.

"Let me get this straight. I'm supposed to think how they think about me when they think about me, and I think about them thinking about me, like, never! Cool! Fire up a big fat one!"

Our town had an incredibly high rate of drug consumption. The CBC stated our town had the second-highest rate of illicit drug use in Canada. Some of the local druggies would, when stoned, gleefully chant, "We're number two. We're number two," then pause, pinch their thumbs and forefingers together, move them to their lips, inhale deeply and say, while mimicking holding a lungful of bliss, "but we're pulling to go higher," then laugh their asses off.

Perspective, lenses, filters, conduits, in their shoes . . . my angle would have been near impossible to convey. I wanted to see our town from the viewpoint of Mister and Stone Pony. Although they were a mystery to everyone, there certainly was no shortage of views concerning them.

I often tried to place myself in a mindset that I thought would be their collective vision of our world. That wasn't easy. It would have required a Vulcan mind meld to get their view, and I saw them as holding one view, one perspective, not two. Not the red man and the black man, not from the singular, powerful experiences of the First Peoples and of the African slaves, but as one. The interesting perspective or view would probably make the stoners think I was writing about them, the stoners. As in, "We're all one, brother."

CHAPTER 14

Stone Pony

I had to be so fuckin' careful about everywhere and anywhere I went and how I got there. As a fuckin' scrawny little Indian with no big brothers or even a pack of scrawny little Indian fuckers for some form of protection. That would have been good. We could have been the Indian version of those fuckin' scrawny Inglis white fuckers.

The two oldest Inglis brothers, even though they were younger fucks than me, beat me up and stole my bike. What fuckin' fuckers! We had to be careful about what type of bike we rode because the two fuckin' white-boy town gangs, the Vipers and the Kings of the South, had their separate bike style. Those fuckin' white boys didn't even realize that a gang that rode two-wheeled, pedal-powered bikes of any type were pussies by definition. It took me some time, a whole bunch of fuckin' paralyzing fear, and a few poundings to come to that realization. The Kings rode banana-seat bikes with high handlebars and streamers on the handles. The Vipers called the Kings' bikes "Fag Wheels," a takeoff on the kids' tricycles called Big Wheels. The Vipers rode three-speed CCM Raleighs, mostly stolen. Nobody bought that bike in the puke-lime-green colour the Kings rode. The stolen bikes were painted that colour. The Kings called the Vipers' bikes "Limey Puke Pussy Pops," intending to slight the Vipers and the British and pussies simultaneously. I was OK with slighting the first two of those fuckin' groups, but slighting pussy? That made no sense.

After having two or three bikes stolen, I learned to weave from the reserve to any point around town via secret paths through bush and marshes, over streams and creeks, on old logging roads, through the woods, over ditches, along fence lines, rock walls, cattle pastures, and fields with animal paths. I got off the reserve because Indians would beat on a scrawny fuckin' Indian with no family for fuckin' protection or likelihood of retribution. Riding was freedom. Freedom from fuckin' fear and fuckin' poundings. Man, this shit that was always falling on my head and the constant motion made me one tough motherfuckin' Indian who, in his own weight class and probably two or three heavier divisions, could scrap the fuck out of most motherfuckers. At least one on one.

On my rides through the secret paths, I often encountered two freaky white kids. I saw them, but they only occasionally thought they saw something. That would be me if those white fucks had decent bush eyes or ears. I heard them comin' every time, although credit to them, for white fucks, they were quite stealthy. I often trailed them and found where they kept their stashes of beer and pop bottles and, occasionally, a *Playboy* magazine. I yanked off a couple of times in their *Playboys*. A couple of times I found them arguing over who stuck the pages of Miss June or Miss September together. It was me. Yeah, you boney white fucks, nothing sticks like scrawny Indian sperm. Made myself fuckin' laugh.

Those kids were branded with the nicknames Bogeyman and Scarecrow, which I thought was pretty fuckin' cool. Something was off with those two. They were smart. They showed me new trails and paths that any fuckin' Indian worth his stones should have found first. Champlain and Cartier didn't have a fuckin' clue. It was Indians who led them to all those so-called fuckin' discoveries and routes. My red-assed ancestors probably got around their fires at night and wondered what these white boys were all jazzed up about. Those rivers, lakes, streams, rock cliffs, forests, fish, and animals had been there forever. It was like everything was the first time they saw a puppy. Look at that thing! That thing is fuckin' amazing." Stupid white fuckin' discoverers. They started fuckin' everything up. Then those robed major fucks, the Jesuits. Save your souls, path-to-God conversion assholes. They were the straight fuckin' line to smallpox and residential schools. You fuckin' Bible totin' priests of all things that fucked us over.

Maybe I'm a little hard on those men of God. The arrogance of the explorers, though, is still laughable. My loincloth-wearin', big-swingin'-dick ancestors knew those white boys with their codpieces on their crotches still couldn't find their own dicks with two hands.

But I fuckin' digress. Bogeyman and Scarecrow. What did white kids have to be frightened about? They were fuckin' white! I guess I didn't know much at that time about social and income classes. And OK, yeah, the biggie, societal evils. These boys were scared of, as it turns out, the same things as I was. Scared about getting the shit stomped the fuck outta them. I didn't get it then, that those white boys were in the same wagon ruts as I was. Scarface, too.

See, my mindset was cowboys and Indians. Indians always took the shit kickin' or got killed. Sure, once in a blue fuckin' moon, I heard the phrase "noble savage." Usually just before that noble got fucked over or killed by the white man or betrayed his own red people, or even worse, made a deal in good faith where the white man, usually aided and abetted by men of the cloth, fucked over the Indian's whole tribe or nation for centuries. The white man knowing the unbreakable contract was unbreakable for only the fucked-over fuckin' Indians. Their religious sidekicks going along with the whole fucking over of the red man. If the red men converted to the glory of God, they wouldn't even want or need the shit fuck pieces of land we gave them, the reserves. How the fuck did you give or cede land to us that was fuckin' ours in the first place, you greedy, cruel fuckers?

Cowboys and Indians. The Indian brave got killed, and the noble savage was transformed into just a fuckin' savage who, maybe someday, might rape our women and steal our cattle. Or rape our cattle and steal our women. Maybe someday. The red threat. Not communists, because those were different white fucks, or those fuckin' yellow bastards.

The Indian was killed or hung, and the fuckin' savage deserved it, primarily for future possible actions. A white man died at the hands of a red man, and everyone got all fuckin' weepy. Even if that fuck had betrayed his promise to the red men and wiped out a village of Indian women, old men, and children when the men were not home. Oh, you fuckin' brave white boys. I'm a little fuckin' bitter! No shit, Kemosabe!

The white guy died, and if he was scalped, the weep-fest reached new proportions, justifying annihilation of the red menace. Fuckin' preposterous. The Church stood by wagging their collective heads and saying if only they had converted to Christ, we could have watched them get ripped off and fucked over at a more Christianly pace.

Occasionally, a white guy would kill another white guy because the lines were clear. The bad white guy had rustled cattle, stolen a horse, wore black (except for Paladin), got his freak on with Ms. Kitty, or kicked Chester. (He had a limp, so he never should have been abused.) We watched *Gunsmoke* and *Have Gun – Will Travel* religiously. Fuck, we would play cowboys and Indians and wanted to be the fuckin' cowboys. We weren't fuckin' stupid. We knew the odds and the outcomes.

I liked Marshal Matt Dillon. He had a kind of sensitive, rational, decent demeanour about him. A white authority figure one could almost trust; however, it was clear there was something off about him. I mean, come on, Matt, get in the game. Ms. Kitty wants you to bone her bad. Get at it, Matt. Ms. Kitty is desperate for your sensitive ways and a good fucking for stress relief. Look, Matt, she runs that saloon, and her customers ain't fuckin' saints. Most of the characters who come in there would fuck a rattlesnake if you held its head. Miss Kitty needs some action.

In just one episode I wanted to hear Marshal Dillon say, "Kitty, bar the door. The sheriff's coming." Sadly, all the good marshal gave Ms. Kitty was that occasional dumb-fuck look from time to time.

Back to Bogeyman and Scarecrow. These white boys were going to find their way. It wasn't going to be mainstream or Main Street. They were too clever and too outside to be on the straight and narrow. These boys were going to have some fun, and probably no one would guess the half of it. I think I could be a part of that.

Anybody ever talks to me seriously or hears these thoughts I'm expressing to myself, then guess the fuckin' obvious. I'm a racist. Well, not so much a racist as I prefer my own kind. At least when they aren't trying to kick the shit out of me, steal something I don't really have, or leave marks on me when they did kick the shit out of me. Not like those white fuckers, especially the Inglis boys. They wanted to leave marks to show how fuckin' tough they were. All three or four of them against the scrawny little Indian fucker.

I gotta stop saying fuck, even if I'm just talking between my own ears. If that crawl space on top of my neck is all fucked up and filled up with the fuck word then how do I expect to fuckin' speak out loud without spouting out "fuck"? If you think in the fuck word, then you speak in the fuck word, and you sound like a fucking fucked-up fucker. That's some pretty deep and scrawny Indian philosophy right there. You will be the fucker you think and sound like. So, fuck that! I'm just going to stop thinking and saying "fuck" right fuckin' now. Hey, that's funny fucking stuff if you fucking think about it.

Our town and Reserve didn't discriminate, at least when it came to me. My shit kickings were equally administered by white or Indian kids. These non-discriminatory ass kickings might have stemmed from the absence of my father in my tranquil domestic life of beatings and fear. My mother was a saint, like those robed dicks only wished they could be. She never laid a hand on me. She loved me as best she could and protected me as best she could. She worked long days and lots of weekends at a white man's resort on the lake. She had to hide her pay packets because she would get ripped off for them by so-called uncles and aunties. She figured out how to protect her money. She got another chambermaid who lived in town to deposit her money in the Canadian Imperial Bank of Commerce in town and bring her four or five blank cheques, so she could pay her bills. We kept very little cash on hand.

Grace, my mother, passed when I was seventeen. Her body just got tired, all the work and all the beatings. Started with my father. Grace would never tell me who that was. My mother deserved better.

By seventeen, I was still slight and wouldn't get past five foot seven, but I was strong, all sinew, all muscle. That strength was my salvation. Not some faith in some foreign God or even our own creator. I was foremost strong.

I have no recollection of my father whatsoever. The last time he was on the reserve, he broke my mother's nose and cracked a couple of ribs. I was nine. He was looking for booze money. No luck, schmuck. Grace was too smart for that, just not quick enough to avoid the closed fist and the stomp of a boot.

I know I was nine because it was my first year playing Y's men's hockey, and I was on the Indian team. Yep, they put four or five of us real Indians on the team called the Indians. The well-intentioned white fucks didn't even get the irony or bigotry or whatever you wanna call it of that whole scenario. The other Indian kids in our age group were on the Smoke Rings. I kid you not! When we moved into the next age group, we graduated to the Teepees and Chiefs. Again, I kid you not! I digress again. Notice how I don't swear much when my mother, Grace, full of grace, is anywhere near my thoughts.

For a long stretch there, probably from age seven to thirteen, I wondered who my father was. I knew he lived in town. I got that much from my mother and assorted and dubious aunties and uncles. There were about eight Indian men from our Reserve living in town. Two respectable citizens married to white women. Man, the kids in those families had it tough. Half-breeds was the description of choice from the enlightened white and Indian folks. Neither one race nor the other. Neither of those two men were my father. Those two families were devout Catholics. The Jesuit strain was what I called them. Thank Christ for that.

Three of the men were town drunks. These, my mom assured me, were not my father. They got beat up more than me. We shared that common bond. The other three were Indian families who had moved off the Reserve of their own free will. All three of those families believed in the traditions of our people but couldn't see or live with that faith and spirit on our Reserve. That's not a joke. In fact, it's very sad.

So, in about 1958 or so I gave up looking for my dad. Well, sort of. I stared at every "town Indian" and all the kids on the Reserve, looking for some resemblance to me. Nothing, never, nobody, no time, no how, nowhere, no one. I didn't figure out who my old man was until Mister came along and helped solve that mystery. That was in 1967 when I was twenty-two. By then I didn't give a fuck.

In 1958 I did have a revelation. The fact that I was as scrawny as hell and short for my age, now thirteen, made me easy pickings. I looked like easy pickings. I was the poster boy for easy pickings. I should have changed my name to Easy Pickens, like the actor, Slim Pickens, except he was as fat as hell. Easy Pickens might have been better than Duke Earl. My mother said I came out screaming at the top of my lungs with both fists clenched, ready for a fight. The creator knew I would be swinging early and often. Earl was her maiden name, so Duke Earl. Nobody calls me that. Nobody even remembers me by that name.

A few years before 1958, probably in 1954 or 1955, when I started playing Y's men's hockey and Legion baseball and was going into town on main roads for games, my visibility made me more of a target. That's when I began using secondary transportation routes for self-preservation. By 1958, I had mastered the woods, fields, and marshes. You can't hit what you can't see or can't find. So, into the bush, into the bogs, and down the deer paths I went. In 1958, I upped my game. Payback, you fuckin' fuckers. I was so fuckin' elusive and slick that I could get away safely. Lickety-fuckin'-split. Still four or five white guys would follow me into the bush. Being chased and scared shitless was still an adrenaline rush, but what the fuck? Time to inflict a little harm.

Pedal like a fuckin' madman, get two three hundred yards ahead, and pull a downed tree, preferably pines with sharp needles and lots of branches across the trail. Tight to a sharp corner. Wait fifty yards down the path, with a clear line of sight.

The Kings of the South were clearly the dumber white fucks. Their banana-seat low-riders were a lot of fuckin' work to pedal. They felt every bump and didn't change course smoothly. Awkward, high handlebars, low axle configuration, I guess.

The Kings came around the bend, standing up to pedal their little bikes as fast as they could go. Three of them ass over tea kettle. The fuckers were all hurt. I could tell. The other two slid their bikes on their sides to stop. Fuckin' chaos, fuckin' mayhem, fuckin' hurt inflicted! Then I heard those tough motherfuckers cryin' and whimperin'. There was blood, lots of blood, on at least two of them. The one guy stood up, and it sure looked like he had a broken arm. I sat on my bike in clear view of it all.

"Hey, you motherfuckin' babies! You guys flew over those handlebars like fuckin' gymnasts. Hope none of you hurt your pussies, you fuckin' pussies. Five of you trying to fight a scrawny little fuck of an Indian and look at ya. All fucked up and cryin' like babies."

And off I rode with howls of "We'll get you" and some very negative, defamatory slurs flowing in my wake. The year 1958 was a good one. The local paper even published a three-paragraph story on three boys injured while riding their bikes on a little-used path. Injuries ranged from a broken arm to a gash requiring seventeen stitches, various cuts, deep bruises, and welts. What the fuck is a welt? Good news all around. Vengeance never visited me on that one. Can't hit what you can't find or see.

That didn't fix scrawny and short. Scrawny like a little scrawny chicken. Was I chicken? Yes and no. Getting shit kickings instead of avoiding them might be regarded as chicken but only by those folks who hadn't gotten a shit kicking. So, hell no. I wasn't chicken, just too smart to get shit kickings. I mean, I can take a shit kicking and have many times, but why the fuck would I? Oops, no need to swear! I made myself laugh again. Taking a shit kicking is just dumb shit. Maybe I'll migrate from fuck to shit as my curse word of preference. It seems less offensive. Yet, calling someone a fucking dumb shit is such an elegant descriptor of some people, like the leader of the Kings of the South. I'd hate to give that up.

If I was an actual scrawny chicken, life might have been good. I would have been the last choice to be killed for supper. Roosters wouldn't try and fuck—I mean screw—me. The plump chickens with big white breasts would have to be sexier, like Marilyn Monroe chickens or Miss June, before I stuck those pages together. Funny, I was still riding my bike on the paths in the mid to late 1960s when those white boys showed up. I wish I hadn't stuck Miss June together the first time we dated. A little scrawny Indian jack-off humour right there.

Couldn't think of an Indian woman like Marilyn Monroe until Sacheen Littlefeather came along. You know, the one who accepted or didn't accept the Oscar for Marlon Brando. Now that was one smokin' Smoke Ring of an Indian chick. My teepee rises for her. She makes my Red Menace menacing.

You know those ads in the comic books, the Charles Atlas ads that show a ninety-eight-pound weakling getting sand kicked in his face? It's always a big white guy who shits muscles, and his name is Buff or Biff or Tad. I knew that Buff was an absolute dumbass because of his stupid grin and haircut. No one wore their hair that way anymore unless they were in the army or a fat old white fuck. There I go again into that crawlspace in my head and use that word, but sometimes it's the fuckin' perfect word.

Now, about those Indian families who moved off the reserve. You know, to get away from the squalor and the high bar of low expectations we had established. One of those families was the Foremosts. That's seriously one seriously fucked-up name for an Indian family. The background skinny beaver damn story was that some white fucks—damn it's hard not to use that word. Conditioning, you know. I have conditioned myself to use that word and variations thereof repeatedly, with universal application. Its applicability in all situations just proves its value. Anyway, the Foremosts and their name. Some white fuck (SWF) said this Indian family were the leading Indians. Leading their people because they were adopting the white man's ways. Therefore, they were the "foremost" of their tribe. Foremost in leading their tribe, which meant to the SWFs, foremost in trying to become white. The Foremosts moved into town, and they thought their lives were mysteriously gonna get better, but damn if those fuckin' Foremosts (FFMs) didn't have a plan. They became fighters.

The FFMs were and still are a relatively scrawny bunch of Indians. There were four FFM boys, and they all took to boxing like fish to water. They were skipping rope, doing push-ups, pullups, running up hills, and became Charles Atlas ninety-eight-pound weakling weightlifting converts. The FFMs' father, one Forrest Foremost. No shit! They called him Forrest. That guy had to get tough as old leather quickly, and grow balls of cast iron. An Indian named Forrest Foremost was almost begging for a beating. Middle name, I shit you not, Francis. Forrest Francis Foremost. He should have gone into the church, then he could have been Father Forrest Francis Foremost. Could have founded his own version of a 4F Club. You know, find 'em, feel 'em, fuck 'em, forget 'em. Not a good club for a man of the cloth, I would guess.

Forrest would have been subject to a world of hurt on- and off-reserve just because of that name.

Forget a simple taunt like "Forrest can't see the forest for the trees." Forrest would have been the tree that everybody and their dog pissed on.

So, Forrest Francis Foremost enlisted in the army, not the priesthood. Smooth move right there. Forrest figured if he was gonna have to fight all the time, he might as well get paid for it. He also figured some advanced weapon training might be pretty good, since he'd grown up hunting and was a good shot. Forrest went into WWII as a sniper and a tracker. He garnered lots of respect from his army buddies and earned a few medals. Forrest had also been fighting all his life, so he boxed as well. He won the military's light cruiser-weight division at 127 pounds and was the Canadian Armed Forces champ. He got into boxing because those white army Fs (not saying the word, just thinking it) needed anybody they could get in the lower weight classes. The Irish guys were good and tough, but they led with their faces. The Indian guys knew how to duck and preferred to miss a punch. The Irish wanted to stand toe to toe. The Indians would rather bob and weave than chuck and receive.

So FFFM qualified in the white-as-fuck (WAF) white man's army, in a low weight class, and got rewarded for beating up white guys. It was a fuckin' scrawny Indian's dream come true. Other white guys, including all the WAF officers, congratulated him for kickin' the shit out of other WAFs. If FFFM tried that off-reserve in his hometown, he would be one dead Indian. Instead, he was given the WAF army's blessing to kick the ass of other WAFs. Now I'm cleverly thinking in acronyms to avoid the F word even in my head. I'm quite proud of this ability and linguistic development.

FFFM came into the army already tough, because he'd been fighting off and on the reserve his whole life. FFFM reminded me of me, and I found that pretty f'n cool. We're two PFC Indians, just like corn and the husk. FFFM was my idol and definitely a hero for this scrawny Indian. So in 1958, I started lifting homemade weights. I set up some stumps in the woods added an axle from a Ford truck, put the wheel rims, tires, and cinder blocks on, and I had a pure Indian bush gym.

FFFM's four boys were all boxing and winning tournaments.

I didn't get my nerve up to go get some training until I was fifteen, in 1960. I started to put some muscle on my frame. I hiked my way through the bush to Mr. FFFM's house. I still took a convoluted route to get there. From the Reserve I took a deer trail that started about a hundred yards behind our house. The bush got thick quickly. The path was more or less a straight line that went about five hundred yards deep into the bush before it cut back to only about twenty-five yards from the Retreat, the local bar preferred by Indians and dumb-as-fuck white men. It was a prime spot for pickin' up empty brownies, empty beer bottles, cuz you know, knock back a couple of store-bought beers before you pay twenty cents a draft before five, and a quarter after five, going up to thirty-five cents after eight when things get busy. People had to be careful in the back of the Retreat. The Retreat wasn't a drinkin' hole for the faint of heart or the faint of fist. A person could run into a couple of drunks, Indian or white, who would try to either pound them or plead for drinkin' money. The Indians tended to plead first and pound second. You know, conserve their energy for the important stuff ... drinkin'. The whites, they pounded first and pleaded second. You know, work up a thirst for the important stuff ... drinkin'. At fifteen, I was only about a buck and a quarter soakin' wet, but all sinewy and lean, not scrawny. I avoided fights by giving the

Retreat's informal beer garden a wide berth when occupied. From the Retreat I cut across the Beer Line, the road that ran from the Retreat bar directly to the Refuge, the other bar outside the town. The town was dry. The road was officially Reserve Road, as the original purpose was being the main road to the Reserve, so cleverly named by SWF. Reserve Road became Beer Line, Drunkard's Drive, Liquor or Licker Lane, or Asshole Alley. Dozens of names. The one-mile stretch from the Refuge to the Retreat from Thursday night through Sunday morning was a major thoroughfare.

Enough of that. I crossed the Beer Line and on the lake side of the road where there was a ten- to fifteen-foot drop. I followed the trail at the bottom, which was a mile to the bridge. The bridge was the only spot where I was quite vulnerable and visible. I scooted my ass across there, veered into the bush, and followed the lakefront all the way into town. Where the lakefront had been cleared, I turned inland and found the trails through mostly marshy areas. I walked through the big park like I owned it. False bravado. On the other side I took a hard right across the CN tracks. Almost straight uphill, skirting the golf course, over a couple of streets, through the cemetery, across the highway, back into the bush, through some marshy areas, farmer's fields, and I came out at the back of Arthur Street. Home of Scarface, Bogeyman, Scarecrow, and the Foremosts.

I knew when the Foremosts trained. Everybody did because it was in the local paper. Monday, Wednesday, Friday, and all-day Sunday. Before and after church. I arrived in FFFM's backyard on a Monday night, right at five. The article said the Foremosts trained from five until eight on the three weeknights. Mr. Foremost saw me coming out of the bush first. I saw their training camp. A three-sided shed with a solid wood platform. They trained there all year. Mr. Foremost thought cold-weather training made people tough. His oldest boy said it was exhilarating. That was Forrest Jr., the eldest. Francis, the second-eldest, said it was cool that they had to shovel snow to train and box just like the other kids had to shovel snow to clean their backyard rinks to play hockey. Mr. Foremost was as clever at assigning names as a SWF, apparently. No imagination. The other two were Fred and—get this—Fillip. The 4F Fight Club. This 4F club could fuck you up seriously.

I stared at the training camp. The weights, the ropes, the boxing ring, punching bags, all kinds of gloves, pullup bars. I took it in, all of it. It was fuckin' magnificent.

Not one Foremost said a word until Mr. Foremost motioned for me to come up onto the platform. "Pick any piece of equipment, and show me what you can do," he said. My eyes roamed around, but the weight bench was the obvious choice. The bar with the big weights looked intimidating, but I bet it was lighter than the axle with the cinder blocks. I laid down, slid under the bar, and grabbed it, ready to lift. Mr. Foremost stepped in and moved my hands closer together. All four brothers from the 4F Club snickered. I sensed I picked the wrong piece of equipment.

"Do ten lifts," Mr. Foremost said. I didn't know if I could do one, but what the fuck. I pushed up and out and brought the bar down and then up again. One. That wasn't too bad. Two, three, four, five. I caught the eye of Fred and Fillip. Their expressions were like "What the fuck?" That inspired me. Six, seven, eight, nine, and ten. Just for fun, eleven, twelve. When I placed the bar back in the cradling arms, Mr. Foremost asked me how much I weighed.

"A buck and a quarter."

"One hundred twenty-five pounds? Is that right?"

"More or less, sir."

"Do you know how much you just lifted?"

"No, sir. I lift cinder blocks on an old Ford truck axle. That might be about the same weight."

"You what?"

"I found an old axle. I didn't steal it. I set up a little weightlifting area in the bush. I used the axles, logs, tires, cinder blocks, and an old bench."

"You just lifted twelve repetitions—one hundred and forty-five pounds each—with relative ease."

"Is that good, sir?"

"It's a Foremost marker."

"What's a Foremost marker, sir?"

"Just a second. The boys might fill you in."

Mr. Foremost looked around at the 4F Club. "Boys, we have a fifth fighter." So it began. For the next five years I was a Foremost fighter. My problem was I couldn't keep weight off, and Mr. Foremost kept sending his boys into the army, as he said, for education and grit. They won numerous provincial and Canadian championships both in and out of the military.

Me? At twenty-one, when Fillip, the youngest, left on a full scholarship to Royal Roads Military Academy, Mr. Foremost and I went out to the platform.

Mrs. Foremost brought us two beers and bent over where I was sitting. She handed me the beer and kissed me on the forehead. There were tears in her eyes and slipping down her cheeks. She never said a word. I thought maybe she was still sad about Fillip's departure the day before.

Mr. Foremost leaned in, and we tapped our bottles together. He took a big gulp of beer, then started speaking. "Well, Fifth, this is the end of the line. First beer I have ever had on this platform, and I'm pleased it's with you. After all these years, all this training, I never thought to ask if you mind being called Fifth. Do you?"

"No sir. Not for a minute. It was more than an honour to be the fifth fighting Foremost. And, sir, I didn't even know you drank."

"Ha, I don't. Or very rarely. Once or twice a year, but only two or three beers. Never when the Foremosts were in training and especially when any of you five won a big fight. I did not want our sons or you to associate winning and celebration with drinking. The two, joy in achievement and alcohol, are not equals. They shouldn't be joined or equated ever. Can you remember that, Fifth?"

"Yes, sir. I can. Good rule. Like all your rules."

"Ha! You say that now. Now that we're closing up the platform. There were times when your eyes flashed anger but mostly confusion over some of the rules."

"Well, sir, you run a tight ship."

"All necessary, Fifth. Fighters need straight lines, square rings to work in. All about containing impulse and bad decisions inside and especially outside the ring. Maintaining composure, control, and discipline within and outside the ring."

"Yes, sir, but some of your rules were just . . ."

"Bullshit? Arbitrary?"

We both laughed.

"It seemed that way at times. Yes, sir."

"They were. Those made you think about what was rational, what was necessary, what was a whim, what was a belief or not, and what you might not understand at that particular moment. They made all five of you think. That was a large part of the purpose."

"They certainly made me think. Sometimes they made me feel lost, and sometimes they felt like home. Like I always knew those things to be true."

"That's good. Do you remember what you looked like when you came out of that bush five plus years ago? As a fifteen-year-old with no sense of purpose and a ton of anger and fear?"

"Yes, sir. A buck and a quarter of scrawny, scared, shitting-my-pants Indian anger."

"Good description. And look at you now. One hundred and seventy pounds of pure muscle and sinew. Not scared of too much and maybe a bit less angry."

"Definitely calmer, certainly less angry, and your training plus the garbage runs have made me feel confident in my ability to handle myself, or run like hell if necessary."

We both chuckled again.

"Man, you sure can run. You took to the hill training runs like a mountain goat. My boys couldn't stay with you. That was your first Foremost marker after the one-hundred-and-forty-five-pound bench press, wasn't it?"

"I love those markers. Every one of them still means something to me."

"As it does to me."

We both looked at the back wall. The Foremost markers covered the platform's back wall. Organized by each Foremost son and me. Best accomplishments for runs, push-ups, pullups, lifts, and big boxing wins. Every significant accomplishment, win, or hurdle passed, captured and celebrated.

"Which fight name did you like the best?" Mr. Foremost continued. "We started with what, the Fifth Dimension, Fore Five, the Earl of Duke, which one?"

"You know, Stone Pony."

"Why?"

"Well, you just said it that day. Stone Pony. Like it was all fact, not fiction. It felt good and strong. Where did that come from?"

"Remember how you five loved to sprint? Race each other? You all loved the competition and the feeling of going fast. And you were the fastest, almost from the start. It was the way you ran. How you looked. Pure force and power. When we started the beach sprints on Sundays, people would not only stop and watch, people gathered at one o'clock sharp."

"I loved how we started. All five of us running fifties in unison. Warming up with ten of them. Forrest Jr. increasing the tempo each time. We all passed you in perfect symmetry. Then we raced. Fifty yards of fury. Whoever finished last was eliminated. It continued. Second race, four runners. Third race, three runners, then two. The crowds that gathered especially, last summer, our fifth and last summer together, we all loved that. You just nodded your head to start every race and smiled after every finish."

"I did that to shine a light on you boys. Five Indian kids demonstrating strength, speed, spirit, camaraderie, joy, and unity. The way you beamed at each other. Openly showing your affection and bond. We were teaching white people about our character. More importantly, the Indian kids who would hang on the edge of the crowds and feel pride in their race, their people. Hardly anyone ever saw us fight, but everyone saw us run. When you ran, every single fibre in your body was taut with power, and your body was glistening with sweat. You're like solid stone and fast like our ancestors' war ponies. Stone Pony."

"Thank you for that name, sir. It's a good name."

"After all this time you still call me, sir, even though I've told you a hundred times not to."

"Sir, you're the first man, Indian or white, I've called sir and meant it as a sign of respect and admiration. Now, I still call you sir because of the respect, admiration, and more than anything, appreciation I have for you."

"Thank you, Stone Pony. That means the world to me, as do you."

"And, sir, as you and your family do to me."

"OK. We better change topics before we start crying."

As if on cue, Mrs. Foremost arrived with two beers. This time, she kissed us both on the forehead and smiled.

"Tell me about the big black man. You've been working with him for almost three years now?"

"He's a good man. Outside of the Foremosts, probably my best friend. We get our own truck and route in four months when I turn twenty-one. We had to wait for my birthday for insurance reasons."

"You're a good team?"

"The best and the hardest-working."

"Good. What's his name?"

"Mister. Just Mister."

"Solid name for a solid man."

"Yes, sir."

We finished our beers in silence with the serenity of comfort, closeness, and care holding us close.

I walked home on the main streets. I liked the long walk. Nobody messed with me anymore. My boxing reputation and the Foremosts' protective umbrella were in place. I usually ran to and from the Foremosts' place as part of my training.

It was sad that the Foremost fighting story was ending, but for me, a new book with Mister had opened. Our own truck route with the sanitation department. We just bought an old truck to do some weekend garbage hauling on our own. Mister helped me enroll in some university courses online after finishing my high school degree. The Foremosts made me take courses if I wanted to train and fight with them. It helped me expand my vocabulary and not say "fuck" so fuckin' much. That word didn't come into my mind around the Foremosts. Funny. Good people drive out bad words.

On the walk, I was thinking of what I'd gained from the Foremosts and boxing. Belonging, acceptance, family, support, and care were all there. With the training and boxing came achievement, self-esteem, respect, integrity, and dignity. I wanted and hoped I could maintain all those things. My best friend now was a big black man, and we were trying to make it in a white world. Trying to get smarter by studying. Working our own garbage business to get ahead, to achieve something.

I just wanted to be a man. Not a red man. Not a colour. Not a stereotype. Just a man. A good man. Doing good things. Mister and I figured we might have to take some bad paths to get to good. We had started a plan. A plan from bad to good.

I also wanted the goodness of kind looks, kind words, and kinder thoughts. I knew I had to earn these things. This I learned and became clear with Mrs. Foremost. She gave all those things as I embraced her family and their ways. I showed respect and received love, care, and kindness. Also the Foremost way.

Mister helped me figure out my father wasn't anywhere near our reserve or town, and that he was most likely white.

Before I left the Foremosts, I thanked Mrs. Foremost again. She kissed my forehead and said she thanked the spirits for her fifth son. I was overcome. I wanted to belong, to be loved.

She handed me this prayer.

Gizhe Manidoo

(Creator)

I'iw nama'ewinan, mata asemaa, minnwaa n'ode'winaanin gda-bagidinimaagom
(We offer our prayers, tobacco, and our ears.)

Miigwech gda-igon n'mishomissinaanig miinwa n'ookomisinaanig jiinaago gaa-iyaajig, noongom e-iyaajig miinwaa waabang ge-iyaajig.
(Thank you for the grandfathers and grandmothers of yesterday, today, and tomorrow.)

Miigwech manidoog iyaajig noodinong, iyaajig nibiing, iyaajig shkodeng miinwa iyaajig akiing.
(Thank you, spirits of the winds, water, fire, and earth.)

Miigwech manidoog iyaajig giiwedinong, waabanong, zhaawanong miinwa epangishimok.
(Thank you, spirits of the north, east, south, and west.)

Daga bi-wiidokawishinaang wii mino bimaadiziyaang.
(Please help us to live a good life.)

Ahow!

CHAPTER 15

Revelations and Surprises

November and December were unbelievable months for me. Every time I turned around, something would surprise me even though it was usually something about me or how I was connecting things and people. I felt like Gomer Pyle on Andy of Mayberry. Golly, golly, golly! Then there were the revelations when things sort of fell in a line for me and the dots connected. My face was both a revelation and a surprise, sometimes both on the same day.

The scars were not fading as much as I had hoped, but they seemed less prominent, which came as a revelation. Then I would catch a glimpse of the scar on my right cheekbone, out of my peripheral vision, and I would shudder at how raw and vicious it looked, which always surprised me. No, shocked me. My beard didn't grow in the gullies or ridges created by the scars. The skin did not fold together nicely on that ridge. It gave me a jagged fault line. When it was cold outside, it looked fresh and raw. I had that fault line from November to April, basically. I still don't regret knocking the crap out of those four cars. The sound of breaking glass and lights were the only slight redemption from the night my mother was raped in our house. My redemption included sixty-seven stitches. From that night you could almost draw a straight line to the death of the man who raped my mom. I hope the coroner's report came back with a "no fault" finding.

The acne surprised me equally whether in blossom or absence. Man, those yellow fuckers bothered me, and I attacked them hard. They were cruel craters, the complete assholes of teen life. Stone Pony and Mister once heard me curse the yellow fuckers. They looked at each other and laughed. Mister said it was nice to hear another colour get called a fucker other than red or black. That was worth a giggle. Stone Pony just grinned from his coal-black eyes.

Money was a revelation. The weekend money was so good. We seemed to be gaining more customers every weekend even though more cottages were closing every weekend. It seemed we were doing some type of security work on the side. Well, not me. I was running more barrels, more lanes. Stone Pony and Mister were doing more perimeter checks and had keys to several homes to check them inside and out. The garbage and security entrepreneurs must have been getting significant cash from the security side of the business. I only figured this out because I was getting more cash almost every weekend. We were working six to seven hours on Saturdays and four to five hours on Sundays. Sunday was becoming my favourite day! After the garbage run, we went directly to the diner or their cabin to consume a big meal with some surprise every week. I loved Jeannie's banter and her meals, but the cabin offered more variety and comfort in being so private.

Omelettes were a revelation, as was egg pie. Stone Pony was the omelette master. Mister always prepared the side dishes. Potatoes, toast, bacon, coffee, fresh juice, and sometimes cornmeal muffins. With a little help from Mr. Clampett, the omelettes, which were just eggs with other stuff thrown in, became egg pie, which I found out was called quiche Lorraine. Mr. Clampett made the pie crust from scratch. Mister said French names made food sound better. I agreed. I was learning to cook, guided by these three men. We went to Jeannie's when the route went longer.

After the meal, we sat in front of a big fire, and I slept for maybe an hour, sometimes two, before I was roughly shaken awake. Time to lift. The routine was simple: legs, chest, back, arms. Three sets of lifts on legs, chest, and back and four or five on arms. Three reps each set. Mr. Clampett lifted some but mostly went through his series of martial arts movements. Everybody was bare chested, and not much was said. I was given instruction and derision given my relative lack of lifting power. Stone Pony was like a machine. He lifted extraordinary weight for his size, which I found out was 5' 7" and about 172 pounds. Mister was 6' 5" and 260 pounds. Mr. Clampett was 6' 2" and 205 pounds. When we lifted and Mr. Clampett was going through his motions, he said with all the colours, sizes, and testosterone we had the makings of some good homo-erotic black-and-whites. I wasn't fully sure what homo-erotic meant, but the sneers from Mister and Stone Pony told me everything I needed to know on the topic.

Mr. Clampett's physique was a revelation. He was one seriously strong man. The surprise—no, the shock—were his scars. He caught me staring at him, or them, one running horizontally across his abdomen, one running from his left shoulder blade to his right butt cheek in a vertical slash. "If your buddies call you Scarface, what do you think they would call me?" he asked. They all snickered. Stone Pony offered up that Mr. Clampett had a beauty on his right thigh as well.

I was going to ask what caused his scars, but Mr. Clampett beat me to it. "Sword," he said, pointing to his abdomen. "Big ass hunk of mortar shrapnel," he added, gesturing toward his back. He patted his thigh. "Combination of three machine gun rounds caught me from the side, and to add insult to injury, a collision with a Cong picket fence." I learned that Mr. Clampett had fallen on a row of sharpened bamboo spikes planted in the ground. The U.S. soldiers called that bit of landscaping a 'Cong picket fence.' "Just two of those outhouse bamboo bastards can do a lot of damage." He laughed and said military advisor work was a little more participatory than it sounded. "They get you to put a little skin in the game and a lot of blood."

I loved the lift. My three sessions a week at school were just so I wouldn't be so badly embarrassed on Sundays. We worked all lift sets together, one after another. Me, Stone Pony, then Mister. Mr. Clampett usually worked in between Stone Pony and Mister or anytime he wanted in. Sometimes he would lift right after me at the same weight. He would stare at me and say, "Watch," then spit out a couple of words, mostly about technique, not speed. "Deep strength, not show. Core, not surface. Better yourself." These words struck like proverbs, relevant rules for everything in life. Substance not presence. The right way only.

Stone Pony and Mister had words for me, too.

"Two more, it's yours."

"One more push."

"Suck it up."

"Breathe."

Every set was three reps with the weight going up each set. We lifted with speed. I struggled mostly on arms. I asked if we could do arms first. They laughed. I took that as a no.

Every week, I couldn't wait to show them I could lift more. That I was capable of more. These were the people in my life I wanted to improve for the most.

"Quiet," Mr. Clampett directed. "Set the mind, set the body, and set the lift. If it's in your head, it can be done. One sequence of willed actions. Fluid. Poetry in motion. Resist the resistance. Gravity is your enemy. Gravity sucks. Think light. Will it."

We kept records on every set and every rep. We looked at these as we lifted. Mister bench-pressed 425, Stone Pony, 280, Mr. Clampett, 355. At the start, I was at 175. These were our personal bests. The others approached their bests but never attempted to surpass them. I was trying to push them every week. After six weeks, my bench press was 190. The Sunday before Christmas, I was going for 200.

Our school board introduced co-ed physical education classes for one of the three gym periods each week. Our phys-ed uniforms were school-colour shorts and a white T-shirt or tank top sporting the school mascot, a gladiator. The symbol was a guy who looked like he was wearing a skirt, sandals that laced up to knee length, an armoured chest piece, and a helmet. The artist's vision never copied well on the clothing. We felt redeemed because he had a spear in one hand and a sword attached at his waist, his hand resting on the handle. Resting on the hilt, I think it was called.

The female uniform was worse. Some kind of one-piece romper that was baggy by design around their butts and breasts. In general, the garment disfigured all the girls equally. Some of the more creative girls made alterations to their rompers, tucking them in some manner to offer a more streamlined garment. We noticed and applauded with more intent gazes, OK, maybe staring, on the verge of ogling. OK, full-out ogling. The gladiator insignia was the same on the girls' rompers as on the boys, but on occasion, a design version slipped by whoever was hired as the morality screeners employed by the school board. A "gladiatress" or "gladiatorette" would appear with curves representing boobs and butts. These designs were quickly changed before a resupply and banned after that school year as "old uniforms."

My thoughts ramble when it comes to girls. Although Woman had provided me with great revelations and insights into women just the previous summer, I was befuddled by any high-school girl. I was horny and hopefully normal in that regard. The degree of horniness was not something we talked about in the locker room or during barrel runs. We tried to talk about it in health class. Those were not co-ed. I should have been confident around girls. I was popular, student council president and all. I had some things going for me. Not stupid and not totally without physical appeal. I was in better shape than most of our high school population, except for the wrestling team, but those cats were just plain weird and a bit freaky in their regimen. The basketball and volleyball players were mediocre specimens, and the wrestlers scared the shit out of them. Hockey, by definition, made players appear physically sound, but only half of my teammates were probably above the low bar set by the volleyball and basketball players.

Back to girls. See how they make my mind wander? I can't think about them too long because it makes it hard—to concentrate, that is.

I attempted the odd date. I got solid, emphatic *Nos* from most of the upper-class town girls when I would dare to ask one of that social class out, but had surprisingly more affirmative responses from the country girls. Perhaps country folk were a little less judgmental or less informed about me and my family. The dating process was difficult without a car, so I did a lot of double-dating. These were a little less pressure-packed and less socially awkward, at least for me. I was better in a group than solo, more at ease. It dawned on me that other than my summer road trip, I had no sense of how to start or build a relationship with a girl. I took to hitchhiking out into the country to visit one or two girls. We would play card games with their families. The dads would eyeball me hard until they got loosened up with a couple of drinks. My nights ended with some necking, usually in the cold, unheated front porch, then I walked to a concession road to hitchhike back to town. My dates were usually on Friday nights. I would leave my date's frosty front porch shortly after 11. Rides were often few and far between, but it seemed worthwhile. I usually was home by 12:30 a.m. It took a good hour and a half to travel the fifteen or twenty miles home. Garbage runs started with pickup at 6 a.m. My social life was not stellar, but girls or young women were astounding. Their physical and emotional warmth, if I could ever figure out how to respond to either, I knew, were something to strive for. Just talking with a girl was more than good enough for me. The conversations were deeper. I could talk school and ambitions.

My backroad hitchhiking always got me wondering what lengths I would go to for a little bit of love. It also occurred to me while standing on some forlorn wintery back road that the warmth that was so recently being radiated in my loins dissipated very quickly from that hot spot. I tried to think in terms of loins, as it sounded biblical and therefore more respectable, after kissing and perhaps a wee fondling of a country-sized breast or two. "Loins" being a sanitized version more appropriate than some of the names guys used like dick, trouser snake, one-eyed python, wiener, Louisville Slugger, Victoriaville shaft, CCM crease cracker, and the list went on and increased in vulgarity. I think we small-town boys had a name for penis for every letter of the alphabet and then some. Some guys had names for their own dicks like Sammy's Slammin' Schlong, Paul's Probe, Tim's Tent Pole, and so on. One guy named Bruce bragged that he asked girls to double-date with him, meaning him and his dick, Robin. You know, Bruce Wayne, so Batman and Robin? I don't think Robin is a particularly good name for a dick. My other observation on Batman was that no one ever saw him on an actual date. Robin wasn't seen out and about either!

Back to girls—I mean women. I wondered whether I was right for any relationship. You know, family history and all. Some, most of our town, judged me as deficient in the potential relationship arena, at least with their daughters. As a frozen traveler of the backroads, my mind drifted to social strata thoughts, about the time my gonads had cooled and started to retreat up somewhere warmer. Travelling north are we, boys? The reality was I was usually hitchhiking south, as my country dates were mostly north or west of town. When I was hitchhiking north to my dates, my nuts were low and headed south, and hitching south to home, my nuts were headed north. Maybe that was why I found women confusing in my current state, no consistency in direction. See how women turn my mental faculties to mush?

Social strata. The revelation was how prevalent the impact of social strata was once I realized what it was and thought about it for a nanosecond. Right, Spock? No shit. Poor Scottie didn't have enough power in the social combustion engines to blast through the stigma zones. Maybe because our high school was such a blend of country and town as well as two wards that were entirely different, one white-collar and one blue. Businessmen versus employees. All kinds of lines, all kinds of biases.

Preconceived notions were almost bred into the population, which became all the more bloody apparent by the education streams. We were all told in grade eight to pick the appropriate stream for our ambitions, interests, abilities, goals, and dreams. Well, my biggest dream, goal, ability, ambition, and interest was to get the fuck out of Dodge. That wasn't all that helpful a guide for a thirteen-year-old who was selecting an educational stream. There were two-year programs, basically intended to get kids to age sixteen, so they could find a basic menial job. Some kids from our ward were turning sixteen the year they got to grade nine. The boys were taking "shop" courses that trained them to do factory work and to learn some technical skills. Some of this education stream was quite practical and offered great skills for everyday life. Every occupational student could change tires, spark plugs, and filters, and perform an oil change. The teachers had well-tuned automobiles. The girls, the young women, were finessed in the arts of life, centering on home skills. They were prepared to be housewives, primarily, but great practical education was achieved in sewing, cooking, and typing. They were expected to be waitresses or secretaries. The expectation, by their curriculum and the prevailing social strata, was they were all likely to become teen mothers and needed to be prepared accordingly.

When I got booted from grade-nine music, an arts and science elective, I was placed in a home economics class with the occupational stream for girls. That was nirvana for me. First, I was the best-looking boy in the class. Competition was scarce, as in none, until Scarecrow somehow got his ass booted from grade-nine art class into home economics as well. I was still the best looking. Second, some of the women in the class were also sixteen, and a good descriptive would be they were "well developed." Scarecrow referred to them as BSHs—built like a brick shit house. They were certainly solid, curvaceous, and voluptuous. Scarecrow was providing me with all the two-dollar words. He once told me to tell a woman in our class that she was incredibly "zaftig," and that was her best trait. She asked me to spell the word for her, and she was beaming as she showed the word to several of her girlfriends. A couple of hours later when she walked across the hall between classes and planted her right boot squarely on my left nut, one could surmise that her trip to the library and subsequent discovery that I had called her big tits her best trait, she found less than charming. I think she needed help interpreting the meaning of the word. It wasn't a surprise that Scarecrow had helped her with the word search.

Some of the girls were from similar situations to mine. Broken homes, wife-beating fathers, or the absence of a father altogether. These girls were as tough as nails, smart in their own way, and usually the girlfriends of gang members. Other women in the class were low key, learning what they needed to know and either weighed down by the low level of expectations set for them or buoyant about acquiring some skills, turning sixteen, and getting out of Dodge. What was strange was that all these different girls just accepted their almost-dictated lot in life and social strata. At least for the moment. Underlying that, in many, there was either a clearly expressed or low-burning fire in them to be more, do more, and be better than where they came from or what was expected of them. By the end of grade-ten home economics, and in their graduation year, Scarecrow and I had come to love them all and care for them like sisters. As Scarecrow once said, "Scarface, these women are like our moms, who have faced or will face what our mothers have already lived through, and that ain't pretty!"

No shit, Sherlock.

Anyway, women. God, they make me ramble!

The other education streams were four-year programs in business and commerce or a five-year stream in arts and sciences. I was never clear at thirteen about the streams, and the guidance I was getting was simply that I was too smart and didn't qualify for two-year occupational programs. Also, I wasn't tough enough, street-smart enough, mechanically inclined enough, or, it appeared, old enough to get in. On the other hand, despite receiving top grades in public school, I wasn't deemed smart enough, soft enough, or studious enough, nor did I have the right, supportive environment to enter the five-year stream. The five-year stream was university-bound, and I was, according to the guidance counsellor, the most likely to get the fuck out of Dodge—though he did express my departure in more polite terms. Something like, "Opportunities for you are likely more abundant in a larger city or out west." Given that there was no university close to our town, I was warned about the academic challenges of the five-year stream and the hard work and money it would take to go to university. They browbeat the social stigma into the kids from my ward, and the majority all filed into the four-year streams. I figured that if I couldn't hack the five-year program, opportunities might blossom for me in occupational and four-year streams. I decided to swim upstream for a while.

I didn't get it during the enrollment process, but the results of the streaming guidance were evident the moment students stepped into their grade-nine homeroom. Everyone I recognized were top students in public school and disproportionately North Warders, the more elite area of our town. That being said, Scarecrow and I, as well as a few other West Warders and some farmers, had forded the streaming indoctrination. Scarecrow had found another two-buck word he could chuck around. In grade-nine history class, Scarecrow talked about the missionary fervour and indoctrination the Europeans pummeled upon the Indians. Our teacher and most of our classmates were amazed by Scarecrow's intelligent questions, which perplexed the hell out of them. "Sometimes you gotta make them uncomfortable about their assumptions, predispositions, and prejudices," Scarecrow told me. "In other words, just baffle the bastards, so they don't whether to wind their watch or shit their pants."

Atta boy, Scarecrow!

Social slotting was evident, normal, and expected. I could clearly see that, but it took me a few years to realize the significance. The stomping boots of social stigma and dogma were pettiness. I mean, if someone lacks confidence about who they are or where they belong, then their horizons get artificially limited and predetermined. They become vulnerable. Vulnerable to the shit-kicking heels and boots of pettiness. Looks can kill—at least part of a person's spirit, part of their joy, and certainly any attempt to cross social lines. My peers in the five-year stream were mostly decent people, and when I pushed them on some of their attitudes and behaviours, they shrugged it off and said that was just the way it was. "Hey, our parents don't hang with those parents, and we don't hang with those kids. You know, likes attract and non-likes detract." This was some new math shit I couldn't fathom.

The pettiness came in comments about clothing, hairstyles, general appearance, mannerisms, and just an outright "bullshit" manner of the "looking down our noses" attitude. Like I said, it wasn't everyone, but it was obvious. We weren't segregated, but we were separated.

I wish I could remember the book or play that triggered the discussion. By then, I was in grade eleven and ensconced in the five-year stream headed to university. It had something to do with those of low birth versus those with birthrights. Either those born with a silver spoon in their mouths or born with a fork stuck up their asses or a comparison . . . something like that. In what might have been a foolish moment, I stood up in our class and stated the values of being a garbage man. The value of the job was denigrated, diminished, and demolished by several classmates. They described garbage men and garbage work so politely. As necessary and physically demanding but not intellectually challenging. The job had a function but did not contribute to the advancement of society or the individual. Required work but not relevant. Physically demanding but not mentally challenging. Most of the class stayed silent. It was me against four or five, with the teacher on the sidelines. One girl, a noted band member who played the flute, attacked the role of garbage man rather harshly. "That role is at the bottom rung of societal benefit and value. It is an outcome of necessity not an outcome of value. It is a role performed by those with limited skills and intellect who lack higher aspirations." She, by the way, was almost as attractive as she was intelligent. I can't remember all her arguments, but she was elegant and even used some examples and quotes from the book or play. I was still standing, feeling humbled and embarrassed and pretty sure my nuts were once again retracting to a safer place. "She's got us in her tractor beam, Captain, and I don't have the engine power to stop her. Beam me the fuck up, Sulu!"

Well, when being publicly humiliated, the best thing to do is attack. At least, I think Scarecrow told me that once. Man, I wish he had been there with some two-buck words to bail me out.

"Listen here, miss. You've never had a day of hardship or shit in your life. You think you're better than garbage men? One thing for certain, we don't play the flute and unless you plan on becoming the next Jethro Tull, that skill is far less valuable to society than cleaning up trash from your shopping expeditions." She did have an outstanding wardrobe. "Another thing for certain, as humble and, in your view, as humiliating as the work might be, we accomplish what we're asked to do, and we don't bitch, complain, or whine. We provide value for our pay, and there is no debate about that ever."

I can't remember anything else that was said. I may or may not have mumbled something about her instrument of choice would be more appreciated if it were the skin flute, at least by the garbage men's union. Some classmates sitting near me thought that was what they heard and started laughing.

The teacher intervened. Her side in the matter was quickly revealed. She verbally thrashed me. Her words were hot and fiery and steamed with the bitter tone and the bile of absolute distaste. That was good because as far as I could tell, she had been mostly comatose in her teaching methodology. We called her "Night Time Nancy" or "Lullaby Lily" for her ability to put us to sleep.

Not that day. She was awake and nasty! My exact recollection of everything she said was vague. At some time in the face of the fury raining down upon me, the humiliation sets in, and I turn off. I go blank to the words, but the sound filters through. I vibrate to the viciousness of the tone and meaning, I quiver on the inside, but I remain fierce on the surface. I'm ice. My mom said my scars burned brightly when I was holding down anger. They were now full crimson. Red tide alert!

Night Time Nancy covered the range of low-birth behaviour, characteristics, capabilities, and the failures represented by my point of view. I think she said my perspective was rubbish, which was a clever double entendre. She was thorough, eloquent, and forceful. She finished with "The only thing you will accomplish or amount to is graduation from Garbage Boy to becoming a garbage man."

Sometimes I should just shut up, but sometimes I just can't.

"With all due respect, thank you for the encouragement," I replied. Night Time Nancy, the Flutist, and her protectors weren't expecting that. Surprise and revelations. "Given everything else you have said, I didn't think I was going to amount to anything. Now you think I can become a garbage man. That's great because the work is guaranteed. It's always picking up, and the amount of trash is just piling up in this town. And, OK, I was just curious, will your speech be covered on the final exam?" That broke the class up.

I was transferred to another English class that afternoon, provided the teacher and my flute-playing classmate a written apology, and was reprimanded by the principal and the head of the music department. All in all, not a bad afternoon. The bonus round? The episode circulated throughout the school within hours. It became known as "The Skin Flute" incident. To tell you the truth, I was proud of that. Pettiness, social strata, and lines between classes were all bullshit. I didn't want to add to those storylines, but I did. People need to push back at times to stand up.

Decency seems to be an elusive trait. Another revelation in behaviour. At least, I can't figure out how decency works or when it comes into play. I have heard the expression over and over about people being decent, God-fearing members of our congregation and community. Well, I must have some degree of decency because most of my life I feared gangs and even GG, the gang girl who nearly busted my nose. You know, the whole fear of God, his wrath will rain down upon us, and hell and damnation mystified the crap out of me. But I knew fear, so I must have had some degree of decency.

Decency for me was the women who came around and helped my mom when she was beat down. Decency for me was knocking the stuffing out of Teddy Porter when he almost raped that girl. That was a decent thing to do.

Decency to me didn't relate directly to sitting in a pew on Sunday morning or Saturday night or whenever. Decency was how people treated others when they needed a hand up. People deemed decent often seemed to be a little bit too judgmental for my liking. But what did I know? I was on my way to becoming a garbage man. Although the sanitation and waste management field wouldn't immediately get me the fuck out of Dodge (FOOD), it would provide the ability to save some coin to eventually get the FOOD. A great acronym. Food, the fuel to rise up and put the pedal to the metal and leave this town in my dust.

Love was a freaking surprise. I fell in love about five times a day. OK, so maybe I was confusing love with more basic instincts. On a more serious note, I was becoming a keen observer of human interaction. I could see the fierce, protective love of family around our town and particularly when I ventured out to the country. Some of the books we were reading were opening up some emotions. I found these were dangerous thoughts for a garbage boy. I was afraid they would make me soft. I had a fierce, protective love for my family. I knew that what I felt for Mister, Stone Pony, Scarecrow, and Bogeyman was a deep, brotherly connection. Call it love if you want to, but for these guys, I had deep emotions and feelings.

Everything about Stone Pony and Mister was a revelation. How hard they worked, their cabin, their physical exercise, their strength, and their wisdom. The bond between them seemed natural, deep, and rare. They were blood brothers. They had been growing this side business for six years. They were buying a second truck and now providing security for cottagers. I know they were raking in cash based on what I was getting paid, now up to $300 to $450 every weekend. Minimum wage was just $4.25 an hour. I was making six to seven times that!

These guys liked to read. One wall near the big fireplace was full of books.

Those bookshelves were weighed down. Books ranging from algebra to zoology. They had high school and university textbooks. They occasionally mentioned they would be cracking the books. They disappeared for a weekend about once every two months. They checked out of the town sanitation department at noon on a Friday, having started their route early, finishing before twelve bells, and then going somewhere.

They had two associates of the Newspaper Crew who could handle the weekend route with me. These guys were known as the FBI. Two tall, strong Indians who didn't say much. On those weekends, we didn't have to get the garbage at most of the places that were normally serviced by Stone Pony and Mister. They said they had done them all on Thursday night before they left town. They didn't return until early Monday morning. They never spoke about their adventures on the weekend, except once in a while, they would look at each other and say something like, "Saturday, remember about two in the morning?"

"Yeah, brother, that was wild."

That was it for the conversation about their Saturday night. Big smiles, little chuckles, and run the barrels.

More than once, I thought of money as a significant revelation. I was giving Mom fifty dollars a week, the little one five dollars, saving like crazy, and buying some clothes, new skates, and decent hockey sticks. Every couple of weeks, I would bring home a pizza or KFC, or we ordered from the Golden Dragon. These little luxuries felt good. I spent a fortune on Clearasil and Snap and should've demanded my money back. Pimples and hope spring eternal, but pimples unfortunately are more reliable.

Despite my world being constantly full of revelations and surprises, combined with my less-than-stellar social status, things were pretty good. I felt lucky. I missed the shit out of Bogeyman and Scarecrow. Occasionally, they would call the house from Columbia or California or Cochrane—who knew if they were actually where they said they were? Those two seemed to be rolling in cash given their travels, and their full-time occupation was now as purveyors and suppliers of the finest quality medicinal herbs one could desire. Surprises were around the corner for all of us.

Revelations were always waiting for me to catch up to them. Reality was often a stone-cold son of a bitch. Reality often didn't end well. Sometimes I wish my thoughts were not so ominous.

CHAPTER 16

The Coroner's Report

The young police officer and the detective knocked on the front door on a snowy Friday night. December 12, to be exact. With Christmas just over two weeks away, it wasn't the early Christmas present or visit I was hoping for, but I had been expecting it for almost four months.

They phoned in advance, primarily to make sure my son was at home. The detective made the call and said he was sure both my son and I would be interested in the findings. That was all he said about the coroner's report and that they would call upon us at about 7.

He made it sound like a friendly visit. "We'll call upon you." Well, la-dee-dah! Should I have tea and biscuits waiting? Perhaps a Christmas drink? My premonition was that a whole bunch of bad was going to land in our home. From the coroner's table to our kitchen table, like a Santa sack full of sad.

"Not a problem, Mom," my son said. "That prick died, probably dead drunk, driving into a telephone pole."

"But son, we did him some damage before that."

He was so calm. "Mom, we might have deadened some of his faculties, but he killed himself. We have nothing to worry about."

We let the young officer and the detective in the front door. They took off their coats and galoshes, and the four of us gathered at the kitchen table. They gladly accepted my offer of tea, and on a whim, I brought out the package of Walker's shortbread biscuits I was saving for Christmas dinner. My son's eyes lit up. He loved Walker's shortbread.

When I served the tea, there was almost no small talk. The detective launched into the coroner's report. It was a very official-looking file folder with the coroner's office stamp and insignia on the outside.

The coroner's report stated the individual died of a broken neck. That wasn't a surprise; however, the coroner had examined all the injuries to the body to rule out any other potential cause of death. The neck injury had killed him, and the coroner was clear on that.

What made the coroner's report interesting was the neck was broken in a manner not consistent, normal, or expected from a car crash. Warning signs were flashing everywhere for me.

"Wow, that is interesting and sort of fascinating," my son said. "Please go on."

The detective was going to continue with or without my son's encouragement, but the comment made him pause. The young police officer rolled his eyes, and the look he gave my son was a clear message: "Shut up and listen."

"Normally, in a car crash like this one, the neck breaks clean with a snap. This is what the coroner describes in his report as the whiplash effect, caused by the vehicle impacting an object. In this case, a telephone pole at a high rate of speed and crashing to an immediate stop. The victim's head would be whipped forward on impact and then snapped back, resulting in a clean snap of the neck."

I didn't like him using the word "victim," which indicated to me the death was someone else's fault, not my former boyfriend's own doing.

"This neck break is consistent with a slower break, a grinding break, where the victim might have even resisted, somehow, against something or someone."

The detective stopped talking and took a good look at both of us. My son asked if they would like more tea or another shortbread. That seemed to both surprise and disturb the detective. It was clear he wasn't getting the reaction he expected, especially from my son, so he went further into his explanation.

"This neck break is more consistent with a slower process than the whiplash effect. Still, the neck is breaking at a relatively quick velocity. A slower process is consistent with some sort of applied rotational force rather than a snap. This break was more of a side-to-side break than the front-to-back break of a high-velocity impact."

The words "velocity," "slower process," "rotational," and "resistance" all felt like words of doom. My son just kept nodding and appeared fascinated by the report.

"The coroner has concluded because of the lack of any evidence to the contrary, that the damn drunken fool broke his own stupid neck. For us, the inconsistency of this side-to-side break compared to the expected whiplash break, the usual nature of a car crash break, is a bit of a concern. Then the question in some of our minds is still out there."

I couldn't help myself. I had to ask. "What question is out there?" My son reached over and held my hand to stop it from shaking.

"The question that floats around in some minds is, did he break his own damn neck in the crash by himself, or did someone break it for him before or after the crash? After all, many people think the prick deserved to die, so suspicions surface and hang around." The detective's words hung there like an accusation until my son spoke.

"Sir, I'm a little confused. Can you simply tell us what the coroner's report concluded?"

"Like I said, the death was caused by a broken neck due to a high-velocity impact from a car crash. Case closed." The detective paused before he continued and gave us some additional facts from the report. "The coroner thoroughly examined several major injuries to the deceased's body. These injuries were prior to the car crash, as documented in previous hospital visits by the deceased and police reports. His jaw had been fractured, his teeth smashed, and he had three broken ribs and a broken nose that occurred about twelve days prior to his death. This was consistent with a hospital report and an alleged fight the victim stated he had been in with Scarface at the Refuge. Allegedly, you sucker punched him and smacked him around with your friends Stone Pony and Mister and several others, preventing him from a chance for a fair fight. That's when you left town to hitchhike to Winnipeg."

My son was exceptionally calm. He didn't flinch or show any outward reaction. He just nodded calmly and firmly. "Sir, that's old news, and those injuries had nothing to do with his death, or you would have mentioned them from the coroner's report. Also, not to be argumentative, but this fight was alleged, not proven it was, in fact, with me."

The detective didn't respond, just continued reading from the report. "The coroner also found three substantial injuries that occurred three to four days before his death. He was struck twice with a blunt object, like the handle of a thick broom or a baseball bat. He suffered more broken ribs and a fracture on his upper right arm. These injuries were not covered in the previous hospital report. The third injury was his nose and orbital bone on his right eye were broken around the same time. This unlucky bastard had his nose broken twice in a week. None of these more recent injuries were necessarily a result of the car crash."

Again, unspoken accusations hung in the air. The detective glared at the both of us. My son's grip was tightening on my hand. I was afraid of what he was going to say.

"You know, sir, I don't think luck had anything to do with his demise or his injuries. I think the outcome was likely a result of his own doing. We appreciate you letting us know the cause of death of the man who raped and beat the hell out of my mom, which somehow you or your office never bothered to investigate. Now, can we offer you more tea or another shortbread?"

The detective and my son had a brief staring match. Neither blinked nor looked away. "No thank you," the detective finally said. "We'll be on our way now."

When they left my son turned to me. "Mom, we didn't kill him. He killed himself." He paused. "Long day tomorrow. I'm going to have one more of these biscuits and then go to bed. Mom, you're going to have to run out and get another tin of Walker's for Santa to leave in my stocking."

He bent over and kissed my forehead, hugged me tight, kissed me again, snatched up at least two biscuits, and said goodnight to the little one as he passed her bedroom door. And for him, it seemed that was that.

For me, I sat at the kitchen table, in the room where I had been beaten and raped, and somehow felt violated all over again.

A Little Peace

Dear God

I know I have prayed to you about this before,
But this detective is clearly judging us, and not favourably or with any compassion.
I thought judgment was yours,
So how can he judge?
Even when he knows, and the coroner says we didn't kill him.

Please God, let this pass us by.
Let that detective find another interesting case to keep him busy.
We deserve to be left in peace.
Give us a little peace, God.
That's all I ask.

Amen.

CHAPTER 17

Christmas Garbage

It seemed like half the population of the big city spent the Christmas holiday in cottage country. They went on refuse overload, sparked by seasonal celebrations, excessive gift-giving, and excessive drinking. This year was a particularly long period of seasonal excess. Christmas fell on a Wednesday, so most schools were out on the preceding Friday. They didn't go back until January 5. That provided sixteen to seventeen days to compile garbage, and they were prodigious in the production process.

Apparently, some university and private school students started trickling north as early as the weekend of December 12. We had extra hours starting that weekend. I received permission for an accelerated exam schedule and finished my exams on December 13. I was granted this privilege because I had work available. Although I wasn't called a hardship case, I qualified for early release because of my family's low income level.

I turned the Lord's Prayer and the other morning announcement duties over to the Rave in my absence. The Rave was raring to go. The first day, he read that Lord's Prayer with a fire-and-brimstone approach that none of us thought was possible. The VP tried to rein him in. Consequently, on the second day of the Reverend Rave's recitals, his delivery closely resembled a Southern Baptist preacher version. The Rave thought the Lord's Prayer was open for artistic interpretation. On the third day, the VP wisely brought in a minister's daughter to recite the Lord's Prayer, thank God!

My early release wasn't all that special. Other students had benefited from an even earlier release, as seasonal workers and due to family necessities. This small group was working at ski resorts out west or headed out on family vacations in the South. I didn't know of one other classmate who got early release because their family income was on the low side.

I wish we had a group picture of the "early releases." My fellow early-exiting schoolmates could have posed with their skis, sunglasses, and tanning lotions, and I could have posed with a garbage can lid. Now, that would be a treasured school remembrance.

Mister, Stone Pony, and I also engaged in some "opening" activities. My employers had expanded their business. They'd bought a second truck and equipped their pickup truck with a front-end plow. The FBI were hired as seasonal help to plow driveways and do some barrel runs. I worked several weekdays with them on barrel runs while Stone Pony and Mister were at their day jobs in the sanitation department.

The opening activities were done in the evenings. Stone Pony, Mister, and I would open the doors, turn on furnaces and water, stack firewood, and occasionally bring in groceries. We also were an unofficial distribution arm for Brewer's Retail as we hauled hundreds of cases of beer into cottage country. My bosses figured out that they had empty trucks going into cottage country that were better utilized with full payloads. Full in, full out, paid both ways. The delivery in was lucrative, according to Stone Pony. They had started a limited service two years earlier and decided to blow it wide open that Christmas. The FBI and I were loading one of the trucks for delivery every day from December 13 on. The last deliveries were emergencies made up to 7 p.m. on December 31. The last delivery was to a gigantic cottage party that was being catered by a local business. The waiting staff included half a dozen girls from my school. We stayed for the party, albeit in the backroom with the caterers, loading garbage out and eating and drinking leftovers. I had a blast for the short time we were there. The only speck of trouble we had occurred when some inebriated upper-crust city woman, I'm guessing in her early fifties, spied Mister and declared her drunken desire for a black man. We had trouble keeping her out of the back areas and kitchen in her pursuit of Mister. Her equally drunk and extremely pot-bellied husband became suspicious, but wasn't coherent enough to understand anything except that an enormous black man was receiving overly friendly treatment from his wife. The host explained that Mister was on security detail to dissuade party crashers and to keep an eye on the catering staff. The fat, drunk, and seemingly stupid husband was appeased, or forgot the nature of the problem he was having, and he conveniently puked in a nearby large trash can that we brought into the kitchen. We chose that moment to leave, and I spent the rest of New Year's Eve at home with Mom and the little one.

I found out when we got back to school that the fat man's wife was found passed out, alone in a guest room in just her panties and bra, at about 3 a.m. by the hostess. No foul play or sex play was suspected, as she had managed to puke inconveniently on herself before she disrobed. She had also covered most of the bedspread in rich, big-city vomit.

The FBI? Yep, that stood for "Fucking Big Indians." They gave themselves that name, and they were friends who I first met at the Refuge as an underage drinker. They were bouncers at the Refuge, didn't drink themselves, taught me some fighting techniques, and were there as part of the whole extended Newspaper Crew that provided coverage for me when I fought the man who raped and beat my mother. That man was now deceased under the somewhat cloudy circumstance of his neck breaking in a rotational versus whiplash motion, as covered in the coroner's report. He crashed his truck into a telephone pole shortly after I broke him up in a fairly significant manner in the parking lot at the Refuge. Part of the mysterious circumstances surrounding his death was the fact that of the three hundred or so people at or in the immediate vicinity of the Refuge, someone should have witnessed a fight that night, but mysteriously, not a single person saw or heard a thing.

Immediately after that fight, the FBI drove me to the edge of town, where I started hitchhiking west with a load of cash and two tickets to Man-Pop, the rock concert in Winnipeg. I had severe cuts and bruises on the knuckles of both hands. The taste of the whisky shot was still in my mouth and on my breath when two blondes in a Beetle gave me my first ride. It seems so long ago. Yet it was only four months back when I hopped into that Volkswagen with blood on my hands. The FBI were my connection with Woman, another saviour and teacher of mine who I met in Winnipeg.

Forget New Year's Eve, which was the usual highlight of the social season for me. Well, really, the only social scene I made. The real world was the deal. We worked solid twelve-hour days except for Christmas Day itself. Some days were fourteen to sixteen hours. Mister and Stone Pony handed me a cheque for $3,500 for ten days of work between December 13 and 24. I nearly shit my pants! They said with overtime, weekends, Sunday shifts, and missing a social life, it was money well earned. It was funny and a bit strange for a kid my age, but I loved the work. The hauling, the grind, the stamina required, the sweat, the companionship, and the silent, solid strength of my work companions. The FBI hardly talked, but I listened hard when they did. They both had degrees, BAs with honours. Mostly achieved through night school and distance education, but with three summer semesters at university. Their degrees were in economics, with minors in business and psychology. They told me that Mister and Stone Pony got them started and paid their tuition and summer-residence fees. These were proud, smart, quiet men. They were skilled boxers and were learning martial arts. Stone Pony and the FBI first crossed paths on the provincial amateur boxing circuit. Stone Pony and the Foremosts had great respect for the FBI's super heavyweight abilities. No one fucked with the fucking FBI or they would be fucked physically and intellectually. They stood apart.

My world was not populated with normal people, if one followed the norms of the day.

I bought my mom a colour TV, making the deal that my own Christmas present was that I didn't have to watch anything in black and white. I called that my *Beverly Hillbillies* clause, which my little sister fully appreciated, and it made her laugh. She had once kicked me hard in the balls for mocking Granny Clampett's wave!

On Christmas Day, I gave my mom a picture of the colour TV and a cheque for $1,000. I told her to get the one she wanted at a Boxing Day sale, and she did that, from Sears. She wanted to give me money back, but I just asked her to hold it for us, to help with the cheques and balances and anything that needed to be reconciled.

My sister was home for a few days and sporting a boyfriend. I was—well—we all were happy for her. He was from our hometown and was a couple of years younger than my sister. A good guy who grew up playing baseball and hockey, always on the all-star teams. He was down-to-earth and, though quiet at times, seemed to be a great match for my sister. He scratched his head over my Christmas cheque when I told him and my sister where the money came from.

He had gone to college and come back to town to work. He was an inside sales and customer service representative for one of the local manufacturers. He knew all about Mister and Stone Pony, the FBI, the Whities, the Brownies, and the Neapolitan Crew. He scared my mom and sisters a little bit when he mentioned that everyone in our town, the surrounding farm counties, and north through cottage country were scared shitless of my bosses and their friends. He also shook his head at how hard and long we were working and said that squared up with all the local legends about my bosses and their acquaintances.

He wasn't being nosy when he asked how the hell I beat the crap out of Mom's last boyfriend at the Refuge and how nobody saw the beating. He said half the town would have paid good money to watch, and the other half would have gladly given me money to stomp the shit out of that asshole. I liked him even more. Mom shut down the conversation on that topic.

On Boxing Day, we were back at it in cottage country on both trucks, and running barrels hard. I worked with the FBI doing about seventy percent of the houses, and Mister and Stone Pony were doing all the special homes for their security and services clients. The FBI could identify every single print in the snow: animal or human. They would see a deer print and say something like, "Buck two twenty, ten to twelve pointer next fall." I liked them except that they were big Maple Leaf fans. When I say big, I mean 6' 4" to 6' 5" and 260 pounds big. Like Mister, just freakin' beef slabs of muscle.

The refuse was startling. We had three full pickup days before Stone Pony and Mister went back to town sanitation. We were on the route from six in the morning to five at night with the two trucks. The FBI bailed at five, took their truck to the dump, and were at the doors of the Refuge working security by seven. The reality was they were big, bad-assed bouncers. The owner of the Refuge had huge, fourteen- to sixteen-ounce steaks waiting for them for dinner every night. Mister, Stone Pony, and I joined them for dinner on that third night.

The surprise was me driving the new truck solo for the next three days in cottage country. I had attended driver's ed classes, as instructed by my bosses, and learned to drive a garbage truck in cottage country. Parallel parking one of the little driver's ed four-door sedans during my driver's test was a breeze. I had gotten my licence on December 5 and had been doing a lot of the driving when working with the FBI.

The solo driving was a rush, a somewhat nervous rush, but still an adrenaline spike. I was mopping up the garbage remnants from my three solo days. Some homes were new customers who saw our trucks and called the number on the side. Turned out my bosses now had an answering machine. Mr. Clampett was doing call-backs and scheduling both new and old customers for pickups. I was very busy as a one-man crew.

On New Year's Eve people were running out of their places, dragging bins and giving me twenty or twenty-five dollars for helping them get rid of the garbage before they returned to the city for their New Year's Eve parties. For those three days, I was finding lots of envelopes with Christmas tips or something similar written on them. I didn't open any of them, but it was not hard to grasp that a hell of a lot of cash appreciation was being received by my bosses. I was on the route until 7 on December 31. At about 5, I saw two barrels three-quarters of the way down a lane that were not on my pickup list for the day. OK, I thought, *just a miss*, although I didn't remember one other miss ever, either by us or a customer. Being service-oriented, the way Mister and Stone Pony had drilled into my head, I decided to stop the truck and throw on my gloves. This was one of the service and security homes, so I had never seen the house. The monster home had a five-car garage and stretched out forever. I knew it backed onto the lakefront, but the water had to be more than a half mile from the house! I was in awe.

The first barrel was as heavy as hell. I had to struggle just to tip it up. I tried the second barrel, which felt like it had nothing in it. I hauled the first one to the truck, hefted it up, somehow avoiding a hernia. I came back for the second and lifted the lid thinking I could just pluck maybe a small bag of garbage out and avoid the run back with the barrel. The barrel was empty, almost. An unsealed envelope was taped to the top inside. The envelope was similar to a lot of the tip envelopes. I pulled the envelope off. The handwritten note read, "Guys, thanks for supplying all the good times." Not a typical note or season's greeting for garbage men. At the bottom of the barrel was all kinds of cash. I carried the barrel back to the truck, opened the passenger side, and carefully dumped the contents on the seat. I shut the door, ran the barrel back, and scooted back to the truck. I entered through the driver's side, squeezing in as I didn't want a gust of wind to blow the loot out. I started gathering the money, separating by dollar value and counting. Lots of hundreds and fifties. Twenty-five fuckin' hundred dollars. What the Jesus H. Christ? I counted it three times. It turned out I loved the look of fifties and hundreds. I was admiring them. I laughed when I realized I was almost salivating and surprised I hadn't popped a boner. The cash was having an impact, so I sorted and neatly stacked the bills. The money had obviously fallen out of the envelope. I put the cash back in the envelope, licked the seal, and closed the envelope.

My cheque for December 26 to January 4 was going to be huge as it was, but given the tip money being hauled in by Mister and Stone Pony's operations and their history of generosity, it made me wonder. Spring break in Florida? New sofa for Mom?

CHAPTER 18

Mister

Stone Pony asked me what my name was, what people called me. My army buddies named me Mister because I was always respectful and polite. A black man named Mister—to many others, that didn't seem right, especially on the white side of my hometown. Where I came from, "Mister" as part of a name or a salutation was always reserved and deemed right for only a white man, not a black man. A black man named Mister seemed to hold power of some kind and caused some fright, consternation, and more than a little anger.

Imagine my pure delight. A white man asks me my name, and I respond, "You can call this black-as-midnight man Mister."

They hesitate, get all tongue tied, and if they're polite, say, "What was that? Why would I call you Mister?"

I see they're confused and try to deepen their bewilderment. "That's right. Yes, indeed, Mr. White, you can call me Mister." My voice goes a little sing-songy, sort of that black, shuffling Negro voice they might have been expecting.

They're now baffled and perplexed, and civility, if they displayed any, is slipping into hostility, and their next words come out as a challenge. "So your name is Mister? You want me to call you Mister? Mister what? Don't you have a first and last name? Or did your parents forget that?"

See, where I come from, black men are not equals, not even after serving two tours in Vietnam.

"Yes, that's right," I say, remaining calm. "Just call me Mister until we get to know each other a little. Then I'll share my given names."

At that stage, they usually walk away or disengage. If I were a smaller black man or there were three or four white men, things would go south from there. It was still the South, and a black man asking to be called Mister wasn't in style. The decision to head north to my father's homeland was easy, and my old army trainer was there as well.

I grew up rhyming instead of talking. When I rhymed, I didn't stutter. Didn't matter much whether I rhymed or spoke and stuttered; I was still likely to get smacked around. Rhymes didn't impress other black folks. Some thought I was making fun of the way our people talked and I was just making a stereotype worse. Acting and speaking like a black-faced white man in a travelling show or on TV whose job it was to get laughs from other white folks by exaggerating the way black folks supposedly talked and acted. Rhyming wasn't a popular way to express oneself on the black side of the tracks. I was small when I was young, up to about age eight. With no father around and no brothers or sisters, I was pretty much on my own and easy pickings for the toughs around our place. Smackdowns were a fairly regular occurrence. Seems Mama had something ruined inside her, probably from a beating from my father, who I never knew and have never had the pleasure to meet. Yet!

On the white side of town, where I rarely ventured, I was obviously just a coon lookin' to get beat up and kicked down.

Then I started to grow, and man did I get big. I stopped rhyming as much and hardly talked at all. My size was giving me some freedom from fear. Except at age thirteen, I had guys eighteen years old challenging me to fight, both white and black. They saw me as big and dumb, mostly because I hardly spoke. Thought they could whip my big dumb black ass. I let them get in a few shots, made them feel good and confident, and when their arrogance had peaked, I would lay them low. That usually took only one or two blows. I gained a reputation and was largely left alone.

Speaking in rhyme had me thinking in rhyme. It was easier, and to this day, I still think in rhyme. Hard habit to break, for goodness sake!

The more I learn, the more I speak real sentences and not in rhyme, even in my own head. I got Stone Pony to study. Turned out he was smart too. We had a lot to overcome. The more we knew, the better we believed things would go. The more Stone Pony learns, the less he fuckin' curses, and I'm trying to help the red man with that. Sometimes I slip up on purpose and curse just for the laugh and to get him off track.

Stone Pony and I share common bonds. We were both preyed upon when young, as we were not very imposing physically in our youth or in our pedigree. The two of us are strong now in body and mind. We also shared the fact that we both had AWOL asshole fathers to find. The Lord says, "Vengeance is mine." Well, Lord, we have fathers that we're going to help you in wreaking some of that vengeance, if you don't mind. You're as busy as hell, so we'll take care of our own miscreant kind with or without your blessing. We're just doing some of your dirty work.

Up to Canada I decided to go. The black man going to the ice and snow. A little town on a lake, maybe find my dad. That fucked-up snowflake. Mama forgot to mention his visit after I was born, about nineteen and forty-four. Came to see his son was the story he bore. Mustn't have liked what he saw. Got drunk, kicked down the door, among the hurts broke Mama's jaw and some things inside her. When I get my hands on that man I'm likely to say, "Hello, good fellow, I'm your son," then kill him with my bare hands.

No trace of the prick, but Mama had tracked him and managed the big trick. It took a long time, but a Canadian passport was mine. Stayed in that small Canadian town, and that passport got me employed. Workin' a garbage truck. Good work for a black boy. I felt the racism, whether American or Canuck. I decided I'd just work for all them mother fucks. And I did. I paired up with this Indian dude. Stone Pony and Mister getting their own route. We scared most of the good townsfolk, but gave them no cause to give us the boot. The Indian and the black man. They're in cahoots. Two different guys without any other friend. Didn't need any but found a few in the end. They were misfits, much like us. We were all searchin' for some kind of justice.

My uncles were cruel and clever. I let it ride and hoped it would get better. Mama's brothers were big, mean mothers. I got their size and some of their wise. Two uncles in jail, the dog pound. Two already in the ground. One other can't be found. One makin' us all proud. Wearin' sergeant stripes around our town.

Where we're from, life is hard for most us negroes. Dealin' with old Jim Crow, making our way best we know. Growin' up big and strong made it easier to get along. Sports channeled my energy and inner mayhem, talking soft and "yes, sirring" and "yes ma'aming." Made my way out to the military. At twenty-one special ops in Vietnam was scary. By sixty-four, was already studying on the GI Bill. Could have told the brass of the Cong to be wary.

Mama dyin' when I get back. Still wantin' me to find my father, askin' me to make him pay or kick his ass. A little, no, a lot of both, if you can make that come to pass.

I always studied hard. Turns out I'm more than a little smart. Tough and strong and all trained up. Special military skills on weapons, hand-to-hand combat, and all the killin' stuff. Teamwork and camaraderie, brothers in arms. Me and my brothers allow no harms. Trained to think before acting. Planning, not reacting. Kill like a fuckin' machine. In the rice fields and jungles, and again in your dreams.

To prey on me, instead of prayin' for me, when I was young the other kids used rhyme to inflict agony.

> You ain't white, and you ain't black
> God knows what came outta your mama's crack
> You ain't American or a Canuck
> You just one stupid-ass mother fuck
> You ain't anything at all
> Your phone ain't ringin', and we won't call
> Nobody can figure what you are
> Except ugly.
> You get hit by a car?
> No, musta been bigger, a big old truck
> Ran you over when you were a little fuck
> Now, you just bigger
> But still the Rhymin' Nigger.
> That rhymin', Your brain gotta be addled.
> You get to actin' strange like you're beggin' to be paddled.

    I don't even know why we had this paddle. They said it came with the butter churn, which we didn't use to make butter, I learned. The churn became a planter for flowers and seeds or other matter. We were careful to line that old butter churn with something, so the wood wouldn't rot and turn moldy. We didn't line it with a potato sack, because that was considered porous. I couldn't figure why a potato sack lining made us *poor us*. We lined that churn with somethin' better. Somethin' that could stand the dirt and the weather. Potato sacks were good for haulin' stuff, fillin' with dirt for baseball bags, and they were tough. Potato sacks felt rough. We had to wear them as clothing at times, when things were tough, and the food seemed to be never enough. A potato sack shirt in the hot season would itch and scratch beyond reason.

    Mama said my thoughts were all "singy-songy," but that's how my mind went along. Mama said us black folks were known by the whites for our rhythm, "But you, son, must have some Canadian craziness from that Army man's chism. Son, it takes you a long time to say somethin'. You gather yourself and what comes out is rhymin' or nothin.'"

    I knew from early days I had a bad stutter. So, just like the churn that didn't make butter, my words would come out like no others. That was the only way I could talk, get things out. The stutter might have been better cuz speakin' in my own tongue, in other's eyes, made me addled, no doubt.

    I was born in Georgia. Folks say I came out rhymin' from my mom's vagina.

My cries had rhythm and flow, and my howls were full of soul. Not bad for a mixture, neither nigger nor white, y'all. Big baby, like his uncles. Not any white at all like that scrawny Art Garfunkel. Man, now there's a white boy, despite that big old afro.

Life began, and from there I became a man. I remember my mother from early on, full of love for me, her son, tellin' me I was a special one. Born in 1940. "Your father a white soldier who hooked me bad. Oh, Lordy, Canadian bastard, never came back to us to stay after the war. Just to lay a beatin' on me and leave me with nothin' but pain, that's all. Someday y'all get your big, bad, black-man self up to the cold. Find him and kick his lily-white ass till he makes us whole. Money would be good from that turd. Don't take anything he says at his word. I did. You came along. Only good thing from meeting that northern dog."

Mama told me something else early on. "Something wrong with you, child. You all mostly tender and mild. Then something snaps, and you go all wild."

I burn for a measure of revenge. Not so much that my "never was my father" abandoned us. More so or all about his beating Mama. Stone Pony and I have a thirst to avenge those poor women, our loving mothers, wreak havoc on the men who beat them and left them to fend.

All that said, I know I just want to be a good man and be seen that way. By all. Black, white, red, and the rest of the rainbow, including mixed blood. When I walk down the street, I hope people can and will say, "There's a good man who does good things for others. He's good people. Bless him."

I don't want people to be scared of the big black man and get the shakes and say, "That negro gives me night quakes." I want their respect only when I have earned their respect. I don't want to be seen or become some jive-talkin' black man, and no Leroy Brown shit for me. That's why I'll talk in regular sentences, walk only as necessary with menace, and make something of myself.

There is a mighty cause calling me. More than some simplistic refrain, like be the best you can be. No. I want to be something. Something to be proud of. Hard for a black bastard, a rhymin' black man to get there, but I will.

Just like I made it in the army. Learn the skills, learn the tools, learn the rules. Think the work, plan the work, do the work, learn from the work.

Watch the edge, cover your back, scan the horizon, stay alert. Ingrain yourself into the team. Build your own team. Have principles, and when necessary, fight the fight.

I carry around a bit of some prayer from W. E. B. Dubois: "Give us grace, O God, to dare to do the deed which we well know cries to be done. Let us not hesitate because of ease or the words of men's mouths or our own lives. Mighty causes are calling us..."

CHAPTER 19

Christmas Dinner

The week before Christmas, I asked my son if his bosses were planning on a Christmas dinner. He said he would check. I told him to invite them over to our house if they didn't have plans. To my surprise, he came back and said they did have plans but would love to come if they could bring the turkey, the potatoes, pies, and three friends.

So, that's how on December 25, 1970, five of the strongest men I would ever meet walked into our house. My son told me to make lots of food. I prepared what I thought was mountains of carrots with maple syrup, peas, homemade biscuits, acorn squash with butter and brown sugar, and three kinds of cookies. One look at that group, and I wondered what else I could cook quickly.

The turkey was the largest I had ever seen. It must have been thirty pounds. The little one said she felt like Tiny Tim in that Christmas movie when the big bird came through the front door. The pot of mashed potatoes looked like ten gallons, and there were five different pies.

The men were Mister and Stone Pony, who introduced me to their three friends. The FBI were the two largest Indians I had ever seen. Pardon me. They were the biggest men I had ever seen, including Mister. They didn't give last names, just Emerson and Webster. The third man, the man with the twinkle in his eye, solid jaw with a cleft chin, and blue water eyes to die for, was introduced as Ulysses. He struck me as a God, and I was smitten from the outset.

My oldest daughter and her new boyfriend had decided to have dinner with his parents. That worked out well for two reasons. My potential son-in-law had some reservations about these men, and we didn't have enough room.

Everything was ready, so we sat to eat. The dining table wasn't big enough, so the FBI brought the kitchen table into the dining room. We draped it with a tablecloth and rearranged the plates and utensils. The little one insisted on sitting with Emerson and Webster at the kitchen table. She was at one end of the whole affair, and I was at the other. The little one said, "Mom, we're the queen and the princess, and these are our loyal servants." Everyone laughed. Without anyone else saying a thing, Ulysses stood up.

"Ma'am, or should I say Queen and Princess, with your leave and at your pleasure, may I offer a prayer or two and then carve the turkey?"

The little one and I laughed and nodded our approval. The men all grinned, including my son, as their sign of approval.

Ulysses asked us to hold hands, and he started the first prayer in what I learned was Chippewa or Ojibwe. The three Indians' heads literally snapped up when they heard the first word of the prayer. We were all holding hands, and I could see that Emerson and Webster's grips almost involuntarily tightened on the little one's hands. Stone Pony's hand tightened on mine. Stone Pony was on my right, with Ulysses on his right, then Emerson. Mister was on my left, with my son next and then Webster. That prayer sounded right and beautiful in my home. I found myself crying and looked up to see everyone was making eye contact. All three Indians had river mist in their eyes. I felt something meaningful and very special had just happened. I felt proud and humbled to be a part of that moment in my home.

Then Ulysses said the Lord's Prayer in a manner and a tone that spoke of God and must have reached God's ear. He spoke in a solemn manner that captured feelings of faith, trust, and passion. I have never been so moved by prayers in my life, and probably never will be that moved again.

Amens and looks of love and trust and of brotherhood circled the table. Nothing else was said as Ulysses carved the bird.

The plates were passed, and everyone was assigned a dish to serve. Potatoes, carrots, peas, squash, buns, cranberry sauce (homemade by Stone Pony), gravy, and the turkey. Eight people, eight servings. Laughter and quick remarks and comebacks about portions. Too big, too small, none at all. Good-natured, goodhearted, good spirits. I felt lucky. Blessed.

They teased and joked. My son drew a lot of the comments. About his driving, his apparent inability to back up, his so-called beard or scraggly facial hair, to which the Indians quipped, "Better some than none." They spoke not at all about their families or homes. They spoke to each other with warmth and in a contagious spirit of closeness and trust, despite the conversation being loaded with sarcasm, complaints against one or another, slights perpetrated, and minor faults and mistakes blown up to mythical proportions.

The little one sparkled at being included. My son was bathing in the brotherhood. I was happy, content, and at peace.

As the plates started being passed for seconds, Emerson asked my permission to speak. I responded with a slight bow of my head and a large grin on my face.

"Permission granted," I said, in as royal a voice as I could muster.

"Ulysses, bless you, my brother. We haven't heard our prayer for giving thanks to the Creator in our language since our grandmother's spirit left to join the Creator. We three Chippewa are proud, mostly quiet men, but this needs to be said. You, Ulysses have touched our hearts, loosened our spirits to fly on eagle's wings to thank the Creator. We thank him for the grace and hospitality of this home and this family. We thank him for our brotherhood with you, Ulysses, Stone Pony, Mister, Scarface, Webster, and me. The Creator has given us earthly bonds that we're grateful for, hold to our hearts, and carry proudly."

When Emerson sat down, through my tears, I saw the sparkle on the little one's face, the swelling emotion and pride in my son, and the knowledge that deep, meaningful truths had been spoken, received, and ingrained. This was drawn on the men's faces.

We continued to eat. The laughter was becoming fuller. Everyone was in high spirits, and not a drop had been drunk.

We cleared the table, all working together, and brought the pies out. Apple, rhubarb, pumpkin, peach, and lemon meringue. All the pies had been baked by Mister. The lemon meringue for Stone Pony. The rhubarb for Webster. The apple for Ulysses. The pumpkin for Emerson. The peach for himself. Mister said next year, despite the behaviour of the other four guests, if they were invited back, there would be eight pies. He said he took requests.

The room was again full of laughter, and despite all these strong men, the room was bursting with love. To think that the big, peaceful man standing there had cooked all those pies, yet everyone in town viewed him as an imposing menace and a threat.

Mister stood up and asked for permission to speak before he sliced and served the pies. I gave him my royal assent.

"I love to bake. My mama taught me. Her kitchen was a safe haven when I was young and afraid to go outside because of taunting and beatings before I got big. Mama made me feel special and baked me peach pies that I, to this day, think are the best food I've ever had or will have. When I told her that, Mama said it was because of her secret ingredient.

"'What's that, Mama?' I asked.

"'Well, I shouldn't tell you because it's a secret,' she said.

"'Please, Mama,' I begged.

"'You won't tell anyone if I share the secret, will you?'

"'No, Mama, I promise,' I replied. Well, I hold that secret more dear every passing year. But today, Mama, please forgive me. I'm gonna share that secret."

This big man then cupped one hand to his ear, reached over and held my hand with another, and gulped in lungfuls of emotion that made his voice catch and waver. "What's that, Mama? It's OK to share with these folks? OK, Mama. Thank you and bless you. Mama had one secret ingredient for everything in her life. Love. I pass that secret ingredient to you all, who I love."

Before Mister's seat could find his chair, I was up with my arms around his massive shoulders and shedding tears on his cheek. He patted my hand, which was on his chest. I spoke in a whisper that turned out loud enough because the room went completely quiet, so everyone heard. "You saved me once. You're a blessing. You have filled me with emotion, and I love you."

I sat down to silence, which Ulysses broke. "Cut the darn pies before they get soggy with tears. Especially the lemon meringue, because a blubbering Stone Pony will make a mess out of that, and I might try a piece after I eat half of that apple pie. And Mister, God bless you and your mama."

Before anyone else could say anything, the little one chirped up. "And God bless us everyone." Her Tiny Tim moment was exactly what the room needed.

The night continued with joy and laughter. Emerson and Webster took turns carrying the little one on their shoulders just like Tiny Tim around the tables. She had to hunch over, so she didn't hit the ceiling when she was on the big men's shoulders. She was so happy. My son leaned back in his chair. I had not seen him so calm and at peace with himself since he was a small boy. I couldn't help from hoping he could stay in the safe, secure place he had found at that moment.

We cleaned up and did the dishes as one big crew, a very different family. As the men were preparing to leave, Stone Pony said he had a few words to say. The kitchen and the hallway where we were gathered became silent.

"First, thank you for having us in your home." Sincere thanks from all the men followed, making me flush with warmth and a humble pride.

"Second, you guys are all working tomorrow, so sleep off that turkey hangover."

Again my home was filled with laughter. It was all such a blessing.

"Third, we six are brothers. That's clear from the blessings we have received in being together today. We thank the Creator for these blessings."

Nods all around, some clasping of shoulders, my son hugging the little one and I, one in each arm.

"Last, no harm shall ever visit this house. You, the lady of this house, little one, and Scarface are on our watch. Our watch will be constant and our concern unwavering. You have demonstrated grace, care, trust, and love. You have not cared what others think or say. You invited us into your home and provided us with a joyous occasion and a safe harbour. No white person, Ulysses excluded, has ever treated us so well. Like family, like sons. We thank and bless you all."

We hugged all those men, and I kissed them on the cheek. I wanted to speak, but I couldn't. I was far too overcome.

"Would you grace us with your company for a Canada Day celebration at our cabin this year?" Stone Pony asked.

I looked at the little one, pulled her close, and whispered in her ear. Then she spoke. "On behalf of Her Majesty, mother of Scarface, and myself, we graciously accept your offer. We'll bring a cake. One cake."

Again, more laughter and hugs as Emerson, Webster, Ulysses, Stone Pony, and Mister left.

We three stood like royalty at our front door, watching the friends we now all three cared for deeply. Loved.

My son started to ask about Mister saving me. "Another time, son," I said. "Get to bed. Work will come early tomorrow."

Selfless Virtue

Dear God
This won't be a long prayer,
Just one of thanks.
You have blessed my family with these five men.
Care and look out for them,
As they will care and look out for us.
I ask little for myself.
I would ask you for a kinder world for them.
I'm certain they won't ask anything for themselves.
God, that must be a virtue in itself.

Amen.

CHAPTER 20

Team Meeting

It felt good when school returned. The morning announcements, the VP's good-natured guidance, Rave and the Ravers, Ms. Librarian, and even the *Raging Rag*. They had missed their announced Christmas edition, so I was expecting a real ball-buster of an edition in the near future. My balls being busted as the main editorial theme, with perhaps a short, swift kick to the nads for Rave. There was nothing I could do to prevent or influence that!

I heard a lot of stories about vacations and ski trips, but more stories about parties, wild ones. I had been invited to a few, but was just too damn tired to go. I slept through New Year's Eve, and my absence from the parties made my legend grow. Rumour was that I had gone to the city for the weekend with Mister and Stone Pony and was partying with models and rock bands. Our town now had a very serious belief that Mister and Stone Pony were minting money with their garbage, security, and a new venture, firewood provisions. The last part was true, as we started hauling firewood right before Christmas. Mister, Stone Pony, Mr. Clampett, and the FBI loaded the two trucks at night, and those customers were the first stops on our garbage routes.

The extent of my partying at New Year's Eve involved the little one and Mom coming into my room just before midnight to wake me up with noisemakers. I stumbled downstairs with them for the countdown to midnight, kissed them both, had a cold beer in a frosted mug with Mom, then went back to bed. Wild, wild!

I was in a bit of a strange place. A mood—whatever you want to call it. Kind of thinking about who I was, where I was headed, and what direction I should be going. I wasn't really feeling solid on a day-to-day basis, not physically but in my head. My status in town and school had definitely changed. I wasn't in a rock band or dating a snow princess. I certainly didn't fit in the right uptight circles, and I played with strange playmates. I always had Scarecrow and Bogeyman, then Mister and Stone Pony, and now the freakin' FBI, not to mention Mr. Clampett, the Brownies, and the Whities.

I was feeling like I didn't have all my shit together. I didn't have a girlfriend, either. I wasn't even dating anyone. No time. The lack of a girlfriend was bothering the shit out of me. I hadn't even kissed a girl since last summer, since Woman, on the way home from Winnipeg. I can't say I was in love with Woman, but I sure felt strongly and deeply connected to her, the truly mysterious Indian woman from Saskatchewan, protector of the weak, the mistreated, the lost, the forgotten, the wayward, and the abandoned.

A girlfriend would be good. The lyrics from "Mr. Soul," the Buffalo Springfield tune, kept turning over in my head. I was just like the words they sang. I would love for any girl to get to know me better. And I am different. And I'm not going to change so I hope she, whoever she is, likes the difference.

Yep, that about nailed it. Any—or at least many—girls, I would be glad if they wanted to know me better. I also had to admit that, given my companions, my work, and my upbringing, I was a bit strange. The beauty of those lyrics was that last thought, "but don't change." I didn't want to change what I did or who I was, but I did want to become better. I thought a girlfriend could go a long way to helping me with all that.

The second Sunday after we got back to school, Mister and Stone Pony declared a big New Year's Eve feast day. They also announced that we would be receiving our holiday and year-end bonus.

I was thinking I might get as much as $500. The business was booming as we entered January. The firewood was a lucrative new business. The Brownies and the Whities were hauling deadfall out of woodlots with snowmobiles and sleds. In February, the FBI were starting as a full-time sanitation crew with the town. They were going down to just two nights a week as security—OK, bouncers—at the Refuge.

The New Year's Day feast was Hawaiian-themed, with pineapple ham and all the trimmings. The guest list had expanded. The FBI, the Whities, the Brownies, Mr. Clampett, me, and a woman I had never seen before. Ms. Cecilia Annamoosie. Apparently, only Stone Pony and Mister knew her, and everyone was as shocked as me when Mister escorted her into the cabin. This was a strange crew. Of the eleven people attending the feast, seven had never been to the cabin. I could see that every newcomer was impressed and almost stunned by Mister and Stone Pony's home.

The festivities started off with Mister stating that before we broke bread, everyone had to introduce themselves and provide a brief summation of their life story. Ladies first. Ms. Cecilia Annamoosie stood up. She was weirdly gorgeous—red hair, brown skin, green eyes, at least five foot eight. Her body shape was hard to describe. She wore a flowing, loose-fitting dress covered by a long shawl that draped her from shoulders to knees. She was definitely not willowy or full bodied. She appeared lithe and at ease, comfortable, and confident in how she looked and who she was.

Ms. Annamoosie stated she was from the Mohawk Nation, born in Quebec, but grew up primarily on the Six Nation Reserve in Brantford, Ontario. She said she was a hell of a lacrosse player, but by age thirteen, when she started to bleed with her moon cycle, (in her world) she was no longer allowed to play with the boys. She made solid eye contact as she spoke. Her voice and tone commanded attention. Speaking in front of that eclectic group of ten men would not have been easy for anyone. Ms. Annamoosie acted like she owned the room, the audience.

"When my lacrosse career bled out, so to speak," she continued, "I focused on my intellect." There were a few muffled snickers and gasps at the way she described the end of her lacrosse career.

"I focused on school. This made me very different from the majority of the kids on the reserve. I studied hard, was an honours student, Ontario scholar, top student, and valedictorian, a first for a Six Nation Indian—and a girl, to boot. That surprised and pissed off a lot of white folks. Shocked and stupefied a lot of Indian folks, especially since most Indian girls my age and younger were pregnant or already had kids. My academic success pissed off a few of my contemporaries of the male Indian variety. My looks were enough to set me apart as it was, and they garnered lots of attention. Brains and lacrosse skills, too! I was a target for abuse. It turns out I was good with a knife and a broken bottle. There were three attempted rapes and three very scarred Indians as a result. Me, you ask? I remained intact.

"I moved off the reserve at age sixteen. I funded myself, working as a waitress. I studied treaty rights. I understood how to get education funding. My university was fully paid. I was accepted to U of T with lots of scholarship money and government funding. I did a three-year liberal arts degree, studying everything: sociology, psychology, economics, philosophy, world history, politics, meteorology, literature. You name it, I aced it! I graduated at the top of my class, a gold medalist. I was accepted to Osgoode Hall Law School at U of T, one of the most prestigious law schools in Canada. I was only the second Indian ever admitted and the first red woman. Not the hair, boys, the skin."

There was a little laughter.

"I finished second to the gold medalist there, articled, and then was employed by a Bay Street firm. I made associate early and was on the partner track, working lots of Indian claims, billing lots of hours. My senior partner was trying to get me to fuck him or at least blow him. I never let that fat, white suburban fucker with a wife and three kids get even a whiff of me. The knife I placed on my desktop when we were working alone at night must have made an impression on him. He kept his distance. I also think that the one time he snuck up behind me and grabbed my tits when I whirled around and grabbed his bag with one hand and told him to look down at his dick he was a little set back—not only by the one hand clutching his tiny bag and dick but the other hand holding that seven-inch razor-sharp hunting knife."

The room let out a collective gasp as twenty balls contracted. Ms. Annamoosie had our full attention.

"Sorry to go on so long, gentlemen, but none of you know me, so I think all this background is essential information. I also think my senior partner was discouraged by my choice of words. As a lawyer, you learn to make a point succinctly and precisely. This is especially true when you're dealing with pompous, narcissistic egomaniacs who feel fully entitled to treat you like shit. My exact words? 'I'll cut your balls off, shove them in your mouth, and watch you bleed to death!' I think I was crystal clear. He seemed to get the message. Just for good measure, I sliced his expensive suit pants about a foot down his inner thigh. I nicked him a little with the knife and told him a good seamstress could fix the pants and recommended he get a bandage for his leg. I also told him I was perplexed at how he would explain the cut and the blood to his wife."

Exhaled breaths, a bit of laughter—but still ten ball sacks feeling vulnerable in the presence of Ms. Cecilia Annamoosie.

"The fucker got his revenge about seven years later. By the way, if you're guessing or wondering, I'm forty-one, single, and happy that way. I know that after the knife story at least half of you are considering marriage proposals. Don't!"

More nervous—but appreciative—laughter went around the room.

"My senior partner and a chief constructed some bullshit enterprise that was set up as some kind of consulting agency for the chief's reserve. They were skimming money through a bogus firm and splitting the four or five hundred thousand a year in billings from the law firm. They were doing nothing. I was the lawyer of record for all the enterprise documents and signed off on all the fund transfers. The money was siphoned out of a black hole of fake consulting entities for which I had written all of the work contracts and documents between the chief's reserve and the consulting companies. I didn't know shit about the companies except that they had all been verified as legit by the senior partner, some legal clerks, and, of course, the chief. Four years into this arrangement, the chief lost his re-election bid and skedaddled to Peru or Ecuador or Bolivia, somewhere in South America. The new chief wanted face-to-face meetings with the consulting firms, but they didn't have faces to meet with. The senior partner hadn't signed one single document, and he had arranged for several unwitting peers to provide oversight for these contracts. Everything was rubber-stamped. I was the only lawyer, apparently, who was hands-on. Although I wasn't disbarred, I was found culpable, and I smelled dirty. Since there was no trace of the money anywhere around me, and the consulting company's fact-checking verifications and legal documents had all been compiled by a law firm that turned out not to exist, no one else was found complicit. Not one law clerk had handled more than one fake file. It was a brilliant scheme. Two point three million dollars gone. The chief, living the good life somewhere in South America, with a one point two million, the other one point one million unaccounted for. The chief's money was verified by some forensic accounting with a bank that turned up wire transfers for it. I figured the senior partner got the rest.

"I was politely and expeditiously terminated, and found myself unemployable. That's the story that leads me to being the lawyer for Mister and Stone Pony and all their enterprises. Just so you all know, I'm extremely good at what I do. You should also know not to fuck with me, intellectually or physically. That's not intended to be threatening or a warning. It is intended to make you feel certain and comfortable about what and who you're dealing with, and guide your behaviour accordingly."

With some raised eyebrows arching her way, Ms. Cecilia Annamoosie sat, and Stone Pony stood up. He nodded to Ms. Annamoosie and thanked her. "The rest of you can give a shorter intro and background, as we all kind of know each other, except for Mr. Clampett," Stone Pony said. "Let's start with the Brown brothers." The Brown brothers were two of the six members of the Neapolitan Crew. The other members were the FBI and the Whities. They were the three two-man squads that provided hospitality coordination at the Refuge.

The Brown brothers rarely spoke. They didn't drink or do drugs. They fought. The Brownies, as they were known, had gone through some disturbing abuse up until age fifteen. The abuse came from all sides, including their father and uncles on both branches of the family tree. The Brownies had an Indian mother and a white father, an unusual combination in our neck of the woods. My father was rumoured to have fathered a child with an Indian woman he had later beaten badly. No one from the reserve had ever stepped forward to claim the honour of being fathered by Art, my father. Why would they? There was no father there to honour—or a father worth honouring.

The Brownies took all that shit and were fighting white and Indian kids all the time. They were called half breeds, two tones, mixed mutts, a darker shade of pale (after the song "A Whiter Shade of Pale"). The Brownies disappeared the summer before they turned sixteen. Turns out they lied about their age and got jobs in Algonquin Park. They blazed trails, cleared campsites, and paddled tourists by canoe on wilderness adventures. They also acted as fishing guides.

That summer, the Brownies matured physically. They grew almost six inches, and eventually would hit six feet flat, the height of their father. Their frames started to fill out. Now, they were described as whisky kegs on stilts. Big chests and the rounded-shoulder, muscled frame of their mother's Irish family. The Brownies didn't emerge from the bush that year until Thanksgiving weekend. Then they drove into town in a Mustang convertible, bright orange, parked their car on Main Street, and stood beside it for two hours. They drew a lot of attention. The word got out that the Brown brothers were back in town, and cars cruised down Main Street to get a look. Many of the cars were filled with past perpetrators of Brownie abuse. If looks could kill, there would have been a lot of dead folks piling up on the main drag.

The Brownies came back with a game plan that was simple and straightforward. They picked four sets of people they were going to kick the shit out of: two of their white uncles who were ten to twelve years older than the sixteen-year-old Brown brothers. Two of their Indian uncles, about the same age as their white uncles; three white gang members from the Kings of the South, who were in their early twenties. Yep, three on two. Then, three Indian cousins in their early twenties. They spread the word on their retribution decisions. Then, the Brownies found them and fucked them up good, one group at a time.

After each ass-kicking, the Brownies drove their Mustang downtown with the top down, parked, and stood by their car. Not a scratch on them, as hospitalization facts and fiction emerged on their former perpetrators. Broken ribs, arms, orbital bones, jaws, and, of course, noses. It was a series of four massacres. The Kings of the South pulled tire irons out, only to have them, allegedly, in one case, stuffed up their asses. The Indian cousins pulled knives. They all had an ear lobe nicked off. The Brownies had never been fucked with in the ten years since. The likelihood of that ever happening was low to begin with, but now, as part of the Neapolitan Crew, the chances were less than zero.

That's how the Brown brothers told their story. They added an interesting fact. Neither could read or write by age fifteen, when they dropped out and filled out. Their mother taught them to read and write after that. They got their grade twelve and were now studying university and trade-school courses. The kicker? They could speak and write in Spanish. A second kicker: good Irish names. The Brownies were Seamus and Patrick O'Connor. They had taken their mom's name.

The FBI went next. The FBI talked almost as one. In the middle of a sentence, one would just take over speaking from the other, and the pattern repeated. The FBI weren't brothers; they were cousins. They grew up skinny and hungry. They got into a lot of trouble for stealing food. They never did jail time, although they should have. They said stealth was their thing, and what made them effective. They were 6' 6" and 6'7" respectively, and weighed 260 to 270 pounds. Stealth seemed impossible at that size. They were always called FBI 1 and FBI 2, or One and Two for short. They didn't look that much alike, but were made very distinguishable by their scars. One's real name was Emerson, and he had a long scar from the top of his right shoulder to his forearm, the result from a knife slash from a fight as a sixteen-year-old. Two had a scar from the same knife fight. His name was Webster, as in the dictionary. They began their story at the knife fight. They were gangly, awkward, skinny teens. Webster's eighteen-year-old sister, Merriam, was gang raped by five or six members of the Vipers. Webster quickly acknowledged that his mother had named them after the dictionary in the hope that would lead them to knowledge or some book learning.

Emerson and Webster planned their retribution. They knew a house where the Vipers hung out, and they tracked the perpetrator's behaviour. On Thursday nights, the gang would buy a couple of two-fours of Carling O'Keefe Red Cap beer and at least two bottles of Hiram Walker whisky. They would sit around and get pissed and brag about past accomplishments; play cards mostly a poker game called Boo-Ray; maybe even plan weekend adventures and jobs. The Vipers planned their crimes while pissed, which might explain why most of them had done significant jail time by their early twenties.

The FBI told us they planned their attack for almost four months. Their stealth made them the best break-and-enter team in the whole area. They never got caught once. Emerson said they studied behaviour looking for patterns and clues. The Vipers would argue about their plans and dispute each other's boasting.

Fights were not infrequent.

A couple of Vipers would step out on the porch together almost every hour. They stepped out to cool their tempers, make alliances, have a smoke or a joint, or piss off the porch. The porch was phase one of the FBI attack. Webster was hidden under the porch and reached up and yanked on a Viper's leg, pulling him down and the one leg through the porch's lower rail. Webster had waited until the Viper pulled his dick out to piss, so the Viper was extremely vulnerable. As Webster pulled the Viper off the deck and began slamming his fists into him, the second Viper saw his buddy go down hard. "What the fuck, man, did you slip?" he asked. Emerson leaped onto the porch and pounded the second Viper across the back of his knees with an axe handle. The second blow was to the back of his neck. The Viper planted face first, and Emerson slid him off the porch. The FBI wailed on the two Vipers until they were a mass of blood and broken stuff. The commotion was not really noticed by the four remaining Vipers in the house. The FBI left their prey and wheeled around to the front door. They counted on some moaning from the first victims to arouse the other Vipers, which it did. As two Vipers headed out to the porch to investigate, the FBI came in the front door. The remaining two Vipers met up with the FBI's axe handles. It wasn't intended to be a fair contest—but six guys raping a girl called for extreme payback, not fairness.

The FBI made only one error. They didn't notice that the Vipers had all taken to carrying concealed knives—switchblades, for the most part. When the two Vipers came back in from the porch to see the FBI flailing away with axe handles and fists, their knives came out. The FBI hadn't fully disabled the other two Vipers, and now it was four on two. No problem. By the end of it all, not a Viper remained intact or mobile. The FBI gathered up the Viper blades, a full bottle of H.W., and emptied the cash from the wallets of all six Vipers.

Webster continued the story. "We were bleeding bad. Got home to the reserve and were stitched up somewhat by my mom and sister. We drank the whisky to numb the pain. Neither of us remembered getting cut during the fight. We vowed never to bring an axe handle to a knife fight again." They both laughed.

The story was legendary in town. The Vipers had sworn revenge, but a number of factors had intervened. First, they were badly beaten. Second, they could only identify their assailants as skinny Indian pricks, which covered more than half the males on the reserve. Third, they kept saying there were ten or twelve attackers, so the suspect pool was not being narrowed sufficiently. Fourth, when they recovered, their continued poor criminal planning led to more jail time for most of them. Fifth, the Vipers were scared shitless by the rage and violence of two skinny Indians.

A couple of things happened afterward. No Indian girl was ever accosted by a Viper for a long time. No Viper came anywhere near the reserve for a longer period.

The FBI succinctly finished their story. They finished grade twelve and got out of town for years. They worked in the oil fields in Alberta and grew massive. They pocketed their money, drank very little, but loved smoking weed and took courses to become truck drivers and heavy equipment operators.

They came back to town because of family problems. Their mothers and sisters were being pushed around by drunken men in their families. That stopped quickly upon their return. They bought a house and a truck. They did most of the hauling and moving around, to and from the reserve. They had a good business going and worked as bouncers at the Refuge. They had been back five years, and both were turning thirty.

Emerson wrapped it all up. "We're proud, independent red men. Don't fuck with us and ours, and we won't fuck with you. If you're our brothers, we'll always have your back. We're quiet by choice, not by capability or competence."

Ms. Cecilia Annamoosie asked if that back-covering went for sisters, which produced laughter around the room.

"That goes without saying," Webster replied, "for all women, especially mothers and sisters." Then he paused. "And that includes you, our new sister and lawyer."

More laughter—warm laughter—and maybe a tear forming at the hard corners of Ms. Cecilia Annamoosie's strong eyes.

Surprisingly, Mr. Clampett went next. He was short, and not sweet.

"If any of you fuckers ever call me Mr. Clampett, I'll cut your pecker off, if I can find it. I'm a veteran of several American excursions, most prominently Vietnam. I have been trained by my country to be extraordinarily good at bad things. My life was OK as a child, not like the shit shows we've heard here so far. I loved the idea of American heroism, military might and order, the discipline and dedication of the soldier, loyalty to our flag, and God and country, but that's all been fucked over by Vietnam. My country is at a crossroads. What I enlisted for may not exist currently. I'm neither a basket case nor a lost soul. I'm a hard case when it comes to loyalty, brotherhood, and accountability to those I love and care for. I have a wife and a son who live in Paris, Tennessee. Yep, Paris on the bayou. I love them, but I have currently lost all ability to socialize within a family unit. They understand, and they don't.

"I was also Mister's primary trainer in the special forces. We served together, and I was his platoon chief in Nam. We have seen and done some shit together. I was born in New Orleans, and my mother, God rest her soul, was Canadian. My father was and is a good military man. I'm forty-plus and when necessary, an extremely dangerous individual. If you want to know more about me, you're probably out of luck.

"My role is front and back security for Mister and Stone Pony. After this little meeting, I hope to have an expanded role as chief of security for all business entities under the auspices of Mister and Stone Pony. I'll likely be a personal security officer for all of you. If you want, call me Captain. My men called me Chief, but that would be confusing with all the Indians in the crowd."

And that was that for the captain. Eyebrows were raised by his mention of business entities, chief of security, and personal security.

I can't say the Whities were the most intriguing part of the Neapolitan Crew, as the FBI, Brownies, and Whities became commonly known for their security work at the Refuge, but they were different and special.

The other Neapolitan Crew members teased the Whities about having permanently drawn the short straw. The Whities were twin five-foot-nine white brothers. They had wrestled through high school and college. They were never separated. They described themselves as aloof and uninterested in most stuff, but they admitted they had always been shy and more than a little introverted. They apologized for the lack of "colour" in their background. Their parents were solid, hardworking, churchgoing citizens. They had a "vanilla" upbringing. Nothing remotely troublesome or a cause for worry—just a plain, low-key existence. Their parents expected them to be tradesmen, garbage men, mailmen, milkmen, or mechanics. An everyday "go to work, do a good job, be a good person, and walk a straight line" sort of life.

The Whities enrolled in a technical college in the big city, primarily because they had one of the best wrestling programs in the country. The Whities both became Canadian college champs in the 172 and 181 classes. They studied electrical engineering, were excellent mechanics, fascinated by and good at almost any emerging technology. At college, the Whities got into weed. They were kind of lost after college and the end of their wrestling careers. They travelled through Europe and Southeast Asia. They became martial arts devotees, starting with Kung Fu and branching out from there. They studied Zen philosophies, meditated, and did yoga. They chuckled when they said they smoked a lot of weed, but only at night, before bed. They said they were mellow until provoked. The Whities' real names were Zachary Thomas and Ezekiel Franklin Whitmore. They were called the Whities because they had always had their blonde hair in a brush cut until their second year of college, when they discovered weed.

The Whities, Zack and Zeke, were the youngest of the Neapolitan crew, at age twenty-seven. They ran their own repair and electronics company. Although not licensed electricians, they were hired for jobs by every electrician in a fifty-mile radius. They were in demand, and were paid journeyman wages or more, despite not having their papers.

The thing they wanted us all to know was that they were methodical, tactical, meticulous, and planned everything. *Calm* was their defining characteristic. For them, even a seemingly spur-of-the-moment bar fight at the Refuge was a predictable event that they planned for and carried out methodically. They were hard to provoke, and their calm and reputation as kung fu warriors stopped most disturbances before they started.

The Whities knew that the Neapolitan Crew was destined to combine with the Newspaper Crew to create some form of enterprise. Zach and Zeke both meditated and got stoned while conjuring up thoughts of what that enterprise would look like and become.

The Whities said their parents had hoped they would become men of the cloth. That was a bit of a problem for Zack and Zeke. They thought their church was loaded with hypocrites, and they found their parents' brand of religion restrictive. Also, the fact that they were on the introverted side sort of precluded them from occupational choices that put them on any form of stage, let alone behind a pulpit. They would rather wrestle with their demons in their own way with weed, Zen, and meditation. The odd shit kicking of brave souls who ventured to tussle with them at the Refuge helped them convert a few non-believers. As in, "For Christ's sake, let's never mess with those short white fucks again, and amen to that."

The Whities also said their parents worried about some of their close associates. When Zack and Zeke heard that, they suggested the Neapolitan Crew, Mister, and Stone Pony attend their church one Sunday to alleviate their fears, but their parents politely and fully declined that suggestion. The Whities hoped no one took offence to that. The reaction was just some good-natured laughter and knowing nods.

There was no need for Mister and Stone Pony to speak, as the group knew their backstory.

So, my turn.

When I started to speak, Emerson held up his hand. "Scarface. Everyone knows your story. You're famous in these parts. You'll be in the care of this whole group in the future. You have no need to talk."

And there it was.

Then Stone Pony stood up. "Now, to business."

CHAPTER 21

Art Thy Father

The Christmas cards arrived on the last day of January, what someone would call *fashionably late* if they were a person who said things like that. The postmark was Vancouver, which was totally foreign in terms of where I would expect Christmas cards to start from and then end up in our mailbox. To my great fear, the handwriting was the opposite of the address, as it was totally familiar. My loafing, cheating, deserting, drunken bastard of a husband sent Christmas cards to my son and me.

So many things were triggered by those two envelopes. I stood wondering if I should let the kids even know that the cards arrived, and wondered if I should keep the card addressed to my son. Why were there no cards for the little one and my older daughter? What messages of hate or anger did they contain? I could take that, but I wouldn't stomach any sappy sentiments. Worse yet, I dreaded the thought that the envelope might contain some appeal to reunite or the slightest suggestion of some type of relationship.

That ship had sailed almost eleven years ago. Art the anchor. He had dragged us down more than once, and that was never going to happen again. That boat wouldn't float.

All these thoughts consumed me even before I opened the envelope. Hell, I just assumed they were Christmas cards. What if they contained cheques? Or bills? Art could do that to me. Raise my hopes with stretches of sobriety, then dash my dreams with a drunken weekend of wiping out my savings with another woman.

Opening those cards was like buying a lottery ticket. I knew my odds of winning were less than tiny, but I still hoped. Art raised my hopes for over seventeen years before he disappeared and dashed them on the rocks of despair, leaving us on the edge of poverty more than once. Then, he took that long walk off a short pier, finally leaving us for what I prayed was for good. I knew he was gone when he left for the corner store on that Sunday afternoon. His mission, a pack of smokes and a loaf of bread. Mission failure.

Then he showed up at our back door with his brother three summers ago, wanting to see his kids. I screamed through the locked back door that this was my house and my kids. He'd given up all his rights. They tried to force the door, but it held. I ran upstairs, gathering the little one on my way, and yelling for the bastards to get off my property, threatening to call the cops, which was an idle threat. Our telephone was on the wall beside the kitchen table in clear view of the back door, where they were banging.

The last thing I heard Art, my loving husband, say was a mixture of these sentences: "I'll break the fucking window, bitch. You let me in now, you withered old slut, or you'll regret it. I'll break your scrawny neck, you piece of chicken shit." Then, things got quiet. My hopes rose that they were getting thirsty from all the yelling and banging, and the two drunks had decided a drink would sharpen their decision-making abilities in facing their current dilemma: to break in and beat up or not. The two pricks had gone on three- to four-day benders with less provocation. I peeked out an upstairs window, and my hopes fell. The car was still there, and no one was inside. My hopes sank even further as I saw the third brother was leaning on the car's hood. Art did that to me. He raised hopes with his silence and then squashed them with his presence.

The silence? The quiet? Why?

My son had arrived home. Scarface, or Garbage Boy, whatever they called him these days, came home to the rescue. Some angry tones and some crunching, crashing sounds floated up. I was torn. Should I rush down and enter the fray or stay where I was, somewhat safe and protecting the little one? Finally, I decided my presence downstairs would only raise the level of anger and potential for violence, so I stayed put.

Whatever happened happened quickly. The car backed out of the driveway, spitting gravel and spinning tires. Their exit was loud—quite the opposite of the quiet, probably engine-turned-off way they'd coasted in. The engine was revving full throttle, and I heard Art yell, "You fucking bastard!" I couldn't make out what my son said, although I heard his voice. Unlike his father, his words sounded calm and controlled.

When I came downstairs, my son was leaning against the doorframe. He had some blood on his knuckles and on his shirt. It looked like he had a bruise forming on his right cheek, and his nose was bleeding. He told me that his dad wasn't much and gave details of the brief fight that had transpired. I told him to wait and then ran next door to beg for a couple of cold beers. Those were the first two beers we ever shared. He was fifteen, and if he could stand up and fight his father, he could damn well drink a cold beer with his mother.

He recounted the encounter, and near the end, he started to laugh. I asked him what was so funny. I didn't see anything funny in fighting with his father. "Mom," he said, "I told him I could see the pack of smokes in his pocket, but he forgot the loaf of bread."

It took a few seconds for that to sink in, but when it did, we both laughed out loud. We clinked our bottles, looked each other in the eyes, which were sparkling with tears of joy, and took big swigs.

I was a mess of emotions. Joy, fear, worry about Art's return, pride in my son for making a stand, and most of all, a deep sense of relief. For reasons unknown, I made a toast to "Art, Thy Father." We laughed for many reasons at that. Reasons both known and unknown and largely unspoken, except for forgetting the loaf of bread. Art the Loafless.

I opened my card with trepidation, a two-buck word I had learned from my son's friend, Scarecrow. It was what I guessed I should have expected. Not much. A simple "Merry X-mas. Hope you and the kids are well. Love, Art." That was it, and somehow it hurt like hell. Love and merry and well? Give me a freaking break. Art the Loafless. Art Thy Father, but he is my Son.

When my son got home, it was late on a Friday night after a hockey game. He went with a few friends to watch a few of his old teammates play for the local junior B team. The team wasn't very good that year, and my son was asked many times to join them. He politely and respectfully turned down the opportunity. He was content with playing for his high school team. He respected the coach. He told me the coach was someone who gave good guidance and lived by a code full of integrity, principles, and character. That was a good man for him to have as a coach. He often said that the code Stone Pony and Mister lived by was similar to the coach's code. I couldn't quite pull those together in my own mind, but both appeared to be good influences on my son.

He came straight home from the game. His friends and old teammates were headed to a party at the Refuge. He had to be up by 5:30 a.m. at the latest. Mister and Stone Pony's truck would be in the driveway by 5:50 or earlier, and the garbage run would begin. I was glad he drank coffee now. Black and strong, he preferred. The fifteen to twenty minutes we spent together on Saturday and Sunday mornings as he ate his breakfast, porridge with brown sugar and a little milk in winter, was a perfect time for us. We drank our coffee and talked a little. What was said didn't matter. The quiet time together did.

When he came into the house, I asked him if he wanted a beer with his dear old mom. He laughed. "Sure," he said. "What's up?"

I got the beer out of the fridge and two frosted glasses from the freezer compartment. It made me think of the small freezer he had bought me for Christmas that was down in the basement. It was crammed full of baked goods and store-bought frozen foods that I had never had before, but mostly it stored leftovers. I crammed it because we could, and that felt good. I poured the beers, and as the heads settled, I pushed his envelope across the kitchen table.

"What's this?"

"A Christmas card from your father."

"What's in it?"

In his voice, I heard a whisper of fear, of dread, and of anger. Three little words loaded with emotions. At least that's what I heard or, more accurately, felt.

"I got one, too. Just a Merry Christmas wish."

"What about the girls?"

"No, just you and me."

He turned the envelope over and over in his hands. He looked at the return address several times, shook his head, and seemed to sigh as he mustered the courage to open it. Strange stuff those envelopes stirred in both of us.

"Vancouver?"

I nodded in response to his astonished question. He opened the card. "He even spelled my name right."

We both spewed nervous little snickers as he read the card. He didn't say anything, just put the card back in the envelope, then a big swig of beer.

"Mom, cold beer in a frosted mug with you—nothing better."

Silence. I couldn't stop myself from asking. "What did he say? What's in there?" I put my finger on the envelope.

"Not much. He said he's sorry but not for what. Merry Christmas, love Dad."

"That's it?"

"Well, there is also a very used, very crumpled five-dollar bill."

I didn't know how to respond to that, so I drank some beer. He drained his glass.

"You know what I'm going to do with the five dollars?"

"No, son. I don't have a clue."

"I'm going to get us the best loaf of bread five dollars can buy." He winked at me and laughed. "Mom. I gotta get to bed. Morning comes quickly."

There was something in his voice, his eyes, his manner. I asked him if there was anything else in the card that I should know. He hesitated, then slowly spoke. "He says he's got his act together, and he plans on visiting us in September."

We looked at each other, both of us feeling anger above anything else. Before I could reply, he put his hand on my shoulder. "Mom, he'll never darken our doorway again. I guarantee you that."

With that, he kissed my forehead and headed to bed. I wondered if he would sleep. I knew I wouldn't. "This man, this taker, can't take anything from us, because we have nothing to give him. Can he?" I asked.

He turned, walked toward me, and stooped over as I sprang up, wrapped my arms around his neck, and kissed the deep scar on his cheek. I held him tight and let tears spill from his cheek to his neck. He let go of the hug, but I held both his ever broadening, thickening shoulders and gazed up at him.

"I love you, son. More than ever. You can make me cry and laugh at the same time. Bread? My God, you keep me stable and grounded."

I couldn't say all that I wanted, because I was being strangled by emotion.

"Mom, I love you too, but not more than ever—just deep, and always, and as always. Goodnight."

That was that. Two white envelopes that screamed doom and fear silenced by two cold beers and an expensive loaf of bread. And that was how we rose.

Straight to Hell

Dear God,
My prayers have been few and far between these days.
It's not that I'm not thankful for our rising,
But as I've told you before, I'm not sure if you have much of a hand in any of this—
Seems to be more our own will, strength, and ability to overcome.

Yet in your presence, I fear two white envelopes.
I didn't see them as two white doves guided by your hand to our hearts.
They had a message of love from a messenger filling me with fear and dread.
Remember, forgiveness is yours, not mine, so don't expect that from me.

As for forgiveness being divine,
Well, divine is your realm, not mine.
My heart is soft and bending for those I love.
My heart is wary and on defence against those who have inflicted pain, sorrow, and suffering.

Forgive away, God; that's your way.
I haven't found that path yet, and don't hold your breath on that one.
As if I think you would take the time to think that hard on me.

Our Father, who art in heaven
His father who is Art in Vancouver,
Hallowed be that name,
Thy kingdom come, thy will be done.

His name won't be hallowed, he has no kingdom, maybe just a squalid room and his will,
will never be done to us, on us.
Except for a five-dollar loaf of bread, eleven years too late.
And that, God and my son, is Art Thy Father in a nutshell.
God, please don't let him darken our doorway.
And God forgive me for this—because forgiveness, that is your strong suit—
But Art can go straight to hell.

Amen.

CHAPTER 22

Take a Shot

Here's my thinking. It had been almost three years. Hey, forgive and forget or fuck 'em. I was still alive, and I had this edge-of-destruction lifestyle figured out. Sort of. I had over two thousand dollars in two bank accounts. I stayed sober from noon on Sunday to noon on Tuesday. Mostly. Technically, one might say I was still drunk when I came to on Sundays. On Tuesdays, I would start drinking when I woke up, if there was any hooch left in my place, which was a very unlikely scenario. On Tuesdays, I always woke up optimistic that I had stashed something from the previous Saturday-night binge. So far, I was zero for forever in that category, but what the hell? Tuesday-morning optimism was something to look forward to, especially after being dry for somewhere between fifty to fifty-five hours. On Tuesday morning, I had a great routine. I spruced up a bit. Washed my hair and armpits in the sink, put on clean clothes, because I spent a buck at the laundromat every Monday, washing and drying my things. A bit of a routine and even the folding helped keep me from drinking, filling every second of time until Tuesday morning. I even folded them fairly nicely. A new skill, ha ha! When the liquor stores opened on Tuesday at noon, I liked to be first in line to ensure I got the fresh stuff. I could buy a bottle of 4 Aces that had been moved to the front of the shelf, where they put the good $1.15 stuff. Then I could officially start my week.

There was a bit of an outcry in my community when they raised the price of 4 Aces from a buck five to a buck fifteen. Mostly because what the hell do you rhyme with a buck fifteen? I mean, "Come alive, for a buck five" is such a classic refrain. How do you replace that? Maybe "Wreck your spleen for a buck fifteen?" That's funny, but it's the liver that gets wasted from drinking, not the spleen. Maybe the spleen does take a bit of a shit kicking from drinking this gut rot, so let's go with that. It's catchy. Maybe I'll copyright that phrase or something. Man, I can be funny. "The liver gets wasted." Hell, I'm an equal-opportunity man. Every body part got wasted. No holdouts: we all got shit-faced together.

I could still get Ruby Rouge for a buck ten. That swill turned my tongue red, and sometimes my piss. That was a worry because I didn't know whether I was pissing blood or just having the old RR railway run through me. Such are the concerns of the serious drinker at the lower end of the social ladder. Lower fuckin' end? Hell, I was drunk so often I couldn't even hold the ladder, let it alone go up the fuckin' thing. Ruby Rouge needed a rallying cry. How about, "Get a friend for a buck ten!" I like it! More copyright revenue coming my way.

On Sundays, I went to a church right in the middle of the freakin' disaster zone that was East Hastings. This minister preached to a few lost souls, a special sermon in the church basement at about two in the afternoon. He knew his audience. He knew we were barely getting mobile by then and starting to get hungry. He went on for an hour. He was fervent. He honestly believed he had a chance of saving our souls and getting us back on God's path. He always included that Bible phrase, "They were lost but now they're found." We all looked around and snickered at each other almost every time he said that line. The common belief and truth amongst us was that we weren't lost; we just didn't want to be found. The minister had that all ass backward. A hungry congregation always thought better of correcting the minster because that would just delay chow time. He meant well, so we didn't want to hurt his feelings.

There were six others who were regulars in my little squad. We came for the hot meal afterward mostly. He also allowed us to shower, clean up, and sleep on cots if we needed a late-afternoon nap. We did appreciate the sanctity and the quiet. Besides, after his teachings and a hot meal, both had the effect of making us sleepy. He believed if we stayed sober for twenty-four hours, we'd be on our way to redemption, sobriety, and leading a life of faith.

He liked me because I had committed, sort of, not officially or anything he should count on as a regular thing, to forty-eight hours of weekly sobriety. That good man of God saw me as a pace setter for the Lord. The Mario Andretti of his ministry. The Sandy Hawley of his horse track. I make myself laugh.

I didn't try to fool him, but he kept saying, "Two days this week, three the next." I hadn't made it that far and wouldn't bet on it for love or money. I was a bit of an aberration as it was. None of my Sunday companions, the rummies and rubies of the streets, make it a real twenty-four hours.

The veteran's disability money kept me afloat, and I had cashed in on my knowledge. My six churchgoing companions were all armed services vets. All WWII war heroes, or so we told ourselves. There wasn't one Legion in the Greater Vancouver area that would let us in anymore. We more than burned those bridges. The last few years, we had cleaned up for Remembrance Day with the reverend's help. We instituted a self-imposed twenty-four hours of forced sobriety, took a visit to the local Sally Ann for some new clothes, and after a shower and a scrub in the church basement, off we went. November tenth was the day of our annual haircut and shave in preparation for the ceremonies on the eleventh. We were a solemn respectful bunch until about 12:30, a full hour and a half after the equally solemn Remembrance Day ceremony. By then, we were achingly thirsty. We knew a tray or maybe two of draft was going to land on our table, free of charge. They made us eat a bunch of sandwiches and soup before the beer flowed. We truly enjoyed the meal, knowing the bread would sop up the beer—or so we told ourselves. This was a myth of the rummies!

We also had war memories. We focused on the pleasant ones at first. A baseball game in the Netherlands, a spectacular whore in France, and some mess hall camaraderie. We chatted often about the excitement we felt when enlisting, through training, and the boat trip over the pond. The pride of fighting for God and country as young, adventurous men. Unfortunately, we found little pride in the actual fighting. It was the illusion of doing something noble that we were proud of until we got there. The fighting was hell, and most of us were scared and just wanted to get home.

After the beer flowed, someone in our little squad of "down and outs" would toast a fallen companion. We all felt obligated to follow suit. The toasts were solemn, real, and heartfelt. Then we slid into the oblivion of loss followed by pain, then anger at the government for forgetting us. The paltry allowance that we had to get by on. We retold some of the horrors that we lived through, and that set off another round of the fuckin' government fuckin' us over. As our voices ascended, our ire built, and our language descended. The veterans, who had managed to put together a good life, and their families started to take exception to our behaviour. We were more or less gently guided out of the hall until next November eleventh.

Most years, the ladies' auxiliary put together a care package for us. The package had toothpaste, a toothbrush, deodorant, and usually a new twelve-pack of underwear. They must have thought we shit our pants a lot or didn't know how to wipe our asses, which wasn't far off the mark when we got incredibly fucked up. As well, there were three or four sandwiches, cookies, and a container of soup. Depending on the year and the Legion Hall, there were other things like combs and socks, which we really appreciated.

After a couple of free trays of draft beer, we would combine resources and buy a third before anyone noticed. Twenty draft beer for three bucks, and we tipped a quarter. I collected fifty cents from each of my six companions to buy the tray. Shockingly, I was the most presentable of the crew, and the hard-assed bartender was most likely to sell me the draft. I also didn't pay. The bartender said the round was on him. He was probably showing generosity to compensate for the numerous occasions he had pummeled on all of us with his meaty fists, just for stumbling into his Legion. I pocketed the money and referred to it as danger pay because sometimes the bartender gives me a swat just on principle. He called it preventative medicine. He figured if he smacked me first and I got a taste for what was coming if I acted up in his bar, I'll be less inclined to do so. He wasn't wrong.

It wasn't a scam, although those guys thought so at the beginning. They took some convincing. I'd set the six guys up to receive their benefits. With the help of Reverend Righteous, we had bank accounts for all the boys, and we all lived in the same building. Still $175 a month for rent. We had established a bit of a preservation society. I handled their accounts. The reverend and I installed the $500 bottom-line safety net. Them sons of bitches, rat bastard, sisters-in-law weren't wrong on that one. I made their cash withdrawals every Tuesday.

We'd go together to the bank and then to the reverend, then back to our building. We all took out fifty dollars. Twenty stayed in our pockets, twenty to the minister. He kept it for us until Friday. Rationing, we called it, just like war time. Every week, where we lived was like war time. Other rummies and the druggies would beat us for a dime. A low cash-on-hand position was good for our health. We got the reputation of never having a dime, so beating us up wasn't worth the time. People had to conserve their energy on Subsistence Street. Couldn't get blood from a stone. We were cagey veterans in our own minds.

The other ten dollars was hidden, mostly from ourselves, in hidey holes in our rooms. We were by far the most spendthrift drunks in the Lower Mainland. I charged them a service fee of seven bucks a month. I kept them organized, and like good soldiers, they followed the line. One of them would break someday, and I'd likely get beat to hell for their passbooks. They couldn't withdraw money from their accounts without me, and I couldn't withdraw money on my own from their accounts. They trusted me. Good soldiers. They called me Sergeant. I liked that.

I had a revelation; well, not really. I had reinvented myself. I was a freakin' war hero. I should have gotten the Purple Star. I was in hospital in Italy, wounded in action. Honest. Whorehouse action. I got gonorrhea. A purple dick, something like that. Purple Star, Purple Dick. Six of this, six of that. Comme-ci, comme-ça.

I was in France, too. Saw some good whorehouse action there. Eighteen AWOLs in three years of military service. I think I set a record.

On the street, people knew I was in the Italian and French campaigns. Wounded in action. Hospitalized in Italy. A freakin' war hero. Whether they believed it or not, well, who gave a fuck? The myth was out there, and that story had saved me a beating or two.

The veteran disability benefits had allowed me to keep my sticks and stones together for over three years. I was managing the streets and as organized as a rummy could imagine or fathom.

I also had a plan. In March, I was going to embark on a path to seventy-two hours of sobriety, maybe increasing my sobriety in four- to six-hour bits until I hit seventy-two hours. My ultimate goal was half a week without a drink, Sunday 8 a.m. until Wednesday 8 a.m. My target date was July, the month of my son's birthday. Then, in September, I'd return home. A freakin' war hero. Three grand in my bank account. The train ride without stops was three and a half days. I sent my son and my wife Christmas cards. Very late, but it's the thought that counts, ha ha!

I wrote only to my son that I'd have two grand when I came home in September. Hedging my bets, given my track record. No sense telling my wife. I had lied to her and let her down almost our entire life. I could've told her I didn't chase skirts anymore. Mostly because I can't, but that was a detail nobody needed to know.

I wrote the cards because I realized I was on a short track to a short end or a fast track to a fast end. It was going to be my last great chance.

Was it fat, slim, or none? I wouldn't have bet love or money on my chances. Even for a war hero.

CHAPTER 23

The Business

Newspaper Crew Enterprises Incorporated was the overall name of the business. Two other companies were created that were owned by the Newspaper Crew. They were Neapolitan Sanitation Services and Cottage Country Consolidated Services.

It was Ms. Annamoosie doing the talking. We had been told not to take notes and just listen.

Mister and Stone Pony had a few goals in mind when they set up their corporate structure. First and foremost was to create business entities with opportunities for everyone in the room. "I'm going to run you through what has happened to date, what is happening, and what the future may hold," Ms. Annamoosie said. "Some of you, like the FBI, know bits and pieces all ready. For all of you, there will be revelations."

We all were very content and relaxed after our big Hawaiian New Year's Feast. Ms. Annamoosie had our attention.

"Neapolitan Sanitation Services and Cottage Country Consolidated Services are fully owned subsidiaries of Newspaper Crew Enterprises. We're going to call Neapolitan Sanitation Services 'NSS' for short; Newspaper Crew Enterprises Incorporated 'NCE' for short, and Cottage Country Consolidated Services 'CCCS' for short. Got it?"

There were general nods all around as Mister walked to the centre of the room and placed a flip chart to the right of Ms. Annamoosie. The flip chart sheet was titled "Organization Chart" and simply had NCE at the top in a square box with a straight line down that branched out and then down to two other square boxes, with NSS and CCCS written in them.

"NCE owns one hundred percent of NSS and CCCS. NSS has entered a contract with the town to provide garbage removal for approximately forty-five percent of the residential business and twenty-five percent of the commercial businesses. The contract starts May first, coinciding with the start of the town's fiscal year or business year. The commencement of the contract also coincides with the retirements of two current sanitation workers or garbage men, as they're commonly called."

This last statement concerning retirement was a bit of a surprise, especially to me, as I knew who those men were. There wasn't one of the eight other current garbage men over the age of sixty, which was way younger than the retirement age of sixty-five.

"NSS has purchased one of the town's existing garbage trucks and purchased a very modern truck of its own with hydraulic crushing and compacting capability. Emerson is president of NSS and Webster is vice president. They will operate one of the trucks and conduct the City Hall paper removal on Wednesdays that Stone Pony and Mister have done the last few years. The contract is for five years. The Brownies, Seamus and Patrick, will be operating the old city truck, and their route is the South Ward. The FBI has the West Ward route."

It figured. NSS had the poor cousin wards. We wouldn't want Indians and half-Indians in the richer parts of the city. Keeping the "White Paper Trail" was a bit of a surprise. The "White Paper Trail" consisted of all the city documents that needed to be destroyed. They were taken to the dump and burned immediately. Those would be two fucking big Indians in the almost total whiteness of that building.

"We'll be using the elevator at City Hall," Emerson said.

Now that was some extraordinary news. The previous City Hall paper disposal crew, consisting of Mister, Stone Pony, and occasionally, me, had to use the stairs. There were going to be some tight white-assed sphincters on those elevator rides.

"We negotiated the elevator," Ms. Annamoosie continued. "All four employees of NSS will be paid higher than the city's employees and will have the equivalent of the city's health benefit and pension plan, if not better."

Mild laughter and wide smiles broke from the normally reserved faces in the room.

"NSS's overall objective by the end of the contract is to secure all garbage routes and services currently operated by the city, including management of the refuse facility, commonly known as the dump. NSS's charter, which includes its business bylaws, allows it to expand into other services and areas. Any questions about NSS operations?"

The Brownies had obviously known this was coming, and they shook their heads. Zachary Whitmore had a question; "Where the hell did the money come from to buy the trucks?"

Ms. Annamoosie supplied the answer. It wasn't straightforward or crystal clear. "NSS will lease the trucks from NCE. NCE had capital savings and leveraged the five-year contract for a favourable interest rate on a commercial loan for the balance."

That answer was like the expanding ripples on a lake's surface when a trout jumps for a fly. We knew how it was done, but where did that fish come from, and how big was it?

"The loan is long term, and the payments are easily covered. NSS will be profitable from the get-go."

Zeke Whitmore had the next question. "How the hell did you guys get a contract with that old conservative mayor and councillor, Sideburns? There's no way they make a deal with a black man and a red man. You know those fucks called you the Lone Nigger and Tonto, right?"

Ms. Annamoosie again answered in a clear-as-mud way. "Mister and Stone Pony leveraged their historical business relationship with city council and administration, as well as their knowledge, intimate knowledge, of city contracts, past and current city deals, and insight into how the mayor, some councillors, and administrators conduct business."

That answer was still mud, but now we knew that our corporate leaders understood the mud. Stone Pony and Mister had dirt, probably piles of it. Stinking, steamy piles of dirty shit-filled mud on those pompous city assholes. The white boys were dirty. Stone Pony and Mister had somehow ciphered through all that city paper being disposed of weekly and found ... what was that word Ms. Annamoosie used? Leverage. Lovely legal shit. Leverage. My new favourite word. Man, Scarecrow and Bogeyman, my whacked-out, world-travelling friends, now *there's* a one-hundred-dollar word. Leverage.

Ms. Annamoosie acknowledged the knowing smiles around the darkening room. "No more questions. Let's move on. CCCS will operate outside the city and will provide the garbage collection, snow plowing, and firewood provision, as it currently does. This change is now a more formalized new business entity of what already exists. Mister and Stone Pony will be co-presidents of CCCS. Within CCCS will be a subsidiary company. That company will provide mechanical and repair work to all equipment under the NCE umbrella. This company is ZZE, an acronym for Zach and Zeke Enterprises."

Mister flipped the page on the flip chart, and ZZE was labelled on a box beneath CCCS.

"Zach and Zeke will operate ZZE. They will be the co-managing partners. CCCS will lease all equipment previously owned by Stone Pony and Mister from NCE, who now holds title to that equipment. ZZE's equipment and facilities will be leased from NCE as well. In the beginning, the Whities will operate roughly fifty percent of the garbage business and seventy-five percent of snow plowing and firewood provision. Stone Pony and Mister will operate the rest. Scarface will be employed by NCE and will be available for all business units."

Mister flipped to yet another page.

"Black and Red Security is what is known as a holding company or parent company. It was created for legal and tax purposes. On all official documents, B and R doesn't have a name, just numbers. The numbers are the business number of the company provided by the government when the business is established. B and R is owned by Mister and Stone Pony. Please flip the page, Mister.

"Clampett Security has been formed as the security arm of B and R and all NCE entities. It has two functions. The first, as you know, will be providing security services to homeowners and businesses in cottage country, similar to what is now provided. The second function is to provide security services for all the other businesses in the NCE group. This includes personal security services for all key operators, the people in this room, and their families.

"Clampett Security does not and will not have any employees. All work provided by CS will be contracted out. The primary contractor is our own Mr. Clampett. He is contracted through another numbered company. CS has a broad and ambiguous charter, which simply means they can operate and provide a whole kaleidoscope of expanding, different, and new goods and services that present as opportunities or needs arise for the NCE group. This allows for growth without changing the focus and core business operations for NCE, CCCS, NCS, and ZZE. That's all you need to know for the legal setup."

My head was spinning. An ambiguous kaleidoscope of operations. Two four-syllable words I had to start using in this situation, and I actually already knew their meaning. The room was quiet and reflective until Mr. Clampett, the captain, broke the ice.

"Remember, don't any of you fucks call me Mr. Clampett." The following laughter lightened the mood.

Then Stone Pony stood up and took over the room. "We start all this for real tomorrow. Mister and I have very serious intentions of growing a monster of a business, although you all have different roles and titles, and beneath all the company names, numbers, and organizational charts, we basically run pails, chop wood, plow snow, keep equipment running, and look after people's homes.

"There are two more business items to take care of today. One is a personal commitment letter or contract for each of you. The most important element in these letters is the non-disclosure clause, which says you're not allowed to disclose or discuss anything ever about NCE and all of this. You will also note that B and R isn't mentioned, and as far as you're concerned, it doesn't exist, and you have never heard of it. This is for the good of us all, especially if anything ever went batshit crazy."

Without knowing the intricacies of business law or holding companies, all the key operators knew, somehow, this made sense. Me too. Call it intuition, premonition, whatever.

"You need to read, sign and hand that letter to Cecilia," Stone Pony concluded. "Take your time."

The letters were read, signed, and handed to Ms. Annamoosie in less than five minutes. Captain never got a letter.

"The second business matter is in these envelopes. This is a letter of thanks from Mister and me. Open it after you leave. We don't want to see grown men and one white boy crying. Don't thank us—yet! There are some instructions accompanying the small gift in each of your envelopes. That's it. Cecilia, please pass the envelopes around." Captain got one this time.

The gathering broke up shortly thereafter. I was getting a ride back to town with the Whities. We opened our packages as soon as we got in the car. So did the FBI and the Brownies. I don't know which one of the other cars the first joyous whoop came from, but it was followed by more. Zeke got out of the car and started howling at the moon. He almost bumped into Captain standing beside the car. Then Zach was out howling. Car doors opened, and seven large men were all laughing and howling away! Mister, Stone Pony, and Ms. Annamoosie were on the cabin's massive porch. I could see their smiles and feel the warmth radiating from those two men, who had created all the commotion.

I just sat in the back seat like a little boy and started to cry and laugh.

The envelope contained a letter with the following instructions. "Bank deposits to be made weekly or better, biweekly in discriminate, small-scale increments of $50–$150. No flashing your cash. No more than $200 on you at any time. No flashy purchases." It also contained $5,000 in twenties, tens, and fives.

Five thousand bucks will make you stop and think. A lot. Like, where does $40,000 in small bills come from? It was like ransom money, when the kidnappers asked for ransom money in small, unmarked bills. At least according to the cop shows and detective movies that was how kidnappers wanted to be paid.

I knew that a lot of Stone Pony and Mister's customers for garbage, firewood, snowplowing, and security services were paying in cash. In fact, that's how the founders of Newspaper Crew Enterprises asked and preferred to be paid. Most customers had no problem with that. So, that much cash was more than possible considering the growth of the business.

When I was thinking through the whole set of businesses, the city contract, and the cash, I thought I should screw college or university and go to work for NCE full time. Soon. Maybe pack in high school after this year, with a grade twelve high school graduation certificate.

I mentioned this to Mister and Stone Pony on Valentine's Day during our weekend garbage run. Their reaction was instant, intense, and definite. Between these two normally stoic and calm men they laid out, very emotionally and emphatically, my "recommended" course of action. Succinctly, it was suggested I finish not only grade twelve but also grade thirteen, then on to university for a business degree, followed by law school. It was clear they had mapped out most of my next decade without any need for my input. Stone Pony had been struggling mightily for a long time to not use the word "fuck" or any of its derivatives (that's a ten-buck word from math class) for a long time. All his "non-fuck" vocabulary efforts were destroyed in about thirty seconds after my comment on achieving my grade twelve as the pinnacle of my academic career. Mister was spouting off unintended rhymes like a jukebox poet. I had set off a maelstrom of verbal violence centered on the idiocy of my suggested academic path.

When the shit-storm settled, and the narrative of "fuck that" and poetic "put me on the right path" finished, then and only then did I timidly and with a smile on my face say, "But how do you really feel?"

Those two men, who I greatly admired, looked perplexed for a second, then broke into grins—small grins, but grins nevertheless. Thank God.

Stone Pony took that small joke as the impetus for a more rational explanation for my academic career. "Listen, you little white fuck, we have big plans for our growth and business venture. We, meaning Mister, the Neapolitan Crew, Mr. Clampett, and Ms. Annamoosie, who all want you to be part of that. What NCE and all these good people don't need is a fuckin' smart garbage boy. We need a fucker who learns business and law and can help the business grow. Right now, you're our designated smart fucker. You got some fuckin' brains, and you should want to use that fuckin' gift to its maximum, you stupid fuck."

Mister picked up the thread from there. "Anybody can run barrels, but doing that puts you in peril. Not accomplishing what you could. Not being all that you should. NCE will need business and legal smarts, not someone who doesn't give two farts. We believe you can be great, and we got zero tolerance for you being second rate."

I was getting their drift. Stone Pony continued with their plan. He was calmer, and the F-word disappeared. "We know you're smart, Scarface. You're not working hard enough at school. Look how hard all the Neapolitan Crew had to work to get some education. You have the straight road, and we will support you, but you must bear down and do the work and get the degrees. We're going to give you all the opportunity in the world, so don't fuck it up with any drop-out-of-school nonsense or other bullshit."

I had to say something. "Guys, I love working with you—always have, always will. I want to be a part of NCE big time, full time, but I'm not even eighteen, and I have trouble planning one week at a time, and you just spat out a ten-year plan for my life! I don't even know what I want or what I want to be. There are a few things I know and feel deep down. Can I share these with you? It would mean a lot to me."

Mister and Stone Pony looked at each other, then nodded.

"Here goes. Top of the list, I need to take care of my mom and sisters and make sure they're safe and doing well. Everything else is second. Is that clear?"

"That's what we would expect," Stone Pony replied. "Nothing less, and we respect that."

"OK then, if I go away to school, how do I do that? Keep them safe, protect them, look out for them, provide for them?"

"We would be honoured to share the responsibility of taking care of your family, keeping them safe and secure," Mister said. "You have our pledge on that. Our pledge extends to the Neapolitan Crew and Mr. Clampett. We will bond to protect all our families. We'll have your family in our arms when you're away to learn. You heard part of that commitment at Christmas dinner."

I believed that instantly. These were all men of their word, and their bond was sure to be unbreakable.

"Second, I appreciate your confidence in me and your vision," I continued. "I would never want to let you down, but I don't know if I can do all of this. University? Business school, then law school? What if I'm not smart enough or can't get into these schools and programs? I can't promise you I can succeed or that I'll even want to go on that path."

Mister shook his head. "We believe you can. We know you're smart enough, and we have seen how you can work with people. To tell the truth, we don't know if you can do this. What we do know is you have a good head and a good heart. Our support won't waver. Ever. We ask you to try. We want you to succeed. We know you will struggle at times, but we believe you can do anything you set your will and your mind to."

The solemn, quiet, calm manner with which Mister spoke, affirmed by Stone Pony's solemn expression, full of both compassion and confidence, almost brought me to tears.

"Third and last thing. I stay involved with NCE through all this schooling."

Stone Pony replied for them and NCE. "You signed one contract with us already. We'll create another contract for employment and education funds. That contract will detail what your employer, NCE, will fund regarding your education costs. You will be financially comfortable as a student. We fully expect you to work with NCE on a continual basis, as full time as possible during school breaks, and part time continuously."

"Scarface, the academic part of your contract will have expected results in terms of grades," Mister added. "NCE will pay you bonuses for achieving certain academic goals. These start immediately."

Stone Pony filled in some more of my future landscape. "Ms. Annamoosie will have the contract for you to review next Sunday after we run barrels. We have given this a lot of thought, and we hope you do. It's a good deal, but you're going to have to prove for the better part of a decade that you're a smart fuck."

"Is that exact wording in the contract?" I had to ask.

"What?" Stone Pony replied, looking a little confused.

"Is it in the contract specifically that I need to be a smart fuck or is that sort of just implied?" I smiled broadly at my question.

"We can add that terminology if you like, with a related clause that requires you not to be a smart ass." Mister said with an emphasis on the "smart ass" part. We were all laughing, but more important was the look in those two men's eyes. That look told me they had unbelievable confidence in me and were backing that belief with their actions and commitments. More important than their words, their bond and their vow to support were given, and I knew that was solid, trustworthy, and honest.

My next comment was from the heart. "I'm in. Just show me where to sign, and I promise both of you I'll do everything to live up to your expectations."

"We know," they said in unison.

And that was that.

CHAPTER 24

Winter Wonderland

Ms. Librarian and I were going on our second date. Valentine's Day. It was a big deal, at least for me. For her? I wasn't so sure. She had boys hanging around the library just to look at her. At least ten guys I knew of had asked her out. She seemingly only went on "dates" where there were a group of people going out to a party or the movies or some other public setting. Our first date was a bowling party with seven other couples. Her father dropped her off and picked her up. Not much chance for romance.

She made my palms sweat and my mouth dry. I know those are clichés, but those are a couple of the more obvious reactions I had around her. Her name was Kristine. Everybody called her Kris or Krissy.

We were going to Angelo's, an Italian restaurant. Her father was going to drop her off. I phoned and asked her dad if I could walk her home. I said we were bringing our skates and that our plan was to go skating at the outdoor rink at Sir John A. McDonald Square, which we called JAMS for short. JAMS was famous for its ball fields, the Dairy Queen adjacent to JAMS, and, of course, the invasion of Mr. Murphy's prized Holstein milkers a couple of years back. That incident may or may not have involved my good friends Bogeyman and Scarecrow. The clean-up of the fields, after the cows had created a prodigious amount of cow crap, involved B and S, under my supervision. Kristine's father hesitated, appeared to think it over, and finally said yes, and highly recommended a curfew of 11:30. That was thirty minutes later than I had expected.

Her dad dropped Kristine off at 6:50 p.m. I had been standing outside Angelo's since 6:37 p.m. I wasn't quite frozen, and at least my palms had stopped sweating.

She wore a maroon coat and a matching hat. Her skates were covered by pink skate warmers. I thought the pink clashed with the maroon. No, I didn't. I looked at her, and I couldn't think of anything. This was crazy. I had previously had sex with six women, including the twenty-three-year-old former Snow Queen, two blondes in a bug from BC on the seventh hole of several golf courses, and Woman, so it wasn't that type of experience that worried me. It was the experience of feeling like I was really falling for someone. Maybe it was infatuation. She made my heart beat faster. Another lame but true cliché.

We said hello and then walked into the restaurant's enclosed porch. I held the door open for her. Kristine entered, turned, and dropped her skates on the floor, then looked me straight in the eyes. "Let's get this over with right now, so we can both relax."

I thought for sure she was going to say she liked me but thought we could just be good friends. My hopes were going to get dashed early and quick.

"Look, I'm nervous, and there's only one way to do this," she said. "So, kiss me right now. I like you, so kiss me right now and then we don't have to worry about it all through dinner."

I started to mumble something, but Kristine leaned in and kissed me. Our lips brushed, and she pulled back a little. "Good start. Gentle, not too urgent. Now kiss me."

So, I did. We did. Our lips moved together softly but with intent. We pulled back and then kissed again more firmly, and she moved her mouth a little to the side. That movement, that incremental increase in friction, was electric or something.

She pulled back and looked me in the eyes. "That was nice. No, that was good, very good, better than I expected. I like your lips on mine. I'm hungry and curious about you. Let's go in."

I was mush. A puppy dog who didn't know what to do next. I felt like if I had a tail, I would have chased it in circles and been deliriously happy, because at that moment, I was deliriously happy.

We hung our coats and were ushered to our table. It was a table for two, right in the dead centre of the restaurant. We were in the spotlight—no, more like the stoplight, because it was the major traffic route from the kitchen, the bar, and the bathrooms. Our table was going to be the furthest thing from a quiet, romantic dinner for two. Once we were sitting and sized up the situation, Kristine leaned in close. "I think my dad arranged the seating. You won't be able to try anything funny out here at centre ice."

We both laughed, and it was good and felt natural and real. Kristine just kept breaking the ice. She reached over and took my hand. That's when Tony Z charged our table. Tony was a big Italian kid in grade twelve with me. He was an offensive lineman and perspired twenty-four seven. His last name did not start with a Z, but he declared himself to be Tony Z to differentiate himself from all the other Italian Tonys in town. The small Italian community in our town apparently lacked creativity in naming their offspring.

"Hey, you two lovebirds, this is a family restaurant." That was his intro. He motioned to our clasped hands and then broke into a bad Italian accent. "You make a man sweat just a lookin' at you." He laughed at his own joke. "Me and Mike A will be waiting on you tonight. I do all the work, and he gets the credit, just like in football."

Mike A was a slick, fast wide receiver. He called himself Mike A because he was the best, and all the darn Caucasians called their kids Mike, whether Protestant or Catholic. Seemed to him that Mike was the only sensible name the Caucasians could think of. Mike A was in charge of our table, Tony, the assistant. Mike A was slick on and off the field. He had that proverbial twinkle in his eyes. He hit the table talking.

"Well, isn't it nice to have the king and queen of the prom visit our humble establishment? You're both eighteen, right? Good. Just needed to ask. Tony and I'll have your evening and dining experience covered from A to Z—get it? Yeah, you're both smart; you get the A-to-Z reference. That's one of my best lines."

Kristine seemed a bit overwhelmed, but she smiled. "If that's one of your best lines, you need to work on your material."

We all laughed as Mike A faked a look of shock and dismay, then fired right back up. "Quick, intelligent, and beautiful. My only question is, what are you doing here with this mutt? Never mind. In some things, there's no accounting for taste. Speaking of which, if you allow me, Monsieur Scarface and Miss Lady Librarian, I'll gladly guide you through the menu and recommend a great dinner for you."

Kristine nodded enthusiastically, which Mike A picked up on and used for a put-down. "Wise choice, Miss Lady Librarian, as this dolt would probably have ordered a double pepperoni pizza. I, on the other hand, will guide you to a truly memorable culinary experience. The rest of the evening is up to Scarface to make memorable, Miss Lady Librarian, and I hope you do not have high expectations. I'm suggesting Caesar salad made fresh at your table by the only guy really suited to be at the end of the alphabet, the constantly perspiring Tony Z. Additionally, I highly recommend a bottle of Mateus, despite being from Portugal and not Italian, as the perfect beverage to accompany your meal. Good? Excellent. Great choices, Scarface. I'll come back with the wine, and after the salad has been served, I'll recommend the main course."

Mike A smiled and winked, and then left. Kristine and I were a little dumbfounded by the pace that Mike A set in making our choices for us. I looked at Kristine with a mixture of wonder, doubt, and bewilderment. My mouth opened, and words tumbled out. "I don't even know if you drink or like Caesar salad."

"I drink a little. Let's hope the skating will wear off the wine, and I have a whole pack of gum to cover my breath. I've never had a Caesar salad, so this makes dinner even more exciting." Kristine was glowing.

"I've never had a Caesar salad either, or Mateus, so we're in the same boat. I have a whole pack of gum too, but honestly, that was for my breath if I got the chance to kiss you. And for the record, I was going to suggest a pepperoni pizza for dinner."

We both laughed, and I realized once again that I was smitten with Ms. Lady Librarian.

"Kristine, what will your dad do if he finds out we've been drinking? I mean, we can send the wine back."

"No, that's fine, all good. Dad knows I've had the occasional drink. So, as long as I'm not staggering or slurring, all will be good. What will your father think? Oh, sorry. Sorry, sorry." Her eyes began to mist up, and she looked totally despondent and innocent at that moment.

"Listen, no problem. My dad never thinks about us, and he even forgot the loaf of bread last time I saw him."

"What does that mean? The loaf of bread?"

"That's a story for another time. More important is what my mother will think."

"Which is?"

"She will ask if the young lady had too much to drink, and if her parents are OK with her having a drink. And was I respectful of the young lady? Then I'll have to burst her bubble by telling her that the young lady accosted me in the restaurant's porch and forced kisses upon me and drank the wine like water."

"You wouldn't tell your mom that, would you?"

"Of course not."

"Speaking of that, please lean over the table."

"Why, Kristine? Are you going to hit me for trying to be funny?"

"No. Lean in and kiss me again."

I did, and as corny as it sounds, the evening was feeling magical. Mike A arrived right then.

"Hey, I thought Toni Z admonished you two already. This is a family restaurant, but romance is good for business. Except the two couples over there in the power corner are clicking their tongues in disapproval. My Uncle Tony, Toni Z's father, says Presbyterians like those folks were born with a board up their ass and wouldn't know joy if it landed in their frozen laps. So, here's the Mateus. This is a vintage bottle, probably corked three months ago. The Portuguese get grapes from wine to bottle to your lips in record time."

Mike A went about the business of opening the wine with the flair I would expect from him. He asked me to taste the wine. I did. He asked if the wine was to my satisfaction, which it was. He filled our glasses and told us Toni Z would be right there to make our salads. I wasn't sure what that even meant.

"Kristine, I hope you like the wine. I don't have a clue whether it tastes like it should."

"Let's toast."

"To what?"

"Well, let's start small. To a great evening. To a culinary adventure. To wonderful first kisses."

"That's a lot for starting small."

"Yes it is, but it's a wonderful short list that we can grow."

I was thunderstruck. *Grow? I think she likes me. Grow? Oh, God, please.*

"To us then and growing our list."

We clinked glasses and drank.

Kristine took an initial sip, then another and another. "This is very good, kind of sweet—or maybe it's the company." She laughed and stared into my eyes.

"Definitely the company. Let's toast again."

"What to?"

"Leaning across the table and kissing."

"Are you going to kiss me again? Right here at centre ice, with the Presbyterian referees' disapproving glares?"

"Yes. We need to see how far we can get those boards jammed up their asses."

Kristine laughed so hard she snorted. We leaned in, kissed, clinked our glasses, and drank our wine.

Toni Z arrived, or I swear I would have been out of my chair and hugging Kristine like the infatuated schoolboy I was.

"Hey, you two, cool it a bit, or get a room. The Presbyterians are going to have heart attacks. I know first aid, but the effort to save them probably isn't worth the tip they would leave. These holier-than-thou tight-asses throw nickels around like they're manhole covers. Now let's get to the making of the salads. Your first Caesar, right?"

We both nodded.

"Now, you gotta have it the right way. So, watch and be in awe. First, the anchovies."

"Anchovies? What are anchovies?" Kristine asked.

Tony Z had wheeled a cart over with all the ingredients. He had a big wooden bowl to make the salad in. He picked up something from a small bowl that looked slimy.

"A small fish that is a delicacy. We coat the wooden bowl with the anchovies for flavour. Don't ask what it tastes like, because it tastes like anchovies. Don't say you don't want it, because then you would have to leave my restaurant."

"OK, OK, Toni, we'll have the anchovies," I said, as both Kristine and I laughed.

"Now the raw egg."

Kristine gave out a little "ew" sound, but Toni Z just kept going and whipped the egg, then smeared it around the bowl.

"Now the main ingredient, the romaine lettuce, crisp, fresh, and chilled. I'll cut the leaves a little. Croutons and our house blend of cheese and a little of our special house Caesar dressing. Voila, this is your Caesar salad."

Tony Z held up the bowl when he finished for us to admire. As he did, I noticed that a number of tables were staring in our direction. Toni Z had prepared our salad with flair and an exaggerated exertion. I was a little amazed and quite impressed by the style, grace, and confidence that Mike A and Toni Z demonstrated. They were just high-schoolers like us. Toni Z put the salad on plates using a long wooden fork and spoon. This he also did with flair. A few tables clapped in appreciation when he finished. We joined in, as we had no experience as to how to respond. A man at a table behind us got up and stuffed a couple of dollars in Toni Z's white shirt pocket and said, "Thanks for the show, son."

In my mind, the night kept getting more and more absurdly magical. Kristine must have been having the same thoughts. "I think I love anchovies, raw eggs, and croutons, despite the fact that I have never had any of them before," she said. "This is magical."

"My thoughts exactly. I haven't had those things either. What if we don't like Caesar salad?"

"We will."

And we did. We ate with amazed enjoyment. Mike A swung by, topped off our wine glasses, and checked to see if Toni Z had made a great salad. We assured him that Toni Z had done a marvelous job.

"But how would we know?" Kristine asked. "This is our first Caesar salad ever—but we love it. Thank you for ordering for us."

"That's good. Now that I have won your trust with the Mateus and Caesar salad, I have a very strong recommendation for your entree. Veal parmigiana."

"What's that?" I asked. It sounded off the charts to me. It was then that I realized that neither Mike A nor Tony Z had brought a menu to our table.

"Trust me; it's delicious. My personal favourite. Only my mother makes a better one. At least that's what I tell her to keep peace at home. I asked the chef to save the last two pieces of veal for you two, so just say yes. Scarface, your role here is easy; just say yes."

I looked at Kristine as she said yes for both of us.

"Scarface, you're in the presence of intellect and beauty. No, not me, stupid—but yes, that is true as well. Miss Lady Librarian, of course. Try not to screw this up."

When Mike A left, Kristine got a very serious look on her face. "There's one thing we need to clear up that will help this evening a great deal—and it has been wonderful so far."

"OK, what is it? And I had better not screw this up!"

She giggled. "No one calls you by your real name. It's Scarface or Garbage Boy, but no one calls you by your real name. I'd like to. Would that be OK?"

I had been living with my nicknames and accepting them for almost five years. She was right. Nobody called me by my first name. Well, a few did. My mother, the vice principal, and my hockey coach. Even teachers called me Scarface, and some people just referred to me as GB.

"Yes, you can."

"OK, then lean in and kiss me again, William!"

I did lean in. The kiss was soft, and I know this is hard to believe, but it was full of meaning for me. Never had I thought or hoped that my name could sound so good. I guess all the fear, guilt, and shame I felt negated any thought of my own name sounding good to my ears. My name coming off those lips just before I kissed them. It was too good to be happening to me.

"Kristine?"

"Yes, William?"

"I'm experiencing an emotional tidal wave over here. My name from your lips sounded so right. Not like I could ever imagine it would. I have been so wrapped up in guilt, fear, anger, and all kinds of self-doubt that I didn't even like the sound of my own name. I preferred Scarface, Garbage Boy, and GB because they had an aura of notoriety and distanced me from, well, me. Does that make any sense?"

"More than a little, and given what I know about your life, it is certainly understandable. I know we have only known each other a little while, but for some reason, I have tremendous belief in you and care about you deeply. And this is way too early in our relationship to be saying things like that."

"Kristine, thank you for your belief and faith. I'll earn it. I promise."

"The Presbyterians are leaving, so kiss me again, William, just to shock them before they go home to be all pious and pass judgment on us."

I kissed Kristine again. That was five times in total before the main course had even arrived. That would shock the shit out of the Presbyterians.

The veal parmigiana arrived, and we smiled as Mike A presented our plates and described the dish and the accompanying pasta. Toni Z dropped a steaming basket of garlic bread on our table and winked. "On the house," he said. We stared at the meal and then at each other and dug in.

"Best meal I've ever tasted" Kristine uttered.

"Best company with the best meal ever!" I replied.

"That's a little cheesy, but so is the veal parmigiana, so I'll let your cheesiness slide."

"How gracious of you, Miss Lady Librarian."

Before we could say another thing, Mike A arrived and asked us how our meals were. We told him they were delicious. He topped off our wine glasses, draining the Mateus bottle. We looked at each other and then spontaneously raised our glasses for a toast.

"To us," Kristine said.

I smiled. "Yes, that's the perfect toast—perfect like you."

"You're the cheese-meister!" she replied, laughing.

"I am, but truthfully, cheesy or not, this is perfect—and from where I sit, so are you."

"That's enough smooth talk, mister. Even a lady librarian can get a swollen head if you keep up the compliments." As Kristine said that, she made a motion with her hands that seemed to say, *Bring it on.* We laughed and ate the rest of our meal in relative silence. The portions were large. Tony Z came by and put half of Kristine's veal, some pasta, and a couple of slices of garlic bread in a take-out container. Almost as soon as Toni Z left, Mike A arrived with what looked like two bowls of ice cream.

"Spumoni. To call it ice cream would be a sin. Perfect dessert to end the meal.

I knew you would want to end with perfection, so I took the liberty of serving the spumoni. Angelo's is the only place in town and probably within fifty miles that serves spumoni. Enjoy!"

We did. Mike A came by and presented the bill.

"This is your Mateus bottle and a red candle. You put the candle in the Mateus bottle and let the wax melt down the sides of the bottle. Something that some folks feel is very romantic and marks a special occasion."

When Mike A left, Kristine leaned in close. "Can I please have the bottle and the candle?"

"Yes, of course."

"William, can you afford this? Can I give you some money to help pay?"

"Kristine, thank you, but I have it covered. I received a nice bonus from my bosses a couple of weeks ago."

We got up, and I went to the cashier to pay. The bill was for sixty-seven dollars. I had never spent that in my life, or even close to that. I had over three hundred in my wallet, and when I opened it, the wad of cash was noticed by the cashier and Kristine. After paying, I walked back to the table and left a ten and a five.

Ten percent was the normal good tip. The fifteen dollars I left was more than double that standard. Mike A called me a big roller when we saw each other at school on Monday.

We got our coats on, picked up our skates, and headed out into the cold. Kristine wrapped her arms around my right arm and hugged me close. I was holding both sets of skates and the take-out bag in my left hand, but the only sensation I felt was the warmth of Kristine's body pressing into my arm and my side.

"This has been a perfect evening so far. I hope my poor skating doesn't spoil it," she said, laughing.

"Don't worry. I'll hold you up. I won't let you fall. I promise."

"I believe that. Do you think we can have a hot chocolate with marshmallows at the Sugar Shack?"

There was a light snowfall, and the temperature was probably in the low- to mid-twenties. Freezing weather, but I didn't feel it. Far from it. I was warm and happy.

"Of course, we can have hot chocolate, but what happened to the girl who kept saying how full she was while eating her spumoni and eyeing up mine?"

"I'm full. I just would love a hot chocolate on a cold night."

"Well then, you probably don't want the marshmallows."

"Of course I do. They get creamy as they melt and are perfect with the hot chocolate."

"Then, two hot chocolates with marshmallows it is."

We walked for about a third of a mile before the lights of the JAMS rink came into view.

Kristine tugged on my arm to get my attention. As I stopped and turned to look at her, she was already on her tiptoes and leaning in for a kiss. Our lips met, and the tentative gentleness was gone. The kiss was still tender but there was also a definite crushing of lips and a slow exploratory opening of mouths and engagement of tongues. The kiss lasted a long time. Her breathing was heavy.

"Whew! That was a good one, William. Even without Dentyne or Doublemint."

We both laughed. There were snowflakes on her eyelashes.

"I tasted spumoni."

"You did not, did you?"

"Definitely spumoni, Kristine. I was grateful it wasn't garlic bread."

She punched me in the ribs. "The next one will have garlic and anchovies."

It was yet another moment of smiles, laughter, and joy in our night. We had only been together for about two and a half hours, but it felt much longer.

It was cold as we struggled into our skates. I felt gallant tying her skates, so her hands could stay warm. Regardless of that, after one lap of the rink, she steered me into the Sugar Shack. I ordered two large hot chocolates with marshmallows. We stood sipping for a few moments and realized we couldn't skate with our drinks. We carefully glided to the home team bench where we sat and quietly took in the other skaters. After a couple of minutes, Kristine nudged me. "Isn't that the youngest Inglis brother, Tommy? You had some trouble with that family, didn't you?"

"Yeah, a little, but it was about ten years ago." I certainly did have some troubles with that family, and so did my mom, which resulted in Mr. Inglis's limp and the Inglis family car windows and headlights being smashed.

"It was a little more than that. My older cousins are about the same age as the two older Inglis brothers you did some damage to. What are their nicknames? Isn't it One Nut and One Eye?" She stared at me with a mixture of mischief, concern, and curiosity.

"Well, I was only seven at the time, and to be honest, the damage done was largely unintentional." I was so glad that she hadn't asked about my mom's encounter with Mr. Inglis and two of his acquaintances. We lived in a small town, and the stories spread like butter on hot toast. More like they melted into the fabric of the small town's consciousness as a mixture of facts, fiction, and outright fable.

"But weren't you scared?" Kristine asked. "They were big boys at that time, almost men, and you stood up to them. That was brave."

I thought for a second or two, and then decided to share the truth. "Kristine, can I trust you with the truth? Sorry, that was stupid. I already know I can trust you."

She beamed back, seemingly more glowing and beautiful than ever. Jesus, I never thought all those thoughts would or could come into my head. I fought through the onslaught of mushiness before continuing.

"Truth is, I was very angry, very ashamed, and very scared. I tried to grab a piece of artwork that Tommy created. It was a very unflattering picture of my family that Harry was holding. He yanked the paper back, and my fingers just kept going until they scratched and gouged his eyeball. George laid a good punch on my shoulder as Harry was dancing around yelling, 'My eye! My eye!' I just wheeled around with clenched fists and, not aiming at anything really, hit him squarely in the balls. Or should I say ball. I felt it squish. After that, the teachers probably saved my life, and George became One Nut and Harry became One Eye. It didn't take long for their respective nut and eye to return to normal, but the nicknames from that encounter have lasted."

Kristine was laughing out loud, another snort—actually, several snorts. I found her snorting sexy. My brain was turning to mush.

"That's a great story. I love it. I know the results are true because even my dad has talked about you as a mere lad giving the Inglis toughs their comeuppance."

"Your dad shared that story with you?"

"With the whole family. The One Nut part made my brother squeamish and my mother blush."

"Has he or anybody else shared other stories about me and my family? We've had some tough goes from time to time." I had always been worried about what others thought about the messy parts of my family life.

"William, it's a small town. A lot of stuff gets spread around. I know some of it is just horseshit. I also can discern there's some truth—probably hurtful stuff, that you can share if you need to or want to. I'll be here to listen, not judge. Tonight, however, is about good things with you, a good person. My dad says I'm a good judge of character. He trusts my judgment. So, don't screw it up, or my old man and I will put a hurt on you that the Inglis brother only wished they had."

Kristine smiled and put her hot chocolate down on the bench, hugged me with both arms, and kissed my cheek. She put her head on my chest. We sat on the home-team bench, stuck out our tongues to catch snowflakes, and sipped on our hot chocolates. Perfect.

We did skate. We did more than a few laps to songs by the Beatles. "Nowhere Man" was one. Also the Stones' "Can't Get No Satisfaction," "There is a House in New Orleans" by the Animals, and, of course, "Sugar Shack."

The walk home was quiet. We stopped and kissed about every fifty yards. I laughed and said we needed fuel to stay warm against the cold. Kristine laughed and said she knew that her kisses were like fire. They were. We stopped our kissing as we turned onto her street. We got to her door at 11:27 p.m. We kissed goodnight, a very respectable, minor peck. I was halfway down her driveway when I heard her door open. I turned around. Her father filled the doorway.

"Good job, Scarface. Home with three minutes to spare, and based on my daughter's perceived level of happiness, there might even be a third date. Goodnight."

He slid inside as he closed the door and I was saying, "Thank you, sir."

I thought I heard a scream of delight as the door was closing, and I smiled. I was a schoolboy walking home in the snow with frozen fingers and toes that I was almost totally oblivious to. Then I started to wonder if the scream had to do with the opening of the take-out bag that contained Kristine's leftovers, the empty bottle of Mateus, and the candle. I started to fear a very unpleasant call from Kristine's father about trying to get his daughter drunk and a tirade on underage drinking.

When I got home, Mom asked me how my date had been. I couldn't stop the smile, and that told her everything she needed to know.

"Did I get any calls tonight?"

"Just one, son, from Stone Pony."

"What did he have to say?"

"Not much. He said, 'Mom, how are you?' And that when you talk in the truck, if you do open up, you always say something good about me. Him calling me 'Mom' and telling me about what you say made me smile and well up at the same time."

We both smiled, and then I had to go in for a hug. Embracing my mom made me "Mush Mellow Man" all over again.

"Stone Pony say anything else, Mom?"

"Yes. He said you have the day off tomorrow because you're probably exhausted from your big date. He also said you worked hard and earned a day of rest. He was laughing as he spoke. Son, I need to tell you, I had my doubts about those two men, but I can't help but start to love them like sons. I hear the rumours around town that they must be up to no good. I think people are just jealous of their success, and this town is extremely smallminded, especially when it comes to Indians and—my goodness—a coloured man."

"They're good men, Mom. The best. That bonus they gave us all was totally unexpected and unnecessary. They pay me well. They also promise to protect us all if that is ever necessary. Mom, I honestly don't see harm coming our way with Mister and Stone Pony in my life."

"In *our* lives, son—and neither do I. Mister already proved that last year. Hey, how about two cold beers?"

"Why not? I ain't working tomorrow! Frosted mugs coming up with two cold beers!"

"Good. And you can tell me about your date."

"I would like that, Mom. I'll tell you everything except the kissy face stuff. Mom, that girl turned my brains to mush. I thought of myself as the 'Mush Mellow Man' on the way home. I want to take you and the little one to Angelo's for a Caesar salad and veal parmigiana and a bottle of Mateus. It was fantastic!"

"That would be wonderful, son! A la-de-da 'look at us' time! Now, spill the beans about the date."

"OK, but did Stone Pony say anything else?"

"No, but he sounded as if he was cold, and it was like he was calling from a phone booth outside somewhere."

CHAPTER 25

The Watchmen

Stone Pony got back in the truck after making the call, turned to Mister at the wheel, and spoke through icy clouds of breath. "It's freakin' cold out there, big man."

"Listen, you skinny Indian, you're talking to a black man from the south who fought in Vietnam. You grew up in this winter wonderland stuff, so you have no business complaining."

"Hey, you big black turd, cold is cold, and despite your racial bias, even Indians get cold."

"Listen, you scrawny prick, calling me a big black turd is lacking a bit of racial sensitivity."

The truck cab was warm from the heater and the bond of their relationship.

"Mister, those university courses really have helped our vocabulary. I hardly drop the F-word anymore, even when dealing with a big black turd."

"I agree, Stone Pony. I barely stutter, and I don't have to resort to rhyming as often to get my thoughts out. Even when dealing with a skinny Indian fuck."

Both men laughed.

"Call me that again, Mister, the big black man with all your sass, and this scrawny f'n Indian will knock you on your ass." More laughter, and Mister put the truck in gear.

"Time to head home, Stone Pony. Our work here is done. We have barrels to run tomorrow."

"Yep, and we're down a man for the day. A good man. Giving him the day off was the right thing to do."

"Yep. He earned it, and we have a big security load of work tomorrow."

"Who would have guessed that our security work would hit a peak around Valentine's Day?"

"Not me, but lots of spring vacations and school breaks coming up, and an early Easter this year. People want to have their needs and security checked off their list."

"For sure. Seasonal business is a good thing. Really smooths the cash flow for the summer season. Mister, did you ever think it would come to this?"

"A little bit, yes. The demand for our services was an open market, although the competition that is coming is a bit scary."

"We're lucky we had the good sense to do some business planning. You still figure two and a half, three years, and we're out of much of the security exchange business?"

"That's the plan. Competition in that field is turning vicious and ruthless. Bad elements are moving in. We gotta be clear of that in three years."

"Amen, brother—if not sooner. Sitting on the kid's date tonight. Hiding outside the restaurant and the skating rink. Trailing him home. I didn't think it would come to this so soon."

"Just a precaution, brother. Rumours are out there about us and our bigger crew. The West Ward has a lot of the old gang members who are rising as our competition. They don't have any use for us, and they have lots of grudges against the kid. Caution is key, Stone Pony. Caution and protecting our own."

"Amen again, brother. Mr. Clampett is recommending . . . what's he call it?"

"Preventative action."

"Yeah, cut the head off the snake."

"Teddy Porter has a lot of connections. He's been in and out of juvenile detention and prisons. His sheet is as long as my arm. Assault with a deadly weapon, attempted rape, arson, and he's suspected of involuntary manslaughter. As if seven stabs with a switchblade was somehow involuntary."

"His crimes accelerated after Scarface beat the crap out of him two or three years ago. The kid saved that cop's daughter from being raped."

"We take out Porter, another gang member emerges. Besides, they're being run from the gangs in the big city. We can't beat those guys. We stick with our plan and exit that business as expeditiously as possible without sacrificing our big plan, our dreams."

"OK, Mister, but if one of our crew, our family, is hurt, Porter is a dead man walking."

"One hundred percent, but as a last resort. Mr. Clampett could take out the whole snake den in a week."

"Yep, but we don't want to activate the captain unless it's a last measure. Love that man and want him safe as well."

"Listen to us, Stone Pony. 'Expeditiously' and 'activate.' We better not let many white folks hear us talking so well. That's another secret weapon and strength of our whole enterprise."

"Everything is fine, big man, but sitting in the cold for four and a half hours watching over the kid brought a lot of our world and reality to the top of my mind."

"Me too. I feel the danger that could snatch us up. Let's stay on track and speed it up where we can. This boom in business now says the summer is going to be huge. Maybe we knock a year off. Out by the end of seventy-two instead of seventy-three."

"Amen to that, Mister. Let's work as hard as we can to make that happen. The kid graduates and is off to university then, so good timing there as well."

"Stone Pony, it's actually beautiful outside—with the snow falling and the full moon."

"Yep. Just like our lives, a regular winter wonderland."

CHAPTER 26

Getting By and Then Some

We're getting by. More than that, really. Back in January, my son came home with a bag of groceries. I asked him what he bought and why he had gone shopping. I hadn't asked him to go. He put the bag down on the kitchen table and started talking.

"Mom, we got bonuses at work from Mister and Stone Pony. I should say from the company, Newspaper Crew Enterprises. Good bonuses. I bought some groceries."

"Well, that's nice and great you got a bonus, son, but why the groceries?"

"You'll see, Mom. You probably should put them away."

"What's the hurry? Tell me about the company. Why that name? Newspaper Crew Enterprises? Where did that name come from? It doesn't sound like garbage pickups or snow plowing or the other stuff you do."

"No, it sure doesn't. The name comes from a poor joke about Mister, Stone Pony, and me."

"A joke? Naming a company after a joke, a poor one at that, doesn't make sense."

"Mom, unpack the groceries, and I'll explain the name after that. There are ten items in the bag. They're all very valuable. Please start unpacking."

I lifted out a package of peameal bacon. Taped to the bacon were five twenty-dollar bills.

"Son, what is this? Is this part of your bonus?"

"Yes. Keep unpacking. Nine more to go."

Next, I pulled out a small bag of mandarin oranges, which we only had once a year, at Christmas. There were five twenties taped to the oranges. I looked at him with wide eyes. He just nodded for me to continue. Next, I pulled out a box of Cocoa Puffs.

"Oh, the little one loves these, but I think it's all sugar."

He nodded. There were ten-dollar bills taped all over the box, ten in total. Next was a two-pound bag of brown sugar with twenties, tens, and fives taped to the bag. Another one hundred dollars in total. There was now four hundred dollars lying on the kitchen table. I pulled off the bills as I unpacked the groceries. Next was a dozen eggs. My son told me to open the carton. Inside was another batch of ten-dollar bills. Another hundred. I looked in the bag and saw five one-pound butter packages. They all had elastic wrapped around them. I pulled them out one by one. Each pound of butter had five twenties taped to the underside. I finished, and there was one thousand dollars on our kitchen table.

"Son, this can't be true. It can't be real. Where did this come from?"

"My bonus, Mom. All those weekends. All those cottages. All the wood we delivered, lanes we plowed, security we did, and, of course, all the garbage we hauled. And it's growing all the time. This is your share of my bonus."

"But, son, it's too much. You need to save it if you want to go to school."

"I'm only giving you some of my bonus, and you know I've been saving a lot. Mister and Stone Pony want me to go to school. They have big plans for the company, and they want me to use whatever smarts I have to help them grow Newspaper Crew Enterprises."

I didn't know what to say. A thousand dollars on my kitchen table. That was only part of his bonus? Mister and Stone Pony wanted him to go to school and planned to hire him to work for the company?

"Son, this is a little overwhelming. It feels too good to be true. Is it legal? Can we trust them? I shouldn't have said that. I know in my heart that we can trust them. This just seems like too much."

"Mom, it's all good. These are good men, and they will always look out for us. Do you want to know where the company name came from?"

"Yes, but first?"

"What?"

"Two cold beers."

"In frosted mugs!"

I got the beers and the mugs, then opened and poured the beers. We tapped our mugs for our toast, and then he told the origin story of the name.

"Last summer, we had just finished what we called the white paper trail. That happened every Wednesday. We took all the files that were considered waste from the offices at City Hall. We took whatever we picked up, and when we got to the dump, we burned it immediately. No one except the three of us were supposed to see or touch those documents. Confidential city documents, old records, all the duplicate report papers from council meetings. Everything had to be taken straight to the dump and burned. Rumour was that Stone Pony and Mister got the job because they wouldn't be smart enough or maybe even able to read the various records and documents, so the confidentiality and security of the council's business was protected. On one particular Wednesday, the other garbage crews watched us as we tossed the cartons of paper to each other, then into a roaring fire. Our job included watching it all burn to ashes. And that day, we got our name."

"OK, son, that's interesting, but I still don't get the connection to the name 'Newspaper Crew.'"

"Well, here it comes, Mom, the best part. There were ten tough men watching us, and their leader started puffing himself up and yelled over to us. 'Hey, you know what you guys are called?' He didn't wait for an answer. He just spouts out, 'You're the Newspaper Crew. You want to know why?'"

"What did they say to that? I mean, Mister and Stone Pony?"

"Nothing, Mom. Not a word. They just took about ten steps toward the men and stopped five feet away from them. Mister crossed his big arms across his chest. Stone Pony had his arms at his sides but was clenching and unclenching his fists. The muscles in his arms from his wrists to his shoulders were rippling, twitching, like they were waiting for release."

"What about you? What did you do? What did the other men do?"

"I walked up a little behind them. Then I stood beside them and clenched my left wrist with my right hand in front of my waist. I thought pressing my arms across my chest would make me look a bit stronger and bigger. The ten men all wavered and took a step back. I could feel the tension. I thought a fight was going to break out. Mister and Stone Pony looked . . . I think the right word would be *menacing*. Me, not so much. I was thinking *ten on three*, and then I looked at Stone Pony and Mister and the ten men. Mister and Stone Pony looked like solid stone, rock hard, and ready to kick the shit out of anything and everyone. The ten men were gulping, swallowing hard, looking around, eyes cast downward. None of them were making eye contact with Mister or Stone Pony. Me, well, I was seeing a lot of shifting eyeballs that seemed to be saying, *What the fuck is happening here? Three aren't supposed to stare down ten.*"

"What happened? You couldn't fight those men. That wouldn't have been fair."

"You had to see those ten sets of eyes. They were all thinking it wouldn't be a fair fight for them. None of them wanted any part of Mister and Stone Pony. I think a few of the eyeballs falling in my direction were an indicator of these guys wanting only me as a dancing partner if things came to blows. Finally, Mister broke the silence. 'OK, why?' he asked. Then the leader, no longer speaking very tough or even like he had anything funny left to say, started talking. "The Newspaper

Crew—you know, black, white, and red all over.' He pointed at each of us when he said the matching colour, I guess to help us understand his humour. That was the punchline—when those ten men were all supposed to laugh and enjoy the good joke by the major wit of their group—but not a snicker, not a smile, not a grin, just a lot of fearful side glances."

"Well, what happened? Something must have happened."

"Stone Pony just stared him down and said, 'That's a strong name. We like it. It fits, because we're the only goddamn crew here who can read.'"

"Oh my God. What did they do? What did they say to that?"

"Nothing. They didn't do one damn thing. I learned then that Mister and Stone Pony radiated stone-cold strength. They intimidated the crap out of ten men. Those ten tough men, and none of them wanted any part of our crew. The Newspaper Crew—especially the black and red members. Scariest shit I ever stood through, but I stood up, Mom. I stood up with those two men because they were brave enough not to take anybody's shit. They would never go looking for trouble, Mom, but if trouble comes looking for them, they're going to answer the call."

"That's a great story, son. Bravery is contagious. You standing up to your father and his brother a couple of years back. That made me braver every day since."

"And two cold beers, Mom."

"And you forgot the bread, Dad."

We laughed, clinked our mugs, made the kind of eye contact that cements the bonds forged through hard times, sorrow, and adversity. Then emerges as love, a belief in ourselves and each other, which forges an inner strength. My son is being forced into being a man of character.

The thousand dollars was well spent. I put it all away for new shingles. The roof needed repair badly, and we also needed some more insulation in the attic.

We were getting by and then some. I had money in the bank and was planning for good things. Things seemed more than good. I knew how to work my dentures after almost three years, so I smiled more often. I had reason to. I was hoping that life could stay that good.

He had a girlfriend. He called her Ms. Librarian. She was pretty and sweet and seemed as sharp as a tack. The first night she visited, she insisted on cooking dinner for us. She made lasagna. My son helped her. He was clearly in deep. Over his head in love. He chopped the peppers and onions and opened the cans. He poured glasses of Mateus for all of us and mixed a little wine with a lot of ginger ale for the little one. The house felt full of warmth. You know—the good warmth that comes from the inside. Ms. Librarian had sparked his inner being, his heart, his emotion, his character. Ms. Librarian told us when she was buying the hamburger that, for a couple of years, she didn't know if my son was fully human. She said she felt that because he didn't smile much, would never fully engage in a conversation or ask her out. She laughed as she said that last part. She was right. He had been in a dark place for a time. She had sensed that and waited for him to come to the sunshine, as she said—meaning her. We all laughed, but my son grimaced at the memory of the dark spots. They were still there, buried deeper now, but they were things that, despite all the warmth and sunshine in the world, would never truly burn away.

I didn't care much for the Mateus. Too sweet for me! I opened myself a dirty old beer—more than good enough for me.

This little girl, Ms. Librarian, Kristine, was helping my son get by and then some.

The kids were doing well in school, and I was doing well at work. Funny to say, but life felt easier. Most people in town, especially those in the North Ward and newer subdivisions in the East Ward, would look at our lives as tough and view us as barely scraping by. Perspective is a good word. Keep your own perspective, ignore the hurtful views, and learn from the caring ones. Perspectives can't hurt you unless you let them.

I was wrapping myself in the warmth of that perspective. Getting by and then some. Only that dark cloud of Art returning spoiled my view.

Getting By and Then Some

Dear Lord,

I feel graced, blessed, and I feel warmth.
Not sure what it all is I'm feeling.
Whatever it is, it feels good. Thank you for that.
Thank you for bringing Ms. Librarian into our lives—especially my son's.
With her, he is getting by and then some.

Thank you for Mister and Stone Pony, our protectors.
No offence, Lord, but they're a bit more reliable and closer at hand than you.
They provide for us as well.
You must like them for lightening your workload.
Maybe you can help them get by and then some.

Lord, we don't need anything, at least at this moment.
Hopefully, it stays that way,
So, go about your business, and we'll go about ours.
Thank you, Lord, because we're getting by and then some.

Amen.

CHAPTER 27

Spring Love and Barrel Runs

The new business structure had started. Newspaper Crew Enterprises was running half the town's garbage routes. The list of cottages we were serving was growing like crazy, and the geographical territory was expanding north and a little to the east. Beginning on May first, we were doing cottage openings. Stone Pony and Mister had hired two cousins of Stone Pony's for the cleaning duties. These two young women were cleaning machines. Another company was born. Crew Cleaning Services, part of the Cottage Country Consolidated Services. The two women were partial owners. Those two girls—well, young women—had to that point in time experienced very difficult lives. I didn't know their history, but Stone Pony let all of us know they were under our shared protective wing. That was all we needed to know.

May first was also the end of Mister and Stone Pony's daily work as a town garbage crew. At least Stone Pony's daily work as a town garbage crew member. Well, before May first, for the last three months, Stone Pony had been focusing a lot of energy on CCCS. That's when the opening and cleaning business opportunity came to light. Mister had explained to me that within a week's period, about ten days before Easter, a half dozen or so clients had asked if they could recommend someone to open and clean their cottages. It had been a mild spring, and people wanted to open their summer spots early. Get a jump on the season. Mister and Stone Pony called another dozen clients who all jumped at the opportunity to get their places opened and cleaned.

Mister and Stone Pony bought a van, cleaning equipment, and supplies. They hired Stone Pony's two cousins, and alongside these women, had opened and cleaned almost twenty cottages. They also had worked the phone and acquired sixty-eight other openings scheduled over the next four weeks. A business was born, launched, operating, and profitable within the first month of existence. The women left freshly baked bannock as an opening gift at every cottage. Crew Cleaning Services was instilling customer loyalty, care, and exceptional service from day one.

I was running barrels Wednesday afternoons, all day on Saturdays, and six to seven hours on Sundays. My steps were light and fast. Kristine had put a spring in my step. I felt different. People like the Rave said I looked different. The student newspaper, the *Raging Rag*, ripped me a new one in their February and April issues. Their last issue in June was sure to be a scathing piece of shit against me, but I wasn't worrying. The anonymous writers/editors were all graduating, and the entire school seemed to know exactly who they were. When the *Raging Rag* issues arrived, the ripples among the student population grew smaller and smaller. The VP categorized them as "one-trick ponies who had shot their collective wad." That made me laugh—especially at his description of their increasing lack of impact and relevance. The VP and I still met with the staff advisor after each issue. He was always indignant, and demanding that I should address the points raised and was perplexed that the VP had not demanded accountability and action. The VP simply categorized the so-called issues raised as primarily personal attacks that were not based on fact, with little if any substantiation—and, most importantly, without any visible sign of support or belief from ninety percent of the student body. The staff advisor exited the meetings perplexed, dumbfounded, and at his wits' end. Those were his words. The VP confidentially told me that the advisor's trip to the end of his wits would be a very short journey.

I had taken the driver's education classes and got my licence on the first attempt the previous December. My family situation and increasing grades had set me up for early dismissal from classes by the first week of June. It was sort of a hardship exemption. My family was deemed poor. A month of extra full-time work would help that. My grades were good enough to get exemptions from final exams. That was new territory for me—and full credit to Kristine, who was studious. After two to three hours of diligent homework together, our studying would flip from books to each other.

We marked June 7 as our four-month anniversary by returning to Angelo's for dinner. I was being cautious and respectful when it came to how far we were going physically. What was kind of strange for me was that I was extremely nervous about sex with Kristine, although her passion more than matched mine when we were doing after-study studying. I had experience with a former Snow Queen who was maybe five years older than me, the two blondes from BC, and maybe a few other girls—just once each—and, of course, above and way beyond all that, was the teaching and lovemaking of Woman and the Seven Motions. Kristine was different in a way that a guy my age would never tell other guys. Special. Handle with care—because I cared, cared deeply. I think she sensed my hesitancy. Kristine would probably be the decider of when and if we were going to go all the way. What a weird thought—and it seemed so juvenile. All the way.

Someday, Ms. Librarian, when you say it will, this will happen in your way and in your time. Someday.

My barrel runs were filled with thoughts of Kristine. Those thoughts made my steps quick and the loads light. Damn, I was becoming a romantic.

I developed my own signature close. I put the lid back on a garbage can or pail and thumped a few beats to Led Zeppelin's "Kashmir." It sounded good to me.

Student elections were going to be held the first week of June. June 7 was voting day. I won in an even larger landslide. The *Raging Rag* arrived in the school cafeteria the day before the elections. They ripped me a huge new one. No impact on the voting. The VP had approached me and instructed, advised, and recommended once again that I take the high road. It worked.

My driver's licence allowed me to drive our garbage route. Stone Pony told me to find someone to work the cottage route with me for the summer. Someone strong, trustworthy, and reliable. I passed the word around but got no takers. The money was good, but it was hard work, long hours, and it stunk. Mister and Stone Pony wanted to cut back to two days a week on the truck—to Fridays and Mondays, the busiest days. They had several businesses in growth mode, and they seemed to be in a hurry for rapid growth.

They gave me until the end of June to find someone, or they would find someone. Stone Pony told me they would find the scrawniest Indian kid or the fattest, laziest white kid possible if I didn't find my own helper.

I wasn't too worried. Hell, it was still springtime, and I was out of school, making money, getting bigger, faster, and stronger. No exams and good grades. Life was good.

And, by the by, I was in love.

I was also mastering the drum part of "Kashmir."

CHAPTER 28

Return of the Bogeyman

I was finishing the Wednesday town garbage route run in the South Ward with the Brownies. As I pulled the truck into the bay at Zeke and Zach's Enterprises, where we now housed all our operating equipment for the Newspaper Crew Enterprises, the Whities were already walking up to the truck. We never got that kind of greeting when we returned for the day, so I knew something was up, and I had a sinking premonition that all wasn't good. Before my feet had hit the ground, Zach told me to call my mom, saying it was urgent. She had called at about 5:15, and it was now close to 6.

I hustled into the Whities' office, shut the door behind me, and dialed our house number as rapidly as I could. My head was spinning through the possibilities. Mom never called and never said *urgent*. Something must have happened to the little one or big sis down in the big city. Her calling at 5:15 meant Mom was home early from work. What the hell was going on? Not another visit from Art? I would kill that prick if he touched my mom.

"Hello, son?"

"Yeah, it's me, Mom. What's going on?"

"Well, the little one got a bit of a scare when she got home from school today."

"Who was it, Mom? If it was Art, I'll break his fucking neck."

"Calm down, son. Everything is OK, and it wasn't your father. Someone else, though. A friend."

"A friend?" I was calming down already, knowing it wasn't that loaf-less asshole of a father of mine. "Who, Mom? Zack said your call was urgent. What's going on?"

"An old friend, son. A good old friend. He was sitting at the back door, looking like something Old Blackie would have dragged home. He gave the little one a start, and she didn't recognize him at first."

Old Blackie was our family dog who had passed away a few years back. The old dog was famous for licking his own balls. Blackie finally caught a car he was chasing. The car had stopped suddenly, and Blackie, whose eyesight was failing, ran full throttle into the bumper. He died on the spot. A broken neck. That seemed to be a recurring theme around our home. He died quickly, and his head was bent back in the general direction of his beloved balls. So, hopefully that was the last thing he saw. His well-licked and well-loved balls. Blackie seemed to have a smile on his face, so that's how we chose to remember the end of his story.

"For the love of God, Mom, tell me who."

"Bogeyman."

Bogeyman, my old pop- and beer-bottle-collecting friend. The best afro on a white kid ever. The almost constantly high dope dealer of weed and hash only, alongside our other collecting friend, Scarecrow. Bogeyman, one half of the globetrotting weed warriors and fine joint providers to our town—and probably to everyone within an eighty- to-hundred-mile radius.

"Bogeyman. Is he OK? What's going on? Is Scarecrow around?"

"No, just Bogeyman. He's bedraggled. He looks bone-tired and skinnier than ever. His hair is gone. He has a deep bruise on his cheek. He looks hurt. Maybe quite badly hurt. He just keeps saying he's OK and asking when you'll be home."

"Tell him in about twenty minutes. I'll get Seamus and Patrick to bring me right home. Mom, can you tell me anything else?"

"Bogeyman says he's hungry."

"Can you feed him something then? Please."

"I tried, son. He insists on waiting for you to get home. He got me to order takeout from the Golden Dragon. It will be here in about fifteen minutes. Bogeyman says for him, Golden Dragon takeout is like a home-cooked meal."

That was more than true. Bogeyman and Scarecrow had more good meals there than at their homes. Scarecrow used to call their meals from or at the Golden Dragon their "family meals."

"Besides you, the only real family they have had for years is each other," Mom said. "Sad but beautiful, all at the same time. Get home quick."

"On the way now, Mom. Keep him safe till I get there. Bye."

I don't know why I added the "keep him safe" part. Danger, danger, Will Robinson. The Brownies had me home in record time. They didn't ask any questions when I told them Bogeyman had shown up at our back door looking like shit and without Scarecrow. B and S had been inseparable for the better part of the last five years. They had travelled the globe together. Now Bogeyman was home without Scarecrow? Something had to be wrong, very wrong. I prayed quietly to myself during the ride home for Scarecrow's safety. Premonitions—worries without knowledge—are a bitch. These guys, B and S, buying dope and partying in Mexico, South America, and all over Europe and who knew where else. They were only eighteen or nineteen. It dawned on me that I didn't even know what part of the world they'd been in last. The last postcard I'd received was from Amsterdam, postmarked almost two months ago. Early April, I think. Somehow, those two had a postcard made of a picture of the two of them, both smoking joints with two beautiful blondes and a table full of draught beers in front of them. The card read: "Wish you were here. No, we don't. The blondes would want you, not us. Having a blast. Amsterdam would blow your mind. Keep collecting. See you in the summer. Love, brother, from the B and S travelling medicine show."

Those fucking whack jobs. I loved them.

The cab delivering the Chinese food was pulling out of the driveway as the Brownies dropped me off. I raced around the side of the house and bolted through the back door. There he was: Bogeyman. He looked worse than Mom had let on. The bruise covered half his face. He looked like shit. When he tried to stand up, he wobbled and favoured his left leg. He stumbled forward and almost fell into me with wide-open arms. Maybe the most awkward attempt at a hug ever. He was sobbing hard, and his breath was catching before his head landed on my shoulder. His stumbling into me should have knocked us over, but he was as light as a feather. His hair was close-cropped—shaved probably not that long ago. His six-foot-three frame appeared to be just skin and bones under his knee-length army jacket. It was almost the middle of June, and Bogeyman was in a winter jacket. I might have been imagining it, but he felt cold. He was muttering, choking words into my collar and neck. I couldn't understand him.

"Mom, you and the little one fix a plate and go."

Mom rephrased my sentence. "We'll fix a plate and go eat outside on the picnic table. You boys need time to catch up and tell each other stories, which will be mostly lies."

Bogeyman lifted his head and in trying to laugh, blew a little snot out of his nose. A bit of mucus landed on my shirt. There was red mixed in with the green and yellow. A colourful and scary piece of art decorating my shoulder. He buried his head on that shoulder. His sobs were deeper and further apart. He seemed to be calming, but how would I know? Mom and the little one got their dinners and headed out the back door. Mom had snapped open two beers and left the bottles on the table. I nodded my thanks.

Bogeyman lifted his head from my shoulder as the back door closed behind my family. He clutched my shoulders and stared into my face. His eyes were water-rimmed and blurry. He was trying to speak again. Either he was becoming coherent, or I was starting to understand his mutterings.

"Scarface, they have him. They have him. They let me go. They just let me go."

I knew he was talking about Scarecrow, but I didn't know who had him, where, or why.

"Listen, man, I need you to make sense and tell me exactly what happened. Start with Scarecrow. Tell me about Scarecrow."

His eyes were bleeding with some inner pain and pleading for something. Understanding? Sympathy? Comfort? I couldn't guess what, as his eyes were completely clouded and obscured with veils of hurt.

"Sit down. Grab that beer and start with Scarecrow."

"OK. I gotta cool down. I gotta mellow. I'm overheating, and I'm cold as hell."

"OK, brother, just take it easy. Let's fill our plates and have some chew and sip on a cold one. Then we'll talk."

Bogeyman was calming down. I filled his plate as he took a couple of swigs of his beer.

He ate slowly, as did I. His face seemed to be relaxing. We ate in silence until his plate was empty. He put more food on his plate. Fried rice, another egg roll, and a heap of chicken balls. He finished his second helping, pushed his plate to the side, and took a long pull on his beer, draining it. Mom came in and got a little more food and fortune cookies for her and the little one. She didn't say anything. Mom looked at the table, picked up Bogeyman's plate, and took it to the sink. Mom got two more beers from the fridge, opened them, and then slipped through the screen door. I was hoping that Mom and the little one's fortune cookies held some good prophecies. When Mom left, Bogeyman began to speak.

"Turkey. Right in the centre of Istanbul."

I had no idea where he was going to take this. What was he going to say?

"It was in the middle of the afternoon, on a busy street. We were high, but not so stoned that we were making fools of ourselves or drawing attention. There were probably a hundred kids like us from the US and Europe all around this area, in the middle of a bazaar and surrounded by shops."

"This was in Turkey, right? The centre of Istanbul, right?"

"Yeah, man. Smack-dab in the hippie mecca that is Istanbul. We had been in the country for three or four days. We got there in a van with some kids from Ohio, coming out of Afghanistan. We were partying—but not hard—and staying in a decent hotel. We had loads of US dollars." Bogeyman stopped talking and picked up a fortune cookie before continuing. "We had been buying hash and grass and selling to mostly American and Swedish kids. We were doubling or tripling our money every few days. We had wired about five or six grand back home, back here, already. Then I think Scarecrow got greedy or careless or something."

"Why? What happened?" I was still grasping that Bogeyman and Scarecrow were in that part of the world, partying and buying and selling dope.

"He came back to the hotel the night before, and he had a huge brick of hashish. He said he paid a thousand US, had talked the seller, a local guy, a Turk, down from fifteen hundred. That sounded like too good of a deal to me, and I told him that. Scarecrow was surprised the guy took the thousand. He would have been happy to pay the fifteen. He figured we would make three or four thousand, depending on how much we smoked ourselves and passed out to friends when we partied."

"Friends? What friends?"

"Acquaintances, really. The kids from Ohio. We were also partying with some Dutch kids we met in Amsterdam about a month before. As you travel, you keep bumping into this caravan of kids travelling around Europe and the Middle East. Strange but true. Scarecrow and I would hear where one group was heading or what the collective buzz was on a cool place to visit or where concerts were happening, and off we would go."

"That all sounds cool, but where the fuck is Scarecrow now, and who took him?"

"Stay cool, Scarface. This is hard for me to tell. Can we have another beer?"

I got him another beer and set it in front of him. His hands had been shaking, but after the second plate of food and the second beer, he was calming down and becoming more lucid. I was nursing my beer and listening to his story unfold and fearing for the ending. Where was Scarecrow?

"Scarecrow's in prison in Istanbul. The police came straight to us. There were at least ten of them. I didn't even notice the cops who came up behind us. They hit us with clubs on the shoulders from behind, and we both fell forward on our faces. They pulled our arms behind our backs and put us in handcuffs. They hooked batons through our arms and pulled us up to our feet. They didn't say a word. As we were walking, being pushed along, they jabbed us in the guts and our backs with batons. The police van wheeled into the bazaar area with horns and lights blaring. It was all like the CSNY song where everything is hazy and fuzzy, doesn't quite make sense and you can't grasp what is happening. Then we were loaded into some type of police van. They were putting on a show of force, a staged lesson for all the immoral Western kids."

"What were you doing? Why would they go straight for you two out of all the other kids?"

"That was obvious to Scarecrow and me as soon as we saw them coming in our direction. They knew Scarecrow had bought a big brick. When we got to the van, Scarecrow resisted a little, and two of them smacked him—one on the back of his head, the other on his right ear. The blow on his ear caused blood to spurt, and Scarecrow was out cold on his feet. I got my leg up, and his chest hit my shin on his way down. Probably saved his face from getting messed up bad, but he still hit his forehead hard on the van floor. More blood. They got us into seats, pulled hoods over our heads, and drove off."

"Did they hit you?"

"Not like Scarecrow, but as we drove along, there were cuffs to the head and baton pokes in the gut, sides, and back. They were working us over. Even Scarecrow, despite the fact that he was out cold. We drove for probably an hour. I could tell we were outside the city, because all the traffic and human noises were gone. The road was quite bumpy by then. They would smack us and laugh. The only words I could make out were 'fuckin' Americans.'"

"What? They thought you were Americans? Did they mistake you guys for some other dudes?"

"No, not at all. When I heard 'fuckin' Americans,' it clicked. Scarecrow had told the locals he was an American from Columbus, Ohio. He said he did that just for laughs. Fuck, we have Canadian flags sewn on our backpacks. I don't know what he was thinking, saying he was American. They came straight for us. They were on a mission. Scarecrow was set up."

"They planned this? Did you have the dope on you?"

"Yeah, it was a setup. That's why the locals didn't bargain or haggle on price. They wanted that brick in an American's hands for whatever reason, and Scarecrow walked into it. Scarecrow had the whole brick, minus what we had sampled and the half-dozen or so chunks we had sold. The cash and the dope were in his knapsack, so they had us dead to rights."

"What happened when the van stopped?"

"Well, I thought they were gonna take us somewhere, rip us off, and maybe tell us to get the fuck out of Dodge while we still could. We heard there was a ton of corruption in Turkey. The American kids laughed about them being ten-cent sheriffs with dollar tastes. You know, cheap to bribe and easy to get away with any of the shit people pulled, like selling and buying drugs in the square. The Dutch kids were telling us that things had changed recently, and the Turks were turning into some real bad motherfuckers. Turns out the Dutch were right."

"So, where were you? What did they do?"

"First thing I noticed when they took our hoods off was that I was sitting backwards, facing the rear of the van. Our backpacks were on the floor at our feet. They had been to the hotel and grabbed the rest of our stuff, including our big travel backpacks."

"What the fuck? That's crazy."

"Crazy from the sense that they planned the whole thing, and Scarecrow stepped right into their trap. Now everything was about to go way off the fuckin' rails for us. Scarecrow had come to and whispered to me to look at the different uniforms. He was quicker to get on his game than I was. There were soldiers with light camouflage green-and-brown uniforms carrying automatic weapons and guys in blue fancy uniforms with metal buttons with holstered guns looking all Paladin-like, except in blue, not black. Their uniforms had shoulder straps with little berets tucked into them and some large silver badges. I couldn't make out the writing on the badges. Whatever they read was bad for us. They weren't UN peacekeepers. I learned later that these were national police, like our RCMP or something. Then there were two guys in suits with thin ties and hats like from gangster movies set in the thirties or fifties. Scarecrow whispered that we were in some serious fuckin' shit. I said, 'No shit, Sherlock.' We both cracked little smiles. Big mistake. Our grins were followed by smacks to our faces with rifle butts."

"You're fuckin' kidding!"

"Serious as the sunrise, as Scarecrow would say. I got lucky. They cracked me on my cheekbone. It hurt like hell—still bruised, as you can see, but nothing broken. Scarecrow wasn't so lucky. The rifle butt broke his nose, blood fuckin' spurting everywhere. He fell into me. The blow bounced me off the seat and dropped me to my knees. Scarecrow's head was resting in my lap, and his blood was covering my crotch and leaking down my pant legs. He was out again. I swear the smaller of the two fucks in suits nodded to the soldiers as a signal to fuck us up. A soldier grabbed Scarecrow by the hair and got him up to his knees, splashed water in his face, and brought him back to life."

"When did this happen?"

"Exactly four weeks ago today, if today is Wednesday, June eleventh."

"It is. Four weeks. Where have you been? Where's Scarecrow? Is he safe, or do those fucks in Turkey still have him?"

"Let me tell you the rest of the story, OK?"

"OK."

"So, with us on our knees, they asked permission to look through our backpacks and search us. Two of the soldiers were holding us by the hair and nodded our heads for us. One of the little suit fucks said in imperfect English, 'I'll take that as a yes, and thank you for your excellent cooperation.' They all fuckin' laughed. There were about twenty of them, and I counted six vehicles.

"They yanked us to our feet by our hair. Scarecrow was bleeding like a stuffed pig, and I realized my vision was blurry. There was blood coming from my cheek and getting in my mouth. I couldn't tell how bad I was bleeding. My right eye must have been swelling, because I could hardly see anything. I took a quick sideways glance at Scarecrow. His nose was really fucked up, bloody, and looking like a flat tire. His eyes were swollen shut. He was a blind fuck in a world of pain. They patted every inch of us, undid our belts, and yanked our pants and shoes off. They grabbed us by the balls and squeezed. When either of us screamed, they whacked the other with a baton. It was the blue uniform fucks inflicting the pat-down pain. The soldiers just held us up. They started to stick batons up our asses. The little suit fuck said to wait. They could do a more detailed ,thorough cavity search later, including our mouths. All of them fuckin' laughed at that.

"The other suit guy nodded to the boys in blue, and the soldiers pushed us to our knees. Scarecrow was barely breathing. At least it looked that way, from what I could make out. They brought our backpacks over and started pulling all our shit out and throwing it around. They weren't happy. The little suit said, 'Gentlemen, where are your passports?' He nodded, and the boys in blue cracked the back of our skulls with their batons. We both planted face first, and the soldiers yanked us by our hair back onto our knees. My head was splitting. I had a mixture of sand and blood in my mouth. Scarecrow was a complete fuckin' mess. I thought he was going to die, and I wasn't going to be far behind. The small suit fuck asked again all nice and polite and mannerly, 'Gentlemen, where are your passports?' Scarecrow wouldn't survive another blow to the head. I nodded toward the soldier holding Scarecrow's knapsack and said, 'In the small bag.'

"The soldier handed Scarecrow's backpack to the little suit. He handed out the drugs and money they had found to the other suit and threw the other shit toward the soldier who had been holding the backpack. When the backpack was empty, he glared at me, walked over, and drifted me a good one in the chin. For a small fuck, he packed a wallop. He yelled in my ear. 'They aren't in here. Where are they?' I said, 'Under the cardboard base at the bottom.' There was a little opening there, and we always slid our passports under the bottom of that plastic-covered cardboard base. He pulled them out and smiled and held his arm in the air, holding the passports like he had discovered America or something. When he took his first real look at the passport colour and cover, though, his victory smile of discovery turned to something like shock, and then fuckin' furious anger. He shouted some gibberish in his Turkish language, but I couldn't make out the words, except 'These fuckin' cocksuckers are Canadians, not Americans.' He was not happy, and he was yelling at the boys in blue about fuckin' Canadian cocksuckers, not motherfuckin' American cocksuckers. As I looked around, I could tell the other nineteen or so were not happy. Someone or all of them had fucked up."

"I can't believe this. Do you need another beer? I sure as fuck do!"

"I sure as fuck do, too, but no. I gotta keep my head on straight to get through the rest of this. Water would be good—just water."

"OK, got it." I poured two glasses from the kitchen sink. Bogeyman took a big gulp of water and then resumed his unbelievable horror story.

"So, when the little fuck stopped yelling, he turned to us and said, 'Gentlemen, you two are cocksucker Canadians?' He grabbed Scarecrow by the chin and raised his head, but that was no good, as Scarecrow was basically out on his feet or out on his knees. He made eye contact with me, and I made eye contact back—well, with one eye anyway. 'Yes, sir, we're Canadian,' I said. He turned and screamed at the boys in blue. One of them said something, and he turned his attention back to us, pointed at Scarecrow, and asked, 'Then why did your friend say he was American?'

"Well, Scarecrow said the local wouldn't stop yapping about the US, the Yankees, Disney, Elvis, Creedence Clearwater, Mustangs, and big-breasted, blonde American babes. Scarecrow figured the deal would go better, smoother, and cheaper since the local said he loved all things American. Scarecrow said he was from Columbus, Ohio. I told the small suit that my buddy figured the Turks liked Americans better because the Turks we met seemed so interested in Americans. Then he went off on a rant. 'We hate fuckin' Americans. They're arrogant pricks. They fuck us over on business deals and foreign aid, and they come here and act like they own the place. They try to fuck our women, bring drugs in, and generally disrespect everything about us. They're scum. We want to arrest them, fuck them up as necessary, and send them back home after they pay for their crimes. You fuckin' Canadians are harmless fucks. You get stoned and don't bother anyone. Now, you buy all this dope and have all this money. Now you're going to get fucked over for breaking our laws.'"

"Man, Bogeyman. How did you get out?"

"Well, all the dope and money was in Scarecrow's bags, so they felt they didn't have a case against me. We found that out after a three-week stint in the prison infirmary. I healed up pretty good. Scarecrow's ear was still mangled, and his nose was still flattened, but he was breathing better. We were taken to a meeting in the warden's office. The little suit fuck was there, and someone in a blue uniform with lots of badges and shit on his shirt—so probably a high rank of some sort—and the warden. The little fuck did all the talking. He said as he pointed to Scarecrow that he had been charged with possession of narcotics for the purpose of distribution, drug trafficking, and the corruption of Turkish minors. There were several other charges, but those were the major crimes that Scarecrow was facing. The little suit said that Scarecrow was facing life in a Turkish prison. We were both standing with our hands cuffed behind our backs. Scarecrow fell to his knees. We hadn't even spent a night in an actual cell, but walked by them on our way in and to the warden's office, and knew neither one of us would survive very long. Our hair had already been cut off, and an orderly had already tried to fuck Scarecrow in the ass. We had one hand free. The other was cuffed to the cots we lay in night and day. Scarecrow fought the fucker off with a spoon he hid from one of our so-called meals."

"What did they charge you with?"

"Fuck all. Consorting with a criminal, drug use, and illegal entry into the country. The little suit said I would probably get one to three years, or I could pay a fine and leave the country. He said the fine was three thousand dollars US. If I paid immediately, I would get my passport back, my return ticket to Toronto from Amsterdam that they found in my backpack, 262 American dollars and 145 dollars in Canadian cash. He pointed to a paper that said we had 3,262 US dollars and 145 Canadian between us when we were detained. They figured my friend should be glad to have the three thousand dollars used to pay my fine and see me return home quickly before they changed their minds. The money was stacked in four piles, three roughly the same size and the fourth less than half the size, with the Canadian money on top. He asked if I thought my friend would agree. Scarecrow hadn't said a word, and neither had I, up to that point. Scarecrow was still on his knees. He lifted his head and looked at the little suit and said one word: 'Agreed.' Then he looked at me and said, 'Take the deal, get the fuck out of Dodge, and get the Canadian Embassy working on my case.'"

"Bogeyman, that's so fuckin' crazy!" I still couldn't believe what I was hearing. Mom and the little one came in the house at that moment. My eyes told Mom to keep moving, and she shepherded the little one into the family room at the front of the house. I heard the TV go on. Bogeyman and I remained rooted at the kitchen table.

"Scarface, I could have died when Scarecrow said that. I started to say, 'Fuck that. I'm staying with my friend,' when the small suit said, 'Wise advice from your friend. Take it. The deal is time-sensitive. You have thirty seconds.' I looked at Scarecrow, and he said, 'Go! Take it. You're my only fuckin' chance of surviving this.'

"Then the blue uniform spoke. 'We'll drop you at the Canadian Embassy. They know you two have been detained. We told them they would have twenty-four hours to expedite your exit from the country.'

"The cards were dealt. The blue uniform produced a paper for me to sign and for Scarecrow to witness. The paper basically listed about ten fuckin' bullshit charges that would be waived upon my exiting the country. We both signed. The pen was being taken from Scarecrow's hand as the little suit put my passport, the pile of US and Canadian cash, and my plane ticket in an envelope with a copy of the paper we signed. He said he hoped I would have a pleasant journey home. He put the three thousand US dollars in three similar envelopes, put one in his jacket pocket, and handed the other two over to his partners. The envelopes disappeared into their pockets. It was then that I realized the corrupt bastards had not written anything about the three grand in the document—just the money they gave back to me. The little suit said one more thing: 'If any of your countrymen want to retrieve your friend from our penal system, the extradition costs will be about twenty-five thousand American. Please don't insult our intelligence by saying you don't have the money. We found wire transfers totaling sixty-five hundred back to a bank in Canada. I advise you to raise the extradition funds quickly. Your friend is going to have lots of new friends in our prison. He will be someone's favourite new friend and playmate—perhaps many someones. My card is in your envelope.'"

I shook my head in disbelief, still not grasping that this could all be true. Twenty-five thousand American? Bogeyman wasn't finished with his story.

"That was it. They hustled me out of the room, and I didn't have a chance to say anything to Scarecrow. He yelled, 'Get me out of here quick!' That's all I heard besides the sound of a boot kick to his head.

"The Canadian Embassy was useless. They couldn't arrange a flight in twenty-four hours. They weren't going to risk an international incident with the Turks over an eighteen-year-old drug dealer. They wouldn't help arrange the twenty-five-thousand-dollar payment either. The Canadian Embassy didn't pay ransoms on thinly veiled bribes. Their advice was that I should get a good lawyer as quickly as possible and get the money together. They did say they would help by pressuring the Turks into a quick trial date, in four to six months, but not to get our hopes up. It might take a year. They added that my friend could well be dead by then, or totally gone mentally. My response to the Canadian Embassy officials was thanks for fuckin' nothing."

"Bogeyman, a fuckin' year? That's impossible."

"What I learned on my way back was that Scarecrow would be raped and beaten by the guards first, and then what was left of him would be settled by the convicts. He wouldn't likely make it a full year."

"We have to get him out. Do you have that kind of money?"

"Yeah. And the connections. The Canadian Embassy bought me a train ticket out of the country. It took me two days to get to Amsterdam, arrange a few things through some Dutch friends, and meet a lawyer, and I've already paid him half of his five-grand fee. He said he has gotten about a dozen kids out of Turkish jails in the last year. All that took a few days, and thirty days after our arrest, this morning, I arrived in Toronto."

"You must be exhausted. You can stay here for a few days if you don't want to go home."

"Thanks. I'd appreciate that. The last thing I need is to go back to that hellhole and have my old man whaling on me and trying to get my cash. Scarecrow was worried about something else—really worried."

"What the hell could that be? Man, he's got to worry about staying alive. Is he? Do you know?"

"Yep, but he's not doing well. I talked to him for two minutes yesterday."

"How?"

"I called the little suit's number on his card. I said I would get the twenty-five thousand if I knew Scarecrow was safe. He said Andrew was getting lots of special attention and making friends. He told me to call back in an hour, and I could speak to him. I did. He was only on the line for a minute or two. He was crying. I could barely make out what he was saying. He was begging me to hurry and get him out. They knocked his front teeth out. They were fucking him in the ass. His words were all slurred. He just kept on saying, 'Hurry, hurry, hurry.' Then that little fuckin' suit came on the phone saying Andrew was very emotional currently. His new friends were playing rough. Andrew didn't like it, and he needed to learn to get along better. 'You should hurry,' he said. 'Andrew might not last, and the price to save him will go up.' I swear, Scarface, if I ever get the chance, I'll kill that little suit fuck with my bare hands."

"I can't believe that fucker was calling him Andrew. I haven't called him that since we were ten or eleven."

"I know—and Scarecrow's real name out of that guy's mouth sounded so fuckin' wrong and evil."

"You said he was really worried about something else. What the hell could worry him more?"

"Mister and Stone Pony's inventory for this fall and winter."

CHAPTER 29

The Salvaging of Scarecrow

I should have figured it out. Scarecrow and Bogeyman had been the major dealers in our neck of the woods of weed and hash for at least four years. They had been travelling around the world. They had more money than I could imagine. Mister and Stone Pony had known them for years. I had never seen the four of them together, not even the night at the Refuge when I left town and started hitchhiking to Winnipeg. Christ, that was just last summer!

Bogeyman thought I knew about the inventory, Scarecrow and him supplying Mister and Stone Pony for their cottage customers in massive quantities. Everybody assumed the inventory coming into our hometown was coming from the big city. In fact, it was reversed. The majority of the supply was coming from our little town going to city people at their summer homes, going back to the city, redistributed throughout the city, most of the province, and by that way back to our hometown. Talk about a circular route!

I was part of a substantial international drug organization. I existed within the inner circle without having a hot fuckin' clue about it all. When Bogeyman told me the deal, everything made sense. The cottages and homes, only Mister and Stone Pony serviced, the wads of cash, the money to buy equipment and land, the security company. Mr. Clampett, the captain, just about fuckin' everything. What a dolt I was.

Bogeyman and I met with Stone Pony and Mister the next day, a Thursday morning.

We had breakfast together and then went and sat at a picnic table in Little Hendri Park. No one bothered us. Hell, no one ever bothered Mister and Stone Pony. They would have bothered Bogeyman, but no one would recognize him without his hair. People never bothered me when I was in the presence of Mister and Stone Pony.

Bogeyman got right into the details. Four fifty-pound bales. The Mexicans had to be paid fifty percent COD on their side of the border. The other fifty percent was when Scarecrow and Bogeyman took possession. The delivery and payment date had been set for August 25. Scarecrow always made the deal and carried the cash. The Mexicans guaranteed the transit to the Cleveland area. Some of their cousins in Ohio brought the goods across Lake Erie where some other cousins, who worked as migrant farm workers, picked it up and drove it to a rendezvous spot just north of our town.

Bogeyman swore the Mexicans would be very nervous if Scarecrow wasn't there. Scarecrow spoke their language well and made them relax. Scarecrow had discussed and detailed all the logistics: different routes, timing, and payments with all the cousins. He was the dealmaker. Scarecrow trusted the Mexicans, and the Mexicans trusted Scarecrow. The trust was such that if a load was a bit light or if the cash was a tad short, they would balance it out next time. "Trust" was not the norm in the drug business.

Bogeyman spit out all the details and was going on until Mister held up a hand to get Bogeyman to stop talking. "None of that is important," Mister said. "First thing is to get Scarecrow home. We'll consult with Ms. Celia Annamoosie. She's our corporate lawyer, Bogeyman, and she will provide legal guidance through her law contacts. It's most likely that she and I will make the trip to salvage Scarecrow. I have knowledge of that part of the world, and Ms. Annamoosie won't be intimidated or tolerate any Turkish bullshit."

Bogeyman had told Mister and Stone Pony the whole Scarecrow saga over breakfast.

"Even if we get Scarecrow back, I don't think he's going to be in any shape for travel and dealing with the Mexicans." Bogeyman's voice quivered as he spoke, the fear for our friend etched on his bruised face and in the soft scratchiness of his watery voice.

Stone Pony took over the conversation at that point. "Bogeyman, you and I will handle the Mexicans end to end. We'll reach out to them and let them know there will be a change in plans. When were you supposed to have your next conversation with them?"

"July twenty-fifth. Always a month before. We call them right at noon. They joke that they want the good news of our order right before lunch. It makes their meal and afternoon siesta very peaceful." His voice was stronger when talking about the deal. It was a comfort zone.

"Well, we're going to make them really peaceful then. Our order is going up to ten bales." Stone Pony had upped the order significantly.

Bogeyman's eyebrows arched, and his voice came out a little high-pitched. "That's like eighty grand! Can we handle that weight?"

"Without question. We keep running out of supply, which has taken the price up to forty-five dollars an ounce. It will likely hit fifty bucks by the end of summer. Supply-and-demand economics. We'll also tell them we'll take another ten bales at the end of October. Do you think they can handle the weight?" Stone Pony smiled.

"Guys, that would be a ton of money at street value." Bogeyman looked and sounded skeptical.

"We expect to gross about two hundred and fifty grand, leaving a tidy profit for resale by our customers." I was mentally checking the math as Stone Pony said the numbers.

Mister jumped back in. "That's likely two hundred and seventy-five grand times two loads, but we're way off topic. The rescue, the salvage mission for Scarecrow. I want to be on a plane by next Friday and have him back here one week later. I had some army buddies who had to be brought back, so I'll gather some intel. Mr. Clampett will be up on this stuff. This is what he would call his theatre of operations."

"Bogeyman, you need to get yourself together." Stone Pony's voice was stone-cold serious.

"I know, man. I feel like shit." Bogeyman forced a laugh. "And I look worse. But hell, I never looked that good in the first place." Everyone laughed at his attempt at humour.

That broke Bogeyman. His small grunt of a laugh flipped into tears, and he buried his head in his arms, resting them on the picnic table. Mister wrapped him in his big arms, pulled him in tight, and held Bogeyman's head to his chest. He was holding him safe from harm, and Mister kissed the top of his head. "We got you, little brother, we got you," he whispered. "We got this. We'll get Scarecrow. We'll bring him home. We got you."

Stone Pony and I could see the sobs that contorted Bogeyman's back and frame even as he nestled in the massive chest and arms of our big black friend. I instantly got the incredible contrast of the strength combined with the tenderness that Bogeyman was wrapped up in.

We were all quiet for a few minutes while Bogeyman settled, then Stone Pony commenced. "We have a basic plan. Mister and crew to Turkey and come back with Scarecrow. Bogeyman and I get everything wired with the Mexicans. Scarface, your role is to build up your new summer helper, Bogeyman. Get him healthy. Get him strong. Can he stay at your mom's place for the summer?"

I nodded in agreement.

"Tell your mom that Bogeyman will be paying room and board of one hundred dollars a week. No arguments on price. Bogeyman, you rest up and keep a low profile through the weekend. You start work on Monday. Mister and I will go and talk with Ms. Annamoosie and Mr. Clampett. We gotta get the Scarecrow salvage plan working." Stone Pony was already standing as he was speaking, and Mister was loosening his hug on Bogeyman.

"Don't call it salvage anymore, please," Bogeyman said. "It's like we're going to get only part of him back. I can't stand thinking that way. I left him. I left him." His voice broke my heart, and he was sobbing again. Mister sat down and grabbed his shoulders.

"Bogeyman, look at me. Look me in the eyes. I need to tell you this, and you need to hear me. I know people who have been held in those prisons. Despite the short time Scarecrow will have been in there, we're only getting part of him back. With time, care, patience, protection, and love, we will get him most of the way back. You're going to need to be strong for him, mentally and physically. That's your main part in this. Get strong for him and for yourself."

Stone Pony took over. "And you never left him. He told you to go. He told you to go, so he had some hope of getting home. Now, because you made it home, we can turn Scarecrow's hope into reality. Because of you, we will bring him home."

With that, Bogeyman's head dropped to Mister's chest, and the sobs slowed and softened. After a couple of minutes, he lifted his head. "What are you two garbage men doin' still standin' here? Get the fuck movin'. Scarecrow's waiting. And you, you fuckin' garbage boy! This sittin' around moping and cryin' ain't getting me strong. Let's go talk to your mom."

With that, the world was starting to orbit in the right direction again.

Mister, Ms. Cecilia Annamoosie, and Mr. Clampett arrived in Istanbul at 7:30 a.m. local time the following Saturday. Scarecrow had been incarcerated for just over five weeks.

The negotiations were quick and amicable—if paying US $20,000 to resolve a planned setup and arrest was an amicable situation. The little suit took ten grand. The blue uniform, who turned out to be a major in the Turkish intelligence and international crime bureau, took seven grand, and the Turkish Army general took three grand. They had asked for $27,500, and politely explained that the extra $2,500 was to pay expenses and some cash for their subordinates. They also shared that "true" Americans were being freed for $50,000. A Canadian was eligible for a "friendly favoured nation" discount. They thought they were funny.

Something they knew or saw about Mr. Clampett scared them. They asked whether Mister and Mr. Clampett had served in special forces, like Green Berets or Navy Seals. The lack of an answer they took as a yes. The blue uniform said that Mr. Clampett looked familiar, that he wouldn't be welcomed back in their country, and he imagined that Mr. Clampett had done some bad shit. Ms. Annamoosie offered $20,000. They took it without much hesitation.

Mr. Clampett's piercing stare and slow nod was described by Ms. Annamoosie as "wet-your-panties scary," and she suggested all three corrupt thugs had stains in their pants due to Mr. Clampett.

They had almost sixty hours to wait before their Air Canada flight on the following Thursday. Scarecrow was delivered to them at their hotel an hour after the money was exchanged. That was a tense hour, waiting and praying the Turks wouldn't renege on their deal. Ms. Annamoosie firmly believed that Mr. Clampett's stare clinched the deal. The three Turk turds believed Mr. Clampett could track them down and kill them before they even knew he was there. They were probably right.

That hour, although tense and worrisome, was nothing compared to the fear that bolted through the three rescuers when they saw Scarecrow.

Ms. Annamoosie described him as emaciated. I had to look up that four-syllable, hundred-dollar word. I noticed I was putting a higher dollar value on strong words since we all received our five-thousand-dollar bonus. Scarecrow was always thin, but now he was sickly, thin, and weak. He couldn't walk and could barely stand up on his own, according to Ms. Annamoosie's crackling voice on the international phone call. Bogeyman had insisted they call as soon as they had Scarecrow back in their arms.

Ms. Annamoosie's voice was strangled by the dueling battle of restraint and emotion, with side attacks of rage and worry. Her fight for control was admirable, but she was losing.

"I need to hear his voice," Bogeyman pleaded. "I need to hear him speak."

Ms. Annamoosie said she wasn't sure he could speak. "His lips are cracked and blood-caked. He is missing most of his front teeth, top and bottom. His tongue is discoloured and swollen. Mister carried him through the lobby and up two flights of stairs to our rooms. Scarecrow's eyes had flashed fear and he thrashed his legs while in Mister's big arms and shook his head as we started to enter the elevator. He buried his head in Mister's chest and clutched the collar of Mister's shirt. We all read it as a terrible horror he was facing from the mere thought of the elevator. Mr. Clampett pointed up to the stairs and said, 'This boy has been confined for some significant period of time in a small, dark place.'"

We could hear them telling Scarecrow that Bogeyman and Scarface were on the phone. They had been trying to get water, some weak tea, and broth into him. His condition wouldn't allow him to manage anything solid. The salvage team had Scarecrow for five hours now. He was going in and out of consciousness, and when awake, he was terrified. He was starting to calm down, and he had stopped shivering. The only words he said were "cold" and "hot." That was what his body was showing. Shaking and clutching for blankets, then sweat beading on his forehead and kicking feebly free of the blankets. Mr. Clampett secured a medical person from the American Embassy who would be arriving within the hour. Ms. Annamoosie described Scarecrow as bruised from head to toe. There was blood caked behind one ear, below his left knee, on both elbows, and on his left wrist. There was blood baked into a bit of shit near his rectum. They had given him a thorough sponge bath to determine the most severe of his injuries. Ms. Annamoosie said Scarecrow had survived a shit-storm of abuse. Mr. Clampett said the three Turks would answer someday. Mister nodded at that comment, and Ms. Annamoosie believed him. They maneuvered Scarecrow into the bed and brought the phone close to his mouth. "Bogeyman, you saved me," he said. "Get me home. I love you guys." And that was it. Ms. Annamoosie said he had craned his neck to lift his head a bit and mouth those words. Then his head dropped back down to the pillow. That simple effort exhausted him. He was back asleep, waking constantly through his nightmares.

Mister took the phone. "Boys, this is going to be a long road back. Scarface, tell your mom—or ask her—if it's OK if we build an extension onto her home. We need to house Scarecrow and Bogeyman on a more permanent basis close to home. Their own families don't work. Talk to her today, Scarface, because Stone Pony is setting things in motion as we speak. Bogeyman, we assume you're OK with this?"

Bogeyman stammered a soft yes. He was still sobbing from the impact of Scarecrow's voice and words.

"We're bringing him home. We're going to get him strong physically and—more importantly—get his head straight about the shit that went down. You too, Bogeyman. Scarface, your boys are gonna need you in many ways. You're going to have to man up again, my friend, but you have that character within you." Mister's words and tone steeled me for the task. His words made it clear I had no choice in the matter, nor would I want one. This was our route together. My fellow bottle collectors, the travelers of secret and hidden paths, the infamous trio of ne'er do wells. I started by collecting bottles with those two, and now we would be collecting our strength of character, and testing that character against the cruel path my travelling companions had walked.

The call ended with Ms. Annamoosie saying to expect them late Friday evening. We would meet at the cabin. She gave us a list of things to buy in preparation. The FBI would pick them up at the airport. Stone Pony would order dinner. Hopefully, they would have Scarecrow standing on his own and eating solid food by then.

When we finished the call, I noticed Bogeyman had added something to the list.

"What's that say?" I asked.

"Eleven words. He said eleven words."

"Really? I was trying so hard to understand him, and I couldn't get past how foreign and beat down he sounded. Eleven words?"

"Yep. Eleven words that have become the best words I've ever heard in my life. Scarface, I'll never forget those words. I can't."

"Tell me what he said, Bogeyman."

"Bogeyman, you saved me. Get me home. I love you guys."

We both stared at each other, hard and deep. Bogeyman's eyes were rimmed with tears. My eyes were probably circled with a slowly dawning comprehension. The bond between the three of us had stemmed from being outsiders, easy pickings for tougher guys and gangs, trodden down by the heavy weight of low means. Accustomed to being the lowest rung on the social ladder, we had grown to be more than those summations of our born-into status. We had climbed in irregular, peculiar, and unexpected ways. Bogeyman and Scarecrow's Turkish sojourn was a frightening setback. Scarring? We were used to that, and so far we had overcome. This too would pass. We would get it behind us and stay in front of it. It was easy for me to think this, but for Bogeyman and Scarecrow? Who knew if they could break on through to the other side, as Morrison sang. We didn't know. We just needed to get at it.

"Listen to me, Bogeyman. We'll get you and Scarecrow past this. I don't think for a second this horror is going to subside quickly, or maybe ever, but you guys have been finding the paths to travel to safety, away from harm, and to some degree of success all your lives. We'll find our way together. We also have a bigger crew behind us and with us. Mister, Stone Pony, Mr. Clampett, Ms. Annamoosie, the FBI, the Whities, the Brownies, and my mom. A veritable cornucopia and kaleidoscope of character. We're rock solid, brother."

My little speech evoked a cracked, crooked grin from my friend. "Cornucopia and kaleidoscope in the same sentence? Two four-syllable words strung together in a coherent manner? Ms. Librarian has had a positive impact on you." We both laughed. "It's a long way back, Scarface. A long, long way. Not so much for me but for Scarecrow. Fuck, man, he may never be the same."

"We can't think that way. We can't show him any doubt. You need to swallow those thoughts. I know it's easy to say and hard to do, but we need to be his guides to come back. This is on us, brother."

"I know. And we must. You know why?" Bogeyman was pleading for me to understand.

"Tell me why, Bogeyman. Tell me why."

"Because he said, 'I love you guys.' I knew he did, but he said it. He loves me, he loves you, and he loves us. He is broken down that much, and his first words are *he loves us*. Guys never say that soft shit. It's seen as weakness. Then there's Scarecrow with the stuffing knocked out of him, picked apart by the black crows in a less than human harvest of his body and soul, and he rises up and says he loves us. This bond is now biblical in strength, Scarface. You get that, right?"

"I get it, my friend, and I love you too. There's no turning back from this. It's our bond, our strength, and maybe our only true form of redemption."

With that, Bogeyman's eyes glistened, and our shared silence cemented the deal.

CHAPTER 30

Stone Pony, the Resolute Core

Maybe it was just the evolving horror of Bogeyman and Scarecrow's Turkish capture and jailing, but suddenly, everything in my world came into focus. My heart and head wouldn't rest easy until Scarecrow was home. I knew that for certain. The other certainty was I knew my direction forward.

The salvage plan had worked so far, although I hated referring to Scarecrow coming home as a "salvage plan." We were going to have to pull him back together. Until then, we just needed him home. Mister, Captain, and Ms. Annamoosie would get him on the plane—get him to safety, to home base.

Whatever the motivation or stimulation was, my mind had stiffened with resolve. I had absolute clarity on the things I wanted to overcome, accomplish, and eventually become. Scarface had asked me, "Stone Pony, you seem so far away and detached. What's going on?" I told him that I was finding my way from all this darkness to my light and my resolute core.

On the degree-of-difficulty scale, it should have been easy, but it was a challenge for me after so many years of fervent and consistent practice. I had really stopped swearing—at least the spoken word. Mentally, the F-word could still go on overdrive. The whole Scarecrow scare was a test of my linguistic cleansing. I could have sworn for a week during that whole mess. I could just have easily broken down and sobbed for a week. I railed at and berated the spirits at the same time I incongruently asked them to keep my spirit strong. The double resolution of not swearing and not sobbing were precariously balanced. For that, I invoked the help and guidance of the spirits.

It felt so good to have one part of my plan working, not swearing, not using the weakness of mind to resort to open vulgarity. Foregoing the descriptive beauty of the F-word, as simple as that sounds, was important in my plan to become a respectable businessman. I knew it took far more than that to be regarded as a good man. That wasn't it. The will to stop cursing was not for or by others but for me. I wanted to be a good man and sound like a good man.

That sounded ridiculously easy. Want to be a good man? Then just choose to be a good man. For me, to be a good man I needed the means to be a good man. A platform that provided stability. My life before the Foremost family was one of running and hiding. It was hard to be a good man when I was buried in the bushes under a pile of negative perceptions and the constant potential of shit-storms of harm. Rising started with the Foremost family. The ring of a family and the ring of the fight brought me up to a level of belief and confidence in myself. Fear dropped down, and possibility arose. I fully believed that the confidence and faith others placed in me was the necessary foundation before self-confidence and faith in myself could fully bloom. At least that seemed to be true in my case. That inner flame was what safeguarded my fire from the winds of hurt, shame, self-doubt, and non-believers. The four winds that could destroy anyone's spirit.

In public, I knew I needed to represent myself as a knowledgeable, capable human being. I did not have to shed my skin colour. I needed to make others shed their stereotypes about my people, my race. I had to make them see me as they saw themselves in as many aspects as they could relate to without me losing myself, my ways, my people. My actions and behaviours were the paths I controlled, and I'd travel them in a manner that could erase the stereotyping cast for me as just another "fuckin' Indian."

I often asked myself why I cared about my people. They hadn't cared about my people. They haven't cared much for me. Even though I learned my father was white, I considered myself full Indian. For reasons not connected to my own upbringing, I was indescribably proud of my Native heritage. Maybe that was the Foremosts. Well, not maybe—for damn certain.

My central truths were few but certain, rock solid. Be a good man, do good things, represent my people with character, stand up, and, if necessary, fight for my people. Be a great partner and a better friend to my brothers—especially Mister and Scarface. Constant care and loyalty to my brethren in our extended family of the Newspaper Crew Enterprises.

And sadly, but true to my core, wreak vengeance on the man who broke my mother—that person being my father. She had never recovered from the broken orbital bone, broken nose, broken ribs, torn-up left shoulder, and broken left arm. Even in what her doctors called a full recovery, my mother suffered from blurry vision in her right eye, and she squinted. She often said her eyesight was like her life—no ability to focus or see things in the right way. Her definition of 'the right way' was the ability to see hope and possibilities for a better life. She said if a person couldn't see it, they couldn't do it, and they couldn't become it. That was her sad view of life until she died. I hadn't developed my Foremost-found drive before she passed. I hadn't shown her a glimpse of the hope, of the possibilities of better things that she needed to provide her with a hopeful vision.

Her breathing was never the same, always sounding forced and harsh. Rasping its way in and out of her frail body like an animal scratching at the surface and then crawling back down into its dark burrow. She walked with a lean to her left. She always appeared to be on a slope. She joked that the downward slope she travelled was caused by her man, my father. My mother used that analogy to explain how men could pull women down and tilt them over. There was nothing funny in her joking—at least not for me. My mother begged me to never pull a woman down or make her tilt or need to fight for her fair share of the Great Spirit's air. This became part of my inner truths that I would never pull a woman down or cause a woman to be tilted to the world and scrabbling to stay balanced on a downward slope. I would never be the kind of man who caused a woman to scrape for her breath. Most importantly, I would never make a woman lose hope.

Bogeyman and Scarecrow also brought home the urgency to move away from our distribution business. The drug business would eventually catch up to us and knock us away from our core truths, either by addicting us to the money or the drug itself or smothering us with connections that we couldn't break or shake. Mister and I knew this, and had been planning accordingly.

Mister and I met with the two local leaders of the Mayhem Motorcycle Club, the MMC. They had been around town for almost a year, mostly recruiting local criminals to be their foot soldiers. The morons who signed up with the MMC didn't fully appreciate their role, which was basically doing all the crime and risking all the time. The MMC would be standing back from the actual crimes they ordered and orchestrated. The locals would be the criminals being caught and jailed.

The remnants and leaders of the two local gangs, the Vipers and the Kings of the South, had all matriculated through juvenile reform schools to prisons. They had long crime sheets, but as of yet had not broken into the big league of crimes. They were gang wannabes, and they saw the MMC as their way to becoming full-fledged, badass, feared criminals. An association with the MMC would enhance their reputation as tough, connected, and feared bad men.

Their desires were fueled by a wanton lust for women, whisky, and money. Drugs were coming up to a higher level in their hierarchy of needs and desires. Drugs provided money, and were a gateway for women and whisky. The MMC was more than happy to feed the locals' aspirations. They provided them with notoriety and increased credibility on the streets just by association. The MMC provided the direction for the locals' actions and took a significant cut in all transactions of a criminal nature conducted on their behalf.

The MMC won the hard-fought and difficult transactions with the major big-city motorcycle clubs. They won or were granted the territory fifty to five hundred miles north of the city and the extensive northwest corner of the province, the Lake Superior region. No other motorcycle gang wanted any part of the cold, distant north. The MMC had to fulfill certain obligations or monetary homage to the big clubs to maintain their territorial rights. They were struggling to meet the expected homage hurdles. The local criminal element recruited by the MMC had proven inept rather than adept. The locals needed to step up their game soon, and in meaningful ways.

The MMC thought the locals would have a better handle on the distribution of drugs in their own backyards. They wildly overestimated the intellectual capacity of the local leaders. Teddy Porter, Blotto, the Inglis brothers, and Mor and Les. These were the brightest of the criminal gang members in the area. The MMC discovered through their big-city lawyers that the cottage-country upper-end folks were being supplied their recreational drugs locally by garbage men. Those men being us—just Mister and me, at present.

The MMC couldn't grasp how the offspring of the rich cottage-country folks were scoring enough dope in the city to sell dope to their friends and locals back in cottage country. That was us as well, but that had never been our intention. We sold dope in big quantities to a customer list of two hundred individuals. They drove back from cottage country with their supplies and distributed product to their associates, either as business favours or selling at a slight markup. The younger cottage-country customers were extremely popular at their universities or workplaces. They were moving serious weight, and that weight frequently moved back to the hinterlands for sale or for personal consumption. The local sellers were facing a very competitive marketplace and were offering an inferior product.

The big motorcycle gangs were supplying MMC product to peddle through their local network that was definitely inferior. Even the local teens referred to the MMC product as "twigs and turds." A person could still get a decent buzz from it, but they had to fire up a ton of joints, and sharing a joint went way down with MMC-supplied product. That wasn't the case with our product. Pure, uncut, and direct from the growers all the way down in Mexico.

The MMC would need to shut down our distribution to fulfill their homage honorariums. That shutdown was likely to be forced and potentially brutal. Mister and I wanted to be clean and out of the distribution business sooner rather than later. In a strange way, we shared the same goals as the MMC.

Mister and I knew how much cash we needed to fund our business platforms. We were pushing to get there by the following summer and get out clean. Pare down the two hundred clients but not transition our client base to the MMC or any other criminal group. Our clients, for the most part, would not have anything to do with the MMC and even less with the local low-rent hoodlums.

We educated ourselves in business and sought advice as necessary. We treated our friends and business partners well. We had a planned exit. We were going to push hard for another year or so and get out. We might sell our pipeline connections, if the Mexicans were interested. That would be their choice, and the Mexicans had indicated that the motorcycle gangs would not be welcomed partners. Especially a second-rate outlaw group like the MMC. Bogeyman and Scarecrow would be exiting the business as well. We needed to be respectful with how we exited the business with the Mexicans. Our western operations out of Winnipeg were run by Crazy Horse, and they would be shuttered as well. Crazy Horse and maybe Woman would move east and join the Newspaper Crew. They would be welcomed. I was resolved to accomplish my core truths.

Mister had found my father. Technically, Mr. Clampett found him. We were planning a surprise visit for the end of the summer.

My resolve to seek vengeance was intact. My vision on that was not blurry. My breathing when contemplating this was deep and cleansing. My walk to this end was neither tilted nor leaning. My core was resolute!

CHAPTER 31

My Boys, My Home, My Work

A Mother's Task: Tend and Mend

It felt like a hospital wing was being built. Everything was moving so fast. Scarecrow was in rough shape. Bogeyman was getting healthy. My son and Bogeyman headed out for work early every morning. I got Scarecrow situated every morning and fed him. It had been almost a month, and he was getting more mobile. The first week, he was sleeping in my son's room and could barely make it across the hall to the bathroom. My son and Bogeyman moved into the little one's bedroom. We had twin beds in there. The little one was bunking with me. The house was calm, but not comfortable. We were crowded—especially with just one bathroom. The injuries that Bogeyman and Scarecrow suffered had frightened the little one. Hell, they frightened me—and I have been beaten just as badly.

Scarecrow would wake up night and day, screaming and sweating. Every time, it took a while to calm him. Sometimes, he shuddered when others touched him. I could see terror in his eyes. He didn't want to talk about what happened to him. Whoever did it to him, whatever they did to him, I hated them. He was broken. Badly broken. We were all doing our best to bring him back, heal him.

Scarecrow started to talk to me at the end of this week, his fourth week home. He revealed a little about what had happened, what had been done to him. He talked about that terrible, hopeless feeling of being powerless. We connected on that point and cried in each other's arms. So strange that two rape victims would come together under one roof in my home.

Bogeyman was gaining strength daily. Weight and muscle were coming back. Running cans, running the barrels, like my son said, was great for body and mind. Bogeyman hovered over Scarecrow when he was home and served Scarecrow's every need. Bogeyman's strength of mind was coming back through his focus on Scarecrow. He had a mission. For my son it was like he had two little brothers to take care of and look out for.

Through all the misery, hurt, and pain in my house, a feeling of a close-knit family was growing. Coming together. Misery and abuse can pull people together. I was coming to love these boys like sons. There was peace in that feeling. They would heal under my hands.

The house was another matter altogether. A whirlwind. The building permits were issued in record time. The back of the house was being built out. A main-floor bathroom was being put in, the kitchen was being extended, and a big bedroom was being added to the second floor. That was nothing. The amazing part was the extension. They were calling it the "boys' wing." A two-car garage with a second floor. The second floor had a small kitchen, a full bath, a living area, and two large bedrooms. I was dumbfounded by it all. Everything bewildered me, from how it was being paid for to how quickly everything was coming together. At times, there were twenty men, all Indians, working on the house and the extension.

Mister and Stone Pony visited me at the house on the Sunday after they brought Scarecrow home. Ms. Cecilia Annamoosie, their lawyer, was with them. They explained how the new addition to the home would become totally mine after five years. The deal was that Scarecrow and Bogeyman would be living in the boys' wing for at least that period of time, maybe longer if necessary. They said they themselves would be occasional guests. The boys' wing would be alcohol- and drug-free. Ms. Annamoosie had some paperwork for me to sign. It was as straightforward as they said. The new addition would be mine, free and clear, in five years. No strings attached. I instantly liked Ms. Annamoosie. She looked like a character and carried herself with character. Strong, independent, confident, and sort of mystical. I trusted her from the moment I met her. She asked if I had questions. I did.

"How do you make this happen? The permits? The workers? The money?" All my questions were half-asked in wonderment and half in doubt that this was actually happening.

Surprisingly, Mister, not Ms. Annamoosie, answered. "The money comes from our business. We're doing well and growing. We might even need a good seamstress like you in a few years to make all our Newspaper Crew uniforms." He smiled as he teased me about being their company's seamstress. When Mister smiled, the room lightened. Everybody's mood lightened. It seemed his smiles had been few and far between. When he smiled, I felt it was sincere, meant for me, and coming from a good place.

"Money isn't a worry and not your concern," Mister continued. "After five years, we might even rent the boys' wing from you on occasion. As for the permits, we have a pretty good relationship with the mayor and some councillors from all the work we've done for and with them over the last few years. We leveraged those relationships to get the required permits expedited."

To Mend, To Tend

Dear God

Well, Sir, there are blessings, and then there are blessings.
I have two young men to help heal,
And if you can help me with that, it would be appreciated.
I know you're busy, so just a little breathing space and healing time will do.
Most church people look at these two as scoundrels.
I hear the gossip, the warnings that I'm putting myself in danger.
Lord, nothing could be further from the truth.
I would rather heal what I can heal.
Isn't that your way, Lord? Helping others?
And if there is sin to be addressed, that's your deal, not mine.
They never had it easy, but these boys made their own way.
They didn't get much given to them, and they asked for less.
I think you're blessed when you get to give people help, hope, and care.
If this is your blessing to me, Lord, thank you!

Thank you for the opportunity to provide comfort.
I pray for their recovery, for their health.
If you ask me if I have a prayer for myself
Something to ask of you, from you?
No, I don't.

Do I have a prayer to share with the world? With you?
If I did, it would simply be this:
A seamstress mends what she can mend.
A mother tends what she can tend.
To these boys, I give comfort as if they were my own
This is my being, my rock, and my stone,
Safe harbour, here within my home.
Give them a peaceful place that they've never known.
I can't say if this is a good prayer or anywhere near holy.
It is just saying what I can and will do.
That's good enough for me.
I share this with you.

Is it good enough for you?
Well, I guess I'll wait and see.

Amen.

    P.S. How's that, Father who art in heaven? A little poem worked into my prayer. Who would have ever thought you would get that from me? Probably not you. Definitely not me!

CHAPTER 32

Mister on Becoming the Elevator Man

Respect is a hard-earned thing. It's not something that comes on a prayer and a wing. It comes from doing the task, doing the ask, doing whatever it is very well and then some. And even your colour with some, with many, you need to overcome. That obstacle of skin is a barricade preventing your victory parade.

I still rhyme in my head. The stutter is gone, but it ain't dead. It lurks inside and can rise in my throat. I can't let it out. It angles up to my lips and seeks the air. I hold it in with an inward glare. The big, black man can't show a fault. That gives enemies of his skin a place to assault.

Even with the rhyming in my head, we have a plan. We had an organizational foundation and a cash flow. Newspaper Crew Enterprises had an upside that we would fully develop and leverage. Stone Pony and I caught the paper trail of some local white politicians rigging the system. Land deals, tax breaks, development contributions, cash and business flowing to relatives and friends. That cash flow was mostly for work not done and services not rendered.

They wanted us to handle all the paper that was being burned by City Hall. They thought we were illiterate low accounts who probably couldn't read—at least not well enough to decipher their deceptions. We got curious when we saw duplicate copies of transactions with different dollar amounts for the same vendor. All the invoices and transactions were filed in sequential order, but there were identical numbers on numerous invoices. There were often two invoices for the same work to the same company with the same identification or billing number. Each one of the invoices had a copy of a cheque attached to it. The cheque numbers were also in sequential order and identical as well. The only difference on the invoices and the cheques was the dollar value. Company A would submit an invoice for thirty and twenty thousand dollars for the same work. That didn't make sense. Then two cheques were made out for the thirty and the twenty thousand stipulated. Only one of the invoices would be stamped and then initialed as paid. The lower-value invoice and cheque were always stamped and initialed as paid. The original invoice was for twenty thousand and vendor company A received twenty thousand. The second invoice for thirty thousand was the fake invoice, a copy of which remained on file. Where the thirty thousand went was the big question.

This was mystifying for Stone Pony and me. It took us more than a while to figure it out, but we started saving those invoices and records.

We had always called it the "White Paper Route." We picked up the files and papers that had to be burned from City Hall every Wednesday. The boxes were always in the controller's office. She was a tiny little thing whose appearance was always impeccable. Stone Pony said that everything she wore looked expensive. Her husband was a big-shot lawyer in town. She always seemed nervous in our presence. That wasn't unusual. We had that impact on most people. Her eyes would dart around the room when we were carrying the boxes out. She would always admonish us not to drop anything or let anything blow away, and to watch it burn down to the last ash. That was unusual. These were supposedly just old papers being sent to be burned. What was the worry? The fact that she repeated this mantra weekly was also strange. We get it already! We nicknamed her Ms. Ash-hole.

We loaded the boxes onto our truck and were to drive it to the dump to burn immediately. Stone Pony and I were so quick with the loading that we decided after a couple of months of running the White Paper Route that we would have lunch before the burn. We would pull over at the park on the edge of town before the dump, and sit in the back of our truck to eat lunch. Curiosity got the best of us, and we started opening boxes and looking through the contents.

Stone Pony got interested in all the numbers and cheques. He discovered the duplications and what he called redundancies. I got interested in the real-estate files. I was amazed at the fact that the same names, companies, and numbered companies seemingly were always involved in the transactions of the city's and surrounding townships' properties. The rich getting richer. Only two law firms ever appeared on the transactions. There was a lot of buying and selling back and forth to the city of the same properties. The lease deals also seemed expensive. The city would sell the land on what appeared to be on the cheap and lease back at a high rate. The companies buying the land from the city were getting their money back in no time. I didn't really figure things out, nor did Stone Pony, for about a year.

We were already taking night courses at the university. We had to take some of the coursework on Saturday mornings in three-hour sessions. When we first started to smell the stink, we enrolled in accounting and business-law courses. The business-law course included strong content on real estate law. We would sit in the back of our truck and rifle through all the papers, accumulating more and more evidence or dirt on the City Hall criminal elements. We found egg salad went best with invoice fraud and were convinced that tuna was best with real-estate shenanigans.

Stone Pony eventually found a way to track the cheques. He had found that in the case of two cheques appearing for thirty and twenty thousand dollars, the twenty thousand would go to the vendor, and then a cheque for ten thousand went to a numbered company owned by the mayor and the councillor. Stone Pony and I found almost four hundred thousand dollars of cheques flowing to the politicians. God knows how much we missed. We didn't tell them how much we had found. We kept all sets of invoices. As we did with all the real estate transactions. We had those two by the balls.

When we confronted those gentlemen, they were indignant, and threatened us with everything they could muster or imagine, but Stone Pony and I had mastered the art of being calm and unflappable. When they finished their rants, threats, and ultimatums, Stone Pony started in.

"Please look at these two invoices. These two and these two you can keep if you like. We have the originals of the original and the original of the fakes!" The politicians were not laughing. Fear had set in. Before they could respond, Stone Pony continued. "This is only the tip of the iceberg with you two. We also have the inflated invoices, discounted land deals, tax offsets, and rebates with about fourteen of your associates in town. You should inform them. We can give you a list of their names, the transactions, the details of how much theft, fraud, and the overall misuse of public funds. The big money is in land deals. You need the list, gentlemen?"

By that point, they appeared defeated. Somehow, they rallied for one more outburst of indignation, which we listened to politely. Until we didn't. Stone Pony nodded at me. Their eyes shifted. They sensed imminent danger. I leaned in close over the table between us and started speaking slowly and quietly. "You know, gentlemen, we don't want to be rude, but let's get some facts straight, OK? Good. First, you're two corrupt motherfuckers. Everything we found has been researched and validated by a pricey big-city law firm and an accounting firm, clients of ours who would like to fuck over two small-town fucks like you. Here are their names and numbers. Stone Pony, please pass the business cards. You may recognize the firms." Their eyes went wide as they realized their way out was becoming very narrow.

"You see, you fucks," I continued, "not to sound or appear to be serious criminal elements, but we own you fucks and your fourteen associates. Now, what should be readily apparent to you is that you need to live in fear every day of a formerly scrawny Indian kid and a big black man. The thing that has changed for you is that up until a half hour or so ago, that fear was only physical. Now, it's mental and criminal. Criminal for you, that is. Oh, and I wouldn't let go of the physical fear part, either. Hold onto that as an absolute truth, because we're still two very scary men. Now, lucky for you, the way through all of this is easy. Notice I didn't say the way 'out.' There is no way out for you. This is a lifetime bind for you, a binding contract. Stone Pony will give you the pertinent details."

Stone Pony started to walk them through our new relationship. "This is, for all intents and purposes, a singularly simple arrangement. You do what we ask. How much simpler can it get? And yes, that was a rhetorical question. You smart fucks understand that word, right? Surprised that we—what do you call us behind our backs? The Lone Nigger and Tonto, isn't it? Surprised that we would know big words? You're funny for racist, white-collared, white-fuck criminals. I don't like to swear, but sitting across from you two, who have been ripping off the citizens in this town for years and stealing their hard-earned tax money for your own benefit, it's just too hard not to call you what you are, which is low-fucking-rent criminals."

I didn't know how much longer Stone Pony was going to rip on those two, so I nudged him back on topic. "Stone Pony, tell the white fucks what they've won."

Stone Pony gave me a quick glance and a smile before continuing. "Here's what's behind door number one for you two. You immediately stop all your fraud and every single aspect of how you're cheating the system. This includes all your friends. You run for office and win just one more four-year term, then you resign. Your primary obligations to us will then be fulfilled, sort of. Remember, we will always have these records, as will our law firms. We have almost five years' worth of material—and get ready for this. Behind door number two . . . ready? While you cheating, dirty pricks are sitting here with your favourite former sanitation workers, subpoenas have been served by our lawyers on behalf of half a dozen real-estate firms and various local vendors for all the transaction records for every year since you two came into office. We're going through a discovery process to see if your town has transacted deals in a competitive manner that has not caused harm or loss to your citizens. The immediate outcome is that all city records will be frozen. You can't go in and change anything. No way out for you boys."

I had to interject for two reasons: because Stone Pony was having all the fun and I had to present another element of our simple plan. "On a personal note, you should now peek behind door number three. You and your friends have done very well from your corrupt schemes. The sixteen of you will have to make amends. Some will be public. First up on that side of the ledger, you will be donating the one hundred and forty acres of land you acquired in the West Ward back to the city. Your plans to develop a suburb are scrapped. This will become a green space and designated home for a new ball field and arena. Whatever you invested out of pocket is gone. You and your friends will get a nice tax write-off. Your donation will build your popularity back up after the stink of the subpoenas issued today and the press releases we have arranged to send to the media. The donation will help you get re-elected. Did you want to see a copy of the press releases we prepared? You will have some hard explaining to do at the dinner table tonight, boys."

I took a moment to savour the looks of bewilderment and the full realization that they were cornered. That look was hard, etching itself into their fake smile lines and creased foreheads. Then I continued. "You got this land at a ridiculously low price through a non-competitive process. You and your friends should meet and discuss how to tighten your belts, as you're going to have some cash drains. We have financial advisors you can use. Us! We won't go into all the details right now, but you will also liquidate all the land you have acquired on the east and north sides of the lake for less than you paid. We know that these were legit transactions, but they were financed by your illegal cash grabs from the city. You will be selling to us for less than you paid. Far less.

"You and your friends need to be prepared that you will be selling off a lot of your personal assets. I would recommend postponing your southern vacations and ski trips. Mr. Councillor, you should sell that ridiculously big boat you just bought; you're going to need cash. It was stupid of you to mortgage your big house to the tits. I guess you were counting on the illicit cash to keep rolling in."

Stone Pony was not rattled or even slightly disturbed that I had broken the planned order of the revelations of our simple plans. Instead, he was amused because he got to study the reactions of the mayor and the councillor. We had them firmly by the balls and then some. Stone Pony took over. "Last thing you should remember. Breaking this deal or seeking to resist in any way or, heaven forbid, fighting back, will not end well for you in a legal sense."

Stone Pony ended the meeting with the clincher. "Just in case you doubt our relative power in the situation, Mr. Mayor, I'm sorry to tell you that that beautiful cottage of yours up north is fully on fire. Don't worry. Your daughter got out safely. She was stoned out of her gourd, but one of our employees was in the neighbourhood and rescued her. He carried her out in his arms. That picture will probably be on the front page of the local paper tomorrow. There just happened to be a reporter and a photographer from the paper in the area at the time. Lucky coincidence? I guess so, and nice to see the locals scoop the big-city press. Your fire insurance? Don't worry about that either. Your policy was cancelled. It seems you forgot to pay those pesky insurance bills on time. The invoices were sent. We have copies, but they were never paid. Looks like one of your fourteen criminal pals was your insurance agent who looked the other way on non-payment for reasons we cannot explain. Your guy won't be getting any claim covered because of your non-payment. The problem is, he can't explain that to his big-city office. We know this is an incredible coincidence, but that big-city insurance company, guess who their accounting and law firms happen to be? That's right. Look at those business cards. Of course, your guy can cover the insurance out of his own pocket, but he's going to take a loss on those land deals, so he might have a liquidity problem as well."

Perhaps our approach with the white-collar small-town criminals might show a little about how I became a Mister.

That was not the way I wanted to become a good man. That path was much different.

My path was one that took me to a higher ground, where my actions spoke for themselves. Where I would live a life of providing. Providing a good situation for others to thrive. The overall business we were growing would provide a solid track and a home for our close friends to grow and prosper. My efforts outside of work would be to embrace and care for those I held close to me: our extended crew, Scarface and his family, and more, I hoped. I wanted to extend my circle of care.

I wanted to pull people up. Elevate. I wanted to be the elevator man! Bringing people higher, with care, concern, and love.

That's how I wanted to earn respect, by embracing others.

Stone Pony and I needed to get clean of the corrupt part of our operations, the distribution end of the business. The politicians would fall off over time after we fully leveraged their wrongdoing. We would exit the drug distribution gracefully in a year or so. We needed to get clear of the bad and get to good!

My rhyming mind had allowed me to overcome my stutter. Hopefully, my business mind, my drive for self-improvement, would help me overcome the wrong we had done.

My mom always told me to drive toward the light. Overlook and overcome the dark. The dark that surrounded a little fatherless boy, being bullied by others for being something of a nothing. My mom believed I was something. If we both thought and believed I was something, that was all I needed. My personal elevator. The army and my mom made me something. Then she died. She passed away as a mother proud of her son. Her heart never stuttered when it came to me. Her love for me made her heart flutter.

I have never forgotten about her desire for me to find my father and kick his ass. I will, and now, I can. I have found my deserting, wife-beating father. His time is coming.

We found Stone Pony's father as well. We're going to pay that man a visit. Mr. Clampett found him. He found my old man as well. I know it's wrong to seek vengeance, but I will. We will.

That may be my last roadblock or detour on getting to my path of light. I'll take that bend in the road, that detour into darkness. That man will pay.

Becoming a real Mister. A path to becoming a man deserving of respect is complicated. Coming from low means and mean lows makes it a hard journey. Getting the means to elevate to respect. I have had to build my own elevator to become the elevator man.

CHAPTER 33

Scarface and Summer Swings

Kristine loved to be pushed on the swings at the park. She said it made her feel like a kid, and that it made her feel free. She could fly. We made love for the first time after a big swing. On a picnic table in the dark. In the park. It wasn't planned. It was one hundred percent spontaneous, and it was grand. Those were her words, not mine. She wasn't wrong.

The swing and the picnic-table sex might have been the apex of my love life with Ms. Librarian, although I didn't know it at the time. It seemed every time we were together, she was more and more weighed down by something. The break came just before my eighteenth birthday at the end of July. We were alone at her house, and she had taken me to her bedroom. She said she wanted to be on top, so she could watch me, see me as she felt me come inside her. No arguments from me. The scenery was spectacular from any vantage point when we were together. Much to my surprise, she came first, and her body convulsed with pleasure, or so I was telling my inner Don Juan self. She absolutely pulled me out of myself and into her in a current. She knew she had drained me and looked at me as hard tears formed in her eyes. Ms. Librarian rolled off, stood up, and started getting dressed. I asked her what the hurry was. I thought her parents were gone for a couple more hours at least. She snuffled out a barely audible "Get dressed, William. I have something to tell you," then she left the bedroom.

I got dressed, went to the can, then went downstairs to find her. All the while I was thinking, *My God, she's pregnant, and we're screwed.*

She was sitting at the kitchen table. My dear Kristine looked more than sad. A birthday card and a small gift box were sitting on the table.

"William, please sit down."

I did.

"William, this is awful. I hate that I'm about to do this."

"Do what? Is everything OK?"

"No. Nothing is OK. Everything is stupid and sad. Please open your card and your gift."

"Can't I wait until our dinner at Angelo's on my birthday?"

"No. It's best to open them now. Please."

"OK, but a birthday is supposed to be a happy occasion, full of joy and love. You know I love you, right? The vibe you're throwing off here is not feeling like joy and love."

"Just open the card and your gift, please. Then I need to tell you something."

I was thinking again, *My God, she is pregnant.* Or was it something worse? She told me she had been on the pill for a couple of years to help with her menstrual cycle, so I hadn't been thinking about that. I was going to ask, but looking at the sadness—almost despair—in her face, I thought it best to just open the card and the gift as she'd requested.

The card was a simple birthday wish. I couldn't remember a word of the verse that was on that card if you paid me. What Kristine wrote I'll never forget: "William, with all my love, Ms. Librarian."

When I started to say something, she shushed me and motioned to the box. I peeled off the wrapping paper to expose a small box from a local jewelry store. I can't remember which jewelry store, and there were only three in town. I took the lid off and stared at a beautiful, fine gold chain. My eyes lifted from the chain to her. I was starting to say something when she shushed me again.

"Let me put this on you. This will look so good lying on your tanned chest. Something so fine and delicate above your strong chest and wonderful heart. When you look at it or touch it, please remember that I love you."

She broke down a little bit in saying that. She kissed my forehead, sat back down, and clutched my hands in hers. I hadn't fully appreciated how tiny her hands were until that moment, although I did realize she was holding my whole world in them as she began to speak.

"I can't be with you anymore. My father, my family are worried that you're moving in a bad direction. Your friends treat me well, and I know them to be good and decent, at least in my presence and to me. There are so many rumours about them, though. Much of the talk centres on drugs and crime and so much money. Scarecrow and Bogeyman's mysterious trips, how they have been so badly beaten and how they look, the fear in their eyes when they make the slightest eye contact. More rumours that they both were in prison somewhere foreign. Mister and Stone Pony buying so many things, running so many businesses, and the money. Always the money. Everybody wondering where it all comes from. Everybody saying they're drug traffickers. Major drug traffickers. My dad's friends in the town police, your own coaches, the men who genuinely care for you, are all worried that you're in with a very dangerous crowd. A criminal and dangerous scene. I feel the same thing. I worry for you constantly—especially after seeing what happened to Scarecrow. My dad won't allow me to see you anymore, but that's not it. I can't live and love you when I'm constantly worried for you."

I didn't know what Kristine was reading from my face. At first, I was hoping she saw the devastation I was experiencing. Then that wave of anguish disappeared when I realized from her voice and her face that this was agony for her. Genuine agony, hurt, and betrayal. The basic fact that my friends, my associations, had jeopardized our relationship and would be our demise. I knew at that exact moment, I would have to choose a path. Ms. Librarian had chosen for me. I was going to protest, to say I could move toward her and away from the whole Newspaper Crew, Bogeyman, and Scarecrow. My mouth was opening, but her fingers touched my lips, and she shook her head.

"William don't say a thing. Don't pretend to choose. There is a certain fate for you to follow. You're painted with a brush of brotherhood. I hope no evil befalls you. God, listen to me. Your Ms. Librarian sounding all Shakespearian. Such pathos, such gloom, such star-crossed love. And I do love you, but just go, William, just go."

I did. The walk home was not like the cold winter's night we shared on Valentine's Day when I was warmed from the inside out, burning with a good fire. Instead, I was shaky and cold in the heat of July. My steps felt awkward. I was staggering from the hard blows of a soft love lost. Remembering her quaking on top of me. The beauty and completeness of her giving herself to me. I put my head down, so passing cars wouldn't see my tears.

The writers and the editors of the *Raging Rag* should have seen me then. They'd tried to bring me down with low words. I had been brought low by high words. *Love you.*

I went straight to my room with barely an audible acknowledgement to my mom, the little one, Scarecrow, and Bogeyman, who were playing thirty-one for nickels at the kitchen table. I sought the sanctity and solitude of my small safe place. The night belonged to mourning, and morning came dark in the bright crack of dawn. Somehow, I knew this good thing, me and Ms. Librarian, would end. Crushed by the judgment and the small-town weight of good and bad. Dealing drugs was not good. Associations earned outcomes. That outcome was foreseeable. Running barrels could be liberating. The physicality shut down the mind, at least temporarily. I'd run hard every day.

The swings of summer. From full romance to being left alone against the wall, not even chosen at the dance. The loss of Ms. Librarian would hurt me for a long time to come.

Scarecrow and Bogeyman were my summer help. We were busy. Thanks to Ms. Librarian's exit, we all had hurts to hide from, run from. Barrel runs, woodchopping, and some landscaping. We were getting brown and firm, and growing our hair. Bogeyman and Scarecrow were getting clean. No dope. No drinks. I joined them, not just in support but because my emotions were too raw. I was still cut wide open by the surgery of separation. I worried about maintaining control. Rage was one sideways look or one poorly chosen word away. I was bottling it up.

Mister and Stone Pony talked straight out about their plans. Sell grass and hash in volume to upwards of fifty people, ranging in ages from eighteen to fifty-five. All their clients had different end customers and intended uses. One of their first clients was a prominent big-city lawyer in his early fifties. He had tried grass once with his soon-to-become second wife, who was in her twenties and, as he liked to joke, had tits in the higher thirties. He took a pound every two weeks. He shared some with his older son and lots with his bosomy wife. Mister and Stone Pony called them Mr. D and Mrs. DD. The lawyer was a springboard to some high-end customers and, in many cases, their kids. Doctors, businessmen, lots of lawyers, dentists, bankers, corporate execs of all types. These were quiet, discreet, well-heeled clients. Increasing the price of the product was never a problem for that clientele. They all had high-service needs and sufficient cash. The clientele soon grew to two hundred total.

Garbage, security, maintenance, cleaning, deliveries, and pickups. Mister and Stone Pony were expanding to do it all. The legit side of the business was booming. The plan was to maximize the distribution branch of the business through the following summer and winter, and then get out of the dope business altogether by the spring of 1973. I didn't doubt their abilities, but the cash flowing in was staggering. They had to wash it through legit business ventures. That explained their sharp, competitive pricing. They also encouraged customers in all their businesses to pay in cash, which would help cover to some degree the cash nature of the dope business. Clever.

Hard work was a panacea, a cure-all, as Scarecrow would say, "for what ails ya." He was ailing. He didn't want to talk about his experiences. He only once said anything that was terribly grim. We were driving in the truck at the end of a solid ten-hour barrel run in cottage country. Scarecrow was sitting in the middle, with Bogeyman at the wheel and me in the shotgun seat. "You know, boys," Scarecrow said, "I never thought I was going to take it up the ass. That still surprises me. Keeps me awake a bit."

That was that. His voice was dead flat. No rage, no emotion of any kind, just dead flat. No inflection, no tone of surprise. Dead flat. The scary sound of forced submission. His mood swung very little all summer except for two high points, if high points were moles on an elephant's ass. He got dentures, and he said filling in the empty spaces with false goods would help fill the empty spaces inside him, and he sort of smiled. The second time, we caught him looking at his image in the big side mirror of the truck. He turned to me. "Garbage Boy," he said, "I'm developing some pipes." He wasn't wrong. The bare bones were filling out with some lean, hard muscles. Scarecrow described his overall mood as morose. He also said he was making a comeback. He swung high and low, but mostly low.

Bogeyman was another story. He was processing. He was processing his own story. He was doing what he referred to as "advanced planning." He talked about the role he could play in the organization. Bogeyman saw himself as a process guy. Figuring things out, organizing, and making them work. Scarecrow had been their front man, the relationship-builder in their dope-buying and world travels. If Scarecrow made the connections, Bogeyman made the connections work. He organized their cash, their transactions, their travels, their banking, and their contact list.

Bogeyman and Stone Pony made another eight-hundred-pound buy. Stone Pony trusted Bogeyman to take the deals and organize the deliveries and payments. Stone Pony and Mister also relied on Bogeyman's knowledge of the trade to help them decide who they could sell larger quantities to safely. Bogeyman also initiated currency negotiations with the Mexicans. The Mexicans needed to dump American cash, as the DEA in the states was on a path of "following the money" as they probed the burgeoning Mexican drug cartels. The DEA was chasing where the US dollars were flowing. Seems no one gave a rat's ass about Canadian currency. The Mexicans could dump and trade Canadian currency with all the Canadian tourists visiting their resort areas. They also could pay their Canadian connections less expensively in Canadian dollars. The dollar was basically at par with the US dollar in 1971, but the Mexicans were trading dollars at a five-percent discount. Bogeyman was now making money for NCE in foreign exchange and taking a cut.

Bogeyman had a physical frame built for hard work. He was building stamina. He loved to run between barrels. His afro was coming back quickly, complemented by a thin 'stache. He described himself as being on a slow, transcendent, upward arc of success. He was swinging slow and steady, building momentum. Analysis was key, he said. I wasn't sure what he was talking about.

Newspaper Crew Enterprises and all the affiliated businesses were flying. The cleaning services had expanded to a third person. The women were stocking fridges and buying groceries for weekend cottagers. The Whities were doing extensive repair and maintenance work on equipment outside of the NCE family, including a lot of work for the city and some interesting customization works on truck frames, load capacities, and engines. NCE was on an upward trajectory.

The city and cottage country were alive. There was an almost-constant festive mood in the air. Money was flowing into the area. Big-city folks spending cash on fixing cottages and buying cottages and spending it in local restaurants, in stores, at the marina, the liquor and beer outlets, and on dope. Lots of dope. Bogeyman and Scarecrow were no longer in the street trade. Several entrepreneurs had taken their place, most of whom were just trying to sell enough weed to get their own consumption needs covered. A combination of Vipers and Kings of the South were beginning to organize together and starting to be more dominant in the street trade, under the auspices of the MMC. It seemed that key members had done enough reform school, juvenile detention, and prison time together to see past their old rivalries, self-interests, and wounds to come together. Teddy Porter was the leader. Blotto was in the mix. Mor and Les were in the circle, as were all three Inglis brothers. Many of my old acquaintances and enemies were united. That didn't bode well for me, but I didn't seem to be on their radar screen—at least not yet. Teddy Porter always swore he owed me, so that was out there, hanging over my head.

Bogeyman and Scarecrow were definitely in their sights. B and S had dominated street sales either directly or indirectly for years. The combined gangs wanted that business at the bidding of their masters, the MMC. Even though B and S were a step back from direct retail sales, they were still supplying a lot of street value. All the locals and everybody else wanted to deal with B and S's loosely affiliated network rather than Porter and his band of hoods.

Mister and Stone Pony were also in their sights. They were now calling their combined group the "All Saints," which I thought was both clever and ironic. Maybe Teddy and crew had done some book learning during their prison stints. Whether they intended to be ironic was unclear, as they were anything but saints. The local police, the RCMP, and the narc squad were paying the All Saints a lot of attention, which was a good diversion for the law enforcement folks as far as Mister and Stone Pony were concerned.

The disturbing thing about the All Saints was they were associating with motorcycle gangs from the city. Primarily the MMC were their controllers. When those guys rolled into town, a lot of sphincters got tighter, the air seemed heavier, and the mood shifted to black-and-yellow caution signs. The big-city gangs were flexing their muscles and starting to look for lucrative markets to push their drugs. They weren't interested in competing for the business. They preferred to monopolize the market. According to Bogeyman's analysis, they were all street pushers and thugs. Their clientele was on the street, in the bars, and in low places. The motorcycle gangs, with the MMC as the territory chief, were looking to dominate the heavy user market and distribution channels. The trade was changing quickly. Bogeyman's analytical overview included an observation that Mister and Stone Pony's "exit plan" might need to be expedited.

Bogeyman and Scarecrow swung from the kings of the small street level, corner nickel-and-dime bag sales to the movers of "weight." Bogeyman and Scarecrow swung from world-class travelers and partiers to stay-at-home sober Arthur Street card players. The boys' wing would be basically complete by the end of August, about a month after my birthday. Bogeyman and Scarecrow enrolled in night classes for the fall. Their plan—well, Bogeyman's plan; Scarecrow was just following in his path—was to graduate from high school by the following summer and take university- or college-level business classes by the next fall. From drop-out dopers to solid academic scholars. No one saw that swing coming.

I ventured alone to the Refuge on the day after my eighteenth birthday. We had celebrated at home the night before, a Thursday night. Stone Pony, Mister, Bogeyman, Scarecrow, the little one, and Mom, all there to wrap me in love and wish me the best. I wasn't Scarecrow-level morose, but I was down. After a dinner of hamburgers and homemade fries and a cake with candles, the party kind of went with my mood. There had been good chatter and a few laughs. Everybody was trying so hard to lift my spirits, but Ms. Librarian had taken away my library privileges, revoked my card, and I was gutted.

Bogeyman and Scarecrow bought me a baseball glove and they bought one each for themselves. Scarecrow's eyes told me that playing some catch, fielding a few grounders, and taking a few swings just might help him come back to himself a little—maybe to second base, but still a long way from home plate.

The red Mustang in the driveway was from Mister and Stone Pony. I thought they had just borrowed the Brownies' ride for the night until they handed me the keys. They didn't even say, "Happy birthday," just turned their heads in the direction of the driveway and nodded. That brought a smile.

Stone Pony finished his chocolate cake and ice cream and said it was time to go. It was a Thursday night, and there were lots of barrels to run in the morning. Friday's bins were always fuller—and even more so in the summer. Summer barrels were always all out, full, and heavy in the city. Full and heavy, like my mood.

Stone Pony motioned for me to follow him and Mister outside. We had already been outside to see my Mustang and start the engine, so I was wondering what was up. Mister's deep voice kicked off. "It's a great car. A beauty. Never drive it on one drop of booze or one toke of weed. Always wear your seat belt. You ever once break those rules, and the Mustang will be gone in a flash."

He looked at me, and my eyes told him I got it and believed him. Stone Pony's turn. He grabbed my right forearm and pressed it to my chest. My hand had been playing with Ms. Librarian's gold chain.

"You been playing with that gold chain all night and looking far away and sad. You probably are. She's gone, and she won't be coming back, you stupid fuck."

That kind of took me by surprise. First, he was working so hard not to say "fuck," and second, he was some fucking angry.

"All the people who love you and will stick with you are here celebrating your birthday, and you, you stupid fucking fucker, ain't even fucking focusing on them for one fucking second. What a selfish fuck. I should ram the fucking keys to this fucking car up your ass. You fucked over those who care for you like an ignorant fuck. Now get your head out of your ass. We don't want your gratitude or your thanks. We want you here with us. Go back in there and make sure those four people know you love them. Respect for those you love is all about staying in the moments you have with them. Ms. Librarian or anybody not there with you or for you should never steal those moments from those who are there with you and for you. You get that, right? And stop fingering that fucking chain, or I'll rip that fucker from your neck in a heartbeat. It ain't a talisman or good-luck charm. It's about loss, hurt, and an empty spot in your soul. It never, never will trump the gains, the joys, and the fullness in your heart those who love you are giving. Tonight you should take the joy, fill up with it, let it drown out the loss, fill the emptiness, and quiet the hurt you feel. Those around you can heal you, so let us in. That's it."

Stone Pony was slapping me to my knees with hot words as effective as when the little one had kicked me in the nuts for my mocking wave at Granny in the *Beverly Hillbillies*. Instantly, I knew these were words I needed to hear.

Mister summed it up.

"We're here. We care, and we will heal you. Let us do our job of providing friendship and kinship. Now, you need to get yourself straight in short order. We know it's only a few weeks since you lost your love, but it's time to turn the corner. We got a lot of work and big plans. You're part of that, big time. Get your shit together. You got anything to say?"

"Thanks. I needed and deserved that. That's what friends do, right? Give you the hard truth in a hard way."

"Something like that. Sorry about all the effing *effing*." Stone Pony made us all smile with that.

"I'm going to the Refuge tomorrow night. Can you alert the Neapolitan Crew to save me from death and destruction? I'm going to get wrecked. Maybe look for a Snow Queen. I'm going to walk there and maybe crawl home. What do you think? Good plan or what?"

"Mediocre plan at best with minimum redemptive value, but go for it, you sad sack little frick." Again, Stone Pony had us all laughing.

I did walk to the Refuge. My route took me through Little Hendri Park where I stopped at the pump for a cold drink of the spring water. Ms. Librarian and I had made love on a picnic table there. We had even talked about hitting that table after dinner at Angelo's on my birthday. I was mixing good memories with missing hopes and never-to-be's or something like that. I walked through town. Lots of people said hi and made small talk. Quite a few asked if I had any weed, and just as many asked if I wanted to do a number. Councillor Sideburns' ample-chested daughter ran to me, bouncing all the way, and gave me the hug of a long-lost lover. I couldn't remember her name. She asked about Bogeyman and Scarecrow, and I gave her a non-answer of sorts. She was still latched onto me, and her chest felt good against mine. She invited me to her place. There would be few people crashing at her place that night, and her parents were away.

I swung through the big park and by the swings and memorialized the inaugural picnic table that Ms. Librarian and I had shared in the biblical sense. Then all the way down an old trail that skirted the lake, coming out of the bush just before the bridge that went over the narrows between the two lakes. Bogeyman, Scarecrow, and I had biked on that trail more than a few times. As I walked, it felt good to clear my head and think of how much the three of us enjoyed collecting beer and pop bottles, escaping the two gangs and beat-downs on our secret paths, and laughed our asses off when we emerged from some trail, safe and together.

How I needed and longed for some cold draft beer across the bridge at the Refuge. It was almost 10. I was making a late entrance, and there was likely a long lineup. I was feeling good—or at least a little more solid.

Crossing the bridge, I saw the lineup snaking around the building. I figured a local band was playing—Flatbush, Zeitgeist, or Thunder Stick. They all played "Smoke on the Water" and Vanilla Fudge's version of "You Keep Me Hanging On." I figured it could be fun. I went to the side door, where the deliveries were taken, and knocked. Zach opened the door, and as soon as he saw me, he broke into a big grin. "Get in here, brother. Happy birthday. We have a pitcher with your name on it waiting for you."

The Neapolitan Crew still worked security at the Refuge on weekends and holidays. The place was a cash cow, according to Stone Pony and Mister. The Neapolitan Crew were making wads of cash at the Refuge. There was no cover charge, but the vast majority of male patrons gladly handed the crew members a few dollars on their way in without being asked. Some patrons even tipped on the way out. Fights rarely broke out under the Neapolitan Crew's watch. The FBI, the Brownies, and the Whities were very effective deterrents to social mayhem.

Zach had a pitcher in one hand and a glass in the other as he motioned me to a table at the edge of the dance floor. The band Flatbush was on break, and my eyes were adjusting to the dark as Zach set the pitcher on the table and handed me the glass.

"Here you go, Scarface. Premium seating with super-premium company." Zeke arrived and smacked down two more pitchers, wished me happy birthday, then sauntered off. At the table were five gorgeous women, likely all two or three years older than me. A redhead leaned in. "Are you Scarface?" she asked. "We hear you're legendary in these parts. We were in line for a long time and then the two big Indians pulled us out of line. They brought us in the side door and to this table. We've been dancing our asses off. We're staying at Candy's parents' cottage on Blue Bay. They told us this was your reserved table, and we could sit here until you came. Can we stay, or do you have friends coming? Or your girlfriend? She must be gorgeous, given how you look."

Man, the chick didn't take a breath. My response was as cool as I could pull off. "You can stay for a while. You might be the friends I was hoping for. There is no girlfriend. Have they played 'You Keep Me Hanging On'?"

"Thanks, and the pitchers, are they from you?"

I nodded.

"And no, they haven't played that song yet. Will you dance with me when they do? Slow. I'm Sandy, that's Candy, then Mandy, April, and Louise. We're all from the city and go to Waterloo Lutheran in KW because we wanted to get away from our parents."

The women all said hi, and they were quite a crew. I filled all their glasses from the pitcher. We toasted each other. The lead singer and the organist came by the table and wished me happy birthday, but mostly they came to scope out the women. My first beer went down cold and fast. The rest of the night was dancing, drinking, and saying hello to a whole bunch of people I hadn't seen since school had wrapped up for me back at the end of May. A few women offered me their condolences on the demise of the Ms. Librarian relationship. A couple suggested they would make an outstanding replacement. Physically, they weren't wrong.

The night was wild. Flatbush was in great form. I danced with every one of the WLU women more than once. Sandy crushed me with her pelvis during "You Keep Me Hanging On," and she made me a little hard. She knew it, and liked her effect on me.

I left with the WLU women, and at Candy's parents place I ended up with Candy or Mandy. I lost the ability to remember their names. At about four in the morning, Sandy woke me up, explained she had gotten a little drunk and threw up but was alright now. We had some fun. I woke up at about nine with Sandy on one side and Mandy or Candy on the other. I smiled. The university women had made a favourable impression. I extricated myself from the bed, which was a big king size, found the bathroom and my clothes, pissed, pulled my jeans on, and headed into the main part of the cabin—well, home. I saw a couple of the WLU women out on the deck and headed there.

"Jesus, are you a model or something?" I think that was Louise, and she was gaping at me.

"Christ, no! Just a garbage boy, or maybe a garbage man. Is that coffee?" My head was a little scrambled, but I was glad I answered somewhat coherently. She and April were sitting on chairs, wearing skimpy bikinis.

"My God, Mandy, look at his scars. How did you get them?" April looked genuinely shocked as she spat out her words. Now I knew that Louise was Mandy, so that meant Candy had had her way with me.

"Knife fight," I said, then laughed as they both gasped.

"Really? No shit," Mandy said. "Seriously, that's so cool."

I poured myself a coffee as they hung there, waiting for a reply.

"I took a baseball bat to a few cars. Some people who had harmed me," I said, which was basically the truth. My scars seemed to stand out in the bright sunshine.

"Can I touch them?" Mandy asked timidly.

"Sure, go ahead." I was standing drinking my coffee as she ran her fingers over the scar on my chest, then the J-hook scar on my neck, and finally the one on my right cheek. Mandy leaned in and kissed all three softly and gently. April stood up and did the same thing, lots of tenderness. They were both standing, each with a hand on my chest. It was erotic.

"Wow. You nailed Candy and Sandy? Now you're going to pop Mandy and Louise. You must have some pecker on you, Scarface." So that was April, and the other one was Louise. OK, now I had the faces and bodies matched to the names. "I peeked in the master bedroom, and those girls are naked, sleeping with smiles on their faces," April said. "Good job, boy wonder."

All three of them laughed. I grinned and scratched my head. April poured herself coffee, and Louise volunteered to make more. She was in just panties and a tight T-shirt that outlined her nipples perfectly. When Louise returned, we filled our coffee mugs and began to banter about the band and the Refuge scene the night before. Lots of laughter and different memories of the same experience. We joked about beer glasses making people look good.

Mandy turned serious with a sad look on her face. "You aren't going to tell us the truth about those scars, are you? I bet the truth is tied to a sad story, and I don't want to hear that."

"The truth is, Mandy, the scars are tied to a sad story that I don't share, so thank you for the grace of not pushing me on that," I said. "The big scars from that event are inside my head and heart now, but I've mostly pushed past them. The healing goes on."

The mood turned somber. April broke through the gloom. "We need a boat ride and beers. Scarface, go and wake up your love dolls, and let's get this show on the road. Mandy, why don't you get the boat ready? Louise and I will get some breakfast rolling. I think those two easy-over-on-their-backs lovers of yours are going to need a kick start to their day. I'm on mimosa duty."

So, off we went. I hesitantly and quietly approached the master bedroom. When I peeked my head in, Candy and Sandy were sitting up and fully covered. That was a bit of a shame, because I couldn't entirely remember their bodies.

"Lover boy! You didn't run out on your new friends!" Candy exclaimed, both of them all smiles.

"Yeah, we thought you might be one of those four F country boys, you know. Find 'em, feel 'em, fuck 'em, forget 'em." Sandy was laughing full tilt.

I knew my response was as lame as shit as it exited my mouth. "Who could forget you two?"

"So, you did fuck both of us. Scarface, we took absolute advantage of you, and we're not sorry." Sandy said, and Candy nodded. They were enjoying this.

"Well, good for you. Now get out of bed. April is making mimosas. Louise is starting breakfast. Mandy is getting the boat ready." Maybe I was staring too hard as I said that because they simultaneously pulled down the thin sheet they were tucked behind. "We need a shower and coffee," Candy said. "How about you get us coffee or shower with us?"

I stared, gulped, and sputtered. "I'll get coffee." I turned and left as they giggled and one of them said, "Poor choice."

My summer was swinging—really swinging—in the right direction. Over breakfast, those five women chatted about a wide range of topics. They were all set to graduate the following spring. At least two of them were headed to law school, another to grad school, Mandy to Europe for at least six months, and maybe Louise was going with her. They talked about women's lib, politics, grass versus alcohol, and their parents and boyfriends, both current and future. I just listened. They got into philosophical discussions and their personal beliefs. Breakfast stretched from before ten to noon. Then Louise, who seemed to be the informal leader, stood up. "Bikini and boat time, girls. Scarface, wear a bikini if you got it, but Candy likely has some trunks you can borrow. The little whore has a big collection." They all laughed at that.

"Yeah, I collected them from outside Louise's dorm room first and second year." More giggles. Those women gave as good as they got.

Then April surprised me. "Scarface, phone the Whities and tell them to meet us at Alfie's marina at one o'clock sharp. Tell them it's the hot bod squad, and they'll be there in a heartbeat."

"Don't you mean hard beat?" Candy's line made them all break up. "Those white boys are all muscles and seriously . . . wait for it . . . flexible. Must be from their wrestling background." The girls roared with laughter and pretended to be shocked at Candy's comment.

We picked the Whities up and began an adventure that lasted until late Sunday night. Boat rides, beer, barbecues, back to the Refuge on Saturday night, a few joints, dancing, and screwing. The quiet Zach and Zeke remained quiet, but it was like Mandy and Louise were their dates. The Whities had small shit-eating grins all weekend. I ended up with Candy and Sandy back in the master bedroom on Saturday night to late Sunday morning. I didn't think about Ms. Librarian once that weekend, which was a relief, a reprieve, and kind of a blessing. Move on. Find a safer path through all that.

We were out on the boat late Sunday afternoon and anchored close to an island. The water was clear and shallow. The bottom was sandy. Louise grabbed two beers and her shoes and told me to grab my shoes. "Let's go for a walk on this little island," she said. We got to shore, put our shoes on, and Louise took me by the hand and led me up a barely visible path. About a hundred yards up the trail, she veered right, ducked under a huge fallen jack pine, and stepped into a small clearing.

"Scarface, you're going to fuck me standing up right here in the woods," she said. I did, but it was more like Louise fucking me. She finished quicker than I expected and appeared ecstatic, frenetically charged, and a little crazed. She bore down on me until I shot inside of her. She might have come again because her back arched, and she moaned. Then she looked me in the eyes and said, "More." She turned around and pressed her back against my chest. "Just play with all my parts." I did. I took direction well in such situations. Her hand reached back between us, and she tugged me to hardness, which was her objective. Louise was tall and willowy, but full and curvy. She moved my hands and fingers where she wanted them and silently showed me how she wanted me to play with her parts. The impact that all this was having on her showed, once again, I was excellent at following directions.

Louise was panting, short little gasps of air. She bent slightly forward and away from me, then guided me inside her. "Don't move," she instructed. She was doing the driving, the riding, the pounding. My depth in her was all from her drilling. The force was all her, foot on the pedal, and she was the whole rhythm section and in control of the conductor's baton. I was just a roadie tending the equipment. Louise got close to an orgasm. "Now, pound it in. Pound me, Scarface, pound me." I was doing my best when she came, and she shook with spasms. She reached back with both arms, one arm grabbing my ass, the other the back of my head, pulling them both forward, pulling all of me into her. I shot like a rocket. She sighed deeply, let go with her hands, and almost fell forward. We had been fucking with just our shoes on.

Louise was a bit catatonic, according to her. "Dress me," she said. I found her bikini bottom and top and summer blouse. I got her dressed. She cracked the beers and said, "We can drink these on the way back. That was some thirsty business, Scarface," and she laughed.

I almost had to carry her back to the boat. Louise was a willowy, wet, wobbly noodle.

Me? I felt fantastic. Drained and sweaty and smiling. Man, that was good. I was laughing to myself with all kinds of thoughts racing through my head, like: *If you feel 'em, fuck 'em, and they faint in the forest, should you go find 'em? Or if a tree falls in the forest while you're fucking, do you hear it?* I was giddy. We hadn't sipped much of the beer, and I finished both of them on the hundred-yard journey back to the shore. We emerged smiling, and cheers rose from our boat and several others moored at the island.

"Uh, Louise, you got a bit of goo running down your thigh." That was Candy. The rest of the hot bod squad, the HBS for short, started laughing.

Louise didn't miss a beat. She took a long finger, scooped the imaginary goo up, and put it in her mouth. "Yum," she said.

Everybody freaked out at that with flash floods of shock and hilarious overreactions. Louise had them back on their heels. "Tasty, high in protein and vitamins, and good for the complexion. Just look at Candy's face. She's a goo-gobbler from way back."

That launched a kaleidoscope of taunts, insults, and disparaging comments on moral character, sexual ineptitude, sexual behaviours, and comparative horniness among and between the five women. The Whities and I just grinned and took it all in. We wouldn't have gotten a word in anyway. They were extremely quick-witted and comfortable with their friendship, which was obvious from the machine-gun rapidity of their exchange.

I finally broke their string of inter-squad taunts. "Thanks to Louise's recruitment strategy, I'm definitely going to university. I think the University of Goo will do nicely." That broke everyone up.

As the hot bod squad continued to verbally joust with each other, the Whities motioned me to look to my left. I did. In the two boats close to us, we saw kids our age drinking beer and passing joints. Nothing extraordinary in those vessels, and nobody I recognized—probably kids like the hot bod squad, up from the city.

The third boat was anchored a little farther away. It had three guys and one lady on board. Two of the guys were big mothers, not quite FBI-size, but big. They were wearing leather vests, which was unusual on a hot day at the end of July, especially out there on the water. The third guy seemed to be staring at me. He looked familiar, but I couldn't place him. Then he waved and motioned for me to come over. I glanced at the Whities, and they both murmured for me to be careful. Before I had turned back around, I knew who it was. Teddy Porter. I didn't recognize him with the curly black hair down to his shoulders instead of his greased-back pompadour look. As I started to walk toward him, I noticed that Teddy had not gained much weight. Porter still had a skinny chest and skinny arms. I was thinking I could rip him apart in a fight. Then I noticed two things. The long knife strapped to Teddy's belt and the letters on the back of one of Teddy's monster companion's vest. "Mayhem MC 1966." The Mayhem Motorcycle Club was one badass criminal organization.

The water was just about waist deep as I neared the boat with Teddy and his companions. I pulled up about six feet from the bow, out of range from getting stuck with Teddy's knife.

"Scarface, how is it that those good-looking, smart, big-city university broads are hanging out with someone as ugly and fucked-over as you and your two albino friends?" Teddy was obviously not worried about mending any fences with me. His voice was loud enough that everyone in the other nearby boats went quiet.

"Actually, Scarface, despite a little meat on your bones, you're uglier than ever, and still look like a dumb shit." Teddy and the motorcycle men all laughed.

I decided to go on the offensive. "Teddy Bear, are you still the little boy who pissed all over himself a couple of years back when I kicked the crap out of you?" I said it with enough false bravado to silence all the spectators in the four nearest boats.

"What the fuck, Teddy?" one of the Mayhem monsters muttered. "This boy put a beating on you? He calls you Teddy Bear?"

Teddy was livid, and looked like he was coming over the side of the boat as he grabbed the handle of his knife. "Fuck you, Scarface, you fuckin' coward. You snuck up and suckered me, and then your fuckin' jerk-off friends knocked me out with a beer bottle and pissed on me. You wait. I'm going to fuck up the three of you someday soon and . . ." He stopped as he looked past me. I turned to see that the Whities were just a couple of feet behind me.

"And tell your white Wonder Bread Boys to fuck off, or I'll fuck them up, too."

"Well, Teddy Bear, that seems like a lot of guys you wanna fuck. Is that the way things are swinging for you these days?" More false bravado. I was questioning my own sanity as the words were coming out of my mouth. Taunting Ted Porter in the presence of his Mayhem Motorcycle Club friends was less than smart.

"Scarface, you're fuckin' with the wrong fucks. But that's OK. You and your whole fuckin' Newspaper Crew are about to have some serious shit rain down upon you. Soon, Scarface, soon. So, tighten up your ass, boy, because you're going to be shittin' your pants and beggin' for mercy." Teddy's threat sounded both surreal and real at the same time. That was not how I thought the conversation would go.

"Shut the fuck up, Porter. Now. You fuckin' moron. Let's get the fuck outta here." Mayhem One's eyes were burning holes in Teddy as he growled out his words. Mayhem Two was already pulling anchor, and Miss Mayhem, leather vest, no bra, was turning on the engine and at the steering wheel. They backed out, spun around, and sped off. Mayhem One cuffed Teddy in the back of the head twice before they were twenty yards away.

"That was a serious threat," Zeke said.

Zach nodded in agreement. "Yep. Those boys are planning some mayhem, and it's coming our way."

"We gotta let Stone Pony, Mister, and the whole crew know right away," Zeke said in a tone as serious as the sunrise.

I offered up an obvious assessment of the exchange. "Boys, I guess I shorted a few of Teddy's circuits, but what the fuck just went down with Porter and the MMC monsters?

Zach stated what we all were feeling. "Good that you did that, because now we've been alerted and can get our guard up, because there's going to be some turbulence in our near future."

Zeke and I nodded at Zach's assessment.

We started walking back to the hot bod squad boat. The other two boats were quiet, and alternated between gazing at us and looking down.

Zach laughed. "How and why did you come up with 'Teddy Bear'? Now that's seriously funny."

"Yeah," Zeke said. "It was hard not to laugh out loud at the reaction. Classic. It was like you called him a pussy in front of the Mayhem boys."

"I'm not sure of the inspiration, but it felt good to call him out that way. Sure provoked him." I didn't know what else to say by way of explanation. What I did know with almost one hundred percent certainty was Teddy Bear and I were going to tangle, and likely my friends were going to be in a battle as well.

With that line about leverage, he shot a smirk at Ms. Annamoosie and Stone Pony. They both snickered and nodded. Something had been communicated that was only known within their circle. I was on the outside, looking at an inside joke of some kind.

"The workers are mostly from the Six Nations down Brantford way. We have done some work with them before, and they had some guys available. They have other jobs coming up soon, so they need to work fast on your home. Are you happy with those answers? Are you happy with your new home?" The way he smiled accomplished two things in my mind. First, I trusted those good folks, and second, everything was going to be fine. I nodded and said yes.

Stone Pony jumped in at that point. "You didn't ask the important question. The reason we're building this big addition to your home."

"No, I guess I didn't, and that is a big wonder."

"Well, it's simple. Those two boys need some close comfort and tending. They have never had much of a family life. Your son is the closest thing to a true family they have ever experienced or been able to enjoy. Scarface cares for them deeply, as they care for him."

Mister took over from there. They were the perfect tag team. "You and your son have faced down some demons and kept yourself rising. Bogeyman and Scarecrow need to be around spirits and souls like that, like yours. Good souls, good spirits, caring folks."

Stone Pony gently lifted my chin with his hand, moved in close to me, and looked directly into my eyes. "Those boys need a lot of healing in a lot of ways. This place we're building is intended to be a place that can make them as close to whole as they can get back to. A place to heal, a place to feel safe, a place to get strong, a place to get over big hurts and larger evils. You have done that in your home. You have overcome hurt. You have overcome evil. We hope you and this home can provide these boys, especially Scarecrow, with the spirit, the heart, and the mind to get over all the bad stuff. To find the strength to rise up and go on to good. That's why this place, this home, and you."

Stone Pony's voice became quieter and quieter as he spoke, almost to a whisper, a soft, warm wind in my ears, catching my heart and tugging out little tears. I was sure Ms. Annamoosie and Mister were feeling the same. We all quietly absorbed the comfort of his voice and his meaning. I got up and hugged him where he stood in my kitchen, then kissed his forehead.

"They will know healing," I whispered. "A seamstress mends. I'll mend them.

A mother tends to her children. I'll tend to them. This is my promise."

Mister broke the silence following my vow, my oath. He was holding back a heavy sob that came out as a snort, a laugh, and a cry all mixed into one. A strange sound all about joy and hope. "This is too teary and weepy," he said. "We need cold beers."

We laughed, and Ms. Annamoosie came and hugged me. "We'll get this done," she said. "We're the caregivers, and these are your new sons, all of them. You're their mom. In your heart is hope and love, and I vow to help you get this done."

Stone Pony stood with two beers clutched in each hand and he laughed. "Let's have a drink, because I'm drowning in tears. Come on, open these, and toast these boys. What do you say to that, Mom?"

We laughed as Mister enfolded Ms. Annamoosie and me in his big arms. "I'll drink to that," he said. That's how it all came about—me getting a big house and a bigger family. It all seemed so good.

I never would have expected something like that to happen. How could I? Getting to that point, that situation? The vow to myself was to do my best to make and keep everyone whole. It was good work. A good way to live. Not that He had been much of a presence in any of this, but the high-and-mighty tea-and-crumpets crowd might even call it God's work. It wasn't, and it won't be. God couldn't take the credit if He wouldn't take the blame. It was the work of a red man, a black man, and a white man, that being my son. The Newspaper Crew, with a little help from me.

Zach stopped us and turned to face Zeke and me just before we got back to the boat and as solemn as hell he said, "Scarface, you will be going to university, but you may be going to war first."

The hot bod squad uniformly agreed that the mood had been ruined. We pulled anchor and headed out.

That's how the summer swung. The absolute high of being with Louise to the low of a pending battle with Teddy Bear and the Mayhem unleashed. There was a strong potential that things would not end well for someone.

CHAPTER 34

Mayhem and Madness

Scarecrow initially described August as *pure bedlam*. He adjusted the description to *mayhem*—and not because of the MMC, but because of our workload. We were working about fourteen-hour days, sunrise to sunset and then some.

Bogeyman said the pace was pure madness, and we wouldn't last. He was going to quit. Then we would get paid on Fridays, and Bogeyman would be first in bed, so we could be up at 5 on Saturday and get a solid fourteen hours in, all at double time. We were running barrels, cutting lawns, trimming trees, removing brush, building decks, and delivering groceries and booze. Stone Pony and Mister were selling weed by the bushel. Money was flooding in.

The boys' wing was almost finished at Mom's house. It was spectacular, as was the addition at the back of the house. I was looking forward to getting back to school for a break.

No real mayhem had fallen on our heads yet. Teddy Porter's threat hadn't materialized. Stone Pony and Mister had called a meeting of the crew after the Whities informed them of Porter's threat and the MMC monsters' reaction. They let the entire crew know the threat was serious. The MMC wanted to control all the drug distribution from outside the big city and through the north. In the big city, they had stern opposition from the Hell's Angels, but they figured they could own the north. It took them a while to figure out who was selling all the dope in bulk in the north that made its way back to the city. The MMC's territorial imperative in the north and the Hell's Angels' market share was being eroded in the Big Smoke. The Hell's Angels didn't want to bother with the boonies, so they gave the north to the MMC. The Hell's Angels expected a kickback from the MMC from the northern sales, and the MMC wasn't making quota. Things were getting tense in the world of motorcycle clubs. The MMC couldn't take on the Hell's Angels. They were subservient to them, and they knew it. The MMC was bound to take on whoever was running the north. The word on the street was they found out from one wasted big-city college boy that massive quantities were being handled by the "Lone Tonto." The college boy told MMC that this motley crew was selling to all age groups and a lot of professionals. They sold to clients who were discreet and credible and could buy in bulk. Lots of that weed was making its way back to the city. The MMC knew that the stoned college boy had messed up the seller's name. The competition was Mister and Stone Pony, who had been nicknamed "The Lone Nigger and Tonto." A black man and a red man were thwarting their ambitions and cash flow and endangering any of their so-called goodwill with the Hell's Angels. The MMC were skating on thin ice, which meant the All Saints were in big trouble, and moments away from getting seriously fucked up.

Stone Pony and Mister, with Mr. Clampett's input, said we had to be aware, on our guard, and careful, because the MMC wasn't going to negotiate territorial rights. The MMC planned on just taking over. That meant mayhem. Stone Pony and Mister revamped their timeline once again, and said they would be out of the distribution business by the following August. Their plan was to build all the legitimate businesses, bankroll them, and let the dope business go to whoever wanted it. They also knew that eighty to eighty-five percent of their clientele couldn't risk and wouldn't buy from the MMC, Teddy Porter, and his associates that populated the All Saints, or the Hell's Angels. They would find more corporate, professional, and far less obvious and dubious supply lines. The MMC liked to fight when they took territory. That added a significant dimension of urgency for an expedited exit from the illicit drug trade for Mister and Stone Pony—and all of us, by extension.

Madness described our work lives, as pending mayhem hung in the air from the last week of July until the last week of August. We were always working and wary, looking over our shoulders. Nothing happened. No sightings of Porter, the All Saints, or any other remnants of the former town gangs or MMC were observed anywhere near NCE operations or around our work. None of the distribution clients had been approached or bothered. None of the Newspaper Crew Enterprises were interfered with. The Neapolitan Crew was still working at the Refuge, and the MMC or local associates never came in that bar for drinks. Mister and Stone Pony took the lack of visibility, encroachment, and interference as the silence before the storm. They simply repeated and reminded all of us to stay vigilant. Mr. Clampett had been doing clandestine surveillance of the MCC, Porter, and the All Saints in town and in the big city. He compiled a dossier (Bogeyman explained the word).

Stone Pony and Mister called another meeting on the second-last Sunday of August. The dossier was presented. In it were pictures, accompanied by the criminal histories of the seven MCC members who had been around town and in the north. The dossier also had eight locals, including Teddy, Blotto, all three Inglis Brothers, Mor (but not Les), and three other former Vipers or Kings of the South. Fifteen soldiers in all, as Mr. Clampett called them. The count excluded four MMC biker chicks and three local gang women. Gloria Gagnier was one of the local women. GG and I had once tussled, with her coming out on top. It wasn't what I would call a fair fight, but that didn't matter in local lore. The legend was I had been beaten up by a girl. There was an element of truth in that, for sure.

Scarecrow shouted out at the mention of Gloria's name. "Double G's double Ds made Scarface a breast man." He relayed the story of my fight with the stacked Miss Gagnier. Everyone enjoyed the moment of levity.

Other than that laughter at my expense, the group was somber and asked serious questions about the threat we all felt. Mr. Clampett handled the questions. He said the MMC was for big, showy disputes, not real gang wars. The MMC wanted to instill fear and intimidate rivals. They would want a public display of force to illuminate their dominance. We should expect a confrontation.

The FBI asked about weapons.

"Us or them?" Mr. Clampett replied. Almost everyone said both. Mr. Clampett nodded and gave us, as he called it, the relevant and recent history.

The MMC were maimers, not murderers, which was relatively good news. Their weapons of choice were tire irons, brass knuckles, bare fists, clubs, and baseball bats, and their women liked rolling pins. They had not killed anybody, and apparently didn't want to step over that line. Mr. Clampett said they had guns, some sawed-off shotguns, and they carried knives.

"Us?" someone asked.

"We have an arsenal. Lots of hunting rifles. We have some explosives. The perimeter of the cottage is fortified with deterrents. We don't intend to fight. We certainly aren't going to launch an offensive. Although I advised Mister and Stone Pony if I took a couple of the locals out of the game, the other six would run for the hills. The locals aren't loaded with intestinal fortitude. Porter talks big, but he would rabbit in a pitched battle. Blotto just wants cash, booze, and broads, with the least work possible and no further damage to his already-ugly, pug-like face." Blotto's nose was permanently spread across a great deal of his cheeks, and his breathing was irregular. In my early days, I often led with my nose in a fight, and Blotto had the same unfortunate fighting style.

"Our families? Are they at risk?" I asked.

"Out of bounds for the MMC," Mr. Clampett said. "Their code of honour. The locals probably would be a worry in that area, but the MMC would hand them their balls if they broke that code. So, no worries."

"I guess we get ready for a fight, a brawl?" Zeke asked.

"Well, we're always ready, but we intend to avoid a confrontation, if at all possible. We don't want any of us hurt, we don't want to draw any attention, and we want to exit the contentious business area sooner rather than later. Our strategy is to stay vigilant, not force or provoke any issue, and let them come to us." Everyone nodded at the seeming wisdom laid out by Mr. Clampett.

"To that end, Stone Pony and Mister are taking off for a week to places unknown. That will take the MMC's eyeballs off target. They're unlikely to strike, because the guys they want to get are the leaders. This is also in their operations manual and code of honour. The MMC measures its collective courage by 'mano a mano' challenges, and that means they fight the leaders. They go for the brains, the belly, and the balls of their opposition."

One of the Brownies offered up the question that many of us were thinking. "How does this work? Do they invite us to dance, or do they just show up at our door?"

"They will let us know, and it won't be subtle. They will interfere with our world in a non-personal manner like burning down a building or stealing a truck. No injuries to personnel, just property. The intimidation is in the threat of ruining everything Stone Pony and Mister have built."

"How do we stop that?" the other Brownie asked.

Mr. Clampett must have been expecting such questions, because his answers were fast and tight. "Generally, we can't. We can put up some defences. All our facilities are gated. Security cameras are in place. Doors and windows have been fortified. We have the German shepherds in the main buildings and yards. Those dogs are trained to deal with intruders. The bright lights and sensor lighting we installed are all effective at making intruders hesitate. We have all the defensive deterrents in place. We're ready."

"Yeah, but how does the fighting part of the brawl work?" FBI 1 asked with a tone of voice that indicated a significant interest in messing up our rivals.

"This is a business competition. It's about controlling a lucrative business. Our competitors outnumber us, and they will leverage their competitive advantage. The MMC have decided their fifteen can adequately handle our nine."

"Nine?" Zeke's curiosity was piqued. "We have twelve right in this room, not counting Ms. Annamoosie."

"They don't know about me, and they don't see Bogeyman and Scarecrow as fighters. The MMC didn't even want to count Scarface as part of our crew, but the town boys, mostly Potter, want to mess Scarface up, so he got included in our count."

"How the fuck do you know all this, Mr. Clampett?" Scarecrow asked, sounding only slightly indignant. "Do they think Bogeyman and I won't fight?"

"First, Scarecrow, relax. Everybody knows B and S are better lovers than fighters." The room needed the accompanying giggle that the comment evoked. "This is another MMC code of honour guideline. They don't fight kids. Anyone under twenty-one. They all have younger brothers and sisters. The MMC doesn't want them or any of their family members messed with. I like that part of their honour system. I respect that. The MMC has reluctantly made an exception in Scarface's case because of Porter's bloodlust for our boy." Mr. Clampett got a round of nodding approvals and recognition with those comments.

"The MMC will fight dirty. They will pick a time and a place, probably eight of them, only three or four of us. Likely Stone Pony, Mister, and Scarface isolated. They're hesitating now only because Mister and Stone Pony scare the shit out of them. They're not even sure two-to-one odds are in their favour or will do the trick. And remember, they make their show of force by taking on their rivals' leaders. They need to take Mister and Stone Pony down.

"The MMC thinks you take out the brains, the leadership, then the house falls. The MMC will be the first wave of attack, two each on Stone Pony and Mister. Two locals will go after Scarface. Two others will hang back, guarding the perimeter in case help or the cops arrive. They won't use guns or knives, but their past victims have been badly broken and bloodied. What they leave behind is not pretty."

"Fuck me. How do we stop that?" Scarecrow asked. "And you still haven't answered the question. How do you know this?"

"I have someone on the inside. That's all you need to know. Safer for everybody—especially our friend on their side. As to how we stop this from happening—we don't. We let them come at us." Mr. Clampett's tone was emphatic, and rang with finality. "They will come. Physical property destruction first, then they execute their plan of attack on Mister, Stone Pony, and Scarface. You know what this is called, gentlemen?" Mr. Clampett wasn't asking a question. He was leading us to his answer. "This is called a setup. We're going to put their prime targets in a vulnerable position. They will come, and then we're going fuck them up."

The room was quiet, and then raucous. The gentlemen knew Mr. Clampett had a plan, and all of us, without even hearing it, liked it and trusted it.

"Mister and Stone Pony are taking a vacation next week. Scarecrow, Bogeyman, and Scarface the following week. Then, gentlemen, the madness with the Mayhem will manifest."

The meeting ended as soberly as it began. The cabin had never felt both so purposeful and so absent of joy. Scarecrow, Bogeyman, and I drove home in silence. Mom greeted us with a big hello and warmth in her eyes. Our responses were muted, and our heads were down. We went to our respective rooms.

Mom came up the stairs shortly after, knocked on my door, and entered. "What's going on, son? You three boys have millstones around your necks. You're weighed down by something. Can you tell your mother?" Mom knew how to ask and open me up, even if just a little.

"Everything is OK, Mom. We just have some business competition that Mister and Stone Pony are worried about. They want us to be a little more careful on our jobs, that's all." Basically, I told her the truth, and it wasn't a bad, unplanned response.

Mom sniffed through that pretense. "Really, what's really going on? Does it have to do with drugs, like the whole town whispers? Or that motorcycle gang hanging around town? Are you in trouble?"

My answer had to skirt with the truth and chase away her fears. "First, I'm not in trouble. In fact, next week, Stone Pony and Mister ordered your 'three sons' to take a vacation. They're taking one this week: their first ever. That's how good business is. Second, that motorcycle gang hasn't bothered any of us. Third, Mom, are there really drugs in town? That's so shocking!"

That made her laugh, and broke the tension, so I continued.

"This motorcycle gang doesn't mess with anybody's families. They have a code of honour. They probably want in on the dope business up here and farther north, but that's not my business."

"OK, son, but be careful. Vacation? What are you doing for vacation? Resting, I hope."

"No. Stone Pony and Mister bought me an airplane ticket, and I'm flying to Winnipeg to visit the friends I made there last summer." That was the truth, and I had learned about it just about an hour earlier.

"An airplane trip? You've never been on a plane. Are you scared or nervous?"

"No, just excited. I'll need to make sure I have clean undies, though, cuz I may shit my pants a little on that plane." That was the truest thing I said to Mom all night. We both laughed.

"Son, this is so exciting. You've earned it. You work so hard. I know you're paid well, but after your heartbreak, you deserve an adventure."

"My whole life seems like an adventure. It really does—highs and lows, now, places to go. I never know what's next, either. This trip is going to be a high. I know it."

That was the truth as far as I could make out. I was looking forward to seeing Crazy Horse and Woman—especially Woman.

"What about Bogeyman and Scarecrow? Are they going, too?"

"No. They're staying put—maybe a day trip or two. They just want to relax, play some thirty-one with you and the little one, and maybe have a cold beer or two on the deck you have out back now. They said they're looking forward to sleeping in." That was the truth, too, though Bogeyman and Scarecrow did have an assignment to carry out.

"Those boys could use lots of sleep, some good meals, and time to heal. I'll feed them well and kick their butts at cards, and you—you be careful, son." She smiled, and I could see she was already planning meals for the week.

"Mom, can you do me a favour when you feed Bogeyman and Scarecrow in a couple of weeks? Can you feed them your hamburger meals? I don't think they ever believed my stories of hamburger meat seven different ways on seven consecutive days, hamburger every day of the week." I knew that would hit a tender spot, and maybe even a scar on Mom's heart. Her smile broadened.

"Those boys will be in love with hamburger meat by the time you get back. These days, there will actually be some meat in all of those meals."

It's funny how when some memories are triggered, they stir up so many emotions and feelings. Sadness, hurt, pain, pride, joy, and some laughs. Those were all playing across Mom's face, and the tears tucked in the corners of her eyes were just visible.

"We've come a long way, Mom, from being held down and beaten down to rising up, way up, so look up, way up—and I'll call Rusty." The *Friendly Giant* reference brought her back to happy. She kissed the scar on my cheek and said goodnight. As I heard her go downstairs, all I could think of was madness and mayhem. What was the madness that was behind my surprise trip to Winnipeg, and what mayhem was waiting in Manitoba? More than that, what mayhem would we be facing when I returned?

Wondering if things would end well would fill my mind for weeks.

CHAPTER 35

Scarecrow: Saints and Scars

I hadn't ventured over to Scarface's room since the boys' wing opened for Bogeyman and me. Tonight, I just had to visit, though, so I poked my head in his door.

"Gotta minute to talk, old friend?"

"Sure, Scarecrow, what's up? There must be something weighing on you for you to make the long trek from the executive wing." We both laughed, which was good to break the uncomfortable feeling growing inside.

"You remember the first time we went to the Golden Dragon? Back before you were Scarface or Garbage Boy, when you were still just a little dipshit collecting beer and pop bottles for cash?"

"Of course, I remember. You were just a scrawny little prick then—and lo and behold, you still are." We both laughed again at our memories and taunts.

"We had some good days, right?"

"We sure did. Collecting everything we could. Facing stiff competition from Odd and Even and the Fortune Cookies, but we found our fair share of bottles." I could see that my old friend was wondering where the nostalgic trip was heading.

"Do you remember when I led us to a case of beer bottles, and there were still eight full ones?"

"Sure do. We opened them and poured them out, so we would have enough money to go have Chinese food at the Rusty Reptile. Remember we used to call it that?"

"Yeah, I do, but we stopped calling it that after our meal that day."

"You're right about that. What's up, Scarecrow?"

"That day was important to me. It was the first time anybody took me out to eat at a restaurant. The Fortune Cookies were there, and they bought us egg rolls. They told us we were good collectors. Everybody in the place was kind and respectful toward us, even though we were just mangy little mutts trying not to get put down or beat up."

"Yep, I remember. We walked right up Main Street on the way home, not even worrying about getting caught by one of the gangs. You were proud of us and happy."

"You do remember. That was a big day. You cared, and you showed you cared by taking me to that restaurant. That might have been the first day I felt someone cared about me. About me feeling good, about me maybe being someone to care about. Anyway, I needed to tell you that felt good, and it still does."

"A big day for me, too, Scarecrow. Now what else is on your mind? What's eating at you besides all the shit we carry, all that you carry? And that's a big load; I get that."

"I probably never told you how much that day meant to me. You were like a saint to me, taking me into foreign territory and making me feel good, feel real. Not like the scared kids we were. Always taking back roads and paths through the bush and marsh to avoid beatdowns and ridicule. We were living in the shadows, and then you took me into broad daylight. I can never tell you how much that meant to me. You were the knight or the saint leading me safely into new lands. I had never felt the warmth of that type of sunshine."

Garbage Boy looked a little bewildered and started to say something, but I cut him off.

"Do you know what I thought about in that prison in Turkey? I mean something that I thought about a lot. Where I let my head go to escape the reality of the rapes and the beatings. Something I would conjure up to ease the pain and escape inside of my own head for a while. Can you even guess?"

My old friend gave me a puzzled look.

"Let me tell you. I thought about us and those eight beers. I saw us drinking them, and they were as cold as ice. We were propped up against that rock wall in the field where that case of twenty-four had been stashed. Drinking them cold beers in the sunshine. Slow and easy. Shootin' the shit, raggin' on each other. Just two kids without a care in the world. Laughing at life.

"That fake memory of actually drinking those beers instead of pouring them out pulled me from the dumps more than once. Fuck me! The dumps? Man, I was depressed, and in dark despair. Would have ended everything in a second if those Turkish sadists ever gave me the fuckin' chance. I was money in the bank for them, and they weren't going to let me go out on my own terms. Then, the thought of you and me drinkin' a cold beer would lift me up. Saved me more than once."

Things were awkward and quiet for a moment, then Garbage Boy ended it. "We can have a cold one right now if you need it."

"Nah, that's OK. Just wanted to share that with you. That prison bullshit messed me up good. Not just the physical shit but my head as well."

"Anybody would be affected that way. You're only human."

"Yeah, I know that, but it's funny what gets you through when you're grasping at anything just to hang on. I remember the first time I showed you the scars on my back from my dear old dad's belt and buckle. That scared you. I figured out in prison why my mom stopped protecting me. Hell, she'd been beaten down so much she couldn't take anymore. He had smacked the fuckin' life out of her, and all maternal instincts had been broken, bloodied, and then buried. My mom was in self-preservation mode. That's where I was over there. Scarred like fuck and just trying to survive. Couldn't worry about cell mates who had been beaten worse than me. Just had to look out for myself. No place for saints in that hellhole. If you could look at the inside of my head, I'm sure the scars would make your sixty-eight stitches look like fuck all. And I don't say that lightly. I know the pain you were in that night both physically and mentally, after what happened to your mom." I stopped to take a breather but was going to continue telling my friend my story.

"Scarecrow, you're OK and safe now. The Newspaper Crew isn't going to let any bad come your way."

"Yeah, I get that. I feel that. Mostly. Yet we both know a shit-storm is coming." Scarface nodded his acknowledgement of that observation. "I liked the old days. Those bottles were our currency. What we found gave us our value, gave us more than a nickel at a time. Those bottles we found gave us our value. Every found bottle, we treated like a victory, a win. Those glass nickels we found represented our success, a measure of self-worth, a way to better ourselves. One bottle at a time, one nickel at a time. Good work for good guys.

"Look at us now! We're still picking up what others throw away. Running barrels. Garbage boys, garbage men. Doing what few others want to. Bogeyman and I discovering riches by selling dope. Touring the world. Women, weed, and wacky times. Mister and Stone Pony bringing us into the fold, striving to get to legitimate enterprises. Leaving the dope business behind. Leaving behind the world that got me fucked up halfway across the world. All this is going to be good. We just need to get past the coming shit-storm. Right?"

"Right, Scarecrow, and we will get past this. Together. Strong and heads up—no more dark alleys and backwoods. In the sunlight. Guaranteed."

"I don't know if you can guarantee that, but that's the plan, and if any mutts can do it, I think it's us. Thanks for listening. Time to hit the sack. Five o'clock comes early. See ya in the morning."

"Have a good night, and we'll have that cold one tomorrow."

I didn't have an easy time getting to sleep. I kept thinking about saints and scars. The saints who rescued me with cash from the prison outside of Istanbul: Ms. Annamoosie, Mr. Clampett, and Mister. They nourished me back to some degree of strength in a hotel room to get me strong enough to fly home. Scarface's mom, the saint who took us into her home and nourished us daily. Mister and Stone Pony, these walking, working saints taking us to a path of righteous behaviour, where we feared no evil and perpetrated none. I wondered how people would regard us if we made it to completely legitimate, legal ventures. Would they look at us like the Bronfmans, who smuggled booze in prohibition, or the Kennedy clan, or any of the white fuckin' legends who pulled themselves up through crimes to legitimacy? No, that wouldn't be for us, because we were mutts from the street. Multi-skinned and multi-breeds. No, there would be no washing us to white or right. We would always be coloured by different brushes and opinions. That was OK with me. I like who we are, understood where we came from, and loved where we were heading. If our journey didn't make us good in people's eyes, well, fuck 'em if they couldn't take a joke. We'd show everyone we were no joke; we were real. We were born with little value and with even fewer prospects, but we were ascending.

I carried scars. The physical scars inflicted by my dad. The perpetual scar of not being valued, not being respected, not being allowed to rise up. No, it wasn't that we weren't allowed to rise up. It was that we weren't expected to. And even when we did, it would never be valued, appreciated, respected, or even acknowledged. No, the bar would just move higher. Our success would always be attributed to luck or illegal acts. Never attributed to worthy traits such as tenacity, hard work, perseverance, entrepreneurial ability, and the intellect to figure out the way up and over the bar. Our bar was set high, and they kept raising the fuckin' thing.

I carried the prison scars. They didn't worry me much, because they were outside of my control. The scars that burned and festered were all about being accepted, cared for, and caring back. A modicum of respect would be nice, too. Maybe I could become chair of the local chamber of commerce. Fat fuckin' chance of that!

And, oh yeah, making something of myself—for myself and the ones I cared about. If I couldn't do that, I would be scarred forever.

CHAPTER 36

A Mom's Mind

My son wasn't fooling me. There was trouble. I could feel it from all three of them—Scarecrow most of all. The courage he was slowly winning back was being attacked. Maybe only in his mind, but he was slipping back into his shell. His words and smiles were fewer and further between. Physically, he built himself back up, but mentally, that was a longer path to travel back. There was fear in him.

Bogeyman was all false courage, a brave front on trembling knees. He was tense and looking over his shoulder, even when looking forward. He was the opposite of Scarecrow. Talking more and telling jokes. Bogeyman was working hard to keep Scarecrow in the sunlight. It was hard work, especially when he sensed the dark of night closing in.

My son? Who knows? His chin was forward, and he clenched his fists. He was preparing for a fight. He seemed to want the battle, whatever the battle was. The Librarian shattered his world. He held no ill will toward her. He even said she had made the right call. There just seemed to be something he needed to end, to close the door on.

I knew without them telling me that trouble was coming. They were facing whatever it was in their own way. Scarecrow kept playing the song "Bad Moon Rising," and my son played "When the Levee Breaks." He sang a couple of lines from that song all the time: Him singing about praying and crying not helping at all was filling me with dread.

I told them to pick some cheerier tunes. They laughed. I laughed along and read their eyes. They were not whole. Something was chipping away at them. What it was, I didn't know, but it was real. In them, I saw, felt, smelled, tasted, heard ... fear, worry, the mustering of courage, the need to take a stand, to stand their ground. To attack, to defend, to run and hide, to stand up and face the demon chasing them or in front of them. It reminded me of the young men with all the world in front of them going off to war. I was a young woman then, in love with Art. Underlying all their bullshit bravery of fighting the good fight for their country and families was the taste and aroma of fear. Fear of the unknown. Fear of what the hell was going to happen to them. The fear was so thick in the air that everything seemed to taste different. It was in their eyes. A part of their uniforms. My boys carried this same hell of the unknown and the wise dread of their enemy in front of them, on them, they shrugged it off and told me not to worry. A mom's mind doesn't work like that. Her mind won't let her rest until she can confront the evil or the worry her children are facing. A mom wants to help them deal with or get over whatever they're facing and reassure them they don't have to face it alone. A mom even believes she can take the burden from them.

Bogeyman also had a song he listened to a lot. The song was by Neil Young, and I liked his music—not as much as Gordon Lightfoot, but he was more than OK. A funny voice, though. The lyrics Bogeyman sang brought me down. The song was called "Don't Let It Bring You Down," but it brought me down. How can that not bring you down? There are castles burning and these boys are looking for someone or somewhere safe. I can provide some of that, at least somewhere safe.

"What castles?" I asked Bogeyman.

"The ones in your head, your dreams, your hopes," he replied. Not a very uplifting answer. Scarecrow and my son nodded in agreement with Bogeyman's answer. That scared me. I told them I pitied them if their hopes and dreams were burning. Almost in unison, they told me that the last thing they needed was pity. They needed pity even less than my worry. I tried to explain that I couldn't help but think that way, feel that way, that a mom's mind works that way. They tried to joke their way out of my worrying and pitying them, but it didn't work for me or for them, and we all knew it.

Ms. Librarian turned my son around for a while, anyway, until she couldn't take all the things that were bringing her down, because she was in love with my son. Bogeyman and Scarecrow were turned around by love and care and hard work and a home. Mostly the home, because they got a family in the bargain. They were turned around until they weren't. I prayed and hoped they would find someone or something that was turning.

Come around, my boys, come around, because until then, this mom's mind feels pity, worry, and a sense of foreboding about how this will end. And don't tell me not to pray or not to cry. Screw Led Zeppelin! I know, better than most, that tears and prayers are often wasted. That's nothing to sing about and maybe that's all I have at times like these.

A Mom's Mind Needs Rest

Dear God,

Cast the demons out,
Out of their way, Lord.
They seem to be walking in a valley of death.
They do fear evil, although they won't ever admit it.

Well, I fear for them, so hear my prayers.
Be there for them, Shepherd; don't make them want.
You really weren't much of a Shepherd when Bogeyman and poor Scarecrow needed you,
Or my son, for that matter.

These three boys tell me not to provide pity.
They tell me not to worry, and they're right,
Because Pity and Worry are twin sisters
Who pull you down, not up.

So, do your job and protect your flock,
So a mom's mind can get some rest.
These boys deserve better than their castles burning.
That can't be the way you want their lives to be,
Can it?

Again, I ask nothing for myself.
Thank you if you have a hand in my current well-being.
I'm grateful if doubtful about divine intervention.
Prove me wrong.
Deliver these boys from evil.

Amen.

CHAPTER 37

Meeting Our Maker

We had thought through our vacation for almost two years. The timing was a little ahead of schedule. Mister wanted to wait another year and maybe take Scarface along. I never wanted Scarface on the trip, ever. He had to make that voyage on his own.

The Camaro flew down the 400 to the 401. We stopped at the Six Nations to say hello to some of the boys who did the original work on our cabin. These were basically the same guys who were finishing up the addition and renovations at Scarface's mom's house. We also had to transact a little business and make sure our alliance was solid. We were exchanging US dollars they were making from illegal cigarette sales across the border for Canadian dollars. They could wash the Canadian dollars easily. We had set up US bank accounts and were depositing money there. Mister was a dual citizen, as was Mr. Clampett, so the accounts were easy to set up. We crossed stateside from Windsor to Detroit. Mister made us get out several times just to stand on busy streets when we got to downtown Detroit. He was laughing about soaking in all the blackness. He told me I wasn't brown enough to fit in, and laughed some more.

The airport in Detroit was jammed. Lots of colour, blacks and whites—but no reds, according to Mister. He was right. More blacks were working at the airport than whites, until we got near the plane—then, lots of white workers. The pilots, ticket takers, flight attendants, and passengers. We were flying from Detroit to Denver, then Denver to Seattle. Mister had flown many times on deployments to Vietnam on military planes and helicopters. He had not been west. Neither had I. It was only my second airplane trip. We had flown to Disneyworld in Florida a few years back.

It got even whiter in Colorado. Not just the snow on the mountains. We landed in Seattle barely two days after leaving our cabin. We rented a car and headed north, crossing back into Canada. We found a motel with a swimming pool, got some beer, sat around the pool, ordered pizza, and lounged the day away.

Mister said he felt great, like a millionaire. I told him, not for the first time, that we *were* millionaires. Weed, garbage, and rich people had been very good to us over the last six years. Our businesses were all strong and profitable. Our legit platforms were stable and growing. Our illegitimate business was incredibly lucrative, but threatened, and becoming increasingly dangerous. It had never been our intent to get that big in the distribution business. Letting it go would not be easy. We had been lucky to date. Largely because we were smart, organized, and kept a low profile—as low a profile as a big black man and a fighting Indian could.

We hadn't been busted, or had our heads busted—yet. Every day we stayed in the weed business, both of those outcomes became increasingly likely. Mister and I were like insurance agents. We determined the cash-out value our plan required. We were probably only six months away—even though we said one year more, we were going to bail as soon as the cash-out dollar figure was hit.

I told Mister that a year from then, we would take a real vacation, spend lots of money, and kick back in style. This trip was about taking care of business, starting tomorrow, in Vancouver, on West Georgia Street.

The person who was the purpose of our West Coast visit had not been that difficult to find. Mr. Clampett had resources across the States and Canada. Our meeting was set. The man we were meeting would never really know the true intent of the meeting. It would be a good payoff for him. His best payday in years. He just had to answer a few questions about his army training and some hometown acquaintances. We were just a couple of guys trying to track down some lost family members. The report we had on our guy was that he was down on his luck, drawing a meagre veteran's pension, staying in a flophouse, and trying to drink himself to death.

We were at the designated corner on West Georgia Street about thirty minutes prior to our scheduled meeting time. We hung in the shadows of a building, although we were still very obvious. A big black man who looked like he crapped muscles and a muscular Indian who projected an aura of menace did not blend well anywhere. We got some stares and then some glares. Not in a good way. People would take a step sideways when they passed us.

Our man arrived about fifteen minutes late. We exchanged hellos. As per the plan, he had been told we would grab a bite to eat from a takeout place and then find a picnic table in Stanley Park. We had a picture of him that Mr. Clampett had procured. He cleaned up good and didn't smell like we had been warned. His small talk included telling us he hadn't been drinking for a day and a half. Instead, he had gone to a mission for a hot meal, a shower, and some new clothes. He joked he was smelling good and looking better. He might even have to go find himself a woman with some of the $250 he'd been promised just for providing some information.

I stopped at a little burger joint and ordered cheeseburgers, fries, and some Cokes. Mister and our new friend kept walking. Mister was dressed in an old army jacket he'd bought from a surplus store that morning. He was also wearing a toque and sunglasses. Me, well, I had on a very cool pair of plastic aviator shades and a cowboy hat that shaded my face. I caught up with them at the first picnic table in the park.

Mister was the first to spot the two guys following us. They sure looked like narcs.

We passed the food around, and our new friend started eating right away. With his mouth full of food, he said he should get the $250 plus expenses for cleaning up. We asked how much for expenses. He said twenty-five bucks for clothes and seven bucks to get cleaned up. "Fair enough," Mister replied.

The narcs split up. One was about thirty yards past us farther into the park, sitting on a bench. The second one was about the same distance away across a path, leaning on a railing. We knew they could both get to us in a hurry, if necessary. It was unlikely that would be necessary.

We explained the process to our guest. Twenty-five questions, ten dollars an answer. The moment we thought he was bullshitting, we would stop paying, and it was game over. Of the twenty-five questions, some were unnecessary. About five questions would give us our answers. We wrote our questions down in advance.

"Full name?"

"Arthur Stephen Smythe."

"Hold on a second. That would make your initials ASS?" Mister asked in disbelief. The truth was, we hadn't known his middle name.

"My parents weren't too fuckin' bright, apparently."

"Birthdate?"

"August 29, 1922."

"Where were you born?"

"Newmarket, Ontario."

"How many brothers and sisters?"

"Three brothers, no sisters. My mother wanted a girl, but no luck for her."

"Instead, she got a prize like you." Mister's contempt was barely contained. We decided that Mister would ask all the questions and do all the talking. My job was to observe our guest and take notes—or at least pretend to take notes.

"Are your brothers all alive?"

"How the fuck would I know? They don't give a fuck about me, and I don't give a fuck about them."

"Hey, man, you just made a quick fifty. Here you go." Mister handed him five crisp tens. "Consider that an advance. The rest, you don't see until you answer the next twenty questions." We decided to give him some early cash and show him we had the bread to keep him hungry.

"Well, ASS, are you ready for the next round? Remember, you bullshit us once, and we might even have to take that advance back—or at least shove it up your ass, ASS."

Our guest's expression registered understanding and fear. Mister was one intimidating black man in those dark sunglasses. Hell, he was intimidating at any time.

"You have any contact with your brothers or your family?"

"Those fuckers gave me a one-way Greyhound ticket from Hamilton to Vancouver three years ago. I haven't seen or heard from them since. My family isn't much for letter writing. No other family to speak of—at least no one I speak to. My parents are long dead."

"Were you ever married? Any serious girlfriends?"

Arthur Stephen Smyth leaned back and laughed.

"That question wasn't meant to be funny, ASS." Mister leaned forward with menace popping from his voice.

"Sorry, big man. It's just that I was married and had a couple of girlfriends along the way. Sort of overlapping."

"You have any contact with any of them?"

"No. Tried to ... what do you call it? Reconcile with my wife a few years back. She wasn't having it. Don't know about those other bitches—the girlfriends, that is. They caused me a lot of grief."

Mister half-stood, reached across the picnic table, and grabbed Arthur by the throat. "That makes me angry, ASS. A man like you referring to any woman you were with by that name is not going to fly. You probably fucked all those women's lives up in some way. You say another word against them, and I'll snap your neck like a fuckin' twig."

I got up and grabbed Mister's big wrist, patted him on the shoulder, and whispered for him to simmer down and sit down. I told him he had to calm down and stay with the plan. The two narcs were both looking edgy and were not trying to even pretend they weren't watching us. Bad form on their part, but they had some skin in this game. Us messing up Arthur wasn't in their best interest.

Mister was crisp with the next questions. Arthur was, not surprisingly, attentive and respectful.

"Any kids?"

"Three. Girl, boy, girl. All with my wife. None with the other ladies, at least as far as I know. Or at least take credit for." That was another mistake by Arthur. Mister maintained his cool, but I almost lost mine.

Mister continued down our list. "Any contact with the kids?"

"None. Well, except the boy. On the same visit where I tried to reconcile with my wife. Him and I got in a bit of a tussle. I wrote him a Christmas card with a note. Said I might be coming to visit in September. Well, that ain't likely to happen, or at least I wouldn't bet good money on it. Don't know why I did that." Art looked more than a little sad about that answer. *Pathetically lost* might be how to describe his look. Shoulders slumped, head down, and a catch in his throat.

Mister plowed on. "Well, you earned another fifty. I assume he didn't write back, so we won't waste a question going down that rabbit hole. You serve time in the army in WWII?"

"Yes, sir. From 1941 to early 1945, some five years. Spent some time in Italy and France."

"Where did you train?"

"Base Borden and then Camp Milner in Georgia. You from there?"

"ASS, we ain't having a conversation here. This isn't a family picnic. Besides, I'm a Canadian, fourth generation—probably longer than your white British ass. Back to the questions. You make any friends down there?"

"Army buddies, and a local girl got sweet on me."

"Do you have contact with the army buddies or the locals, the girlfriend?"

"No. The girlfriend said I got her pregnant, but that couldn't have happened; the timing wasn't right. I straightened her out on the timing and her general recollection with some persuasive and gentle guidance."

The veins on Mister's neck were throbbing, but he stayed calm. "Nice to know, but we're more interested in your army buddies. Any contact with them—particularly Sergeant Roy?"

Art's brow furrowed. "That Irish French fuck? He busted me probably a dozen times for being AWOL. Out after curfew both stateside and in Italy. No contact with that prick, that's for fuckin' sure. If I did, he wouldn't have those officer stripes to protect him. You boys looking for him?"

"Well, ASS, that's our business—but yeah, you could say so."

We had verified what we had wanted. Army time in the States, a dalliance with a local girl who he basically admitted to beating, and he remembered the name of his platoon sergeant. Next, we had to verify some things back home. We needed to be a hundred percent sure this bedraggled old fuck was Scarface's dad to satisfy ourselves that our next steps were justified. There was one other major part of Arthur's backstory we needed some certainty and closure on as well. The guy was building our case that he was unsalvageable scum.

"When you got back home, was there any trouble?"

"Well, I made eighteen years of domestic bliss." He snorted and laughed at his comment, then continued. "It worked for a while. A daughter and then our boy, but the whole time, I was rolling downhill. You know, booze and broads. Not holding a job. My wife was becoming more and more bitter, being a pain about it. Guess I can't blame her. I wasn't really Ward Cleaver." He finished with a little smirk.

"Thanks for the background, but any troubles?" Mister growled.

"Yeah, some with the law, just minor drunk and disorderly. Some woman made some trouble. Again with the pregnant shit. We got that straightened out. Her brothers made some noises, but weren't tough enough to follow up."

"We heard you played some baseball."

"Yep. Loved baseball. Three championships in a row. Played for the Refuge bar team at shortstop."

"Play against some teams from the reserve?"

"Now, those red fuckers can play some ball. No offence intended, quiet man. They could do everything. Run, hit, throw, catch—and smart plays, all the time."

"That local girl who falsely accused you of getting her pregnant, was she from the reserve?"

"Yeah, and she was a hell of a ball player, too. Liked to drink and liked to—well—party."

"So, be honest now, it's important to tell the truth here. Did you get her pregnant? It seems that charge follows you around. You must be some virile stud or something."

"Honestly, I don't know. I don't want to offend the quiet man or anyone, but as I said, she liked to party, and I wasn't the only white guy she partied with."

Now, I was the one who had to hold back the fury. This drunken, lowlife piece of shit casting aspersions on a member of my own tribe. I wanted to break his fucking neck right there. Mister put a hand on my shoulder and gave me the *simmer down* look.

I did, barely.

"Are you sure that's the answer you want to give? Because the so-called quiet man is kind of twitching like he thinks you're full of shit. I'll give you another chance to get your answer right, and I'd be careful because if the red man here doesn't hear truth in your answer, and I take my hand off his shoulder, he might squeeze the truth out of you."

"Maybe. Probably. Her brothers, her family, and she sure did think so. So, likely yes, likely."

"So now, that makes me wonder. The local girl in Georgia. Think hard now. Truth-telling is way better than a serious beating from a serious black man followed by a quiet red-man ass-kicking. Was she black, and did you get her pregnant?"

"Does that count as two questions? Never mind. Forget I asked that. Just trying to lighten the mood. She was black, and yeah, likely my kid."

"Any trouble with her brothers?"

"Well, her and I had a little fuss, and her brothers wanted to speak to me. See, we were deployed back to Camp Milner to debrief our training and pick up some personal effects. I saw the girl and the kid. He didn't look much like me, dark with curly hair. Looking at him, I wouldn't have thought there was any white in him."

"OK, ASS, you're almost home free with two hundred and fifty dollars. Party time for you and getting yourself a woman. Be careful, and don't get her pregnant."

ASS looked up at Mister and smirked. He was looking talked-out and thirsty. I figured he would get too drunk to find a woman with his windfall.

"Those brothers ever catch up to you, either my colour or the red man's shade?"

"No, but I heard they looked for me for a while. I wouldn't want to meet up with any of them. Is that why you're here? To find me and tell them?"

"No, ASS, no worries there. Question twenty-four coming up. You ready?"

Arthur Stephen Smyth was getting the alcoholic earthquaking tremors for a drink. Doing the rummy rumba in his seat. The booze beat was coursing through him. ASS was almost quivering with anticipation of his first swig. "You ever beat those two women? Think and answer truthfully. Either a whole lot of pain or a whole lot of money is coming your way."

His head went down. He clasped his hands together on the table in front of him, almost like he was praying. His eyes were closed. When he opened them, he glanced at both narcs. I realized he had spotted them and was clearly aware of their presence. Situational awareness, Mr. Clampett would have called it. Probably developed from almost a lifetime of looking over his shoulder out of fear. Knowing he was vulnerable and had some atonement coming. There was sweat on his forehead, and he kept licking his dry, parched lips.

"Yeah, a little bit of a tussle with both. Didn't mean to hurt them. They both put a lot of pressure on me to do what they said was the right thing. It was only supposed to be a little fun with them, not kids and all that. I was married. I'm sorry if I hurt them a little bit."

Mister and I looked at each other. He sat down and motioned for me to speak.

I took a few deep breaths to stay calm and cool. "Arthur, you call broken arms, broken noses, fractured orbital bones, broken ribs, teeth knocked out, black eyes, and smashed mouths a little bit of a tussle? What kind of man does that? You're a fuckin' incredible piece of shit. Do you know how bad the two of us want to fuck you up? Wipe the fucking ground with you? Cut your balls off and stick them down your throat? Do you?"

ASS was frozen, paralyzed with fear as he watched Mister grind his big right fist into the palm of his left hand. Mister reached over and grabbed him by the throat again. ASS appeared to stop breathing. At first, he didn't even seem to notice the knife cutting through his pants and slicing into the skin of his inner thigh, near his balls, if he really had any. ASS winced a little, but our words and Mister's fist were implying more hurt and menace than the knife prick to his leg could ever inflict to this prick—or his prick.

"We would stomp your worthless ass, ASS, but those two narcs you've been eyeballing have been eyeballing us for a couple of days. Probably not too wise to mention that you know us in any way if they come and ask you questions. They look like men of menace. Just tell them you know the streets around here, and we're looking for a couple of guys who ripped us off on a dope deal in Seattle. Actually, ASS, the big man and I think those two are gang types, like the West Coast Mafia. We don't want to fuck with them and have them look at us as competition or anything like that. You sure as hell don't want to be connected to us. Last question. Ready?"

He looked again at the two narcs, West Coast Mafia, whatever they were, then nodded.

"Do you have any idea who we are?"

His eyes went wide but vacant. He stared at us, but no lights came on. "Nope, not a clue. You're dangerous-looking, and I don't think I would forget for a second if our paths had crossed. Honest."

We didn't say a word. Mister handed over the two hundred we owed. Arthur took it and shoved it into an inner pocket. He looked like he was going to shit himself.

"Can I go now?" he asked. "You guys ain't going to work me over or anything, are ya? I won't say anything about being connected to you. I'm not, am I? Forget that. I don't want to know. You two frighten the fuck out of me—far more than those gangster types."

I took the lead and gave him our final questions and answers.

"You have no idea of who we are?"

He just shook his head. He was done talking, out of fear and probably from withdrawal symptoms.

"Think very hard. Think about the questions we asked you."

ASS displayed no sign of understanding. Nobody home. Not a sliver of light going on.

"We're your sons. Your flesh and blood. We grew up big and strong and are doing OK. Our moms, not so good. Before they both passed, they suffered. Passed way early, too—mostly because of you."

His mouth was flapping, opening and closing like a fish out of water, gasping to live.

"We aren't going to hurt you. We just want you to know we exist and that someday your sons might come looking to settle the score for their moms. You ought to be looking over your shoulder, around every corner, behind every door, and keep your head on a swivel—because someday, we will be there. You have that to look forward to. Anticipate that every day for the rest of your life. Now, you tell anybody you had your sons visit you, and we will end you right then, you miserable, cowardly fuck. You got that straight?"

ASS nodded. He had pissed himself. The stain had a pinkish tinge. His piss was mixing with the blood from the little cut I had administered. Blood and piss.

"Those two narcs, they want us, not you. We'll know if you say one word about us. We have sources. How else could we find your miserable ass? Are we clear?"

ASS nodded and looked at his soaked crotch. Mister finished our reunion with dear old Dad.

"ASS, one mention of us, and you won't wake up the next morning. Glad we met you, because we want to thank you for staying out of our lives. Do the same for your other son. We ain't asking for that. We're telling you that. We will all become less friendly and a lot more fierce if you come anywhere near us. We intend to be more, become more than anything you could ever imagine. You had no part in any of that, nor will you have any part of our futures. The traits, the character we have that allows us to become something is all due to our mothers. Not you, you miserable fuck. Your genes, we apparently didn't inherit. Because we ain't miserable, cowardly, woman-beating fuckups. Not even close. The safest spot in the world for you is right here. Drunk in your pissed-in pants and silent about your three sons. See you, Dad."

The sneer in Mister's voice as he said "Dad" was as sincere as it was sinister. ASS heard death in that word. It's amazing how tone, volume, and diction can turn a word that should be full of love, trust, and respect into hate, hurt, and potential doom.

We didn't glance back. We headed to the parking lot a mile or so away. The drive back to Seattle took three and a half hours—lots of border traffic. We got the last flight with a connection to Detroit, spent a few great nights living the life in Motown, and saw the Tigers play.

On the drive home we took the Detroit-Windsor tunnel, a new experience for both of us.

We made a business stop with the Six Nations, then went straight home. The cabin felt good, welcoming, and somehow, it had fewer dark spots. Maybe that was all in our heads. Not one word about ASS between us. Not one word from the two narcs that Dad had broken his vow of silence.

Mister and I checked an important black spot off our list. Well—white spot, we said when we celebrated at a White Spot before leaving BC. Meeting our maker, well at least the other half of our making, seemed somehow anticlimactic in the rear-view mirror, putting Arthur Stephen Smythe behind us.

The narcs knew everything about him now. They were paid to monitor his behaviour for the next ten days. Make sure ASS didn't say anything about us to anyone. They had to make sure he showed up for his next meeting the following week. Art's demise was well underway, without our direct intervention.

CHAPTER 38

Pissed Pants

"I told you! I don't know who the fuck you are."

When I said that, the big black fuck reached across the table and grabbed my throat again. He moved so quickly I realized he could snap my neck like a twig in a second. It was a bad, bad situation. I just thought I would get another drink before I died.

The black man was scary, but that red fuck looked worse. His fuckin' coal eyes were burning with a hate hard-on for me. He told me to look down. I felt the knife against my nuts before I saw the blade. He cut my new pants and sliced my thigh. I couldn't scream, because the big black man seemed to be permanently closing my windpipe. I was thinking about fainting, but something told me that wasn't an option.

The big black man had already stuffed a wad of cash in my jacket pocket, the two hundred and another thirty for my expenses. The knife cut a little more as the red man said, "Look, he's pissing his pants." I hadn't noticed. The narcs looked nervous, but weren't coming to my rescue.

The Indian told me that the meeting had never happened, and I was lucky I didn't know who the fuck they were. Even though they told me who the fuck they were. Then they got up and left. Left me sitting at a picnic table wearing my pissed pants. I watched them leave. The narcs or West Coast Mafia split shortly after. The warm piss sensation had turned cold. The fuckin' bastards. Neither had finished their meals. I sat there in my piss and blood, getting a good, full belly before I set forth to go on a fuckin' bender to end all benders. At least that was the plan I was thinking through over lunch. I made myself laugh. Yeah, my business lunch. Two hundred and eighty bucks in my pocket. A very productive lunch.

Hey, maybe my wife could sew my pants back together. After all, she was a good seamstress. The problem was these were scared-the-piss-out-of-me pants! Can anyone fix that?

Fuck those fuckers. I would rat them out in a second if the narcs asked me. I could tell them where they were from and some names. The women's names they were asking about. My fuckin' bastard sons, black and red. If I ratted them out, I would just head to the hills for a few months. Pay a couple of months' rent in advance and head up Grouse Mountain, live like a hermit for a couple of months. My plan for redemption, I was putting on hold temporarily—probably permanently. That little Indian fuck had probably stirred up shit about me with the Natives. They would fuck me up royally if I showed up around there. Sorry, son—no family reunion in the works for now. Fuck it. Face it. That last chance at redemption was a fantasy anyway.

The food was gone. I was sober, so I could smell the piss stink. I got up and wrapped my jacket around my waist. The jacket hid my piss-soaked pants pretty good. Go home. Wash up. Change. Get to the bank. Deposit one eighty, then go fuckin' snake eyes wild! Now that's a plan. Maybe toast my boys, but not out loud. A hundred-buck bender. I was going to try for a whore on East Hastings. I had been eyeballing one for a few weeks. Red hair, even though she was Asian-looking. Maybe she had a new slant on things. Made myself laugh at that—*slant* and *Asian*. Guess I wasn't a proper man, always thinking in negative terms about other colours and races.

They had made me piss my pants. My leg was bleeding. Who gave a fuck? The narcs sure as fuck weren't worried about my health, so those guys had to be some type of gang or mafia outfit.

It was just a scratch. I had experienced worse just from falling down drunk. It was amazing I hadn't broken an arm, a leg, my back, or my neck on those five flights of steps up to my penthouse. It was more likely I would break something going down from my penthouse on the fifth. Down or up, who gave a fuck? Broke was broke.

I forgot how much I liked French fries and Coke. I remembered I used to like rum and Coke back in the days when I could afford mixed drinks. Or more truthfully, took the time to mix a drink. Why the fuck would one water down any good alcohol anyways?

I set off home, thinking about a red-headed whore and a hundred-buck bender. Stopped in at the bank to deposit the $180. Good thing the bank was on the way and before the liquor store, or the deposit would've shrunk or never been made. My passbook was stamped, and my account balance was $2,984.77. More money than I had ever had in my life. Not bad for a man who had just pissed his pants.

Maybe I could go somewhere else. Fuck that hometown reunion shit. It was certain that visit wasn't going to be much fun, at least for me. My reception would be cold and hostile. Hostile! Like in *hostiles*, as they called the Indians in those Western movies. I'm a funny man.

Yep, a red-headed whore and a bender to remember. Except I wouldn't remember. I would remember not to say a thing about the black man and the red man. That fear could not be pried out on a measly hundred-buck bender. No, that fear could only be pried or loosened off my tongue on that particular topic during at least a two-hundred-buck never-ender. Who was I kidding? After fifty bucks of booze, I wouldn't remember a damn thing. Hell, by the second jug of 4 Aces, I wouldn't remember my full name—even though Arthur Stephen Smythe ain't a real mouthful or a mindful.

I headed up to the fifth floor, entertaining myself with thoughts like, *I'll take the fifth on the topic of those menacing fucks, since I was on my way up to the fifth* and *No comment, Mr. Narc* and *I'll drink to not remembering to remember what I shouldn't remember.* By the time I reached my room, I had almost forgotten those two men. The smell of piss and the need for a drink were dominating any thoughts I would have for the next couple of days. And maybe a red-headed whore.

CHAPTER 39

Winnipeg and Away

The Whities drove me to the airport in Toronto on Saturday morning. I had a phone call from Mister and Stone Pony on Friday night. They were all pumped up about the Detroit Tigers game they had seen that day. Mister was pumped because he was surrounded by black people. Stone Pony was pumped because the visiting team won. The Cleveland Indians. Those good men were in good spirits, and as giddy as schoolboys on a field trip.

On the way to the airport, the Whities talked about our experiences with the hot bod squad. They had been hanging with them from time to time all summer. They said their own parents would not have approved of some of their summer activities. Neither would have the hot bod squad's parents, so they had that in common. We all laughed at that. All good remembrances, and we'd all thoroughly enjoyed our university educations to date.

We did discuss the MMC and Teddy Porter in a more serious manner. We ended that discussion in agreement that trusting in Mr. Clampett, Mister, and Stone Pony was the only smart course of action. We also agreed on what an absolutely intimidating and scary piece of work Mr. Clampett was. None of us ever wanted to be on the opposite side of him, even though we realized we didn't know anything he did or was capable of. Me? I had immense respect for him from the day I met him walking up the lane to the cabin. The man could be a ghost—and not the friendly Casper kind—anytime and anywhere he felt like it.

When I said goodbye to the Whities, they wished me good luck and told me to have a blast. I felt a special bond of brotherhood with them. Deep. Real. Important. Solid.

Then I turned around and looked at the airport terminal. Man, was I out of my comfort zone. I played with the necklace Ms. Librarian had given me, and my spirits sagged more than a little. How did I get from here to the plane? This part of the adventure would require concentration and take my mind and my heart away from Ms. Librarian—or so I hoped.

I had never studied signs and markers or the pattern of crowd flows so diligently. I must have looked hopeless and lost. Half a dozen people plus airport workers asked me if I needed directions or help. I was like a salmon swimming upstream for the most part, but I kept getting help along the way. I mimicked everyone in front of me through the bag check, ticketing, seat assignment, and every single step to my departure gate. I sat down in gate area W12, quite alone and two and a half hours early for my flight to Winnipeg. I was revved up. It was nerve wracking and exciting at the same time, doing something way different than I had ever experienced.

My hair was tied back in a ponytail. My scars on my cheek and neck were highly visible. Even though there were other longhairs around, I stood out. The dark brown of my skin and the strength in my upper body were on display. When I peeled off my jean jacket in the check-in line, my tight muscle shirt revealed some decent arms, a solid chest, and a flat belly. Mister and Stone Pony told me how to dress. They said I should stand out from the crowd. I did. I was picking up some mixed vibes. Some admiring glances, or so I thought. Some peace signs from fellow longhairs and some attention from a group of what I thought were thirteen- and maybe fourteen-year-old girls.

There were other looks—looks that I was more accustomed to. Looks of disdain and disapproval. The overt and obvious looks that discounted my worth based on my appearance. I played naming games with my deep discounters. The woman in her fifties with a cake of makeup all over her face was the Dowager of Disdain. The businessman was Executive Executer. His assessment being my asset value was of minimum worth. The well-dressed, Cleaver-like family expressed unanimous judgment and disbelief at my rude and slovenly appearance. The security guards, the furrowing of their brows, snide comments to each other, and the clear sphincter-clenching recognition that if I was truly trouble, they would need assistance.

The unintended gawking at my scars. I couldn't blame anyone for their curiosity on that score. The check-in line bent around several times. One businessman who I estimated to be in his late forties seemed particularly entranced by my scars. As we passed each other on one of the lineup loops, I made direct eye contact. I could tell he found that both threatening and offensive, so I leaned in a little closer and gestured at my neck and cheek. "Knife fights," I whispered. I also laughed a little, which served to further intimidate the poor man. My laughter was at the thought that he might be a lawyer, and had just filled his briefs. I was certainly getting noticed, and following Stone Pony and Mister's directive on that score.

It wasn't until I was sitting at the gate, anxious for something to do, when I really studied my ticket. Seat 2B aisle, then in smaller print below were two words in bold type: "First Class." If Mister and Stone Pony's goal was to make me conspicuous, my seat on the plane would do the trick.

I fidgeted some more before going to a little variety stop near my gate. I bought a *Toronto Star* and a Coke. I was too nervous to eat. I went back to my seat and turned to the sports section. There were three or four positive articles on the Maple Leaf hockey team, even in late August. I drank my Coke and read the stories. A man in an Air Canada uniform came to the podium in front of the entrance ramp. I thought it was a good time to ask as inconspicuously as possible how one went about boarding the plane, because for me, that sounded more like a pirate term than a pilot-related term. I thought the Air Canada man was maybe the pilot. I walked up to the podium as he finished his announcement and asked him how to get on the plane.

He smiled. "You walk on. First flight?"

"Yes, sir."

"Let me see your ticket."

"Here you go, sir."

"Well, you're a polite young man."

"Yes, sir."

He laughed. "Jesus Murphy, son. You're flying first class. You know anything about what that means?"

"No, sir, not a clue."

"Well, young man, it means the following. First class boards the plane first. You will be served a drink and a snack probably before the proletariat is allowed to even get on the plane."

My eyes went wide.

He was grinning, enjoying this. "Son, I'm happy for you. I must warn you, though, you're going to freak out the other first-class passengers. You play in a rock band or something?"

"No, sir. I'm your basic high school student and a garbage boy."

"This is too cool. Are your parents rich or something?"

"No, sir. It's just my mom and baby sister. Mom is a seamstress, and we get by. We make do. My employers bought me my ticket. They consider me a good, hard worker, and this is my reward."

"Well, in that case they should have sent you to Hawaii or someplace exotic instead of Winnipeg. Even in first class, some might regard a flight to Winnipeg as a very limited reward."

We both chuckled at that.

"Well, sir, I have some friends and history in Winnipeg. My experience there was sort of exotic." My thoughts were flying to the two blondes from BC, Man-Pop, Crazy Horse, the march from the Golden Boy and the Legislature to Blue Bomber Stadium, the bands Chilliwack, Iron Butterfly, Led Zeppelin, and, of course, Woman.

"OK, son, if you say so. Exotic Winnipeg. That's a new one for me, and I've been helping people fly all over the world for almost thirty years. Son, in first class, you're served a hot meal, including dessert, and offered free drinks. The stewardesses are going to fall in love with you. They'll bring you seconds and serve you drinks steadily. Don't get shit-faced. That's bad first-class form, and bad for the stewardesses."

"No, sir, I won't get shit-faced." We both laughed. "I'll also do my best not to frighten the other first-class passengers."

"OK, son. Your employers aren't dope dealers, are they?"

"No, sir, just hard-working garbage men who started their own business on the side. The sanitation business has really grown for them." No one had ever asked me that question before. Mom danced around it, but never asked directly. She was probably afraid to. I was glad she hadn't, because I didn't think I could lie to her.

"Listen, son, people will be curious how a longhair like you, dressed like you are, can afford a first-class fare. People will be suspicious, cynical, and dismissive—especially in first class. The people passing by on the way to their seats are going to be shocked, curious, and maybe upset. First class is seen as a privileged zone. You don't fit the privileged look."

"Any advice on handling that, sir?"

"Yes. Smile and say hello, be polite, and don't appear privileged. You got the appearance part of that covered." We both laughed at that.

"Thank you, sir. You're a good man, sir. Thank you."

His eyes welled a bit as he spoke. "I have a son, probably a couple years older than you. He looks like you—well, sort of. The long hair, big sideburns, blue jean jacket. He doesn't have your build or your scars. He's a good kid, but people write him off just on his looks. This includes friends and family all based on the first impressions created by his current style choices. He is studying for a doctorate in comparative religions. I hate that surface judgment. You know what I tell my son in situations like this?" He leaned closer to the side of the podium and bent over slightly in my direction. I say, 'Fuck 'em!'"

I pulled back a little bit and looked closely, seeing the shine of anger mixed with the mirth in his eyes before leaning back in. "Yes, sir. Fuck 'em, if they can't take a joke or a toke."

We both were smiling as I walked back to my seat.

The boarding was on time, and I was away to Winnipeg with visions of Woman dancing in my head. The warmth of her body against mine last summer as I shivered with the severe cold I had suffered. Beneath blankets of fur, and then her making love to me, teaching me the Seven Motions. I also smiled broadly at memories of the two blondes from BC and golfing at night on the seventh holes in northern Ontario and Falcon Lake.

The businessman who was in seat 2A gave me a head-to-toe look of disdain and dismissal as I sat down. He even asked if I had the right seat—twice. I just showed him my ticket. He said something pompous and prick-like. I can't remember exactly what he said, but it was something that sounded like, "Anybody can sit in first class these days. That's why I couldn't get a Friday night flight out." I was going to let it go, but then he said, "You should at least put your jacket on if you're going to sit in first class."

He broke some sort of barrier with that, so I leaned in closer to him and gave forth, "Mr. Businessman, here are a few things you should know and just think about." His head snapped back. His tone had been full of disdain and dismissive in nature; mine was full of threat and maybe a little terrifying. I continued in that voice. "First, these scars are from knife fights, so there isn't much that scares or intimidates me. Second, the men I work for can buy and sell your sorry ass four or five times over. That's why I'm sitting in first class. Last, sit back, shut the fuck up, and enjoy the flight. This is my first flight ever, and a miserable, judgmental asshole such as yourself isn't going to ruin the experience."

I was talking a lot tougher than I felt. The effect was successful. Mr. Businessman scrunched over in his seat as close to the window as he could. His eyes were wide open, and he was a whiter shade of pale. I love that song!

The stewardess came with bowls of mixed nuts. "Gentlemen, would you care for a beverage before departure?" I nodded in deference to my travel companion in seat 2A. He asked for a scotch, a Chivas Regal.

"I'll have the same but a double, and so will my buddy," I said. "You can bring me a beer as well—Molson Export if you have it."

"Will do, sir. Would you gentlemen like water for your scotches?"

The businessman nodded.

"Me too, just like my buddy. Thank you, ma'am. Thank you so much. It's a real privilege to be sitting here. I fully understand that and really appreciate your kindness."

That floored them both. The stewardess blushed. The businessman got some colour back. The drinks were served, and 2A couldn't help himself. He tried to lighten the mood with "You're a scotch drinker? That changes everything, ha ha."

"No. That changes nothing. You're still a pompous ass. Never had scotch before. First time. You better hope it doesn't fuck me up too badly. I get drinkin', I get to fightin.'"

I had just bought myself about three hours of silence. He pounded the Chivas Regal. I took a big swig and then held my urge to spit it out as it burned its way down. When I regained some control, I glanced over at 2A. He had a slight semblance of a smirk, so he probably saw that Chivas Regal and I had experienced a rough start. I leaned into his 2A solitude. "Mr. B., that's some strong shit there. I guess it's what you call an acquired taste."

He just nodded. Smart play on his part.

I swear to God everyone stared at me as they boarded the plane. Young girls giggled, a couple of stoners flashed me peace signs, and businessmen did double-takes with expressions of astonishment. You know, that *What the fuck?* look. Families were a mixed bag. Young kids gawking, some mothers edging them to the other side of the aisle, and some young women—OK, just one—with a look of lust—at least in my imagination. It was fun to be such an intense person of interest. The detective used that line a couple of times when asking me about the death of the man who had beaten and raped my mom. I was—and so was my mom—a person of interest in that death for a period of time. That man did not end well.

The takeoff thrilled, bewildered, and frightened me all at the same time. The meal was great. A filet mignon with fried potatoes and honeyed carrots. I didn't take a second scotch, but 2A was absolutely pounding them. The stewardess recommended one of the red wines with dinner. 2A nodded, and I said, "Same as my buddy." He was fully shit-faced and passed out halfway through dinner. The stewardess leaned over me to get his tray as the businessman nodded forward, almost laying his head in his dinner. She must have seen my glance at his steak and offered me another filet.

"Miss, your perfume is quite nice," I said. "Could you tell me what kind, please? Because if I ever get a girlfriend, it would be fantastic if she wore that fragrance.

And yes, another filet would be wonderful."

She was fully blushing and said she would write the name of the fragrance down for me.

More steak, more wine, and every five minutes or so, I gave 2A a shot to the ribs with my elbow. He'd be bruised and sore in that spot tomorrow, and wonder what the hell had happened to him. I was laughing my ass off, although in a silent and respectful manner, as a first-class passenger should.

Ah, life was good, and I was drunk.

Landing was rough—at least from my perspective. Everybody clapped, except for the passengers in first class. The stewardess, whose name was Elaine, told me if I needed assistance, I could wait at the top of the gate, and she would guide me through the airport. I waited, and everyone gawked at me again as I stood at the top of the ramp.

Elaine walked me through the airport to the baggage carousel. Winnipeg only had two baggage carousels, so getting oneself or one's luggage lost wasn't an issue. Elaine handed me a package of Air Canada matches and a small bottle of perfume that she said she liberated from the on-board sales inventory. She kissed me on the cheek and walked away. The matchbook cover had her name, phone number, and a note saying she hoped my next girlfriend enjoyed "her perfume." I was dumbstruck.

I spotted my bag, grabbed it, and headed to the exit. Mister and Stone Pony told me a ride would be waiting for me—and there they were, Crazy Horse and Woman.

My smile was splitting my face. They charged me at the same time. The three of us were in our own little world in a three-way hug that blocked the exit. The little lineup waiting for us to move took in the spectacle.

An Indian with long, black hair and a fringed jacket and boots, a statuesque Indian woman in blue jeans, a cropped top, barefoot, and stunningly beautiful, and me, the shortest of the three, blondish-brown ponytail, long hair, wispy beard, in jeans and a muscle shirt. We could have been the Canadian version of the Mod Squad or something. We moved out of the doorway and headed out to Woman's well-traveled Pontiac Strato-Chief. As Woman always said, that was a good car for an Indian princess like her.

We chattered away and just wallowed in each other's company. It was just after 3 on a beautiful, late-summer afternoon. We parked near the Manitoba Legislature and went to the park across the street. I told my two friends that I had been drinking on the plane and could use a snooze. We found a spot at the base of a big elm, and I laid down with my head in Woman's lap. Crazy Horse drifted over to a group playing frisbee and joined in. Someone was playing music, and the sounds of Chicago, Lighthouse, Creedence, and others filled the park. The haze in the air was from all the joints being passed around. Nice vibe. Not much seemed to have changed in the almost full year since I had been in that exact spot.

Woman smiled down at me. "You look good—strong and tanned. Not like the sick child I drove back to his mom. You look like a man. Are you at peace with the world?"

I tilted my head, so I could look fully at her face before replying. "Woman, you know you're stunning, right? Knock-down, drop-them-to-their-knees gorgeous. I've thought about you a lot. How you cared for me, nursed me, and loved me."

"If I could blush, Mr. Scarface, I would be blushing. Well, I think I am, but you can't tell with this wonderful skin I'm in. Scarface, there's something in you that pulls out the woman in me. You have an aura of kindness and caring about you and an aura of hurt and pain as well. You exude trust, loyalty, and an inner courage. It's easy to fall in love with you."

When Woman finished, I didn't know whether to shit my pants or wind my watch, laugh or cry. Thankfully, she bent over me, raised my head from her lap with one hand, then kissed my forehead, my lips, and the scar on my cheek. "Be quiet," she said as she let my head fall back into her lap. "Rest for a while. I'm content in our silent moments. Best not to say anything. Just feel your emotions, think your thoughts. They will all flow into me. Be still. Close your eyes. Rest."

I was asleep in a moment.

CHAPTER 40

Voyage

When I woke up, we hustled over to Crazy Horse's place, an apartment building close to the Fort Garry Hotel. His place was unbelievable. It had three bedrooms and two baths. I showered up and put on a good shirt, which meant a shirt with sleeves. Dinner was at a restaurant close by called Mother Tucker's. A very attractive redhead showed up at Crazy Horse's pad, and the four of us walked to dinner. Heads turned. The two women were opposites in skin and hair colour, but they were both knockouts. We were the textbook version of what hippies looked like. I didn't know about Kathy, the redhead, but the three of us didn't classify ourselves that way, or any way.

At Mother Tucker's, there was a bit of a scene. The entrance was jammed, as was the small seating area in the bar, and the bar itself was lined with people waiting for tables. I heard people muttering about the wait time, even when they had a reservation. The crowd was all white, and not one of "our kind" was anywhere to be seen.

Crazy Horse politely and respectfully manoeuvred his way toward the hostess desk. A man standing beside the overwhelmed hostess looked out over the crowd and spotted Crazy Horse. "Monsieur Le Cheval, just in time. Your table just cleared." The sea of humanity between us and the hostess station parted. I think mostly because of the attractiveness of the two women, but probably a little bit from the shock of seeing two long-haired freaks and their girlfriends ushered to the head of the line. After the white, freaked-out sea closed in our wake, I could hear the muffled sounds of consternation, incredulity, and a general exhaling of "What and how the hell did that just happen?"

Dinner was unbelievable. Martinis and escargot to start. First time for both for me. Caesar salad made at the table with a bottle of Anjou. Prime rib for Crazy Horse and me, grilled shrimp for the ladies. With dinner, a bottle of Beaujolais for the men. The ladies finished the Anjou.

Talk was animated. Well, Crazy Horse was animated, as was Kathy, whom he referred to as Red Rock. Woman and I were a bit subdued. Even if we wanted to contribute to the conversation, there weren't many gaps or lulls for us to take advantage of, and we were OK with that. Woman held my hand under the table for most of the meal. That anchored me. Woman was grounded and of the earth. Touching her always planted me firmly.

I learned a thing or two that surprised me. Crazy Horse was connected to Stone Pony and Mister in the dope business. Crazy Horse's setup was similar. He serviced large wholesale clients in Lake Winnipeg, Lake of the Woods, and Falcon Lake—basically, Manitoba's cottage country. The supply network was connected. An extension of the same Mexican family of cousins brought the weed across Lake Superior through northern Minnesota. There were cousins all along the way. Some worked seasonally for Mennonites in Manitoba. The Mennonites had done lots of missionary work in Mexico. Crazy Horse said the Mexicans appreciated the Mennonites bringing some of their countrymen to a higher ground through worship. They joked that they were returning the favour by bringing highs to Canadians, including any Mennonite brethren who wanted a toke or two. Interesting how international trade worked. This Manitoba joint venture with NCE benefited from increased volume buying. Crazy Horse would also exit the business in a year. He had already started a cottage opening/closing/repairs and maintenance business. That legit business was booming.

After dinner, we headed back to Crazy Horse's. As we left the restaurant, we had all become immune to the stares. The man who ushered us in thanked us for coming, and Crazy Horse palmed him some serious cash. On the short walk home, Crazy Horse and I fell behind the women.

"Good to see you, brother," he said. "I mean, Man-Pop was so fuckin' outrageous last year, and then boom, you were gone. Woman said you had some serious shit back home. Someone got killed?"

"Well, someone died, and my mom and I had some bad history with that man. Neither one of us killed him, but in the span of a week, we both laid a beating on him separately. I was out here with you at Man-Pop the night he passed out and away on his own."

"Oh, then that's all cool. You're off on an adventure of some kind tomorrow. Red Rock and I will cover for you. Say you've been here with us all week if anybody asks. I doubt they will."

"An adventure? News to me. Where am I going?"

"You really don't know?"

"Nope."

"Well, Woman will fill you in. You two are leaving in the morning—probably a peace or a rescue mission if Woman is involved."

"OK. Crazy Horse, it's good to see you too man. Blood brothers. I still have the scar on my thumb. I think it's my favourite of all my scars."

"Don't get sentimental on me, Scarface. We can't be acting like pussies."

"I'm glad you're connected with Mister and Stone Pony. They're good people. I'm also glad you're leaving the dope distribution business in a year. That business is going to get really criminalized with hardcore motorcycle gang-based assholes and dangerous men."

"You're right, brother. We maximize our cash intake for a year and then get the fuck out of Dodge."

It was only 10, but I was tired and eager to go to bed—hopefully with Woman, but I didn't know if that was going to happen. Woman and I slept together, and I mean slept. She didn't say anything until she slipped into bed. "Just hold me tonight." I did as I was told. I had a full belly from two big meals and a lot of drinks. I wasn't drunk, but I was a little foggy, and way too mellow.

When I woke up it was about 6 a.m., and Woman was gone. I threw on my jeans and got a T-shirt out of my bag. My travelling suitcase was my hockey bag once again.

Woman was in the kitchen, drinking coffee, fully dressed. "You look rested."

"I am, and you look beautiful."

"Scarface, we have a mission. I've already showered. You should, too. We have a long day ahead. We'll leave as soon as you're ready. Here's a coffee. We'll grab a bite at a little place I know. They bake bannock fresh each morning."

I took the coffee. "OK. Can you tell me where we're headed and why?"

"When we're in the car. We'll have lots of time to talk. Go and get ready." She motioned with her long arm toward the bathroom.

I showered, brushed my teeth, got dressed, and packed up. I looked at the alarm clock on the dresser as I left the bedroom: 6:27 a.m. New day, new adventure, and time with the mystery that was Woman. My saviour, my mentor, my lover, my teacher, my infatuation.

I left a note for Crazy Horse. Woman told me we would be back on Friday. My ticket home was for late Sunday night. I was looking forward to hanging out with Crazy Horse and a weekend would likely be enough for my sanity and sobriety.

We drove for almost two hours. We barely talked. Woman played a Joni Mitchell eight-track in a player she had installed in the Strato-Chief. When it finished, I popped in *Déjà Vu* by Crosby, Stills, Nash, and Young. I loved every song. Woman sang along to Joni. I sang along to CSNY.

The title song, 'Déjà Vu' did make me wonder. This all felt familiar, yet I felt things were shifting. That my feet weren't solid, I wasn't braced for what was coming. Like the ground was shifting underneath me, some force was moving me to endings, conclusions outside my control.

And with Woman I was wondering, but I was waiting. The reason would come to the surface eventually. Time in her presence was, for me, somehow mystical. Calm. A time to reflect. Think about myself, think things through. Two hours of silence with Woman, and I learned stuff about myself. When she reached over and squeezed my hand, my heart thumped.

She seemed to look into me and see whatever I was feeling. She knew what I was thinking. "It's time to heal your hurt. Close a door, correct a wrong, several wrongs. You need to close this door. If not, you will always wonder when it's going to open. This door of yours, whenever it opens, hurt comes in. That's your mission. Close this door!"

That was how Woman talked. I didn't know what it meant, but I knew what it meant, know what I mean? This wasn't a riddle, and it wasn't gobbledygook. Woman talked in parables, and my mind was illuminated with images from her words. I saw the door closing. I was kicking it closed and then putting a bar across. It wouldn't open when I was done.

"Don't ask questions. Just look inside. We'll talk tonight under the stars and furs."

I was content with that. I knew where we were heading, or at least I thought I did. We pulled down a country road, dirt and gravel. The Strato-Chief handled the road like she was home. After about five miles through the dust and fields, a little cabin appeared. A faded sign read, "Wanda's Welcome" with a blurry picture of home-baked bannock. It was 8:53 a.m. As I stepped out and stretched, my nostrils flared with the smell of baking, and I was instantly salivating.

"Easy, William." She smiled as she said my name. Have you ever had something seemingly so simple come along and bend you to your knees? In my deepest places, I just wanted to be William. Just a simple man, a better man than my father, just a good man. Woman calling me by my name weakened any resolve I had for the pretense of the muscled, notorious Scarface or Garbage Boy. I just wanted to be a boy, unleashed. What I wanted to be unleashed from wasn't all that clear to me. Everything? Nothing? Reputation? History of me? Woman saw the impact.

"Hold me," was all I could say.

"Always." The perfect one-word answer, and I fell into her arms. Woman could make the ground solid under me and stop the internal quavering of my spirit.

That was the mystery of her, of Woman.

"Pull yourself up, William. These are friends. This place, this food, is solace. Strength for our mission. Strength for healing through sorrow. Strength for moving beyond. Moving forward. Closing the door." Woman was breathing wisdom and the ache of my own being into me.

"Come. Let's eat. Let's meet Wanda." With that, Woman led me into the restaurant.

Wanda wasn't anything like I expected. My mind pictured a wizened elder. Instead, she was a girl—well, a woman in her early twenties, vibrant and glowing. A stocky build, a whole fire of life in her eyes, a star rising. They hugged, kissed, patted each other's backs, hugged again, and swirled together in a bond of deep love. I watched, absorbed, and knew that Woman had performed some miracle with Wanda. When they came out of their embrace, Wanda looked at me. "So here you are, Scarface, the warrior, the man-boy who holds hearts with his glance. You have mine because you have Woman's." Wanda walked as she talked and stared into my eyes, and her eyes told me that we had shared hurt. Not the same hurt, but deep hurt. Her eyes also told me that she had risen above the hurt, the pain, the sorrow. What of my hurt did she see, feel, intuit? She hugged me, and it felt familiar and comfortable.

"You look sad, Scarface. How could you be sad in the presence of Woman?" Wanda's question was serious.

"Not sad, Wanda. Woman called me a name, and it meant everything." As the words stumbled out, I wondered if they made any sense.

"Woman has that effect on people, and I sure as hell ain't Wanda." They both laughed as Woman came to my side, and they both hooked one of my arms and pulled me further into Wanda's restaurant, or "I'm not Wanda's restaurant." The aroma of fresh-baked bannock was intoxicating in its wholesome fullness.

"Breakfast is almost ready. I cooked the bacon early and threw the eggs in the pan when the chief pulled up. Kenton is tending the eggs, toast, and hash browns. He's probably burning the toast or forgetting to flip the eggs, probably sweating and swearing because he wants everything perfect for Woman. He doesn't give a shit what you think, Scarface." Again the women laughed as Wanda hustled through saloon doors leading to the kitchen and bellowed at Kenton in Cree. Woman smiled and gestured to the table in front of the window, and I moved toward it. Woman went to a coffee pot and poured us cups. By the time she set our coffees down and sat, Wanda and Kenton were bursting through the saloon door carrying heaping plates and a basket of bannock. I was salivating in full, open-mouthed hunger.

"My name is Tumble. This is Kenton. If you ask for ketchup, we'll kick your ass. Well, I will. Kenton is a far gentler soul than I am. Eat. We'll join you after the best breakfast west of Winnipeg is in your tummies."

Woman and I tucked in and were quietly enjoying the meal. I had to ask: "Tumble?"

Woman smiled, and I saw the emotion in her eyes and heard it in the trembling tone of her first words. "Short for Tumbleweed. At least, that's what they called her when I recovered her from the streets of Regina."

"What's her real name?"

"Donna Red Cloud. Which was or maybe still is appropriate. She comes from La Ronge up north in Saskatchewan."

"Recovered?" I was getting good at asking short questions.

"Recovered, exactly. Her mom and grandma are both single moms and asked—no, begged—me to find her and bring her home."

"This isn't La Ronge."

"No, smartass, it isn't. Better place for her than home. Tumble was abused by an uncle—probably a couple of uncles. One is dead now. The grandma says she had nothing to do with that passing. Most of the community holds a different perspective. He froze to death in the area they call the Triangle after drinking some home brew with Grandma. He had lots of bruising and blood caked and frozen on his nose and mouth. A couple of young boys found him. RCMP said the bruising was from him falling. Nobody argued with their findings. Nobody cared enough to even think about another explanation. He wasn't a man of or for his people."

"So, La Ronge would not have been safe for Tumble."

"Not in her mind. Tumble thought, felt, and sort of knew that once a victim, always a potential victim in her hometown."

"Sad. I'm sorry."

"Sad is good. Sorry is not. You had nothing to do with this, and sorry keeps people down. You need to lift people up, inspire their capabilities, and bring out the good."

"That's what you do, Woman. Isn't it?"

"Yes. That's my journey."

Sadness clouded Woman's eyes with her words, but her voice was strong, resolute, and proud.

"Woman, sometimes I catch this shadow of sadness in your eyes, your words, your movements. What is your sadness?"

The little inhale of breath was more visible than audible before Woman answered. "My sadness, my woe? Not a path we will travel today or for a long while, William, but we will. I'll share someday."

"I can wait. Whatever your sadness is, it's already touching me. Everything about you does."

"You're trying hard to become a good man, aren't you, William?"

I loved hearing my name coming from her lips. In a manner similar but different to the way I had loved Ms. Librarian saying my name. I nodded, and Woman smiled.

"Or are you just trying to get into my pants through sweet, soft, seductive chicanery?"

"Both." I was getting good at one-word answers as well. We both grinned, and Woman reached across the table and grabbed my hand.

"Be a good man, William. Your mother needs that. It's her life wish." She paused. "I need that."

Woman stared intently at me as she said it. My eyes and heart were registering the depth and meaning of what she meant by my mom's "life wish." I nodded. Woman's gaze drew back, and she registered something of herself for herself.

"William, I need that. More than I thought."

Tumble rumbled into our world.

"More coffee. Ooh-la-la. Holding hands at Wanda's. How perfectly high school prom night. You two need a room?" All three of us grinned and giggled. This mood was good.

"No, this boy here would be too overwhelmed."

Tumble poured us more coffee. She asked if we needed anything else.

"No thanks," I said. "We're all good."

"I'll give you another ten minutes to finish your prom date. Then I'll be back to talk."

As soon as Tumble was back through the swinging saloon doors, Woman began. "As to Tumble's story, she was turning tricks for dope or cash on corners in Regina's whore district. That district is mostly populated by Indian women. She had been at it for two years and was only eighteen when I grabbed her bedraggled, drugged-out, skinny ass from those streets. She fought me for about a minute.

Some pimp-like asshole started to intervene, but my backup was two stone-cold warriors who resemble your FBI, just not as big. Mr. Pimp Wannabe retreated like the coward he is. My version of the FBI went back a couple of days later and helped him with some behaviour and attitude teachings."

"How long ago was that?"

"Three years, at the end of this week."

"Why here?"

"Kenton's grandma was the original Wanda. Kenton is a recovering alcoholic. Four years sober. I brought him back home, cleaned him up, got a local elder to guide him. He's a good, clean man now. The restaurant makes a little money. Kenton knows he owes me, and he owes our people, who helped him. He provided a safe harbour for Tumble. She cleaned up and has been sober for three years. It was a tough start. The same elder who helped Kenton helped Tumble. She was a big part of Tumble's recovery. I think they're a couple now. Kenton is twenty-four or twenty-five."

"He looks ten or twelve years older than that."

"Eight years of hard, dangerous drinking will do that. From age twelve. We recovered him for his grandma. Don't know where his ma and pa are. The fuckin' residential schools almost annihilated my people. We'll be generations recovering. Kenton's grandma just passed a year ago. She was good for them both, plus the local elder, another good woman."

"Why did they call her Tumbleweed?"

"She was just blowing from one bad man to another like a tumbleweed. No roots, no home, no worth in her mind. She would bump up against someone who used her for a while, then just let her blow away when her street value diminished. This was usually when she made less money hooking than the cost of what she was sticking in her arm or snorting up her nose."

"So sad. That must make you furious."

"Fury does no good. Recover. Stabilize. Nourish. Guide. Protect. Hope. Those are my tools. Fury and anger are just the boiling of the pot, not the making of the meal of living."

"What is our grand vacation plan, Woman? Are you just driving me to dining spots around the prairies?"

"That's quite a transition from Tumble to travel. You want to know your plan?"

"My plan? I thought, hoped, it was our plan."

"Well, it is, and it isn't our plan."

"That's a little vague."

"We're driving through Hobbema, stopping at Sweetgrass tonight. From Hobbema, we're driving to Banff. We'll stay around Banff Sunday through Wednesday morning, then you go on your own a little farther. We'll meet back at the cabin we are staying at on Wednesday night and retrace our steps back to the Peg by Friday. Details to follow."

"OK, and I have a mission? A purpose?"

"Yes. We'll talk tonight under furs and stars. And yes, William, tonight we will be lovers."

I shut up. I wasn't going to say something to ruin that! Tumble and Kenton came out and sat with us. With all our coffee cups full, Tumble started talking, telling me her whole story and telling Woman all the things that were keeping her clean and straight. When Tumble finished, my heart ached, and my anger was being vented through deep breaths. Kenton told his story of recovery on a straight and narrow voyage. Mostly now, Tumble and Kenton were saving each other. I was not proud to be a white man during their storytelling. If I had to describe the moment, I would have talked about the redemptive healing power of love and trustworthy people. I would have talked about the weight and scars of oppression and disgust in the treatment of a people different from us who are deemed lower in worth like my mom and me, only worse. Far worse. I would have also talked about the judgment of others and wondered aloud where God was in all this. But Woman steered all thoughts back to inner strength, managing our own path, and leaning hard into love. As she spoke, I fell more in love with her.

At the end of Tumble and Kenton's talk, Woman looked at me. "William, Tumble, and Kenton have given you a great gift," she said in her heart-honing voice. "They have shared who they were, but more importantly, who they have become and how they're evolving to the best of their souls and spirits. This is a great gift, and you owe them for that, you understand?"

I nodded. "Yes, anything."

"Just two things, not anything." Tumble and Kenton looked hopeful and emotional.

"What, Woman? What do I owe?"

"You owe them a bond and a promise. You owe them the bond of trust. That they can always trust you to protect them on their path. That's your bond. Your promise is to respect them as people, as people you care for, as people you embrace into your voyage to your best soul and spirit."

"Oh, Woman, this I promise, and I bond to Tumble and Kenton."

With that, Woman had us all stand up and embrace as a whole and singularly. Then we left. When we were driving, after about ten minutes, Woman spoke. "Did their stories touch you?"

"Deeply."

"Good. We're headed to Sweetgrass. About eight hours. We'll sing and enjoy the drive. You can reflect on life, love, and mostly about others. About decency, about caring, about understanding, about relating your own story to your own future. About guiding yourself in a good direction."

"OK, that's deep. I'll try."

"Try hard, William. On this voyage that you're on, you need to understand who you are, how you will heal. Heal yourself and then you can heal others. That's what you need to do, William."

"Heavy stuff, Woman. Heavy thoughts."

"It is and always will be. If it wasn't heavy, it wouldn't be worth the carry. Don't ever confuse it with a burden. This voyage, this path, is the weight you were born to carry."

"How heavy is your carry, Woman?"

"Today isn't about what I carry. It's about what you will carry."

"Can I think of one other thing, Woman?"

"Depends on what it is."

"Can I think about you?"

She did a quick turn of her head and broke into a beautiful smile. "A little bit would be OK."

Then she was quiet. So was I. Maybe fifteen minutes later, Woman spoke again. "William, you're thinking of me; that's nice. Thank you." That was that for speaking. We drove and sang to James Taylor, Neil Young, Joni Mitchell, and others. Woman had a nice eight-track collection. The eight hours seemed to fly by. I did think, a lot. It was difficult. I kept thinking I needed to be centred. I kept staring into an abyss of hurt, then replacing my own self-absorption with thoughts of Tumble and Kenton's hurts, then recalibrated, and thought my hurt was minimal. Yet the chasm of hurt, shame, doubt, and pain gaped open like the hungry mouth of a nightmarish beast, bloody fangs and torn flesh on its tongue. *Healing will kill this beast?* I wondered, and then I slept.

At Sweetgrass, we met a few people: a couple of female elders, some young women, and the chief. I was welcomed, and apparently, they knew who I was. They talked in English and Cree. I was paying attention, and my ears picked up when one of the elders talking in Cree said CBC and pointed at me and motioned as if she had a stick and was picking up garbage. They all laughed, and I grinned. The chief embraced Woman and shook my hand. We went back to the Strato-Chief, and Woman opened the trunk. We pulled out a big rucksack, my hockey bag, and a small backpack. As we started walking, one of the elders came and handed Woman a pack. We were headed up a narrow path on a slight rise, just outside the town, when Woman broke the silence. "We have dinner, we have furs, we will have the stars, and William, we will have each other."

I was simultaneously deeply emotional and aroused, and smothered a laugh/cry. The walk was a little over a mile and a half. Down the other side of the rise was a small, fast-flowing river. A lean-to shelter was on the far bank. Woman took off her boots and jeans and waded across. I followed suit—or un-suit. She built a fire from wood that had been gathered there, apparently for us. She opened her rucksack and spread furs on the ground beneath the lean-to. She opened the pack and said it was time to eat. We ate sandwiches quietly and drank water. Woman kept the fire going, even though it was just 8:30 and still light. "Let's bathe, William."

Off came her T-shirt, bra, and panties. I struggled out of my jeans and shirt and followed her to the river. She turned toward me, naked, proud, and beautiful. "Off with the undies, white man. The Natives want to see what gifts you're bearing or baring. We can already see that your totem pole is standing."

Yep, I was more than erect. I pulled my gonch off and ran into the water. The river was cold and only about five feet deep. We swam and hugged. I performed the juvenile back float maneuver, saying look at the lighthouse on the rocks. Woman joked that the light was redder than it should be. She had soap and shampoo and said we should bathe each other. We did. Woman assured me her breasts had never been so thoroughly cleansed. I came in her hand. We both laughed at that, her with joy and me with embarrassment. As I bathed Woman, I felt something under her left breast that extended to the top of her hip bone. As we dried each other, I saw it, a long scar, mostly healed, probably eighteen jagged inches in length. Woman followed my gaze.

"A bottle. A Crown Royal whiskey bottle. Supposedly really good whisky. I didn't taste any. I kicked the bottle from one of their hands as they were raping me. When they were finished with me, the biggest of them said I needed to be taught a lesson. He said he was going to cut off my left tit for spilling good whisky. He called me a worthless Indian slut. I fought. Hard. He cut me bad. They all thought he had gutted me. He said I would soon be a dead Indian slut. I still had my left tit, and I lived, William, and I live."

Her head fell on my shoulder. Her body wracked with sobs of remembrance, of terror, of horror. Again, the beast with bloody fangs and flesh on its tongue rose in my mind. The sobs became less intense, quieter, slower, and her body increasingly limp. Woman's head rose, she turned my head then kissed the scar on my neck and then my cheek.

"William, we all have scars on the surface and deep within. You have learned some of mine. I know most of yours. Feed the fire. I'll be waiting in the furs. William, come and heal me, and I'll heal you. I believe deep scars are healed with deep trust. Deep trust is in your head and in your heart, and there is tremendous deep trust in the physical. William, understand that trust trumps lust. Come to me only in trust. Clear your mind of everything else. Come to me in trust."

I fed the fire. Then I walked to Woman, waiting in the furs, in a mist. A fine mist of elusive but dawning comprehension. We held each other. The stars broke the dark one by one as the fire dimmed. Then we trusted. Woman guided me once again through the seven motions. The hunger was ravenous, the harvest of body by body was sensuous, deep, and rhythmic. We moved. We blended. We cried. We laughed. We gasped. We sighed. We danced under the furs to the constellations' delight, and the full moon winked at us, enamored by the sight. And I felt whole. I felt my sinews, tendons, muscle, and joints all achingly whole and healing. I felt the healing power of giving my heart and soul. Trust is the abandonment of self in the arms of another. Woman, Woman, Woman. Etched on the inside of my eyelids, tattooed on my veins, stitched into my scars, pulsing through my heart beats. Woman, Woman, Woman.

We were up early, packed our gear, forded the stream, dressed, and walked to the car. We shared coffee and fresh bannock with two elders. Woman and the elders talked in Cree. As we got up to leave, one of the Cree elders rubbed a cream, some sort of a poultice, on my cheek and neck scars. She motioned for me to lift up my shirt. She applied her medicine. She tugged on my belt. I undid the belt and slipped my jeans down. The healing ointment was applied on my leg scar, followed by another medicine. That one stung more than a little. The elder grinned as I grimaced. Woman placed a pouch of Export A tobacco in my hand that I knew to give to the elder. Then we were off.

Again, quiet and peaceful, all the way to Hobbema, which took about six hours.

Woman had some business to take care of with some people on the Reserve. She said it was OK if I just waited at the car. I got out and sat on the car's hood. It was as hot as hell. I took off my shirt, draped it behind me on the hood, and laid down. I must have dozed off. A couple of kids woke me by tugging my feet, and I sat up.

"Are you a hippie?" The kid and his buddy were probably only seven or eight. Standing back about twenty feet from the Strato-Chief were eight kids who looked about my age. They were looking me over, sizing me up.

"No, I'm not a hippie. At least not full time yet. I'm a garbage man."

The young kids' eyes went big, and behind them the five guys and three girls laughed.

"A garbage man? Wow, you came to the right place then. There's a lot of garbage around here. You gonna take it away?" That was the other kid; those young boys weren't shy.

"Not today. We're just travelling through."

One of the little guys ran back to the teens. The guys had a definite edge to them, but they seemed friendly. The kid came scampering back. "Hey, garbage man, my sister wants to know where you got all the scars."

As soon as I heard the question, I decided I was going to fuck with the assembled youth of Hobbema.

"Knife fights," I said, followed by a dramatic pause. "You should see the other guys. Carved like a turkey dinner."

I heard gasps from the girls. The boys straightened up a little, tensed up, and really started looking me over. They all took a step or two back and were shifting their weight from foot to foot. I didn't know why, but I had strapped a hunting knife that Stone Pony gave me to the back of my belt. I pulled it from its sheath, put it in front of my chest, and ran the tip over the scar on my neck. Everybody got quiet and took another step back.

"This is a good knife," I said.

One of the girls edged forward. "Did that shit hurt? I mean, it looks like someone carved you good. Like a jack o' lantern or something." The whole group laughed, and so did I.

"Yep. Hurt like a son of a bitch. There's another scar on my leg. Sixty-eight stitches in all." Now I was telling the truth.

She edged closer. "Can I touch them?"

"Sure." It was always a bit of a circus or a show-and-tell with my scars. Sometimes it was just a shitshow of abuse and ridicule, but that wasn't the case that day. She was genuinely curious. I let her stroke all three. We didn't speak as she touched me. Her hand lingered on my chest. She seemed entranced. One of the guys called her name, and she walked back to her friends.

Woman came just then. She stopped and looked the scene over. "Time to go."

So, I got in the car, and we were on the road again. I waited another fifteen minutes or so before commenting, "That was a little strange back there."

Woman was quick to respond. "What did you expect? A good-looking white man, half nude, with all those scars on a reserve. Might draw a little attention. However, William my dear, that was only partially about you."

I laughed. "Hell no, Woman, that was all about me. I'm intriguing and notorious. Even Cree elders know about Scarface the Garbage Boy."

"Hate to burst your bubble, but I have recovered five kids for that tribe. Three girls and two boys. They were all in that group, gawking at you. Everyone wants to know more about me, Woman, the recoverer of the lost and stolen."

Woman was solemn, so I went quiet, and she continued. "That tribe has seen too much hurt, so they're very grateful for my interventions. They have some money. They're helping you on your voyage."

"How?"

"You'll find out on Wednesday."

That was it for conversation. I was learning to be mellow with a bit of mystery. We drove for about three hours to Banff. We went to a small grocery store in town. Woman bought some food to last us a couple of days, and we picked up a pizza and got back into the Strato-Chief. We ate as Woman drove. After about a twenty-minute drive, we pulled down what seemed to be a logging road. We bumped along for a couple of miles before Woman made a turn that I didn't see coming onto a road that was more a trail. I knew there wasn't much sense in asking where we were headed, so I bumped along in silence. Then the trail ended in a small clearing with a log cabin. The cabin was the opposite of Stone Pony and Mister's grand home. It looked a little run down and weather-beaten. I saw a little lake at the bottom of the hill.

We spent the next two days and nights just being with each other, simple meals, walks on trails around the cabin, skinny dipping, and long, slow "trusts," as Woman called them. Two idyllic days and nights. Lots of small talk about big things. Life, love, care, healing, and hope, amongst others.

Then on Tuesday night, Woman unveiled the next portion of my voyage.

"Tomorrow, early, at six o'clock, we leave. We're driving to a small airport where you're flying to another small airport outside of Vancouver. Friends will pick you up. You have a special meeting set up on Wednesday afternoon. You'll fly back late Wednesday evening. I'll meet your plane, and we'll begin the drive back to Winnipeg."

"Woman, that's a travel plan, but what's the purpose? Where's the healing? In the meeting? Who is it with?"

"You will answer all those questions yourself. That's all we will speak of this."

That was it. Of course, there was the evening and night with a fire in front of the cabin. The sleep under the furs and the stars continued to sweep me into a place of peace and ease. My mission, my voyage swept from my mind.

Woman always reminded me to breathe, just breathe. Making love, sleep, wake, love, sleep. No visions, no fears, no nightmares. Truly the calm before the storm, I kept thinking and reflecting as we bumped down the trail, the road, and then the two-lane highway to a tiny airstrip and a lake. The float plane had the same tribal symbols as those at the Hobbema Reserve. This was how they would help me on my voyage. Few words. Only the trust-filled goodbye in Woman's eyes.

My pilot didn't say much, just basic safety instructions. The takeoff from the water was a rush. Another new experience. Flying through and over the Rockies was breathtaking, scary, and unreal. The landing, the touchdown, was impossibly smooth. We taxied to the dock and then the pilot nodded goodbye. "Tonight, six o'clock."

The one man on the dock nodded and beckoned me to follow. It was about 10:30 a.m. He said little, just, "We will grab a bite. Your meeting is at twelve-thirty. No need to tell me anything. I know—don't know—who you are."

We pulled up at a beat-up looking restaurant. My driver got out of the car and headed to the back of the place. He returned with two plates of food covered in foil and two coffees. We ate in the car, saying nothing. I wasn't hungry. I was getting wound up. Whatever my voyage was, Woman never said. I was wondering how it would heal me. My driver took my half-eaten plate. "Mind if I finish this?"

I nodded. For a smaller man he could pack it away! Then he took our paper plates and cups to the trash, came back, started the car, and away we went—to who, what, where, or why, I didn't know.

He motioned in a circle. "We have a few extra minutes," he said. "I'll drive you around Stanley Park to see some sights. When I drop you off, I'll point to a table, and you just go sit there and wait. You're required to always wear the sunglasses, jacket, and cap, which you'll find in the backseat."

I didn't even bother asking why. Stanley Park was beautiful and alive, crawling with people of all kinds. It was a Heinz 57 mix for me compared to home. We stopped at exactly 12:30 p.m. He reached into the backseat and pulled up a large brown bag and then launched into directions.

"Put this stuff on now, and don't take the jacket or cap off at any time. There are sandwiches, potato chips, and pops in the bag. The guy you're meeting will be hungry. Sit at that picnic table straight ahead there. See it, about fifty yards, out there in the open?"

I nodded, and my tour guide continued. "Sit facing the water. Don't go for a walk. If you have to piss, there's a public washroom about a hundred yards to the left of the table. If the guy you're meeting has to piss, go with him and then walk him back. You have until four o'clock if you need that much time. I'll be back and will pull up right here. Your flight is at six. Any questions?"

"Yeah. Why all the bullshit cloak-and-dagger secrecy and spy stuff?"

"I don't have a clue, man. I had to write all this shit down and memorize it, or I wouldn't get paid."

"What if I'm done before four?"

"Then someone will call me at a payphone where I'll be waiting, and I'll come and get you."

"Are they paying you well?"

"Yep. Way more than what someone should get paid for driving you, waiting around, and then taking you back to the plane. A big payday for me and for less than seven hours of work. Hey, I'm not supposed to talk to you or answer any questions. Please don't say anything. I only got half the money up front, and I don't want to blow my payday."

"OK, good enough. I wouldn't want to screw that up on you. Anything else?"

"Yeah, man. The mystery of all this is driving me fuckin' crazy. I was contacted by a friend of a friend. I don't know anything or really have anything to do with this. So good fuckin' luck to you, and see you at four. Put the glasses on and get out."

I turned and looked out the passenger window. "If you're mystified, I should share with you that I'm totally in the fuckin' dark as well! So, brother, we both are living with a mystery. At least for the moment."

As I turned from the car, it hit me like a lightning bolt. Maybe being with Woman had put me in some sort of fog. It was then I knew why I was there and who I was going to meet. I thought I was going to puke up the bit of food I'd eaten.

CHAPTER 41

Our Father Who Art

I was barely ten yards from the car when I saw a man taking a seat at the designated picnic table. I stopped walking as he sat down on the side of the table facing away from the water. His head was on a swivel, glancing in every direction, including mine. He didn't appear to notice me or take any second looks toward me or even in my general direction. I started walking toward the table and noticed a clean-cut guy in shades sitting at a park bench about fifty yards to the right. He stood out, because in that part of the park, only longhairs seemed to be passing through. About ten yards from the picnic table, the guy, who I assumed must be the guy I was supposed to meet, stared and squinted. The sun was behind me.

"You the guy I'm supposed to meet?" he asked.

I nodded and had to stop myself from saying, *Hello, Dad.* "I guess so."

"Well, at least you're a fuckin' white guy."

"Last time I checked, I was."

"Another smart mouth like those other two fucks from last week."

"Well, I don't know about them, but if you didn't like them, I probably would."

"Listen, you look like a young fuckin' longhair fuckin' faggot to me. I'm here because I was forced to, despite the money—but you got the money, right? If you don't have the money, I'm fuckin' walking, despite those two fuckin' narcs."

"Narcs? Money? What are you talking about?"

"You better know what I'm talking about! Look around and you will see the narcs. Not like you. Short hair with them fancy aviator glasses sort of like yours, but they have the real kind made for real, serious assholes. You know, the ones where you can't see their eyes."

Well, I knew where one was sitting already, so I looked left and, sure enough, about twenty-five yards in front of the bathrooms sat an identical-looking, out-of-place guy.

"OK, I see the narcs. But the money?"

"Yeah, two hundred and fifty. Fifty up front and two hundred when we finish, which at the latest is at four o'clock. That's the deal, and why I signed up. So, you got the cash or not, kid?"

I opened the brown bag and didn't see any wads of cash in there. I thought I would check the jacket pockets before I fished around in the egg salad sandwiches, which the aroma from the bag informed me was our lunch menu. Sure enough, inside the inner chest pocket was a packet of something. I pulled out a brown envelope and peeked inside. It was stacked with cash. I counted five tens and handed them across. My father snatched them and stuffed the tens in an inner pocket of his raggedy-ass jacket.

Art was succinct and informative about how things were going to go. "They said you would lead the conversation. Ask me some questions, so get at it. It's your dime."

I was staring at him the whole time. He was smaller, sicker-looking, and smelled more of booze than at our last encounter over three years ago. He looked destitute, broken, and nervous. He kept scanning around. Couldn't keep his eyes or head still. It was like he was expecting something bad to happen. His body and face had little twitches going on. I guess he didn't like the silence.

"What the fuck, boy? Start talking, or give me the rest of the money, so I can start walking."

I took my glasses off. "Hey, Dad," I said slowly, "you remember the last words you said to me three years ago?"

Now I had his full attention. His eyes were riveted to my face before he took all of me in. The way recognition dawned on his face was priceless. I couldn't describe his expression. Shock? More than a little of that, but what else was mixed in? Fear? Definitely. Joy? Non-existent. Bewilderment? A ton.

He recovered quickly. "What are you doing here, you little fuck? Except now, you're a big fuck. You came all this way to fuck over your old man? I got a knife, and I'll cut you some more. You're probably some kind of long-haired faggot now, without a man like me around to teach you some respect and discipline."

"Take it easy, Dad. I asked you a simple question. No need to get all fuckin' brave, tough, and insulting. Do you remember the last thing you said to me?"

"No I don't, and I don't fuckin' care to. You came all this way to test my memory? Then you're wasting my time. My brother and I were very drunk, and you sucker punched me, you little fucker."

"Hold on, Dad. Where's the love? Let's get a few things straight. You tried to break into our house, and you were threatening my mom. I happened to arrive home at the right time. You suckered me. Good shot right on the beak then *blam*, I gave you a solid knock-down kick to your nuts. Dad, I was fifteen, and I kicked your ass. Your brother didn't like the odds of going one on one, and he backed down real fast and hauled your sorry, beat-up ass outta there. But the question is, Dad, do you remember your last words to me?"

He wasn't saying anything, but his eyes were dancing all over the place. His bottom lip was quivering, and he had to lock his hands together to keep them from shaking. "No," he said finally.

"Lucky for us, then. I do. The parting words from father to son after you had deserted us eight years before that, with not so much as a Christmas or birthday card in between, until this year, and certainly no money to help us get by, and you can't remember what you said, dear dad of mine?"

"No. I was drinking."

"You're always fuckin' drinking, you asshole. Your words, Dad, they were so incisive and clever that they've stuck with me all this time."

He almost looked hopeful, like he might have said something meaningful, wise, or a lesson to live by. He looked curious.

"Dad, you said two words with great sincerity, although they were somewhat garbled because I mashed your gums and lips into your teeth, and you were bleeding badly. So was your ear. Your voice was a little squeaky, which might have been caused by the solid boot to your balls, but Dad, you were brave enough to say, 'Fuck you' as you safely sped away in your brother's car."

"Like I said, I was drunk."

"No, you weren't. You had been drinking, but you weren't drunk. They cleaned you up for some dreamed up re-entry into our lives and gave you a couple of shots for courage."

"My brothers always poured stiff ones."

"I bet they did. Their plan didn't get too far, did it? Mom wasn't going to let you into her house, and then I showed up."

"I could have made it a lot worse for you that day."

"How? Neither your brother nor you had the balls to take on a fifteen-year-old. I had my good old reliable Louisville Slugger as a deterrent to the sloppy, cowardly drunks who were—and still are—the Smythe brothers."

"I ain't a coward."

"Yes, you are. You beat up women. I never heard a tale about you fighting a man. I, on the other hand, have had lots of fights with tough guys—largely because of you."

"Yeah, I heard when I was in town you hadn't won many—and even a girl took you."

"True, Dad, but in the last three years, that's kind of changed. I've filled out, so to speak, and can more than hold my own. You're a big credit for that. The day I smashed your mouth and watched you clutch your balls. The terror and scared-to-death look as you fell down the back stairs. The fear in your brother's eyes as he saw me clutch the Louisville. Yep, you Smythe lads taught me a lot about myself. You threaten someone I love, then I have the courage of ten. I think I fully got a backbone when you were fully losing yours."

"Fuck you. I was drinking. I wasn't ready, and my heart wasn't in it. I didn't want back in that hole you call a home. My brother's wife wanted me out of their house and their life. She said I was a bad influence, but it was my older brother who taught me to drink. She thought my wife would take me back in. She said your mom had a big heart and was a bigger sucker for bad men. Guess she was wrong about that. My brother should have smacked some sense into that bitch of his."

"Careful, Dad. Careful how you refer to women. I got a hair trigger when it comes to that, but listen to you chatting it up, really earning your two-fifty."

"Fuck you, and stop calling me 'Dad.' You say it like you don't mean it anyway."

"I don't mean it. You're right. What should I call you?"

"Call me Art. Use my fuckin' name."

"Yes, sir. Art it is. Our father who Art."

"What's that Bible bullshit about?"

"Well, Dad—I mean Art—when you left, we missed the bit of your pay cheque that wasn't going to booze. Things were tough, very tough. Man, if I had known we were meeting, I would have brought hamburgers or a meat pie."

"Now, what are you talking about? Is your brain fucked up from all the beatings or what?"

"Could be a little bit touched in the head, Art, from all that shit and abuse. You better hope not, because then I wouldn't know good from bad. Good would be kicking the shit out of you for all the shit and abuse we had to go through—but let's get back to the biblical shit, as you so elegantly put it."

"You sure like to babble about nothing."

"It's good to talk, Art. You know, let it all hang out. The biblical stuff? Our father who Art. Well, that comes from the frightened, confused mind of a seven-year-old boy watching his Mom scrape by, make do, and hope for the best. Five pounds of hamburger meat that had to stretch over seven days of meals. And she did it week in and week out."

"That ain't Bible shit."

"Patience, Art. I'll get to it. Mom thought it would be good if I went to Sunday school after you left, that it would be good for me. Not church, just Sunday school sometimes—and just for me. No one else in the family could dress well enough to attend the Lord's house. Did you know God was so into the latest fashions, Art? I sure as fuck was surprised by that."

"Bunch of high-faluting fucks hiding behind Bibles. That's all that shit is."

"So, not a man of God, Art? No need to answer that. This isn't Sunday school. I never went very much and not at all by the time I was eight. It was the Lord's Prayer every day at school. You see Art that was one confused seven-year-old that you abandoned. He was still hopeful there was something good about you that he could clutch onto. When someone asked, 'Where's Your Father?' I said I didn't know. I even drew a family Thanksgiving picture in grade two, and because you were out of the picture, as most people were saying, my drawing had you out of the picture. A classmate drew a picture of our family, though. It included you with a beer in your hand and your arm around an Indian woman. The picture showed Mom with her big pregnant belly, my sister, me, and Blackie, our dog. You remember Blackie, right, Art? There was good old Blackie in the picture, licking his balls."

He couldn't contain himself. He smirked a bit. I glared that away for him.

"Now, the artwork was poor quality—mostly stick figures, poor use of colours, lack of composition and dimensions according to Mrs. Blunt."

"Mrs. Blunt, that old withered—"

"Don't say it, Art. That would be bad for your health."

"I have a knife."

"Fuck the knife, Art. I'll shove it up your ass if you say one more bad word about any woman."

He understood from my tone and my eyes more than the words that he would be mightily harmed if he said one more word on that topic.

"Art, you should learn to stay away from certain topics. Now, back to the biblical shit. First, that grade two piece of art was about and included you, Art. Told a story. An accurate story. You did drink a lot. You did have an Indian woman from the reserve on the side as a girlfriend. Apparently, you knocked her up and then beat her down. The rumour in town has always been that you left because her brothers were going to come after you. Mom was pregnant about seven months at the time of the drawing; incredibly accurate, you agree? And Blackie did lick his balls a lot." I laughed at that.

Art wanted to laugh along but was squirming a bit, probably wondering what a knife up his rectum would feel like. I saw pain in his eyes as he spoke. "You know I'm a war veteran. I've seen a ton of shit that can fuck you over."

"We'll get to that, Art, but remember we need to cover the biblical shit. So, the hopeful, scared-shitless seven-year-old tried to grab the drawing from a couple of tough thirteen- or fourteen-year-old brothers of the artist. He ended up poking one in the eye and smacked the other in the testicles so hard, the guy almost lost a nut. They both were required to go to the hospital, and they acquired the nicknames of One Nut and One Eye. The seven-year-old was viewed as a legend—but likely a soon-to-be dead legend. Here's the biblical part, Art. The seven-year-old didn't pray for protection, forgiveness, or worldly things. He prayed that the Art in 'Our Father who art in Heaven' was you. That was where the seven-year-old figured you had fucked off to. Heaven. Our father who Art in Heaven. Get it? Then I could tell people where you were—and Heaven was, you know, a good place. How fuckin' pathetic was that seven-year-old to have a hope like that? Pretty fuckin' sad, right? Laughable, comical."

"I didn't know that."

"Well, how could you? You didn't write. You didn't call. You didn't send money. Art, you did nothing. You might have been in Heaven or Hell, but most likely you were just drinking your life away. Then you sent a letter saying you were going to visit this September. That's just next week. What the hell, Art? You think for a second you're welcome, or that we want you in our lives? Are you fucking crazy? You come near us, and I'll kill you with my bare hands."

"OK, OK, relax. I was drinking when I wrote that. I have no way of getting there anyway. Your two friends who visited with me last week made it clear that my presence would not be welcomed."

"My two friends? What the fuck are you talking about?"

"Your two friends. The only thing I overheard from those two narcs was that they referred to them as the '"Lone Nigger and Tonto."'"

He had to see my face drop, but I was glad I had put the sunglasses back on.

"I don't know who you're talking about."

"Sure, you do. Your mouth opened like a flapping fish."

"These guys, did they mention my name or anything?"

"No, but they asked me a bunch of questions. Paid me two hundred and fifty bucks. Stupid fucking questions about me and women and my army time. If people like those have money to throw around, I'll sure as fuck take it. Then I was told to come to another meeting and make another two-fifty. So, what the fuck? They didn't kill me the first time, so I showed up, and here we are. A family fuckin' reunion and all."

He started to snicker, but my look, even with the sunglasses, deterred any joviality he might have been feeling.

"Anything else about those two?"

"Yeah, that black man is one big dude. The Indian man is a scary-looking fuckin' native who has gone fully off the reservation. Those two I don't imagine get fucked with much. They were very curious about some babies I might have had a hand in making."

Again, a little sneer, like he was rather proud of himself. I took off the sunglasses. I wanted him to sense some real danger. "Listen, Art. Be very careful what you say about those two guys. They didn't kill you, but there's nothing stopping me."

He took that threat seriously. He coughed up a little spit that was dribbling from his lip to his chin.

"OK, I wouldn't want to antagonize a mean shit like you, and I want my money, so what do you want to know?"

"That's a better attitude. What else about those two guys?"

"Well, those two narcs were here with them."

He gestured to his right and left and then continued. "The narcs came and told me to clean myself up and get ready for a meeting today. They said there was another two-fifty in it, so I was motivated—and, to tell you the truth, curious. And it's easy money, at least so far. Besides, no one has shown any interest in me for three years. My family sent me out here on a one-way Greyhound bus ticket that was marked *no refund, no exchanges*. That was right after the foiled attempt to . . . what do they call it? Reconcile? Yeah, reconcile, with my family."

"Anything else you're leaving out?"

"Yeah, the most important thing for them."

"What's that?"

"Well, it's such bullshit. I didn't feel it was worth saying."

"I'll judge that. Now spit it out."

"They said I'm their fuckin' father. They said they were my sons. They said to stay the fuck away from them and you. All three of you are my sons. Fuck, I'm Fred Fuckin' McMurray. My three sons."

I should have put the glasses back on, but he saw right away. He misread my reaction.

"I knew it. Those fucks lied to me. There's no way those two bastards are my sons. Your look told me they ain't your brothers. Those fuckin' lying bastards making me think I got a coon and a buck for sons."

My left hand was on his throat, my right pulled back ready to smash his jowly, alcohol-fucked-up face into mash. I saw in my peripheral vision both narcs were already coming in our direction, so I let go and pulled him into a standing position. As I let go of his neck, the release of pressure must have triggered another release. His piss was staining his crotch before his ass hit the bench. He was whimpering and sputtering.

"They called me ASS. You know, Arthur Stephen Smythe, A-S-S. What fuckin' sons would do that? And you, grabbing me by the throat, choking the piss out of me. Well, fuck the lot of you!"

"Art, let's talk about your army history."

I could see he was a little taken back by the abrupt change in topic, but it seemed to settle him. He rattled through his training in the States and, as he called it, his experience with the big black man's mother. He was telling his whole story now. How the war had fucked him up, made him a drunk, and made him lose his temper. He said it was no excuse, but that was occasionally why, when he was drinking and feeling fucked up by war memories, he might have hit a woman or two. He was earning the two-fifty for sure. Problem was, I knew his war record—and his record before the war. He talked about the Indian woman who he had as a girlfriend, said he was sorry about what had happened to her, then spoiled that by saying it could have been one of her brothers who beat her. The Indians were crazy that way. I had to choke down my anger when I heard that comment.

He finished strong, saying he was sorry for how things worked out with my mom and with the family. He had just become a no-good drunk, fucked up by the fuckin' war, and said our family deserved better than him.

At least he finished with the truth.

"Art, thanks for sharing. Did you enjoy the sympathy party you just threw for yourself?"

His head came up, and his sobbing stopped. His alcoholic self-con job hadn't worked.

"You know, Art, your war story doesn't work. First, you had been in jail five times for being drunk in our hometown prior to the war. You lost at least seven jobs, one house, all our furniture, and even Mom's wedding rings. Let's talk about your war record. Nine AWOLs during training, nine more overseas, a stint in hospital in Italy. You know, when I first saw that, I had a brief burst of pride. My dad, a wounded war vet, fighting for his country. I shouldn't have read the actual documents detailing your time in the army any further. Gonorrhea. That creates a discharge—and not of the honourable kind, right, Dad? Do I have any Italian brothers I should know about?

"You never served near the front. You were a driver at the rear headquarters, driving generals, drinking your brains out, and screwing whatever came your way. Man, the horrors of war really fucked you up, or was it the whores of war? My guess would be the latter."

I was on a roll, and I wasn't stopping. "Somehow, along the way, it seems three women fell in love with you. All you did there was bring hurt and misery into their lives. You got them all pregnant and beat them. Then, they experienced the horrors of war. Their time with you was a war. They all survived you, Art—barely, but they did. Your war cry should have been 'hurt and desert.' So, take your sympathy tale and shove it up your lying ass."

"You done? Give me my two hundred and leave me the fuck alone."

"Had enough, Art? Enough truth for one day?" He nodded, but I kept going, "Yeah, I'm almost done with you. Just a couple of loose ends to tie up. I want to be perfectly clear with you. Are you listening?"

He made brief eye contact and nodded. He was starting to get a little ripe in his pissed pants.

"Art, this is the end of any family reunion, ever. If I see you anywhere around our town, I'll end you. It will be your ultimate demise. You understand?"

He nodded.

"Here's your cash, ASS." Man, that felt good saying that. "One last thing before you grab the money. You mention that we met or that you met those two men, those two good men, last week, and we will finish you, quick and ugly."

With that, I handed him the envelope with the cash. He snatched it and buried it in an inner pocket of his jacket. I walked toward where the car dropped me off and stood at the curb. Within five minutes, my ride arrived. When I got inside the car, only then did I look back. Art was eating an egg salad sandwich. The narc on the right was still there, and it was then I spotted a phone booth about forty yards behind him. The other narc was standing beside the phone booth. He must have called my ride. It was 2:45 p.m.

"Ready to go?" my driver asked.

"To the airport, James." My last sight of Art was watching him furtively glancing around as egg salad spilled from his mouth.

"Our father who Art."

"What was that?" the driver asked.

"Nothing, nothing at all. Just putting the last nail in an old coffin of hurt."

CHAPTER 42

Closing the Door, Letting in the Light

When the plane landed, Woman was there waiting. Her embrace felt good, like a starting point of coming back to wholeness. I had never fully understood that there was a void in my life from not having a father. Woman drove. We didn't speak for a few hours. Woman always knew when it was the right time to speak. This drive wasn't the time.

What I was realizing as we drove is that I couldn't miss something I never really had. The void that was Art was a black hole. I felt that darkness was closing quickly as we drove. I thought about the darkness in Woman's life. Now, *that* was pure evil. I wondered if her darkness was a gaping void.

We retraced our steps and spent the night in the cabin outside of Banff and then stopped at Hobbema. I stayed in the car and didn't draw much attention. We camped at our private lake at Sweetgrass and stopped for an early dinner at Wanda's. It was good to see Tumble and Kenton again. They felt like old friends. I felt connected to them. The four of us all carrying our scars, within and without.

Woman and I didn't say much to each other until the long drive from Sweetgrass to Wanda's, then we said a lot, with Woman leading the conversation. "Did your meeting help?"

"I don't know."

Before I could say anymore, Woman put her right hand up to my lips to hush me. "It's important that you know. I don't know about your meeting. We won't speak of where you went or who you met. We can speak about what in you has opened or closed. If there is healing for you. If there is a way forward for you from this meeting. Take your time and think before you say what you feel."

I had been thinking of my meeting a lot. On the flight back through the Rockies, through the nights in Banff and Sweetgrass, except for the long spells of total enchantment and convergence with Woman. On the drive from Banff to Sweetgrass. It was about an hour before I was ready to speak. Slowly accumulating my thoughts and feelings and organizing them in some form of emotional and cohesive structure.

"Woman, I'm ready to speak."

"Good, William. I'm ready to listen."

Her saying my name was like snapping the cap on my bottle of feelings and thoughts. Then, they just poured out. "There is good and bad in all our lives. Here, driving along alone with you, is all good. I feel whole and clean with you. It's a strange way to express my feelings, with the word 'clean.' I mean, being with someone I trust, I don't hide anything, don't pretend anything. I can just be myself. Be real, be true, be as pure as possible with another being. I soak that up as healing. I feel good, strong, grounded.

"On the other side of my world, my meeting already seems so far in the past, yet it was less than two days ago. Then, I felt shattered and dirty. Unclean. Every second during that meeting, I thought that bad things were just waiting to pounce, tear, and scar. I retreated and acted with a protective exterior of fierce, barely controlled rage. I was feeling that nothing good could come from that connection, ever. I was feeling the power to destroy, the power of being the predator, to seek revenge. All those feelings and realizing there were capabilities within me that could unleash forty lashes and more. That's when I saw the self-destruction lying within. There would be no healing in that. No healing in pummeling for revenge. No healing in a brutal beating. No healing in killing. This presence, this capability to wreak Old Testament vengeance that was in me, I believe was born from him. His neglect, his abandonment, his cruelty to others. This is his gift to me, those horrible traits and possibilities. To shut those down, I must close him out. End him. Remove him from my life, my thoughts. There is no healing through him—only darkness. A black, strangling void choking out the goodness, the light, and healing. So, Woman, you ask me what has opened, what has closed? You ask if there is healing? If there is a way forward?"

I paused and glanced over at Woman, who I didn't realize was pulling the car to the side of the road. I waited until the car was stopped and she had placed it in park before I continued.

"You probably have guessed that I met my father."

Woman nodded. "I felt all along that this trip of yours, this voyage, was going to be about your father. After this meeting, is a door closing? Is there healing?"

"Yes, but the answer will come in steps. First, closing the door, then ensuring that the malignant pieces inside my body are cut out, with no re-entry point or chance of return. Shut the door. He will stay out of our lives. The physical part is the easy part. The emotional part is far harder. I can tell you that after standing on the precipice of murderous intent, the climb to higher ground requires a relentless examination of who I am and who I want to be. I have started closing the doors of anger, hate, and revenge. Well, maybe not closing—but sealing them off. This is necessary, because behind those doors, the darkness of despair, ill will, and the ugliness of hate are lying in wait. I can't let that stuff seep through. Then, I turn my mind from the closing and sealing of the doors to my own personal dungeons, and demons and look toward the light. Woman, you're part of the light."

I stopped talking to catch my breath and my thoughts and to turn my mind to the doors I wanted to open. "It's like a dream tunnel, where I see the light shining and walk toward it. My walk is not fully confident because of the darkness and doubts I'll probably always harbour in some buried inner recess or crevice. I know they can re-emerge if prodded, poked, or stirred. With you, I feel pulled toward the light. Then, I think of your own dark experiences. The recesses of internal blight and strife you must bury. This makes me think about your way to the light. You recover people. You help fix brokenness. You do so with a fierce faith in yourself. I believe that you model the ferocity of good action for me. You're a part of my healing that instructs me to self-heal. So, healing is coming. That door is opening. Thank you."

I took a moment to settle, and Woman placed her hand on my chest. "Breathe," she said.

I composed myself somewhat and then continued. "Then, there are the other healers in my life: my mom, Stone Pony, and Mister. Probably by extension, Mr. Clampett and the whole Neapolitan Crew. Strange mix of teachers, yet all cut from the same cloth. They're all warriors of what I feel is the right way to heal. By guiding myself to my own good. Doing and acting in a manner that will bring good to me and others. All these teachers—Mom, Stone Pony, Mister, and you—stand up and fight or struggle to gain their own good, which is often for the good of others. Mom persistently works to make do and get by with an independence that is borderline heroic, at least in my eyes."

Woman nodded. "Your mother is brave. She's a warrior. You come from the good things inside her. Never forget that."

"I promise I won't. Then, there are Stone Pony and Mister, who persist through a work ethic that none can match as they face bias and stereotyping. The kind of irrational hatred and utter disdain that would halt and destroy most men. They persist with their pride intact. They endure with a humility of spirit that is anchored in souls of steel fire. They're biblical, and they will overcome, driving themselves so they can create an empire of opportunity to give hands of healing to those they embrace into their fold. Their will will be done.

"They heal themselves by doing what no one thought they were capable of doing. Their mission: getting to a place where their fold consists of and embraces many. Uplifting and healing all who come their way, the duality of creating good through doing some bad. Balancing that and then exceeding on the good side of the ledger. The balancing of books. Their credits will far outweigh their debits in the long run. Their need for reconciliations will recede."

Woman nodded. "Those are good men with good intent and good hearts. Rising above their low means despite the high expectations, that they were destined to be failures from birth."

"Then there is you, Woman, a totally different pathway to my light. When we blend, there is healing. Our physical times take me away, and I feel good, strong, and, most importantly, whole. Beyond the body and to the heart and mind. You take me on journeys, Woman. You transport me. I hope I don't sound like a horny, lovesick teenager. I am. You make sex whole. You commit fully. I feel it in every sinew, I see it in every glance, hear it in all your sounds. Your aromas cascade over and through me, and I taste all you are from all you give. And I'm greedy for you. I'm filled up when we finish. I feel so strong and pure. You heal me, and so healed, I sleep. There are no dark places in that sleep."

Once more, Woman nodded. "You're good for me as well. I also feel whole and full of peace when we're together."

"So, Woman, dark doors are closing and sealing, but some darkness gets through the cracks. Doors to light are opening and can be gained. Healing comes in the arms and bonds of those I trust and love. And Woman, I love you."

It was good that Woman had pulled the Strato-Chief to the side of the road. She was weeping. She bent her head to the steering wheel and clutched it with both hands at ten and two. For safety? For control? Slightly lifting and turning her head she spoke. "William, I told you a year ago I would always be there in your heart, and you in mine. We heal each other. You're the only one I have been with since men tried to destroy and diminish me to nothing. You were given to me as a gift. A gift of love. I'll always love you. That was meant to be before we met. I know we're not destined to be together forever. We're meant to be together only on our voyages. The next time we're together will be my voyage. You will help me toward healing. To the closing of dark doors and finding light. We'll speak no more of this love today. We'll let it rest in us quietly. Our love does not need to be questioned or examined. It needs to rest and thrive deep within us. That is our health stone, our healing hearts. Sacred and pure, between us."

I started to talk, but Woman shushed me with two fingers to my lips. She pulled the Strato-Chief back onto the road. We drove in silence. We ate an early dinner at around 5 at Wanda's. Tumble and Kenton were glad to see us, but they were busy. Wanda's was packed. I was the only white person in the room. Tumble joked that they usually didn't serve minorities, but in my case, an exception could be made.

The two hours to Winnipeg were travelled in silence—no music, just the Strato-Chief humming along the highway. When we passed the "Winnipeg 20 miles" sign, Woman reached over, and we held hands.

"Woman, I know you don't know all that happened with my father, but I must tell you something. As a child. I thought, hoped, and prayed that the prayer 'Our father who art in Heaven' was a reference to where my father was. Heaven's a good place, and that was my hope. because all I heard about my father was bad. Well, my father, "My Father who Art," is my father no more. My father soon will be no more. I'm certain of that. He will drink himself to death or meet a quick demise because of his drinking. That will close a dark door. That will help in the healing for many. Me, not the most, others certainly more, as he has been their personal demon."

Woman nodded, and nothing else was said. She pulled the Strato-Chief to the curb, five or six houses down the street from Crazy Horse's apartment. Then she turned off the engine and slid over on the front seat. Her two fingers went to my lips again. "I'm not staying."

My eyes protested and pleaded.

"William, I have two young girls to recover. That's my mission of healing today. Besides, if I believe the romantic things you've said, my healing of you makes you sleepy, and you need recovery time."

Her fingers had not moved from my lips, and though I had much to say, foremost of which was pleading with her to stay, I knew to say nothing was the right thing for us at that moment.

"William, the next time we journey, I feel you will be helping recover me. Be prepared to heal me in all ways, beyond the physical. Be ready, William. I'll need you."

With that, Woman removed her fingers from my lips and leaned in and kissed me. It was Woman's kiss to give, and mine to receive. A gift given fully. As Woman's lips parted mine, she pressed her hand to my heart, grabbed my right hand, and pressed it to her heart.

"William, close your eyes."

I did.

"Think of me, William. Think of us."

It was all that I could possibly be thinking, and my mind was full.

"William, heal."

Woman removed our hands from our hearts, scooted over behind the steering wheel, and stared forward as she started the car. I got out of the Strato-Chief, opened the rear door, and grabbed my bag. Woman pulled away from the curb. Gone. The Strato-Chief's taillights soon disappeared. I was left on the curbside but with no sense of loss. I felt full.

The two days with Crazy Horse were rip snorters. Food, drink, and weed. We almost got busted on Portage Avenue at about 2 on Saturday morning. Crazy Horse and I were both standing on a *Winnipeg Free Press* paper box, whooping at the moon, the August full moon, the Sturgeon Moon, according to our Cree brothers. This was according to Crazy Horse, who also said the August full moon stood emotionally for freedom and our sense of being in the world.

We chose to freely whoop our way down Broadway and up Portage, retracing our steps to Man-Pop last September. Crazy Horse was joyously celebrating our freedom and our sense of being in the world. We were beings. Free beings of value and worth. Of course, our beings had maybe a few too many beers in them.

Crazy Horse replicated his climb atop a *Winnipeg Free Press* paper box from almost a year earlier, and I felt obliged to join him. We were short a few thousand kids and our ten Cree warriors, but our spirits were strong. The police were surprisingly polite. They rolled up in two cars, and four officers circled us. They politely asked if we two drunken fuckin' Indians wouldn't mind getting down from there.

"Certainly," Crazy Horse said. Then, he leapt in the air, did a 360, and landed on his feet. The officers were all reaching for their guns. I jumped tentatively to the ground, wondering how the hell I got up there in the first place.

Crazy Horse took command as he landed and saw the nervous move of hands to guns. "We're not Indians; however, we're more than a little fucked up and drunk."

Crazy Horse is pure muscle, and has shiny black hair and the magnetic good looks of a movie star. He feels dangerous but looks charming and exudes a charisma that can mesmerize. The cops held still.

"Sorry we caused a disturbance. My shy friend here is Scarface, from Ontario. I'm Crazy Horse from St. Boniface. He's white and somewhat ugly. I'm Metis and more than a little good-looking."

The cops were astonishingly frozen by Crazy Horse's monologue. The younger officers at first one and then a second, flashed recognition. The first officer to speak, who looked like he had not quite reached puberty, spoke in a startled manner. "You two? You're the crazy fucks who led the peace march to the stadium last year. You're on the same paper box as last September with all the dancing and drumming fucking Cree. Right?"

Crazy Horse and I both nodded. We were sensing this encounter was going to go from bad to good.

"Yeah, you two were all over the papers and a full-on spot on the CBC national news that they showed for days. These two had girls taking their shirts off and showing their tits. I remember the captain's daughter took her T-shirt off, and the captain wanted to club you guys if he ever caught you."

"I wish we had that power," I said, "but those women had their own naked vibe flowing."

One of the older cops smiled as he removed his hand from his gun. "It is you two fucks. What a day that was! We were expecting a riot, and you two pied fuckin' pipers had everybody marching along quietly and peacefully. No fights, nothing. Even stopped marching for the red lights. Our Captain McConnell is too much of a hard-ass anyways."

All the cops laughed, and none of them had hands to guns anymore. Then the pre-pubescent cop spoke up again. "And the rack on the girl. I should have been arrested for ogling."

The laughter of the four cops sounded good. "Yeah, I looked too," another one said. "I couldn't help but look at all the chicks. They were writing on those T-shirts. You were so disappointed when McConnell's daughter put her shirt back on. Remember what I said to you?"

"No. My brain wasn't working. No blood flowing. My blood was all getting channeled to my dick."

"Exactly! I said, 'Is that your baton in your pants, or are you just happy to see me?'"

Again, the four cops laughed. Then they told us to shut up and get off the streets. They even asked if we wanted a ride. We politely declined. Neither Crazy Horse nor I had any desire to spend time in the back of a police car. Besides, he was probably carrying a couple of dime bags. We walked drunkenly and as quietly as we could back home. Blood brothers, arm in arm.

Sunday was quiet, just lazing about on the grounds of the Manitoba Legislature.

Crazy Horse and I said our goodbyes at the airport. First class on the way home. I knew the drill, as an experienced traveler. I wore my shades. I was really hungover. I enjoyed the meal, slept, and didn't mind the gawking that came in my direction as a longhair way out of place in first class.

I did experience the same type of bullshit with another businessman. "Got the right seat, son?"

I was a little surly, a consequence of being hungover. "Let me check your fuckin' ticket, bub," I said. "Make sure *you* should be in first class. Why don't you sit down, shut the fuck up, and leave me the fuck alone? That behaviour is recommended and a very, very healthy course of action for you to follow."

He must have been just a junior vice-president or something, because he followed directions well.

Stone Pony and Mister picked me up at the airport. We spoke very little until we reached my driveway.

"Two things," I said. "First, I'm proud to be your brother, under one condition. Don't speak. Please listen. The condition is we're full brothers—none of this half-brother horseshit, agreed?"

They both nodded in agreement.

"Second. Our father who Art is our father no more, right?"

They both nodded again.

"A father, he never truly was," Stone Pony said. "Our father will be Art no more. He will hurt none of our families ever again. We'll talk of that father no more. He ceases to exist for us and ours. We went there and closed that door. Say nothing to anyone about our meetings with Art. All our tracks are covered. No one will know of our meetings with Art. Ever."

We all nodded.

"We need to become blood brothers again soon," Mister said. "Now, get some rest. Big work week coming up. Looks like you'll miss the first week of school again. You're eighteen now, so you can take a hardship absenteeism without your mother signing any forms. We took care of that for you."

Back at home, I felt good, though I was wondering what would happen next.

CHAPTER 43

Bogeyman: Fat Hopes and Thin Dreams

When I first met my two best friends, Scarface wasn't either Scarface or Garbage Boy. He was just himself, which wasn't much in our town. Just a kicked-around kid scraping by. Scarecrow was and still is ahead of the game. Smarter than us, figuring things out beforehand and on the fly. Survival of the quickest and the invisible was how Scarecrow referred to our early lifestyle. And that's how we operated, quick and unseen. Except for Turkey and except when it came to baseball for a few summers. Then, we were seen, and we were something on the field, at least for a while.

Then, shit happened. Dope shit. Scarecrow and I getting all freaky and hip with all the shit of the late 1960s and early 1970s. We went from tools to cools and nobody's fools. At least that's how Scarecrow described our evolution, and he wasn't wrong. Scarecrow and I had turned sixteen, and Scarface was still fifteen when Scarecrow and I started smoking a ton of weed and selling a ton more to support our recreational drug use. Recreational drug use was a new term, and we fully embraced the lifestyle it implied. Hell, everybody appreciated and needed recreation.

That summer, the three of us put a beat down on Teddy Porter, although Porter only saw Scarface, who did most of the beating. Scarecrow did knock him out with a full bottle of beer to the back of the head. The three of us were all sipping cold beers. Scarecrow and I were stoned out of our gourds. We were hanging around a field that was frequented by teenagers for some illegal toking and drinking. You know, recreational activities.

Porter pulled into the field and was trying to "recreate" himself with some chick. He got a couple of beers out of the trunk of his car and stupidly left the trunk open. We considered it an invitation to an open bar. We snuck up and liberated the almost full two-four of beer. Porter was too busy asserting himself with the chick to notice the theft. We thought it would be cool to see how Porter flipped out when he went to get another beer. So, we were just chilling, drinking beer, and listening to the crickets fart. We were all knocking back the free beers when things got heated and out of hand in Porter's car. Porter wasn't taking "no" for an answer, and we could see and hear the chick struggling. The seriousness of her situation wasn't registering with Scarecrow and me. That wasn't the case for Scarface. That boy snapped into action!

He covered the fifty yards to Porter's car in record time. We had barely gotten to our feet when Scarface ripped Teddy off the fighting and scared girl. He must have hit Porter a dozen times before we got to him. Porter had freed himself and pulled a switchblade on Scarface when Scarecrow hit him in the back of the head with a full beer bottle. Porter was out on his feet. Our brains were processing the scene and what happened when Scarecrow and I simultaneously realized that Scarface had saved that girl from what look liked a certain rape.

Scarface walked the girl home. Turned out she was someone we all knew, a good kid, and fifteen years old, just like Scarface. Her father was a cop, and that scored us all some good karma down the road. We threw Porter in his backseat, and Scarecrow pissed on him. I followed suit. We poured a couple of beers on him and took off. Scarecrow muttered to himself, but loud enough that I heard: "All square, Teddy Bear. Almost."

We cut through the fields to the nearest corner store and phoned the cops from the payphone. Scarecrow muffled his voice and told them there were some kids drinking and maybe fighting in Christie's field. We doubled back and hid about a hundred yards from Porter's car. We hid in the wheat field and watched as the cops hauled Porter's pissed-on, beaten-up ass out of the car. We sipped on Porter's cold beers and enjoyed the show.

Life took a swing up—one might even say high—for Scarecrow and me. We grew our hair, and because we knew how to score and sell dope, we were instantly very cool. Girls liked us, and guys needed us. Life was good. We started travelling and making connections. We became major suppliers of recreational drugs, just grass and hashish—to our local community and beyond. Soon way beyond our home turf. We made connections in Mexico, and we figured out a set of logistics that made our supply lines almost invisible. We found a local connection who could move bulk weed, and we moved the bulk weed to them—"them" being Stone Pony and Mister. Nobody knew we were connected back in those days. Our business dealings were quick and invisible. It was a solid partnership. Nobody, especially the cops and the narcs, would have guessed that we were capable of that. Acting dumb and stoned cemented the impression. The stoned part was accurate, but everybody miscalculated our smarts.

Turkey was fucked up. I'm happy we both made it out alive. Now, we're part of something that is something. We're moving from illegal to legal endeavours. We're gaining strength and maybe wisdom. We're still cool—just way more cautious.

In Amsterdam, we rolled fat joints and had thin Dutch girls straddle us as we "shot-gunned" them. Blowin' smoke mouth to mouth was far fuckin' out, and the Dutch girls loved the smoke and the straddle. Scarecrow and I had fat hopes and thin dreams. Hopes to get high, make some cash, and have some female companionship. We didn't dream much. No sense dreaming, because we didn't dare to think or dream of possibilities, given our background and current occupations. Fat hopes and thin dreams seemed to work for us. Is that a metaphor or an analogy between the joints and women and hopes and dreams? Who the fuck knows? I don't, and I don't care much, either.

With my upbringing, deadbeat dad, and disappearing mom and all, I didn't dream much. My mom must have studied Scarecrow's playbook. When Dad was turning nasty, my mom got invisible and quick. Dad was lost with no one around to hit, so he just drank himself into oblivion, which worked out well for everyone. "Hey, Beav, not the home life dreams are made of." Wally always the sensible older, helpful brother. "Geez, Wally, I guess you're right." The Beaver is always a good foil to our reality.

I hope a lot, but I don't dream. My hope when I was younger was for a full belly. I thought getting fat was a luxury. Scarecrow informed me that a few centuries back, being fat was a sign of power. I think my yearbook quote would be "Power to the pleasantly plump"—if I had finished high school, that is.

With all that was going on with the MMC and the All Saints, the NCE going forward as a legit enterprise and Scarecrow and I getting strong, my dreams were starting to fatten up. I tried to keep them thin, because dreams can get starved really thin, really quickly. Luckily, I knew how to diet in the dream department.

Now I was part of something, and the success of NCE was a big, fat hope. I had never been more full of hope. At least not since Scarecrow and Scarface took me as a brother-in-kind, a brother-in-arms. I can work with hope, but I can't work with a dream. Hope seems real; I feel it. Dreams are fantasies and mind-fucking non-tangibles.

At least that's my view. I'll take fat hopes over thin dreams any day!

CHAPTER 44

Fred Fuckin' McMurray

The egg salad sandwiches were good. So were the salt-and-vinegar chips, and the Mountain Dew was cold. Who would ever buy Mountain Dew to go with egg salad? I was fucked up. I knew that, but whoever thought egg salad and Mountain Dew was a combo, they were seriously fucked up. I made myself laugh, which is hard to do with a mouth full of egg salad while sitting in pissed pants.

My Mountain Dew was bottled by Clem and Clara. Now, what the fuck is that all about? Thanks, Clem and Clara, for all your hard work to bottle this lime-green or yellow swill just for me.

I was feeling a little giddy sitting there in Stanley Park with another $250 in my pocket. The two narcs were apparently still on duty, just watching me. I wondered if I should invite them over for lunch. The second egg salad sandwich was filling me up. My curiosity was getting to me, so I opened the other brown bag, which was at the bottom of the bigger bag. It was scrunched in there, and I was wondering if maybe they brought me dinner, too—or even better, left me a big bag of cash or some good booze. I looked in and saw it was just some cloth or clothing or some horseshit like that. There was a note. I picked it up and read it aloud to myself. Don't know why the fuck I did that.

"Dear Dad. We brought you a change of clothes just in case you pissed your pants again. We also want to be perfectly clear on a couple of things. First, don't ever visit any of us, ever! That would be a very serious mistake. Second, never mention our visits—to anyone. The narcs are on our payroll. They will know if you open your fuckin' mouth, so don't be stupid. Now, go get drunk, you spineless prick. All our love, your three sons."

Well, fuck you, boys. I had already decided not to visit, but after meeting you fucks, who would want to?

I looked around, and the narcs were still there. I got up and walked over to the washroom. I changed my clothes. Well, my underwear, socks, and pants. The bag had all the replacements I needed, plus a shirt, jacket, and a pair of runners. I changed my shoes, too—kept the old pair, but threw my pants and other stuff in the garbage. I washed my legs, balls, and even my ass good, and used up a ton of public soap and paper towels. I thought I was smelling as fresh as a daisy when I came out of the bathroom.

The narcs were still there. I went back to the table and pulled out the rest of the egg salad sandwich and the chips. I had Clem and Clara juice left, and in a moment of pure inspiration, decided it would be an interesting mix. My jacket had lots of pockets. From a big pocket that was low on my right side, I retrieved a mickey of Hiram Walker whisky and uncapped it. Is Hiram a Jewish name or something biblical? Who the fuck knows, and who the fuck cares? I get thoughts like that when I'm giddy. I carefully poured a third of Hiram in with the Clem and Clara. Now we had a three-way going. Fuck it. I'm funny! Hey, Clara, I hope Hiram ain't too stiff for you. Clem sounds like a limp noodle, and you know old Hiram is a badass with a hard-on.

Wow, first taste says the three of you play well together. Clara and Clem were helping me start on my about-to-be bender. So was the egg salad.

My three sons? Imagine that. I'm Fred Fuckin' McMurray. He didn't have a wife either, did he? Just old Uncle Charlie to help him. Well, my three supposed sons were all strapping, strong bucks, big, strong men. Well, the Indian wasn't tall, but he was all muscle, wiry, and coiled like a spring. That red fuck could mess a person up in a minute. Those eyes of his were colder than a witch's tit. Nothing but menace in those eyes, at least when he looked at me. I would rather mess with the big black man than that fuck of an Indian. Man, he was just itching to go all warpath on my ass. That prick cut me. He knifed my leg. I thought he was going to cut my balls off.

Those strong, healthy men, those sons of mine, they had money. They had come a long way just to tell me to stay the fuck away. That didn't make sense. They must have had money to burn. Hey, maybe I could write some more letters and tell them I was planning a reunion trip. You know, visit all their mommies. Maybe they would pay to keep me away, like a divorce settlement. Separation pays. Yeah, fat fucking chance of that! They would kill me before that ever happened.

My three sons! Incredible! Clara was just about done, and Clem too, so I poured another third of Hiram in the Mountain Dew bottle. Hiram burned a little more without as much of his yellow friends in the mix.

Yellow? That's a nice colour. Three sons, let me think about this. I'm a fucking stud. I get with a woman, and she gets pregnant. Yep, a genuine hard dick of a stud. They should appreciate my value. Put me on a farm, a stud farm, like a retired Triple Crown winner. Use me for breeding purposes. Clearly, I get results.

Right, Hiram? Now I'm talking to a whisky bottle. A short one at that. Maybe I should invite the narcs over for a drink. What do you think of that? Only if they bring their own booze. Now, I had a rhyme going in my head.

Any colour, anywhere, any size is fine
Get them pregnant every time
Red, white, black, or yellow
I'm the right fellow
Short and fat or thin and tall
I'll fuck them all
Knock them up, then knock them down
Make a baby and get out of town!

I'm a funny guy! Sometimes, when I'm drinking with a few friends, I'll whip off a couple of rhymes. Then we all get tanked and argue about the rhymes and how they went.

My fuckin' sons thought I might piss my pants again. They brought me a change of clothes. What bastards! Thoughtful bastards, though. In reality, just two out of the three were bastards. The white one was legit, but he was a little asshole.

Well Hiram, we're drinking by ourselves now. Clara and Clem have skedaddled. But let's put you in the Mountain Dew bottle, for old times' sake. I'll finish you off and get straight to the bank, deposit $150, and then get fucked up. Hey, I didn't get any expense money this time. So, the only non-bastard is the cheap bastard. I crack myself up.

Let's add my good qualities up. First, I'm a virile stud. Three women, three kids. Second, a fucking war hero. Purple heart. Purple dick. Six of one, half a dozen of the other. Third, I can rhyme like a fucking poet. I've done that since I was a kid. Fourth, I can fucking swear like a fuckin' artist. Always have and always will. I wonder if these things are hereditary.

Oh yeah, and I'm Fred Fuckin' McMurray! My three sons.

CHAPTER 45

Mom's Eye View: Different, Defiant, Thy Will Be Done

He came home different. Like he had figured something out. He was calm. Easy. When he spoke, he smiled. He talked about how in one year, he felt five years older. In a good way. He told me not to count on him having more maturity, just being more worldly wise. He talked about Crazy Horse, Winnipeg, Sweetgrass, Banff, the prairies, steak dinners, and good times. Every so often, he would say something about Woman. He said that was her name, Woman. I asked what her real name was. He looked puzzled for a second, and then laughed. "It's Woman."

Scarecrow and Bogeyman just looked him over. Their collective wisdom and insight was that he had scored some really cool shit. That, for them, fully explained the Mr. Mellow who had returned to us.

I was not happy that he was going to miss the first week of school again. He had the hardship permission slip that he could sign himself now that he was eighteen. Hard work had helped him so far, so that in and of itself wasn't a bad thing. He seemed happy and content. Whatever happened on his trip seemed to be all for the good. They say the Lord works in mysterious ways. Well, if he had some hand in this, then what's the biblical phrase? Thy will be done. So be it.

He was leaving the house before 6 every morning with Bogeyman and Scarecrow in tow. That week, they didn't get back to the house until after 8. They had asked me to pack big lunches, but not to cook dinner for them or the little one and me. They brought home takeout. Monday was Chinese, Tuesday was Kentucky Fried Chicken, Wednesday was pizza, and Thursday was A&W. They told me Friday, there would be a big surprise. All of our meals seemed to be a celebration.

On Thursday night, the conversation was heart-lifting at first, and then it took a strange, unexpected twist.

"This all seems so right," Bogeyman said. "The family having dinner together and feeling good."

"Yeah, surreal compared to where we were a few months ago," Scarecrow added with a bit of sadness. "This is good. I feel better, not quite whole but making a comeback."

We all went quiet at that. The little one filled the silence when she spoke. She rarely spoke up at dinner. "At school, kids and some teachers asked me about the house. They're very nosy about all you boys. A couple of kids laugh at how strange and weird my three brothers are. I didn't know what to make of that all week until today." She paused. She certainly had grabbed our attention from our A&W Teen Burgers, onion rings, and root beers. Not an easy feat with the appetites of these three young men. "Today, I told them all that I have three strong brothers, and I love them."

Those words made those young men little boys again.

"I told them I love them because they're good and they're funny. I just look at them, and I know they care for and would do anything for my mom and me. I told them that I was blessed and thankful, and that I felt special. I felt safe. I felt protected. I felt loved. I told them I might have lost a dad, but somehow, I gained two brothers, so I'm doing alright, thank you very much."

The little one stopped and smiled as her ears filled with the muffled sounds of three young men, her brothers, and her mom stifling sobs and tears.

"Thank you, little sister," Scarecrow said, "and you're right. You're protected, safe, and loved."

"I think little sister deserves an increase in allowance for sticking up for us," Bogeyman said. "I say a dollar a week from each brother."

The boys all nodded.

Lord, is this your will? I wondered. *Three brothers to protect, care for, and love her? Then thy will be done.*

It's amazing how easy it is to crash from joy to worry and fear. They call it premonition or intuition or something like those feelings, those senses. I went from joy and a full heart to fear and a racing mind. Somehow, the feeling came over me that things for our family were going too well, and something bad was lurking around the corner. Why couldn't my brain leave *good enough* alone?

Three brothers. That was how I was thinking of them, and how I wanted to think of them.

They told me they would be home by 7 on Friday night and that they had cold beer and wine ready. They said they would clean up, and dinner would arrive at 8. They told me to set the dining room table and relax.

When my son came bolting through the back door shortly after 5 on Friday, I was a little surprised. I had just got in the door myself a few minutes before and barely had time to set my things down, say hello, and hug my little girl. He started talking right away.

"Mom, we have visitors coming at six. Go get changed. I'm going to clean up and grab a quick shower. I'll be right back down, and we can talk then."

"What? We're having visitors for dinner? Who?"

"No, not for dinner. Let me shower, change, and get my head on straight, and I'll explain what I know when I come back down. Just hang on for a few minutes, OK?"

"OK."

Well, it looked like my premonition was on the mark, based on my son's words and actions. I changed quickly, fussed with my hair, and came back downstairs. I told the little one to go to the neighbours' and play. I decided to walk her over and asked my friend if she would mind my girl for a couple of hours. She said that was fine and that the little one could join them for dinner. My friend is a good friend—the kind who knows when not to pry. I scooted home just as my son was coming back into the kitchen. I couldn't help thinking how good, strong, and controlled he looked.

"Mom, sit down, and I'll tell you what's happening—at least as much as I know. I honestly don't think we have anything to worry about, but we have visitors who we would prefer not to be welcoming into our home arriving in about twenty minutes. I want you to be calm and not worry."

I couldn't hold back. "Well, I can't be calm if I don't know what's going on, and so far you've just managed to scare me and make me worry, so now, please tell me what's going on."

"OK, Mom. At about 4:30, Stone Pony and Mister pulled up to our truck. They told B and S to finish our route and our other work. They also told B and S that there was nothing to worry about, but I needed to be home with my mom. I knew something was up because they were driving two vehicles—Stone Pony in mine, and Mister in a company truck. Before I drove home, they told me what was up. They told me not to worry and to tell you everything was OK. You know I trust and believe them, right?"

"Yes, and so do I, son. They're good men. Please go on. Who's coming?"

"Our old acquaintance, the detective, and that young cop. The young cop somehow tracked down and then called Stone Pony. He told him he was bringing the detective for a surprise visit at about six. Mister and Stone Pony came to get me and tell me to get home."

"Why is he coming? Did you get into any trouble when you were away?"

"No, I didn't. All the young cop could tell Mister and Stone Pony was that it had something to do with a dead man who was close to us."

"My God, they can't still be after us for that, can they? That was a year ago, and witnesses said they saw him at least two days after I last saw him. You were out in Winnipeg when they found him. How can they still be thinking we had anything to do with his death? He broke his neck when he crashed his drunken self into a tree."

"Yeah, Mom, that's why I say don't worry. That detective has never seemed to like us much—and remember, a lot of his buddies wasted a lot of time chasing down the golf thing. So, maybe he's still pissed."

I smiled at his mention of golf, but I was still worried. "Son, what is it, then? He must have a reason."

"Maybe he just wants to rattle our chain a bit. Remember, he told us about how his neck was broken, that the break wasn't consistent with how a neck breaks in a car crash. Maybe he's just being a prick. Who knows? But we'll find out soon enough."

I knew things weren't going to be very pleasant from the first words out of the asshole arrogant detective's mouth. "You folks come into some money? I sure couldn't afford these fancy new additions on a lowly detective's salary—even with twenty-five years of service."

Normally, my son would just suck it up and back down, but not today. "Funny—I understand good detectives make a decent living. I guess if you pool a garbage man's and a seamstress's pay, you can do alright. But you got a big pension coming soon, right?"

He didn't find my son funny at all, and he showed his cards early. "You know, you long-haired smart-ass, there are a lot of us who think your mom's boyfriend had some help killing himself last year. Most of us think you two had something to do with his demise. A hand in that murder."

"Let me stop you right there, Magnum PI. In reality, 'most of us' is only you. All the reports say he killed himself through his dead-drunk driving at the tail end of a three-day drunk. So, it ain't murder, and you're way over the line. Not only can we pay for the addition to our house, but I think this is police harassment with no grounds, and for your information, Magnum, we can also afford a lawyer to protect our rights. Aren't I right, Officer?"

My son looked at the young police officer as he finished talking. The officer looked extremely uncomfortable and said, "This is the detective's house call."

This only sent the detective, who was fuming already, further into the red zone.

"You fuckin' smart-mouthed, hippie freak, you think you know a thing or two? We'll see when I handcuff you and your precious mom and parade you out your front door. We'll see then, you—"

"Stone Pony and Mister, you hear the threats that Marshall Dillon here is making to me and my mom?" my son asked.

As if on cue, those two men walked from the kitchen into the hallway where the confrontation was taking place. I had no clue they were there. They both had two beers in their hands.

Stone Pony looked directly at the detective and lit into him. "Yeah, we did, Scarface. Luckily, we dropped over for some cold after-work beers. So fortunate that we can listen in and now observe police intimidation. Settle down, Columbo, and loosen your tie. Your face is bright red. Hell, you got a good Indian look going there. You could almost be my brother."

The detective was almost vibrating with anger, clenching and unclenching his fists. It looked like he was going to say something, but Mister picked up from where Stone Pony left off. "Yeah, you should mellow before you have a heart attack or something. You should probably—and this is just a friendly suggestion—stop clenching your fists, because it looks like you're fixing to punch somebody."

The detective couldn't take any more. "You two shut the fuck up and get the fuck out. This is a criminal investigation, and I'll charge you two with interfering with a police officer doing his duties."

My son re-entered the exchange. "Whoa, back up, Officer Friendly. First off, these two gentlemen are invited into this house. We just opened the door, and you walked right in uninvited. Second, what criminal investigation? You haven't said anything about that, which I think is breaking legal requirements. So maybe, sir, with all due respect, and to use your exact and uncalled-for language, maybe just maybe, you should shut the fuck up and get the fuck out, unless you're going to be somewhat respectful and treat us with a bit of decency, as is required by law and probably the oath you took twenty-five years ago."

The detective was clearly processing my son's words and the whole scenario before he spoke. Never in his wildest dreams—or nightmares—did he imagine an Indian, a black man, and a longhair would stand up to him. I thought his head was going to explode. He looked like a comic strip character when they show steam coming out of their ears.

"You can all shut up now. This is not a criminal investigation—yet. I came to be respectful. To show my respect. I have some information for the family members. Maybe your two guests should leave."

I had had enough of this arrogant ass, and I knew he would browbeat us and step way over the line if we were just on our own. I heard a car pulling into the driveway. My son looked out the kitchen window. "It's B and S. They came home early."

That was my cue. "Whatever you have to say, you can say in front of these two men, and you should wait until those other two boys are here as well."

"With all due respect, this is a personal family matter, and you might want to hear it on your own."

"If that was the case, you would have knocked on the door with hat in hand and waited to be invited in," I replied. "You would have been respectful instead of making snarky comments. I say this in front of this young officer. I don't feel safe or that my rights will be respected by you. Whatever you say now, my feelings won't change about you, and I'm going to make damn sure the chief of police knows how you treated me. All these men and this young officer saw and heard your disrespect."

B and S came in the back door to the kitchen. They stood behind us, beside Mister and Stone Pony. My son unexpectedly took my hand. "Spit it out," he said. "Make it quick. Then get out of here."

The detective was seething, but then he smirked. "OK, have it your way in front of your esteemed house guests. It seems your husband has passed away, ma'am."

He stopped and studied our reactions. I took in a short draw of breath. As far as I could tell, the five men around me had no reaction. Not even my son.

"He was found dead at the bottom of the stairs in the flophouse where he was living," the detective continued. "His neck was broken."

"Where was he?" my son asked.

The detective's eyebrows rose. "You mean you don't know?"

"No, or I wouldn't have asked. And where's the decency and respect? No, 'I'm sorry to inform you.' So, like I said, spit it out and then get out. By the way, is that your usual approach to informing people of the death of a family member? If so, you need to work on that—maybe some remedial training in decency would help."

The detective was once again back on his heels. He hadn't expected or prepared for such back talk. "Vancouver. His neck was broken. Sound familiar? He was found last Friday."

My son took a step toward the detective, and Mister and Stone Pony moved up and were at my sides. The detective took a step back, and his eyes flashed fear. My son's voice was low and dripping with promise. "Listen, Detective. You make one more insinuation, and I'll ensure that your professional existence is a living hell. Everyone in this room knows that you just attempted to intimate without a shred of proof. Three things are going to happen now, you low-rate thug. One, you're leaving. Two, I'm calling the chief of police and telling him exactly what happened, and playing the tape for him. You see, Mannix, your powers of detection are missing. I hit 'record' the moment you knocked on our door. You didn't even think to look to see if we accidentally left a tape recorder on. Third, I'm calling our lawyer—and not to prepare a defense because we don't need one. I'm going to check with her to see what legal grounds we can proceed with against you."

With that my son looked at the young police officer, gave him a nod, and leaned behind me and hit the "stop" button on his tape recorder. Then he turned back to the young officer. "Do me a favour and get this piece of shit out of here. I just found out, from a complete asshole, that my father is dead. In a manner my mom and I should never have had to face or hear."

The young officer grabbed the stunned detective's elbow and slowly spun him around. They were out the front door quickly. The detective couldn't restrain himself, shouting from the front steps. "You haven't heard the last of this from me."

My son strode toward the door. The detective seemed frozen, and his hand went to his gun. He looked scared.

"Officer Friendly," my son said, "I want to share the last words my father said to me just over three years ago. They fit this occasion, almost perfectly. You ready? All ears, Columbo? Fuck you."

The detective turned on his heel and walked to the police car with not so much as a goodbye or a "kiss my ass." The young officer looked at us, mostly at my son, rolled his eyes, shook his head, and followed the detective to the car. We watched them get in the police car, the detective punctuated his exit by slamming his door, and they pulled out of the driveway. As soon as they left, my son turned to us. "Bogeyman, get you and Scarecrow a beer out of the fridge. Let's all head out to the back deck."

We all filed through the house and out the back door. Boogeyman went to the fridge and got the beers for himself and Scarecrow. Mister and Stone Pony handed one of the two beers they were each holding to my son and me.

"Well, that's a bit to digest," my son said. "The passing of my father is only surprising in that it hadn't happened earlier. I'll talk to the young officer. He's sort of our friend—or at least he's more respectful of the law-and-order process. I'll find out what happened to Art."

With us all gathered outside, Mister spoke up. "I have a toast to make—well, actually, two toasts. First, to family. This big extended family right here, and to all our families."

We clinked our bottles, and I took a deep swig. There were tears in my eyes.

"Second, to the departed—for no other reason but as a sign of respect for the dead. There's no sense kicking someone when they're already down and gone. To our father, who certainly Art not in Heaven, thou are done. You will no longer haunt our minds, blacken our hearts, or throw shadows over our souls. May you rest in peace. Lord, thy will be done."

The religious toast from Mister set my mind spinning. Still, we all clinked our bottles and took a drink.

"Let's all sit down and enjoy the rest of this day out here on the deck," my son said after draining his beer. "Scarecrow, can you call Angelo's and ask them to add two more dinners to our meal? Those who need another beer, grab one. We need to talk a bit about all of this. Mom and B and S, I will need a minute with my employers to talk over bereavement pay and leave."

There was a bit of a giggle all around before my son continued. "I might have been a bit more tactful with the detective, but he's been gunning for us all along, so it's better to show him we won't be bullied or intimidated by his dime-store detective-novel tactics. Let's enjoy tonight's dinner and thank the Lord we're all together. You guys are going to love this meal."

"First, I could use another beer," Scarecrow said. "Second, you called him 'Officer Friendly.' Now, that was funny. Scarface, you were defiant. You stood up to authority and something that was wrong. We need to defy what's wrong and what can hurt us. We need to be strong. You, Scarface, are showing strength. We need to face everything like this head on. No fear. That will be the difference-maker in all the shit we might face. No fear. That difference will instill fear in those who would bring harm against us. They don't expect strength; they expect weakness. We're not weak, especially when we're together."

No one spoke, but there were lots of physical signs of absolute approval of these words.

Then Mister and Stone Pony and my son headed off the deck and into the boys' wing. Scarecrow went to the phone. Bogeyman pulled out a chair at the table for me. We both sat down with our beers. I glanced at my watch to check the time, 6:22. What had just happened? What had I just learned over what seemed to have gone on for hours, but was just a few minutes? Art was dead. Broken neck. Sound familiar? That was one thread of my thoughts. My son's no-fear, no-bullshit response to the detective was the second string I was pulling on. Was that smart? He was defiant. He was strong and, as the kids say, "in his face." Would that come back to bite him, to hurt him, to hurt us? The third loose, lost random string of wool that was unraveling in my poor head was Mister's toast to the not-so-dearly departed, Art. Our father? Art wasn't even a sliver in Mister's life, but he said, "our father." I didn't realize it, but my son must have shared the deep hurt inflicted by his dad. It bothered me that he hadn't shared all that pain with me. I did feel a surge of gratitude that he could share that pain with Mister and Stone Pony. I planned to thank them for that at some time.

I was looking over Bogeyman's shoulder and noticed my son was upstairs in the boys' wing. At the same time, I realized Bogeyman was holding my trembling hand and saying something to me.

"It's all going to be fine. Nobody here has a thing to worry about. Your boy, your family, we're all safe. No harm will come your way. No harm will come Scarface's way or the way of anyone of us due to Art's passing."

With that, my head slumped onto Bogeyman's shoulder, and I wept small tears as my brain swirled in circles of larger thoughts. Scarecrow had joined us at the deck table. We sat and drank our beers. I got up and got us three more. We sat and made some small talk. For some reason, my brain switched tracks, and I was thinking about Scarecrow. As I looked at him, I marveled at how this young man, only three months removed from being abused in a foreign prison, was now comforting and protecting me. *Yeah, God, you work in mysterious ways. Can I admit something, Lord? I'm not sad Art's dead. I could be capable of breaking his damn neck if he came near my kids and me again. You took care of that for us. Do I thank you for that?* Lots of strange thoughts.

My son, Mister, and Stone Pony came back onto the deck. My son filled us in on what had just transpired. "Everyone, we're going to have an impromptu wake of sorts and a talk before dinner. I called the chief of police and talked to our lawyer, Ms. Cecilia Annamoosie, and I invited someone to talk with us. Dinner still good for eight o'clock, Scarecrow?"

Scarecrow nodded. We all sat on the chairs around the big picnic table. Everybody was settling in with a new round of cold beers, and I was feeling more than a bit dazed. Right then, a police car pulled into the driveway. My thoughts were instantly dark, thinking that the detective had returned. I looked at my son, but he touched my arm and smiled. "All good, Mom. This is who I invited to talk to us."

The young officer got out of the car, and he started straight in. Art had been found in the stairwell by another resident. He had fallen the eleven steps from the fifth floor to the fourth floor of the building where he lived. The evidence gathered at the scene indicated he was falling-down drunk. Apparently, he must have tumbled and fallen. He had multiple injuries from the fall, including some broken ribs and a broken nose. There were no injuries that would indicate Art was defending himself in a fight or an altercation of any sort. Given the alcohol smell on him and the condition of his clothes, it seemed he had been on quite a bender. The young officer said the only unusual thing about the death was that there was no indication he had tried to protect himself as he fell. The Vancouver police had already ruled the death accidental. The young officer said he had seen the incident report that described the deceased as "dead drunk" by several witnesses who had seen him shortly before his fall.

My son thanked the young officer.

Just as the officer was leaving, he turned back and looked at me. "Ma'am, my condolences for your loss, although in my opinion, it wasn't much of a loss. Just so you all know how I feel. That detective, by the way, is a one-hundred-percent asshole. There is no investigation. He had no right coming here. I heard over my car radio that the chief was ripping him a new one back at the station. Seems the chief got a call from an angry citizen about police intimidation, browbeating, inappropriate language, and lack of respect and decency. Just for the record, he's off the case, because there never was a case."

As the police car pulled out the driveway, my son made a toast. "To that fine young officer and the chief of police." We all laughed, but my head was still clouded with dark thoughts. A foreboding that this wasn't anywhere close to being over.

Then, my son filled us all in on what he had learned and what would transpire. "We're going to get a copy of the police report. It clearly states no foul play was suspected or involved. We need to make a quick decision on what to do with the body and his few belongings. My thinking is we bury him in Vancouver. We pay for what they call a vagrant's burial and erect a small cross with his name, date of birth, and death. Tell them to send us his personal effects only. That would be jewelry, if he had any, wallet, ID, papers, that sort of stuff. Give all his clothing and other stuff away. Nobody has to go to Vancouver, but somebody could go. I'm thinking we won't, OK?

"I'll phone his oldest brother, and if they want to do something different, they can have at it. There is little reason to believe they will. They were the folks who shipped him out west on a Greyhound. Very unlikely they want him back now. I would like to keep this quiet. In many ways, his death has absolutely nothing to do with our lives. I asked the chief if he could keep it quiet as well. He said he would, but you know it's going to get out. Mom, do you want to drive down and talk with big sis, or just call her?"

"Just call." I was satisfied with that. I didn't have the energy for a drive.

"OK, then that's all settled. Mom, you and I can go in and make those two calls. Dinner should be here right at eight."

With that, we got up and went to the phone in the kitchen. My son phoned his so-called uncle first. It was a short conversation. Art's oldest brother indicated that the family wouldn't be paying for or doing anything for his brother. So be it. The call to my oldest was a little harder. She was OK and said she had not thought about him in years. So, that was that. We came back outside as a cab pulled into the driveway. Mister paid the cabby, and we unpacked the food on the picnic table on the deck. The little one was staying over at her friend's house for the night. The meal was veal parmigiana, spaghetti, Caesar salad, and garlic bread. Loaves and loaves of garlic bread. There was spumoni for dessert. It was the meal my son had experienced and loved for the first time, only last February, with his girlfriend, Ms. Librarian. The loss of that love was far more painful for him than the loss of a father who never was.

Scarecrow opened two bottles of Mateus wine. I stuck with my beer.

We didn't say much at first. Then the men started joking and kidding each other about work and how much they were eating. The food from Angelo's was great. In the company of those men and those boys, who were becoming men far too soon, I felt safe, secure, and loved. Art's demise slipped quickly from my mind. That was that—or so I hoped.

The Way

I'm sure not the one who can point the way for these boys, these men.
I wonder if they're on a good path.
If you had some steering or direction, we would all listen.
I like the strength in my son.
I'm not sure about the defiance, though.
Any thoughts you would care to share?

I don't think a recommendation of meekness will fly.
These five men and I, we have been meek enough for a lifetime.
We won't go looking for trouble.
I sense trouble is hunting us down.
I can feel that in these men, these boys.
They're readying themselves for something.

With your infinite wisdom and power
And certainly, all glory be to God, and then some.
If you can, prevent whatever they feel is coming.
That would be a true blessing—
But that's not your style, is it?

The kids these days would say you're a laid-back God.
You let things unfold and see what happens,
See who comes to you and who doesn't.
I know these men probably aren't headed your way,
So, if you can bend a little, come halfway
To help them in their hour of need.

They're going to need a way.
I don't know if it's a way in or a way out, or both.
The Bible says you're the Way.
We don't need you to part the seas or anything truly biblical.
Just a little path, a little light
To help us find the way we need.

Amen.   P.S. If Art is with you, bless him; he needs it. If he did make it to your side of the fence, that would be a head scratcher.

Thy Will be Done

Dear Lord
I know it's been a long time between prayers,
Then all this.
I do feel thankful tonight, so thankful,
For Art's passing.
Should I thank you for that?

That seems wrong, but I'm grateful, relieved.
He was a dark shadow
With potential to hurt us,
Hurt our hearts, burden our souls.

Now, *poof*, he's gone.
Like some magic trick, he is no more.
Was that your will?
Well, if it was, Amen to that.

Thy will be done.

Amen.

CHAPTER 46

School of the Surreal

I didn't go to school on Monday. I extended my hardship work leave. I didn't go to work either. Stone Pony, Mister, and I met on Monday night and talked through our visits to our recently departed father. Stone Pony told me at the outset that our father's passing was none of our business and that nothing could be gained from discussing the details of his death.

I had only a couple of questions for them. Were they worried about the two narcs in the park? Were they worried about any of us being spotted with Art? They said not to worry about the narcs. They weren't narcs, and they weren't a problem. They weren't worried about any of us being spotted with or connected with our father. In fact, none of us had been to Vancouver. The tracks of our visits were invisible, and that was that.

I went straight to the VP's office on Tuesday morning. I had arrived at school early. I guess I had just got up at my usual working hours and headed to school. I drove my Mustang, which looked stunning, into the student parking area. The VP gave me a big smile, shook my hand, and welcomed me back. I asked if I was still on probation of some kind, and if I could have my old job back of making the morning announcements, including saying the Lord's Prayer. He agreed. Although my campaign manager had done an excellent job in my absence, the Rave knew he was just keeping my seat warm.

Most students and faculty were surprised to hear my voice. I got a little choked up during the Lord's Prayer. I reflected on that later. We forgive those who trespass against us. *I sure as hell ain't there with you on that one—at least yet, Lord.* Amen to that.

Just a year ago, I had come back a week late for school. Mom's boyfriend was dead, and the police were at our house. Same asshole detective. Déjà vu, which was also my favourite album, *Déjà Vu* by Crosby, Stills, Nash, and Young. Almost cut my hair. I think I was letting my freak flag fly.

We had been through so much. I truly felt like a grown man in a teenage wonder world. My classmates wondered what was next in our graduation year. I was wondering what freakin' life I was living. So, the school environment was not grounding me. Seeing Ms. Librarian again was like a swift kick to the old nut factory. Old and quaint and totally inadequate expressions barged into my brain. About how I felt upon seeing Kristine. Sayings along the lines of, "His stomach sank, his heart throbbed, his eyes swelled, his throat went dry." Nope, a kick in the balls was the most accurate description. It was painful. What I managed to do was give Kristine what must have been a very mixed look of pain, disdain, loss, and my anger, all rolled into one. She didn't deserve that. Her family forced her into that decision. She had approached me with a big smile and a glow in her eyes, and I killed them both. I hurt her and then I walked away, not saying a thing. I showed her!

Well, no I didn't. I showed me, me! Still hurting, still wounded, still caring, still loving and scarred. I should have turned around and apologized. Told her I understood and still cared for her deeply. I was too much of a wounded, self-absorbed little boy for that. Just a garbage boy, not a man.

My popularity or notoriety seemed intact. The staff advisor for the *Raging Rag* looked at me with utter contempt. I knew what Ms. Librarian must have felt from the look he gave me.

Missing a week of school always seemed to set jaws to flapping. It was rumoured I had hitchhiked out west. Close to the truth. When I was asked where I had been, I just smiled and shrugged. "Places." The mystery of my non-answer was like pouring fuel on the fire. My trip was fervently and definitively reported as my going to Mexico, the Rockies, Winnipeg, New York, California, Chicago, and Ohio. The latter two destinations were explained by my infatuation with CSNY's *Déjà Vu* album. Go figure. Kilgore Trout.

I was leading the student council, playing football, and studying hard. The weekends were full of work—and I mean full. Saturdays were a minimum of twelve hours. Sundays at least ten hours. I had no social life. That surprisingly seemed OK. Bogeyman, Scarecrow, and our little family looked forward to Friday or Saturday night card games. Horse race, Rummoli, and thirty-one were the games of choice. Chips and dip. Sunday-night dinner was a takeout meal. My life seemed quiet and peaceful. The only black spot was that prick detective. He dropped by near the end of the month to tell us he thought we might want more details on Dad's death. On our behalf, he had asked his counterparts in Vancouver to take a closer look at the case.

Dear old Dad had been in the ground for three weeks. No one was in mourning. That prick was trying to rattle us. It didn't work. He left without a thank you or, as Mom would infrequently say, "without a howdy-do or a kiss my ass," which made me laugh. That black cloud was hanging out there. Two deaths at our doorstep in just over a year. What tragic luck for our family. That's how that dick detective left a cloud hanging over us.

He did drop some unsettling tidbits that his Vancouver buddies turned up. Apparently, Art had mumbled a couple of things that a bartender remembered. The bartender recalled that Art mentioned three things: most notably he said he was Fred Fuckin' McMurray, with three sons. He said that several times. He talked about the two narcs who were looking to bust him. Last thing he slurred out was a rant that women were always trying to trap him, getting pregnant on purpose, trying to tie him down.

The detective asked if any of that meant anything to us. We said no, not a clue. The detective studied our reactions. He got none. We were emotionally so divorced from that man that his ramblings didn't—couldn't—affect us.

"Oh yeah, one more thing," the detective said. Who did he think he was, Columbo? He said the bartender heard Art laugh and say, "I guess the family reunion I planned is off." Did we know anything about that?

Mom said we got a letter back in June saying he was coming for a visit in September.

Mannix jumped on that. "You still have the letter? Where was the postmark?"

"No, we threw it in the garbage. The postmark was Hamilton. His brothers live there."

"Thanks. Maybe I'll follow up with them. Just one more thing, though. You were travelling recently, right?" He tried to drill a hole through me with his eyes.

"Yeah, I took a one-week trip."

He chuckled. "Any golfing on that trip?"

"A little." I smiled back and met his eyes hard and square. "I visited friends in Winnipeg and Sweetgrass and spent a few days in Banff."

"Not Vancouver?"

"No, and we didn't know the prick who abandoned us was living there, but we already told you that. Right, Columbo?"

That made the detective's anger flash. As he stood up to leave, he dropped his bomb. "Look, you two. There are two men dead with broken necks. You were travelling just before their deaths both times. Interesting. I ain't done with this. Stick to golfing, son. Crime ain't your game."

He thought he was leaving with a big, ominous threat.

"Hey, man, you need to relax a little. Get a hobby other than us. Does anybody know you're here hassling us again? My golf game is good, so thanks for asking. You mustn't be getting any rounds in. That must be what's making you so uptight, right? Remember my father's last words to me? Yep, you do. Fuck you!"

He slammed the door behind him.

"What's the golf talk about?" Mom asked. "I don't understand."

"It's a sexual reference, and I used that terminology to be polite. Remember when I was asked on CBC how I got to Winnipeg last summer?"

"Yes. You said golfing."

"Yep. I got a ride to Winnipeg from just outside of town with two girls from BC. We were all squished into a Volkswagen Beetle. We couldn't find hostels to sleep in, with so many kids hitchhiking around. We pitched tents on golf courses, the greens of the seventh holes to be exact, and things just happened. We ended up having sex on the golf courses. So, I got to Winnipeg by golfing."

Mom blushed. "Son, was it safe?"

"What, the sex?"

"No, driving all squished in together in that little car."

"Oh yeah. They were careful drivers."

Mom seemed OK with the answer, but I knew she had to chew on that revelation for a bit. In truth, they were not careful drivers. They were slow drivers given that they were perpetually stoned—always at least one joint for breakfast, which set the agenda for the day.

Despite the detective, which Mister and Stone Pony told me not to worry about, life was moving along. Fall turned to winter, football to hockey, and work to more work. I had Wednesday and Friday afternoons free after 1:45 p.m. If there wasn't a practice or a game, I went to work. Money was rolling in.

On the last Sunday of every month, Newspaper Crew Enterprises had a business meeting. Ms. Annamoosie would walk us through the business development. Business was booming. Mister and Stone Pony would lay out the business plan. We all seemed to fixate on being out of the dope business by September 1 of this year.

Part of the business plan was my accelerated education. My marks had steadily climbed. Just before Christmas, I received an early acceptance to the University of Guelph in honours BA studies. Early entrance meant the spring semester, starting in May. My early graduation requirements from high school would be accomplished by mid-April.

High school was surreal as it was. This accelerated plan just made it more so. In my mind—when I let it drift, which was far too often—there was an abundance of heartbreak, coroner's reports, Teddy Porter, and death. I tried to keep a tight rope on my head because the paths my mind travelled were a bit on the dark side. Most days were good. I liked to study, to read, to think. Hockey was good that year. The coach had principles that taught us leadership, commitment, loyalty, and integrity. After finishing the year by just making the playoffs, we won our regional championship. An English teacher opened my eyes and mind to thinking critically. The only gap in my life was the intimacy of a close relationship. Memories of Ms. Librarian and Woman filled that gap in a good—though agonizing—way.

Mister and Scarecrow proposed an academic and business plan for me to follow. First, University of Guelph and get the prerequisite undergrad degree, excelling there as an honours student, then an MBA at one of the top three schools in the country. My part was to get the grades.

As far as work, I would work in the business every second weekend and full time during all breaks. The owner of the accounting firm that NCE used was going to instruct me in all the basics of accounting, and I would take all the business courses I could access at U of G. The goal was that in two years, I would know the basic accounting details and how the books were constructed on every business line in all the NCE companies. How the businesses were all amalgamated into one overall set of financial statements. I liked numbers, so that was all good.

Mister, Stone Pony, Scarecrow, Bogeyman, Mr. Clampett, Ms. Annamoosie, the FBI, the Brownies, and the Whities were always admonishing me to keep my nose clean. Encouraging and motivating me by continuously expressing their belief in me. Every time I heard their support, it meant the world to me.

I was so pointed toward the future and making it real that the day-to-day of high school didn't seem real. It was a strange existence when my immediate activities were focused on high grades and immersing in the intensity of sports, when those activities were just transit routes and outlets for the real stuff down the road.

My transition mindset blinded me to most of the gathering storm.

CHAPTER 47

*Leaping Over Laments:
A Librarian's Tale*

I had been thinking about this for months. I made it all the way to Sunday at the end of August before I was knocking at his front door. William's mom opened the door, hugged me, and asked me to come in. We talked about small things before I blurted out why I was there.

"I love him. I can't stand being apart from him. So, here I am."

"Do your parents know? Is your dad OK with this?"

"I'm exerting some independence here. My dad set me up with the sons of respected families over the last few months. Those boys respected my dad enough not to go under my blouse and try to get into my pants for two hours maximum. Your son is not like that. When my dad tells me he has a problem with William, I'll tell him that. My mom says I should follow my heart. So, here I am. Where is he?"

"Well, they have these company meetings once a month at Mister and Stone Pony's, and that's where he is now."

"Do you know what time he'll be back? Do you mind if I wait?"

"I don't mind, but I think it will be late. He said he might even stay over. I certainly will tell him you came by."

"OK, but you must tell him I love him, and I want to get back together. William is a good boy, a good man. I know he still has big feelings for me."

"He does, although he's trying not to show it. The return of his Ms. Librarian would mean the world to him and our family. I'll tell him, and I'll also tell him he's an idiot if he doesn't run back to you."

"Thank you for everything. I'll go now. Tell William he can call me late or early tomorrow. I'll be up and waiting." With that, I left and started the walk home.

I had spent enough time lamenting my loss. It was time to act like a woman who knew what she wanted—and I wanted William. I had mustered the courage over the last few months to stand up to my father and maybe educate him on a few facts about our town and the respected leading families.

I was also smart enough to know that I was just a teenage girl going through all kinds of changes. Like sex. A girl was a slut if she did and a cock tease if she didn't. It wasn't like that with William. I could just be me, and he followed my lead and my needs. He was so understatedly confident in everything and with everyone. He just needed the chance. I thought I could help bring him to daylight. Above the bar of small-town put-downs.

I needed him to call. I felt he needed to call. That look he gave me at school. I didn't understand the anger I saw in that look until I stepped back and realized how he must have felt. Dumped by me and trashed by my father and my dad's peers. Was that what a garbage boy deserved or just what he could expect? Was it right? I didn't think so. Had my reputation been "sullied," as my father said, by an association with William, the lowly garbage boy? I didn't care. They underestimated him—and even worse, they underestimated me.

I would stand up against small-town prejudices. I wished his friends didn't deal dope. I also wished the police weren't always so interested in him and his family. I didn't want him to fly low, under the radar. I wanted him to soar, and I wanted to be beside him when he took full flight—when *we* took full flight. Maybe I was just a romantic teenage girl, swirled around by emotions and the uncertainty of this stage in life. Then again, maybe I wasn't. Maybe I had a good grasp on what I wanted and how things should be. That was what I would find out.

I wanted to find out with William.

CHAPTER 48

Corporate Raiders

Every month from early winter through late spring, the growth and success of NCE was stunning. The injection of cash from dope sales was increasing at such a rate, it was hard to believe. Turning off that tap in September would be hard. The Manitoba division was sending bales of cash east. The prairies, led by Crazy Horse, were in constant harvest mode. Those flatlanders liked to get some elevation by getting high—apparently a lot. More impressive was the legitimate growth of all the independent businesses under the NCE umbrella. I knew enough about accounting by May to understand that the separate entities were all viable and profitable. Even before washing cash through them. The house cleaning and prepping business produced a high profit. The core garbage-disposal business was experiencing what the accountant called "economies of scale."

When I came home from Guelph for the May long weekend, my studies in Economics 101, Accounting 101, and Intro to Statistics were already valuable. English, Intro to Psychology, and Intro to Sociology were all enjoyable and fascinating. I was living like a recluse in the cement-like dorms on the U of G campus. I lifted weights every day with a couple of football players and engaged in some obligatory howling at the moon every Thursday, pub night, with some dorm mates. Life was good. School was not easy, but it wasn't hard. I had uncovered my own high level of ambition.

There were a couple of dark times. Our friendly neighbourhood detective dropped by on the Saturday evening the weekend I came home. He had heard I was back in town. Said he wanted to check on my well-being. He just wanted to remind us that he was working diligently on our behalf, of course, to ensure the real cause of Art's death was unearthed.

I thanked him for his efforts on the departed's behalf before informing him we didn't give a fuck. This time, I pre-empted him from entering our home. I told him he wouldn't lay any shit on my mom's shoulders. He had a snarky smile on his face the whole time. As he was walking back to his car, he turned back. "My line of inquiry is focused on those two narcs that your dear departed dad mentioned. I figure, somehow, those narcs know most of your associates are drug dealers. Maybe they thought your old man had some insight there. You know, family connections and all—so I think that's kind of interesting, don't you?"

That fucking weasel, acting so smart, like he was on the verge of breaking some big case with his brilliant detective work.

"Knock your socks off, Joe Friday. I can tell your golf game is still for shits."

"Funny man, Scarface. Funny man. Speaking of funny, we still have no clue what your old man's Fred McMurray reference means. Must have been his rum-soaked brain playing games with him."

"Or maybe, Monsieur Poirot, it was his favourite TV show, and remember..."

"Yeah, I know, fuck you!"

"Right on, Link. Now you're getting it. Fuck you—and like my old man, you're very clever."

With that, I turned and went into the house. That guy was a dog with a bone. He was getting to me. I was going to keep up my front of defiance and aggressive denial.

The other dark cloud was the Mayhem Motorcycle Club. Mr. Clampett informed us at the May meeting that they wanted Mister and Stone Pony out of the distribution business. They didn't like the competition. The MMC wasn't sure about our group's full involvement in drug distribution, but they knew enough that they wanted NCE and affiliates out of their market. As exiting the drug business was Mister and Stone Pony's game plan anyway, the MMC wouldn't be a long-term issue. Negotiations had begun. Mr. Clampett said the MMC were professionals. The only real threat was the MMC's local affiliates doing something idiotic. He didn't think the locals, led by Teddy Porter, were smart enough to mount any plan that was clever or brave enough to be truly threatening. We all agreed with those observations. However, Mr. Clampett cautioned us that stupidity and a latent revenge motive could cause the All Saints to take some type of action. This was likely the longer Stone Pony and Mister remained in the drug distribution business.

Mr. Clampett advised us to be smart, avoid conflicts with the All Saints, and keep our eyes and ears open for trouble. I hadn't seen any warning signs, nor had the others.

My plans changed a bit as the studying ratcheted up near the end of the semester at Guelph. I was only coming home every third weekend from June first onwards. The semester ended in the last week of July. I achieved an eighty-four percent average. I was ecstatic. Driving home in my Mustang for the long weekend at the beginning of August, I was feeling on top of the world—at least in my little corner of the world.

The NCE business meeting on Sunday was all good news. Revenues were up, and so were profits and salaries. The MMC negotiations had gone well. Mister and Stone Pony would be out of the drug distribution business, but not until early next year. Seems the MMC needed to arrange supply lines. All local sales would be taken over by the MMC on September first of the following year. Mister and Stone Pony would handle all bulk sales through the end of the year. There would be no handover of a client list. The MMC understood that, and didn't want to deal with that well-heeled group anyway. Those clients were too recreational in nature, and the MMC believed there was more profit in their own network of street sales. We all laughed about that given the profit margins Stone Pony and Mister had achieved and the willingness of their clientele to accept price increases without negotiating.

Mister and Stone Pony were informing all their bulk clients to place big end of the year "going out of business" orders, even offering some volume discounts. The cash inflow was expected to be huge at the end of the year and into January. Scarecrow and Bogeyman had set up large, profitable deals with the Mexicans. Manitoba operations were exiting the business in the same way at the same time. It was going to be a very coordinated exit.

They were also advising their clients that engaging with local suppliers would be a bad plan. All the local distributors would be criminals. That was all that needed to be said. Their clientele started seeking other supply lines and placing large "going out of business" orders.

August was a blast. Running barrels and accounting lessons. It was good to be home. Everyone was healthy and strong. Turning twenty was a big party at the Refuge. I met up with the university hot bod squad again. More good times. Life was good. A future, maybe a bright future.

The August business meeting was on the last Sunday of the month, which was August twenty-ninth. The U of G semester started on Thursday, September second. I was going to be set up living off campus in a one-bedroom apartment about a mile and a half from campus. I was heading out on Wednesday morning.

The NCE gathering was a bit different. Mr. Clampett was off on family business. He had been gone for about a week and a half. Business was great, the mood was upbeat, and we all seemed to be on some type of natural high. I was surrounded by good, strong men. Scarecrow and Bogeyman were healthy and folded into the team. We were a band of misfits, but we fit well together.

Mister and Stone Pony asked me to stay over at the cabin. I was glad to. They were going to lay out my personal plan for the next year. I was excited and had some ideas for myself and about the legitimate paths the business could follow that I wanted to share. They were open to my thoughts.

The rest of the crew left at about 6 that evening. Mister and Stone Pony seemed to be distracted. They walked around outside. I fell asleep on a big, comfy rocking chair on the porch. They woke me up about half an hour later, and we all went inside. Mister poured coffees, and the mood became serious and intense.

Stone Pony leaned into the conversation. "Tonight's the night. A bunch of locals—five or six, maybe more—are going to hit us. They're being led by your boy, Porter. They want to get at just the three of us. The rest of the crew doesn't know. Neither does the MMC. This is Porter and Blotto believing they're showing initiative, and Porter seeking revenge. Mr. Clampett has one of the locals feeding us information. Porter wanted this takedown before you escape back to school."

"Why not have the other guys around? At least even the odds. This is a hell of a time for Mr. Clampett to be away."

"Look, Scarface," Mister said, "we have this covered. We have a plan. They're hitting us here in our home. They wanted it isolated. You know, no interruptions, nobody to interfere. That's how we want it, too. The MMC won't be involved. Remember, that's not the way they do business. Porter and the locals are counting on the element of surprise. What isn't a surprise is you're their main objective. Porter wants revenge. He negotiated a chance for revenge upon you with the MMC."

"I feel so special," I joked.

The men laughed. Then Stone Pony provided the next piece of the picture. "The biggest surprise for Porter isn't that we won't be surprised, but that you won't be here when he arrives."

"How's that going to work?"

"We'll show you." With that, they led me into Mister's bedroom. Mister pulled a trunk away from the foot of the bed. Stone Pony moved the rug that had been beneath the trunk. Mister pulled at a corner of the floorboard, and a trap door opened. I saw a ladder built into the side of a shaft and a tunnel heading off.

Mister followed my gaze. "They're coming at dusk. You're going into the tunnel. There's a knapsack at the bottom of the ladder. In the knapsack is a flashlight, a flare gun, water, and the ignition key to the little outboard boat. The tunnel runs about two hundred yards from the cabin and comes out on a ridge just before Cedar Ridge Creek. The tunnel is four feet high, three feet wide, and solidly framed. It is straight and flat, with just a little downslope when you get close to the exit. The exit looks like a grate on a storm drain. It swings open easily. We need you to shoot a flare up when you get there, so we know you're safe. Take the boat across the lake. We'll give you a call at your house when everything is finished here."

"What? You guys are going to take on five or six guys? No. I'm staying."

"No, you're not. We've got this wired. Six of them ain't going to make it as far as the cabin. Trust us. Mr. Clampett is going to eliminate three or four of them before they get to our driveway, let alone the doorstep. We're going to deal with Porter, Blotto, and Mor. End of story. Mr. Clampett never left town. You know he can be a ghost. He parked the boat for your ride yesterday. Scarecrow and Bogeyman are going to leave your car parked at the town dock. That's why we had them drive back in your car. That's all they know. We're going to teach the three local leaders a couple of finer points of negotiations. The MMC will be OK with that. They say the locals need to learn their place and do business the right way, not emotionally."

We just hung out after that. I asked a couple of questions about how they were going to manage the situation. The takeaway from their answers was that it was best for me not to know details. I called my mom to tell her I might be a little late or stay over; I wasn't sure yet. The business meeting had covered a lot of heavy ground, and we were talking our plans through. Mom told me about Ms. Librarian, and my whole being was washed with a feeling of peace. Man, all we had to do was push the local yokels back, and Ms. Librarian and I could be together. I almost called her, but I preferred to see her and tell her how I felt. She guessed right when she told my mom she knew I had deep feelings for her.

I went into the tunnel at about 8:50 p.m. with instructions not to move until I heard three taps on the trap door.

Probably about the time I went into the tunnel, the locals were creeping toward the cabin—at least that's what Stone Pony was guessing.

The three taps came about twenty minutes later. My eyes had grown accustomed to the dark, so for the first thirty yards or so, I didn't turn on the flashlight. It was surprising how quickly I became accustomed to new experiences and new environments. When I turned the flashlight on, I started moving pretty fast, given my hunched-over form, necessitated by the height of the tunnel. I always felt I was a little claustrophobic, and this experience confirmed it. The tunnel seemed to dampen the sound of my footsteps, but I could hear myself breathing. *Slow down*, I kept saying. The adrenaline was flowing, but it wasn't an adrenaline rush. It tasted and felt different. I felt caged and useless. My thoughts were about running to get out of the tunnel and then doubling back to help my friends. The tunnel was amazingly straight, and in probably three minutes, the moonlight was coming in the shaft, so I turned the flashlight off. That gave me some relief. Getting out of an unfamiliar situation always provided some relief, some comfort. That truly was the light at the end of the proverbial tunnel. The wire gate was attached to a solid brace. The latches were on the inside—two of them, one on top and one on the bottom of the right side. If anyone had studied the end of the drain from the other side, they would have thought it peculiar that the latches were on the inside.

I unhooked the latches, swung the gate open, and sat on the edge of the tunnel with my feet dangling in the air a couple of feet off the ground. The moonlight was great, lots of stars in the sky, and I breathed deeply. I was feeling sort of relaxed, like I had escaped. I was pondering my plan to double back when I thought I should locate the boat. I looked toward the creek when my eyes caught a glint of metal in the moonlight.

There was only a split second between the moment I heard the bang until I felt a searing pain tear into the left side of my gut. The sound and a flash was recorded almost precisely as the pain registered. I fell forward, landed face first, and was awkwardly rolling, sliding down the bank to Deep Cedar Creek or—as it was more familiarly known—Shit Creek. My momentum stopped with my left side in the water and my right side on the bank. My right arm was hooked into a branch, which was keeping me from full immersion in the creek—or in the shit, given my situation. I didn't even hear them coming, but I recognized Porter's voice as soon as he opened his mouth.

"Well, look what we got here, Blotto. The tough guy, Mr. Scarface himself. Mr. CBC. Mr. President. You ain't looking so hot right now, Mr. Big Shot. Looks like you're gut shot. I would say I'm sorry about that, but I'm not."

Blotto cut Porter's gloating short. "You stupid fuck. Those Mayhem guys said no guns, no killing. You just fucked us over, man. Those guys don't like their directions being ignored. You just brought a pile of shit on us, Porter."

Their words were registering. Gut shot. Killing? Was I going to die half-in and half-out of Shit Creek, bleeding out? Talk about hitting the high bar of low expectations. The water was darker all along my left side, and seemed to be thick, like engine oil floating on the surface. My blood shining in the moonlight. What had Crazy Horse said about the moon back in Winnipeg? He said it was the Sturgeon Moon or the Blood Moon. That seemed about right.

Porter kicked the back of my head before he took a step toward Blotto. "Stop your fuckin' whining, Blotto. My story is going to be that this rat came scrambling out of the hole, looked like he had a gun. I shot before he could shoot me. End of story—and fuck the MMC if they don't like it."

Blotto's anger subsided quickly. "OK, OK. What are we going to do now? Are you going to finish him? Are we going up to the cabin?"

Porter grinned at me as he pondered his options. "Well, lover boy here is done. Look at all the blood in the water. He's going to die slowly and in a lot of pain. No sense wasting another bullet on him. Besides, I don't want to make any more noise. Just let him keep bleeding out. Then the critters will come and get a good feed. Maybe before he dies. I'm going to use this tunnel. The other rats in that cabin won't be expecting that. You watch Garbage Boy as he bleeds out for about ten minutes, just in case he thinks he can do something heroic. Then you take the boat back, like we planned. We'll see you at the Retreat in an hour."

Blotto nodded. He looked relieved to be getting out of there. Porter headed into the tunnel. Blotto turned to me, and I could hear Porter bumping his way up the tunnel and cursing as he kept hitting the walls or the braces in the ceiling.

"It wasn't supposed to go down this way," Blotto said, sounding surprisingly sincere. "One of our guys was out night fishing and saw a boat sneak up the creek and not come back. He thought it was just an Indian getting crayfish, but the boat never came back. He told us that Deep Cedar, I mean Shit Creek, was right near the Lone Nigger and Tonto's cabin. Porter said we should make sure to shut down any escape routes, so the two of us came out here by boat. Porter's gut feeling was right. Sorry about the gut shot. Porter wasn't even supposed to bring a gun. He's been bragging how he was going to rip you apart with his bare hands. Says all your muscle doesn't make you tough. Guess we'll never know about that."

I was in pain and scared and maybe dying, but I had to get it out. "Blotto, everyone knows, especially Porter, that one on one, I would destroy him. You know that. He knows that. Tell him for me that he's a fuckin' coward, and he will always be a coward. Now, Blotto, I'm going to do you a favour."

"How are you going to do me a favour? You're gut shot and dying. What are you going to do? Give me your girlfriend's phone number?" Blotto's laugh turned to fear with my next words.

"We knew you guys were coming. Mr. Clampett is out in the woods and has probably got two or three of your guys already. I guarantee they will be messed up good. Porter is going to be trapped at the end of the tunnel. Those two wild men in the cabin are pure muscle and bone, and they have their knives, bows, and hatchets and will be putting notches on all your hides. My favour to you is telling you to get the fuck out of Dodge, because they're going to have all your balls hanging from a string in about an hour."

Blotto grimaced and was already edging toward the boat. "I knew it. I told them you guys were too smart not to be ready. Fuck it. I'm sorry about you getting shot. Fuck it."

Blotto could handle a boat. As nervous as he was, he had the outboard started and was gone. I had to move fast. Where was the backpack? I got my left arm out of the water, latched onto the branch, and pulled myself out of the water and up to my knees. I could see the backpack. It had dropped on the little dirt ledge below the tunnel entrance.

I tried to stand but couldn't. What a fuck of a way to die. I crawled up the bank, got the backpack, and pulled out the flare gun. Thank God it was already loaded. I pulled myself up to the tunnel opening. The pain suddenly didn't seem too bad. Maybe I was going numb. I steadied myself as best as I could and held my right arm with my left, with my left elbow resting as flat as possible on the tunnel floor. What had Stone Pony said about the flare? A thousand feet straight up before it burst, or was it five hundred, unless it hit something? Well, this shot was either going to hit part of the tunnel or Teddy Porter. I could hear some noise in the tunnel. That had to be Porter. I figured I better get my shot off.

The recoil from the flare gun was enough to throw me off balance. My knees and feet dug in, so I didn't wind up in Shit Creek again. There was an impact. The flare burst in a great flash of light that seemed to be all the way up the tunnel. I heard some yelping and thumping. Porter must have met the flare. I hoped they were well acquainted. Pulling myself up again, I yelled down the tunnel. "Come on, Teddy Boy. Come on back here, you fuckin' coward. I'm dying to light you up like Canada Day fireworks." I instantly thought that maybe that was a poor choice of words for someone who'd been gut shot and might be dying.

The loss of blood was affecting my thinking. Come back here? Porter had a rifle. I had a flare gun that I was scrambling to reload. Sure enough, a rifle shot echoed down the tunnel. Porter must have put that one in the dirt because no bullet came whizzing by my ears. The flare gun loaded easily enough, and I was ready to light Teddy Bear up again. There was scuffling and thumping a long way down the tunnel. I tried to boost myself up to get a better look up the tunnel when the pain roared in. My left hand went to my gut instinctively, which was the only limb offering me any support. The fall backward ended in a slide back into Shit Creek. I was half-submerged in the creek with my head propped a bit above the water. The sky was clear. Full moon. The Sturgeon Moon. It was called the red moon because sometimes it looked a little red from the summer haze. Good moon to die under if I was about to die. Stars. Lots of stars. I heard my name being called.

"Scarface, what the fuck, man? Scarface? Mister, come quick. He's here. No, no, Mister, he's hurt bad. Blood everywhere. He's been shot in the stomach."

Mister came tumbling out of the tunnel, dragging a load behind him.

"Is he breathing? Get him out of the water. He saved us. Porter was waiting in the tunnel with that rifle. He would have killed us both. Scarface, you shot that flare. Look, the flare gun is still in his hand."

"He's breathing, barely. What about Porter?"

"He's dead or almost dead. We clipped him a little with our hatchets, hardly any blood. The back end of those hatchets must have crushed something in his skull."

Stone Pony turned to see Mr. Clampett coming down the other side of the creek. Mr. Clampett surveyed the situation and then took charge.

"Look, boys. I heard everything you said. The other three locals are tied up back at their cars. Scared, just messed up a little bit—flesh wounds, not anything they won't recover from. Porter, we need to deal with. Scarface, we must get some medical help fast. Get them both in the boat. Stone Pony and Mister, pull yourselves together. Now!"

The bodies got loaded. Porter was thrown into the boat like a sack of dirt and came to. He was mumbling. Incoherent but still alive. I was loaded in very gently. I couldn't speak; I was barely aware of what was happening. Mister put a life preserver under my head. The captain wrapped some tensors over the gut shot, from a little medical kit he had pulled out of his knapsack. He packed the hole with some gauze and ripped Porter's shirt off and tore strips to hold everything in place. "If Scarface is breathing, it isn't perceptible," Mister said.

Nice word, *perceptible*. That's a five- or ten-dollar word right there.

"You two head back to the cabin," the captain said. "Use the tunnel. At daybreak, come back here and clean everything up, including the tunnel. Leave no signs.

No evidence. Blotto must have taken off in the boat they brought. The other All Saints were eager to fill me in on that part of the plan, as they wanted to avoid being messed up any further. I'll connect with the MMC. The upshot will be that this corporate raid never happened. None of the other locals saw Porter here. Blotto will be convinced he wasn't here either. There were no corporate raiders."

"What are you going to do for Scarface?" Mister asked. "What about Porter, or his body?"

Before the captain could answer, I mustered the strength to speak. "Guys, I'm weak. Tell my mom and sisters I love them. I love you, too. This isn't ending well."

CHAPTER 49

Captain Cover-Up

I was working this all out on the fly; that's what a good captain must do. And I was the captain. I was going to follow the shoreline, stay out of the moonlight. If Porter died on the way, I'd stash his body in a secure spot up the lake a little. We'd find a permanent resting spot for him later. I was going to get Scarface to an old fishing camp and get him some medical attention. If he could still use it. We'd come up with cover stories for whatever the outcome turned out to be. I needed to move if Garbage Boy was going to have any chance at all.

I started the boat and headed down Deep Cedar Creek, leaving two silhouettes of sunken despair with the knowledge that their protégé might be dead or dead soon. The Sturgeon Moon was looking awfully red.

I marveled at the beauty of the night and how loud the tears dripping from my beaten-down face sounded as they hit the boat deck. I marveled that one of my passengers came to and spoke.

"Mr. Clampett, this ain't ending too well, is it? Tell everyone I love them."

That was the extent of the conversation under the watchful eye of the Blood Moon. I didn't bother answering. Porter was clearly going to die, his skull crushed. At least it wasn't a broken neck this time. I navigated the boat about fifty yards up a small creek and dumped Porter's body. *Let the crayfish have at him*, I thought, *at least until I get back*. "Come on, William, hang on," I whispered. Even though I knew he must already be gone, or soon would be. I heard a few more faint moans and words, something about "in my time of dying." Then nothing.

I thought through the cover-up on the ride. After I dumped Porter on the bank of the creek, I couldn't detect any breathing coming from William. A veil of tears? Fuck that; I was drowning. There wasn't no veil in the world that could stop or hide that.

These boys had to disappear: Blotto, Porter, and Garbage Boy. There would be more questions than answers if they were found in any shape, breathing or not. The plan for Garbage Boy first. I'd have his car taken from the parking lot. Not by Scarecrow or Bogeyman, but by one of my operators. I had five on call that night, not including the Doc I had stashed at the cabin down the lake, just in case things went sideways for any of my boys. And things had gone more than sideways.

Fuckin' Porter bringing a gun to a fistfight. Breaking the rules of his bosses, the MMC. Whatever the outcome for Garbage Boy, his body wouldn't be found, dead or alive, for some time. The story would be that he couldn't take any more of the mayhem surrounding the NCE and fucked off somewhere in his car. I would make sure the operator driving his car would have it seen somewhere, so witnesses could account for Garbage Boy's departure.

Porter was the hard part. He was crayfish meat for the moment. Then, I got inspired in my thinking. We would get the boat that Blotto and Porter took to Shit Creek and smash it somewhere. I would plant some evidence of Porter's demise at that scene—maybe his shoes, belt, and that comb he was always slicking his greasy hair back with. Nothing with blood on it or even the remote chance of gunpowder or flare residue. I would double back later and pick up that stuff from Porter. He definitely wouldn't be needing it or missing it. I would stage the scene at the island where the hot bod squad had taken the Whities and Garbage Boy.

Blotto, given he was still breathing, I was thinking, might be the hard part—but with a little consideration, he would be easy. We knew some stuff about him. In addition to him going along with Porter and breaking the MMC rules that night, there was more stuff—secret stuff—that would make Blotto quite unpopular with his contemporaries. When I got to the Doc's cabin, I needed to make some phone calls. I'd send one operator to steal Garbage Boy's car. Another to steal Porter's. Two more to secure Blotto and convince him to disappear. I knew where we would send Blotto. He would be driving Porter's car and heading south to the Florida Keys. I'd provide him with some getaway cash. I'd also threaten to reveal Blotto's misdeeds and character flaws, and that big fat ass would be in Porter's car in a heartbeat, getting out of Dodge. Blotto would get to live and come out of his shell down in the Keys.

The fifth operator would be getting the boat the two All Saints had used and meeting me at the island to stage the wreck site and evidence of Porter's demise. Porter and Blotto would be assumed to have split because they had run afoul of the MMC. Very plausible—and in reality, true about them being offside with MMC.

Three missing bodies all at once would create a lot of questions. The police would ask about them, but no one would have any answers except me and my operators, who would all be long gone, without a trace. Blotto, Porter, and Garbage

Boy would not be found. I was too good at this for there to be any fuckups. The American government had trained me well.

I just couldn't let myself think about him. William as William. Thinking of him as Garbage Boy made him a little more disposable. He was a good kid who didn't deserve this shit, this ending. Maybe I'd retire after this, because I couldn't lose any more young men on my watch. I would get Mister, Stone Pony, and the Newspaper Crew through any crisis arising from this, and then I would be done.

The Blood Moon seemed to be looking for more blood. Maybe she'd get some—maybe a lot. I hoped she wouldn't.

CHAPTER 50

Bottom of a Boat: In My Time of Dying

The moon looked very cool from down where I was. I sure as hell wasn't expecting to die that way. In the bottom of a boat. Gut shot. I couldn't speak, and I couldn't keep my eyes open. I could hear things, though. The captain was mumbling, and the engine was humming. I could smell blood and oil. Something kept bumping into me. I thought it was Teddy. I wasn't sure about that, or very clear on anything. The bottom of the boat was cold from the water, and that felt OK.

Things were flashing through my mind. My life wasn't flashing before my eyes—well, maybe a little. I was thinking more of future things that I was going to miss. Ms. Librarian jumped to near the top of that list. *Kristine, I'm sorry I was such a dick this past year. Mom, little one, and big sis, I'm so sorry I'm leaving you like this.* I was going to miss all the things I would have done with a girl, my girl. All that family stuff. The stuff of life. Graduations, everybody growing up, Mom retiring, weddings, birthday parties. All the day-to-day stuff. The "just being people" stuff.

I was going to miss people. The NCE crew, Mr. Clampett, Ms. Annamoosie, Crazy Horse, my hockey coach, the VP, Rave, the young cop, Miss Librarian, and all sorts of good people. They were all flashing through my mind like those picture cards I used to flip through and see a movie. My mind was looping the big six in my life: Mom, Scarecrow, Bogeyman, Woman, Mister, and Stone Pony. I wanted a life with them. I didn't want to leave this life. I couldn't see anything about what we had already done and been together; all I could see was what I wanted to do with all of them. Just be together. That would have been good enough. That was all I wanted. And there I was in the bottom of a boat.

Why were the lyrics from the Zeppelin song, "In My Time of Dying," so clear in my head as everything else went dark and fuzzy? Those words bouncing around in my skull were capturing everything I was feeling. I don't want anybody to weep, or moan, or grieve, I just want to make sure I make it home, dead or alive. And maybe Scarecrow and Bogeyman, can snap the caps on some real cold, cold beers with my mom and just say good-bye, William.

Where did the moon go? It was dark, cold. There wasn't any light at the end of that tunnel or at the bottom of a boat.

CHAPTER 51

Brothers in Blood and the Lost Boys

Five stages of grief? Maybe for some psychologist. Maybe. Mister and I didn't know anything about stages or how to sequence and classify our feelings. Stages? How many stages are people supposed to feel? Who gives a fuck about that babble and drivel? We were twisted balls of rage and guilt who wanted revenge on the world. Between the two of us, Mister and I counted and experienced disbelief, a feeling of overwhelming blue, numbness, anguish, pain, an inability to forgive especially ourselves—and rage, rage, rage. We had to swallow the rage. All six of our stages we felt were paralyzing in their own way. They suspended, obliterated rational thought. Could we relate to words like "sadness" and "grief"? Barely. For Mister and me, those words and feelings were insufficient and not of our world.

Four days had passed since the failed corporate raid. Blotto had taken a long trip, as had Porter. The MMC informed the rest of the locals that Blotto and Porter were being banished for a spell until they learned to listen to directions and follow MMC principles. The locals were too scared to probe for details. Blotto nervously convinced the rest of the All Saints, in a hurried farewell address, that Porter and he were lucky to be leaving with their nuts still attached.

It was surmised that Scarface had just blown town. We told the cops, his family, and our crew that at the NCE meeting, he had seemed distracted. After the meeting, he had told Mister and me that he felt overwhelmed by work, school, and personal stuff. His car was seen heading west. No one had heard from him.

Some rumours circulated that he had been killed by Porter and Blotto, and that was why those boys had beaten it out of town. Those rumours had more than a little merit, and were taking on a substantial amount of belief, even with the police. Porter had been very vocal about getting revenge on Scarface.

Porter's case became a little more interesting when the cops found a small outboard boat wrecked on an island usually reserved for partying. They found Porter's belt, shoes, and his comb. The comb was Porter's signature accessory, and even had his initials carved on the handle. Speculation was that Porter had gone for a boat ride and maybe wrecked the boat. Blotto and Porter had been seen in a boat the night before they disappeared. The police were thinking that maybe Porter hadn't run, or before he could run, had been knocked off by the MMC. The speculation included Porter getting knocked off because he had offed Garbage Boy and broken MMC rules and needed to serve as an example to others.

The cops' heads were spinning.

Scarface's car was missing, so the cops—mostly Scarface's favourite detective—thought things didn't add up. Three people disappearing at the same time was more than a little suspect, and rumours, theories, and speculation were rampant throughout the town. The whereabouts of the three boys was the major topic of conversation everywhere. The detective called in some help from the Big Smoke, the big city. Four homicide detectives landed in town, and that set tongues wagging and heads nodding. Somebody had killed somebody.

Garbage Boy was on the national news once again, this time accompanied by the other two "lost boys." Just yesterday, the headline in the local paper read, "Praying for the lost boys." The same hypocritical church ladies who had descended on Garbage Boy's mom and house after the great cow pond desecration and catastrophe had begun holding fervent prayer meetings for the three lost boys.

The local detective, when queried by the local paper and the CBC national news, was dumbstruck about the reference to "lost boys" and the apparent outpouring of sympathy and feeling of loss. He couldn't restrain himself. He provided a bit of Blotto and Porter's criminal records and current suspended sentence status. He noted that both those "lost boys" would be in prison for five to seven years with one more violation. He suggested that they "got lost" to avoid jail time and wagered that a crime would surface attributed to them, and it would amount to serious jail time. The detective was actually helping cover the disappearance of Blotto and Porter with some believable rationale.

The detective was a little more wary when it came to Garbage Boy. He said he found it interesting that people who moved in the same circles as Garbage Boy were often found dead. He didn't make any direct accusation, but his pondering added fire to the rumours already circulating that Garbage Boy had bested Porter in some sort of fight, and Porter was dead. Many of the Newspaper Crew and a lot of the town had heard that was exactly what the detective thought. He was giving his theory some oxygen to get those fires burning.

There was one thin lead on Porter. Apparently, he had crossed the border through the Windsor tunnel about two weeks after he had disappeared. He was driving a car remarkably similar to Garbage Boy's. As far as the possible tragic drowning, Porter's body hadn't turned up yet, which was surprising in a shallow body of water like Lake Hendri.

Scarface's mom and sisters were completely distraught and in a state of suspended animation. Scarface's mom wouldn't hear of having a funeral until a body was found. The truth was she didn't believe and couldn't accept that her son was dead. None of us could. We would take care of Scarface's family. At least on that side of the ledger, things would be good for them.

Scarface's mom talked to us all about debits and credits, like she methodically tracked in her bank book. Reconciling and correcting any errors that one made in a bank book. The thing was, she couldn't reconcile her son being missing or dead. Everyone thought he was dead, killed by Porter or someone. The books weren't balanced. They never would be. How could they be? She balanced and reconciled all she could in every other aspect of her life, but not this!

She gave up praying.

It was Mister's idea, but I called the entire Neapolitan Crew together. We met at the cabin on a Thursday, four days after what we could not have imagined would be the worst night of our lives. At least so far.

Mr. Clampett had been and was still tying up loose ends all week. We hadn't seen him since the Blood Moon on Sunday night. He called early Monday morning and told us that Scarface was gone. He told us to clean up the ground around Deep Cedar Creek and not to leave a trace of anything that had happened there, to cover the end of the tunnel with brush, so it was totally invisible. He also told us that he had put Porter's belt, shoes, and comb in the small outboard boat and staged a crash. He assured us that the boat was not traceable to any of us. He told us not to tell the Newspaper Crew about Porter, Scarface, or anything that went down on Sunday night. He also told us that Scarface's car had been taken care of and to get Scarface's mom to report it had been stolen. If we could point a finger at Porter for that theft, it would be good.

The captain, our Mr. Clampett, told us we could rise above all this sorrow. He said he had a lot of containment work to do, and we wouldn't see him for a few weeks.

We informed the Newspaper Crew that Scarface left shortly after they did the night of the meeting. We told them we didn't know anything that happened after that.

Scarface's mom reported him missing to the police on Monday afternoon. Bogeyman and Scarecrow had gone to work in the morning, and Garbage Boy had been a no-show. That's when she called us to ask if he had stayed over on

Sunday night. We told her he hadn't stayed. Then she phoned the cops and reported him missing. We hated lying to her, but it was better—and only natural for her to be the one reporting her son as missing.

We also agreed not to tell the Newspaper Crew anything about the corporate raid or the outcomes. If they didn't know, they couldn't say anything. They would all be left in the dark and hurting.

The Thursday-night meeting was quiet, almost serene, as we sat in a circle of shared sadness. Bogeyman, Scarecrow, the Whities, the Brownies, the FBI, Ms. Cecilia, Mister, and me. I called the circle a time of solidarity, solemnity, shared sadness, and loss. I asked each person to share one remembrance or one thought about Scarface, about Garbage Boy, about William.

The emotion was overflowing. Scarecrow and Bogeyman wept loudly and openly. They shared many stories that made us laugh and cry. Mister stuttered through a poem he wrote. The stuttering flowed into his lilting, sing-song poet's voice, which was full of sorrow and anguish. I recited an old Indian story of passing on, and how the spirit of Scarface would be with us forever.

Mister cut his thumb first. Then we all cut our thumbs. Each member of the Newspaper Crew walked around the circle sharing their blood, thumb to thumb, blood brothers (and sister) forever in the name of Scarface, Garbage Boy, William the Lost.

CHAPTER 52

Lost Boys, My Ass

The big-city homicide detectives ended up working the three cases for six weeks before they shut things down. They surmised Porter and maybe Garbage Boy were dead, likely in a boat crash. The local detective was allowed to keep the three files open but was told he could only work them on his own time. Nationwide alerts hadn't turned up anything on two of the "lost boys."

Before the big-city dicks left town, Blotto had turned up in the Florida Keys. He called his mom from the Keys and told her that Porter hadn't left town with him. Blotto was thinning down and establishing his sexual preferences in a more open, tolerant community than the gangs had provided.

That was all anyone knew. Nobody had heard from Porter and Garbage Boy, including family and friends. Except for the alleged sightings of Porter crossing the border at Windsor in Garbage Boy's car and Garbage Boy headed west in his car. The alleged sightings were conflicting, and the big city detectives were dismissing them.

The theory that had gained traction in town was that Porter and Garbage Boy had fought, and only one had died. The big-city dicks provided some credence to this line of thought when they released a statement, "The history of animosity between the two men is sufficient to believe that foul play could have occurred. However, there is no factual evidence to support this theory. The high water of the spring run-off might release one or two bodies, and when found, a coroner's investigation will be held to determine cause of death." When pressed for a follow-up to the statement, the lead detective in charge of the case speculated that Porter was possibly alive, as the sighting of him crossing the border in Garbage Boy's car was reasonably credible. That was it from the big-city dicks.

The local detective wasn't shy about sharing his sentiments about the remaining "lost boys," especially after a whisky or two. His perspective on the matter was crystal clear. The thought of these three characters being "lost boys" nauseated him. The town was lucky to be rid of them. Garbage Boy had killed Porter, possibly in self-defence. It was likely that Porter had ambushed the kid, and Blotto was there. Somehow, the kid got the advantage on Porter, then Blotto split. Hell, the kid was nothing but muscle, and Porter was a skinny prick with a switchblade.

That boy wasn't going to be stopped by a greaser with a pin pricker. The local dick knew that Blotto was a fat-assed coward and would have booted it as soon as the tables turned on Porter. The MMC probably ordered Blotto out of town to get rid of any of the disappearances causing blowback to them.

When the big-city detectives were sent home, the local dick had another moment in the spotlight. His opening quote was certainly newsworthy: "Lost boys, my ass!" He proceeded to spell out how gullible and hypocritical the local church ladies were, comparing the boys to "Peter Pan, Tinker Bell, and that whole fantasy world. Read the criminal records of Blotto and Porter. These are sinners, not saints. As for the much-missed and grieved-over Garbage Boy, he's somehow connected or related to possibly three suspicious deaths."

That was the last interview he was allowed to give to any news outlet. He vowed privately, to anyone who would listen, that he wasn't done with this case. He also let everyone know that Teddy Porter would be found, dead. And that dear departed lost boy would be found with his neck broken. Broken in the rotational fashion, not by a whiplash motion. In the customary broken neck demise of all those closely associated with Garbage Boy.

He was going to be the one to bring Garbage Boy to justice, even if the kid was dead.

CHAPTER 53

Lost

The question in my mind, from the night the circle of blood brothers rose and departed was, "Are we all lost now?" Mister had the same question.

Mister and I had lost our real, shared blood brother.

We felt totally lost without him.

The Newspaper Crew was black with anger, red with fury, and absent of white.

Now, many things may not end well.

ACKNOWLEDGEMENT

First and foremost, I want to recognize the support, encouragement and critical input from my wife Deb. She has always been the initial editor for all my writing. Her criticism is sharp, direct and laden with the intent of making these stories 'good reads'. Deb challenges the flow of the story, the necessity of some content and words, points out where more clarity is necessary and at the same time recommends what might be missing. Let's be clear at times we disagree. Strongly! This truly is a give and take process. It isn't easy because I am very possessive and loyal to my words and story. What I appreciate most is Deb's willingness to provide her insights even as she has learned that I can be defensive, ornery and stubborn about changing the story content or even a singular word, but the process works. Our differences of opinion are often resolved over a glass of wine. I guess being together for over 50 years gains you that type of great relationship and trust.

Our daughter Lauren, chipped in with both technical and marketing expertise. It seems I have some strong woman in my life, as Lauren has also pointed out where I am lacking in either perspective or knowledge. I think Deb And Lauren exemplify one of my favourite song lyrics from Neil Young's Ambulance Blues that I paraphrase as 'nothing like a friend, who tells you you're just pissin' in the wind.' It is hard to tell someone you love that they may be doing something that just doesn't help them or in this case help in telling Garbage Boy's story or in bringing the book to market.

Our daughter Meaghan just tells me "you need to hear me, really listen to me." And then I step back from my own noise and let her wisdom filter in. Thank you, Lauren, Deb and Meaghan, for being the people that keep me straight and whack me, just literally of course, upside the head when I need it the most.

Then there is our oldest, our son Mike. His role, in my support infrastructure, is more like the Springsteen lyric from Jungleland. Mike is like the poets in Jungleland, he stands back and lets it all be and when the moment is right he takes an honest stand.

Music, like my support team, played a large role at important times in the writing of Garbage Boy.

I have great appreciation and respect for the professionalism of Cam, Julianne,

Shelby and Geoff at Friesen Press. Thank you for your knowledge and guidance throughout the process.

One Great City, Tim and Scott, thank you for supporting and partnering on the crazy idea of launching a book with a companion beer. Garbage Boy Golden Ale is gritty, authentic and original just like Garbage Boy.

And last but as they say definitely not least, thank you to the readers and especially that group of patrons who took the leap of faith and purchased multiple copies of Garbage Boy to support a Canadian author finding his way in a very tough market.

Sincerely,
Michael

SCARRED: The Prequel

Scarred was published in 2019 and now serves as the prequel to Garbage Boy: The High Bar of Low Expectations.

Scarred tracks the path of Scarface aka Garbage Boy and his mother over a decade as they struggle to ascend in the face of adversity. The boy faces the ongoing everyday battle of being an easy target for the local gangs and tough guys. The mother struggles to overcome a brutal rape and raise, as a single parent, her three children.

They 'make do and get by' all the while rising in the face of social class stigma and the swirling cultural shifts of the late 60's and early 70's.

Scarface is accompanied by his eclectic group of companions, including his close friends Bogeyman and Scarecrow and his bosses Mister and Stone Pony. The underdog story ends in an unresolved death and more mayhem on the horizon. The mother and son become 'persons of interest' in the death.

Their humble prayers go largely unanswered as they weave their way through abandonment and abuse to some for of ascension.

Follow Michael McMullen

Facebook: Michael McMullen Author Page

Instagram: michaelmcwrites

LinkedIn: Michael McMullen Author

Website: www.michaelmcmullenbooks.com

Up Next from Michael McMullen

Leaving Lisa

Lisa was a "rock star" by her late teens. Mo was a waitress and pregnant by 17. Smackin' Mackin was getting football scholarship offers in junior high school. Guy was excelling at school as a preview to climbing the corporate ladder. These four disparate personalities get entwined by a chance intersection at GoHo's Diner in their adult live's. The characters move forward parallel to each other and precariously balance on whether they should somehow collide or combine. They have all now lost something and simultaneously are trying to leave something behind. Leaving Lisa is about losing and moving on.

Easier said *than* done.

Look for Michael's third book 'Leaving Lisa' available late 2024

Lost And Found: And The Shot Gunning of Mrs.D

Death brings closure. Or does it? In 'Lost and Found' you are not sure of what has been lost.... forever. The main characters in the book find parts of themselves, they find others and they strive towards healing. They also struggle and are blanketed with the searing pain of loss. Some don't seek healing, they seek revenge or something even more tangible. Whatever is lost or found there is no resolution until the fate of Garbage Boy is clear. We need a 'body' to close that chapter, actually make that two bodies.

Lots is happening in the interim as Mister and Stone Pony continue to grow the legitimate parts of their burgeoning business empire while trying to jettison the drug trade. Scores need to be settled with the Mayhem Motorcycle gang, or do they? There seems to be a lull before the storm and the entry of Mrs.D and her big time, greasy lawyer husband are the start of another maelstrom of good intent and bad outcomes or is it bad intent and good outcomes. Depends on your perspective.

The crew from 'Garbage Boy: The High Bar of Low Expectations' returns with all their uniqueness.

Scarecrow, Bogeyman, the FBI, the Whities, the Brownies, Mr. Clampett, Ms. Cecilia Annamoosie, Ms. Librarian, Crazy Horse and Woman. Which of these will get lost? What and who do they find?

And then there is always Mrs. D and her shot gun ways.

Look for Michael's fourth book in the summer of 2025.

Printed in Canada